WINTERSTOKE

Winterstoke

L. T. C. ROLT

FABER & FABER

This edition first published in 2015
by Faber & Faber Ltd
Bloomsbury House
74–77 Great Russell Street
London WC1B 3DA

Printed by Books on Demand GmbH, Norderstedt

All rights reserved
© The Estate of L. T. C. Rolt, 1954
Introductory remarks © individual contributors, 2015

The right of L. T. C. Rolt to be identified as author of this
work has been asserted in accordance with Section 77 of
the Copyright, Designs and Patents Act 1988

*This book is sold subject to the condition that it shall not, by way of trade or otherwise,
be lent, resold, hired out or otherwise circulated without the publisher's prior consent
in any form of binding or cover other than that in which it is published and without a
similar condition including this condition being imposed on the subsequent purchaser*

A CIP record for this book is available from the British Library

ISBN 978–0–571–32602–0

Introduction to the 2015 Edition

L. T. C. ('Tom') Rolt (1919–74) was famed as a pioneer in the appreciation and preservation of Britain's canal network both as a means of transport and a source of pleasure. His 1944 book Narrow Boat inspired the founding of the Inland Waterways Association (IWA). Rolt also set up the first organisation to save and run a railway, The Talyllyn Railway Preservation Society. He was furthermore a lover of motorcar craftsmanship, and joint founder in 1934 of the Vintage Sports Car Club (VSCC).

Rolt was a forerunner of our current green movement, with many of his written works weighing the relationship between modern technology and the natural world, in particular his 1947 book, High Horse Riderless. His other publications include a three-volume autobiography, now reissued as The Landscape Trilogy, and many distinguished biographies of engineers, including Isambard Kingdom Brunel (1957), Thomas Telford (1958), George and Robert Stephenson (1960), James Watt (1962), and Thomas Newcomen (1968).

Rolt was twice married, to Angela Orred (1939–51) and, in 1952, to Sonia Smith, who survived him. With Sonia he had two sons, Richard (b. 1953) and Timothy (b. 1955).

Winterstoke (1954), the history of a fictional Midlands town, is perhaps Rolt's most unclassifiable literary production. Writing in Landscape With Canals (1972), the third volume of his autobiography, Rolt had this to say about Winterstoke in a chapter entitled 'The Truth about Authorship':

While Sonia and I were living in Laurel Cottage, the little furnished house we took at Clun, I conceived the idea of concentrating a number of actual historical happenings in the English Midlands upon one imaginary industrial town. The book would present the story of the growth of this archetypal town and the fortunes of its chief families from the days of the first monastic mill on the river to the present day when the presence of an

INTRODUCTION

atomic research establishment on the outskirts of a huge blackened town struck a new apocalyptic note. The book ended with the bewilderment of the town's 'labour' inhabitants on finding that, despite the fact that their elected representatives had nationalised the basic industries, the gap between wages and process had continued to widen until the prospect of starvation became very real.

It had always struck me that, despite its overwhelming importance in the story of mankind, far too little attention had been paid to the Industrial Revolution in the worlds of literature and art. I was resolved, in my small way, to remedy this deficiency, my object being not to glorify but to explain and to awaken understanding. It seemed to me that with this book I had hit upon an ideal vehicle to give the whole course of the Revolution a concise and dramatic shape. I called my imaginary town, and the book about it, Winterstoke. I invented the name because I felt it had a suitably dour and foredoomed ring to it; it was only subsequently that I discovered there was a real Winterstoke in Somerset, near Taunton, but no matter.

I began by drawing two maps (which eventually appeared as endpapers) of Winterstoke, one *c.*1790 and the other modern. I lived with those maps for six months and during that time Winterstoke, which was in fact an amalgam of Stoke-on-Trent and Coalbrookdale with bits of Wolverhampton and Derby thrown in, became intensely real to me. I walked its shabby streets, the towpaths of its blackened canals or the bank of its stinking river, the Wendle. I smelt its acrid polluted air, I knew its pretentious Victorian buildings and statuary, and was equally familiar with its every colliery, ironworks and factory. I hoped I could make my readers share this knowledge with me and see Winterstoke for the terrifying urban monster it was, typifying what English history over the past three hundred years had all been about. But such hopes proved in vain. For although I thought, and still think, that the book rang wholly true and that what I wanted to say could not have been said in any other way, the fact remains that it fell between every kind of stool, being neither fact nor fiction. As the reviewer in the *Daily Telegraph* justly observed:

INTRODUCTION

Fictionalised history is ninety-nine times out of a hundred productive of fallacy; either by the subordination of fact to the requirements of the plot, or by over-simplification, or by gross partisanship on the side of the hero. But *Winterstoke*, by L. T. C. Rolt, is the hundredth case.

This was very nicely put, but unfortunately the hundredth case only went to prove the rule. I had not any great expectations, for although I knew that *Winterstoke* was one of the best things I would ever write, I also knew that it would be a difficult book to sell. But I was unprepared for the catastrophic result. Sales were so minimal that they did not even cover the paltry £100 advance on royalties which I had received. I do not believe that the book was even remaindered; I think it was mercifully pulped into oblivion, a kindlier fate for an author's brain-child in such circumstances. I was later told that the book had been shortlisted for a well-known literary award but a miss is as good as a mile and this was cold comfort. The happiest outcome of this melancholy publishing episode was that *Winterstoke* brought me my best friend in the world of publishing, John Guest of Longmans. John wrote me a genuine fan letter when he had read the book, suggesting a meeting in London. I write 'genuinely' advisedly and with emphasis because letters from publishers' readers are often designed, by flattery or otherwise, to attract new authors to their publishers' lists. In John's case this was not so, although he had cast bread upon promised waters, for it would not be long before I should beat a path to Longmans' door.

*

The author's widow, Sonia Rolt, recollected in 2014 the following conditions and circumstances around the writing of Winterstoke.

Tom and I were leading a nomadic life with baby Richard. It was not yet possible to come to the family home with the hope of occupation as our home. Tom's mother, Mima, was still very much alive, and as with Tom when he was a baby, Mima had not found a way to accept with any degree of comfort, let alone any delight or hope, what is commonly regarded as normal family life.

We were quite cheerfully accepting the open door from those

INTRODUCTION

on my side who were prepared to welcome us, chiefly my aunt Peggy. But we felt we should be on our way. So our great friends the Trevors – Meriol, Tudor and their mother – offered help. Tudor had recently finished building a house of many rooms, Aller Park at Welcombe, on top of a high shoulder above Marsland Mouth on the North Devon Coast. It was in a most spectacular position. One little room became Tom's writing room. It seemed to suit him down to the ground and he wrote under the window gazing away and away down the great flank of the valley; grass on one side, matched by woods of dense oak on the other, the trees low and cropped by the great Atlantic gales into something with the appearance of sheep's fleece.

Winterstoke was hugely important to Tom – a summing up of all he knew and had learnt, expressed in this way. He was happy in spite of life's difficulties; he had a companion – me – he had a son – Richard – he had friends, who loved us and were happy for him to write and work in their place.

That's why it was so terrible when, many months later, standing by the kitchen door at Stanley Pontlarge, we opened the post together to find the first royalty statement from Constable for the new book. It was not just the money – it was as if all that he could do and had done had been rejected. I have not fully understood it till now. I offered to go at once to work in Cheltenham – fatuous on my part.

We picked ourselves up and the phrase, 'Of course, Constable could never sell my books,' came to be currency – which takes us on to Tom's association with Longmans and John Guest. But that is another story.

*

The author's second son, Tim, reacts to Winterstoke *from the vantage of 2014:*

Winterstoke was written between May and September 1953 when my father was forty-three and had just become a parent for the first time. In 1944 Tom had experienced unexpected success with his first published book *Narrow Boat*. Nine years later he might already have had intimations that *Narrow Boat* would be the book with which he would forever be associated. His in-

INTRODUCTION

tervening books had not sold in anything like the quantity of his debut. He had also endured a tangled and bruising human experience when the nascent canal organisation, the Inland Waterways Association, to which *Narrow Boat* had given direct rise, blew up in his face. The politically volatile and strife-torn IWA had expelled Tom, along with many others, in what came to be known as the first of three 'civil wars' within the young and conflicted organisation. Tom's first marriage had also broken up and his days of living on the canals had ended when his boat *Cressy* was found to be irreparably rotten.

Tom had moved on from waterways to railways, starting the Talyllyn Railway Preservation Society, the first organisation of its kind set up to save and run a railway with a mainly volunteer workforce. Tom had worked as the manager for the Talyllyn for the first two critical and successful seasons of this enterprise, but had, in the autumn of 1952, decided to focus once again on his writing career. Even so, while setting up and running the Talyllyn, he had found the time to write two books: *Railway Adventure*, an account of his time with the Talyllyn, and *Lines Of Character*, a kind of Proustian celebration and evocation of small, remote, mostly defunct or soon-to-be-defunct railway lines.

Winterstoke would mark a first (and only) venture into long-form fiction. Eschewing the dominant psychological forms of narrative fiction, the book instead takes more the form of an essay, or even, one could say, a Brechtian *Lehrstück* or lesson play; it is a book of ideas and by no means a conventional narrative. More accurately it is a book that attempts to make sense of the material world and the British landscape as my father saw it in 1953.

In order to accomplish this, he looked back – initially, at a youthful, handwritten and unpublished effort of his that he had entitled *Strange Vista*. This narrative he had written in direct response to his experiences as an engineering apprentice in Stoke-on-Trent in the late 1920s and early 1930s. Witnessing and experiencing first hand the bankruptcy of the steam-engine builders to whom he was apprenticed, also the wider and devastating economic effect of the 1929 financial downturn, had a profound impact on the young Tom. He sought to give this

INTRODUCTION

some kind of literary form in *Strange Vista* and with *Winterstoke* he turned again to this idea.

Now he imagined every detail of an imaginary Midlands town and fleshed it out with maps and a detailed geography. Rather than providing rounded-out characters and a psychologically based narrative, the book takes the form of what we might now call socio-economic history. My father looked further back, deep into the past, to pre-Reformation England before land enclosure. He imagined a complete world and followed it, diligently, over time. The book traces the story of a single town over nine centuries.

There is rigour and a depth of thinking to create the world of the town over such a span. In taking us through this ebb and flow of human endeavour, my father, who had left school at sixteen to pursue an engineering apprenticeship, proves himself to have an enormous depth of understanding and an intuitive sense of history. But he also reveals his prejudices, politics and peccadilloes. In the first chapters the writing is sketchy and idealised. By the time we reach the eighteenth and nineteenth centuries there is more flesh on the bone and it feels like this is the epoch with which the writer most strongly identified.

When we reach the 1950s, the then present, the writer really reveals himself – and not in the best of lights. The full extent of his prejudices and 'small-c' conservative politics are harshly exposed. I found reading the conclusion dispiriting and depressing: so *this* was how my father thought. How very much at odds he must have been with the times he was living in. It seems amazing that I am even here to relate this. Yes, there may be some truth in what he has to say about the 'nanny state', the soul-less nature of 1950s Winterstoke and the pessimistic outlook for the future post-nuclear world. But from a 2014 perspective it seems such a prejudiced, blinkered and partial view; it has the effect of lessening the impact and authority of much of what has gone before. I guess my father was trying to write something that would stand outside time, yet he only succeeds in writing something so very much of its time – the cold war dread of nuclear annihilation hangs very heavily over the book.

At the heart of *Winterstoke* there is a deep yearning for a way of

INTRODUCTION

life that has been lost. I think it is a truism that as we get older we start to view the world around us through the lens of our own finite life. Our fast-changing world can all too easily be seen to be set on a misguided path and bound for inevitable destruction, when in fact what we may really be experiencing is only our own approaching demise.

I feel in *Winterstoke* my father is grappling with this sense of his own finite time. When he writes of a world in danger of going off the rails, he may really be writing about his own impending mortality. The nuclear bomb casts an indelibly dark shadow over the narrative of *Winterstoke*. When I spoke with my mother in 2014, she confirmed that the November 1952 test explosion in the Pacific of the first hydrogen bomb had an especially powerful effect on my father's outlook. This book is filled with foreboding for the future.

Yet there may be a hope in it too. If there is a sense of it being an elegy for a lost time, there is also the sense of the book being the writer's honest and thorough attempt to understand the past – a long hard look into the past as a way to understand the present. Remember, this was a book written in the aftermath of the Second World War when people were very much looking forward, building new worlds and knocking down the old. The rhapsodic *Narrow Boat* may unwittingly have provided the foundations of a looking-back mentality and set in motion the wheels that would save the canal network.

Winterstoke does not provide a single simple message; rather, the book illustrates an intractable dilemma – how spiritual life and the material world may or may not be reconciled with one to another. There may be no easy answer to this, but just by setting down the question Tom provides a hope. *Winterstoke*'s revisiting of the past holds out the prospect that our real-life choices for the future can be made with an enhanced and fuller understanding. The author is asking that we value the past, and learn from it. We certainly do not have to come to the same doom-laden conclusions that his book offers.

It now is no surprise that the book was so resoundingly unsuccessful on its publication. It was so much against the current of the times. Now we can regard Tom as a seer in many ways, but

INTRODUCTION

then he must have seemed a voice crying out in the wilderness, spectacularly out of sync with the 1950s zeitgeist.

The world has certainly turned since it was written. Now, arguably, our country is beset by a 'looking-back' mentality. Heritage Britain is everywhere. Sixty years on, what would my father make of this? Would he see it as a good thing? Or would he scorn it as no more than a nostalgic and vain attempt to turn away from the present into a safer and cosy, but essentially unreal, past. (Poundbury, anyone?) What would he make of 'new' developments such as 'sustainable energy' windfarms or genetically modified crops? Much of what preoccupied him in *Winterstoke* is, of course, very much still with us: his 'sinister wired enclosure of the Atomic Research Establishment' might have shut down in the 1980s, the premises now occupied by a new business (a heavily grant funded biotech research start-up, perhaps?), but the nuclear question lives on. We have an ageing generation of nuclear power stations and an ongoing and ostensibly ever more pressing debate about how to provide energy for our ever more precarious seeming future – the holy trinity of 'clean', 'sustainable' and 'safe' being the current misnomers of choice within our twenty-first-century lexicon.

Taking a cue from the two maps in the book, it might be amusing to imagine a map of Winterstoke as it could be today. The railway line now turned over to a cycle path? Or, more appositely, some part of the railway revived as a volunteer-run tourist steam line? (With an attached bookshop selling a choice few titles by L. T. C. Rolt.) Newly completed ramparts and concrete dams enclosing and channelling the River Wendle after recent catastrophic flooding? A controversial and much-fought-over wind farm on High Hanger Hill, while nearby banners protest about proposals for a fracking plant?

Throughout the town, mobile phone masts are likely dotted here and there? Perhaps a struggling volunteer-run town museum and library, with fading exhibits detailing some of the illustrious deeds and doings from the past? And servicing the town's changing spiritual needs, a yoga and meditation centre housed in the former ironworks? Next door, one of three successful private gyms? (Two of which might be located in former church

INTRODUCTION

buildings?) A popular and thriving mosque housed in another far less prepossessing former industrial building? Emberley Old Hall now a tourist attraction with an annual 'sealed knot' re-enactment of the 1645 sacking? An artisan cheesemaker located in one of the much-restored outlying farms? (His cheese Old Blue Wendle, 'tangy, zesty, with just a hint of smoke'.) A heritage-themed architect-designed retro village of bespoke, high-specification detached houses expanding on the former Emberley village? The deep colliery now all gone, turned into a landscaped skate and recreation park? And dotted round the outer limits, at least a Tesco or two (or is this more of a Waitrose place?), along with the all-night petrol station and the burger franchises on the dual carriageway?

In terms of my father's written output, *Winterstoke* occupies an introspective mid-point. It might be paired with *The Clouded Mirror* (1955), a book of four essays taking up many of the themes touched on in *Winterstoke*. In the vivid writing and stronger characterisations of the central sections of *Winterstoke*, which deal with the Industrial Revolution, we sense Tom has found his métier. This, of course, is the world he returned to in the series of engineering biographies he would go on to write and for which he would come to be perhaps best remembered. There he is both authoritative and engaged, no longer peevishly crying doom and destruction.

I may wish my father had peopled the landscape he created in *Winterstoke* with some flesh-and-blood characters, but perhaps that would be to essentially misunderstand the book, undermining its rigorous purity of purpose and distracting from the harsh lesson in hand. Engaging characters and enveloping narrative storylines would not be true to its somewhat severe purpose. So Tom sketches his past with broad confident strokes, whisking us ruthlessly from era to era, to the dispiriting conclusion.

So why read it now? Are there things we can still take from it? Certainly the central theses of the book are as valid as when it was written. Can the capitalist ethic continue to be sustained in a world of limited resources? Can the finite material world ever be reconciled with the spiritual infinite? These questions are as clearly relevant now as they ever were. *Winterstoke* was a plea

INTRODUCTION

to understand and appreciate our past as a way to enrich and inform our life decisions in the present, for all of our futures.

My mother tells me that Tom received a glowing letter from John Betjeman saying that *Winterstoke* was the best thing he had written and that the book should be on the syllabus for every school. But that, of course, never happened. The books I remember from my school days were all about creating a bright modern world, not posing difficult and intractable questions; and certainly not positing the possibility of human extinction.

Winterstoke may also shed light on Tom Rolt the man – not a very kindly light, I find. For the man revealed here is full of fear and prejudice. But, then, we must remember the time from which this book comes. The 1950s in England may have been an especially fearful and forbidding period; and the writer unconsciously and truthfully reflects this.

WINTERSTOKE

*When the usurer hunts the squire as the squire has
    hunted the peasant,
As sheep that are eaten of worms where men were
    eaten of sheep;
Now is the judgement of earth, and the weighing of
    past and present,
Who scorn to weep over ruins, behold your ruin and
    weep.*

G. K. CHESTERTON

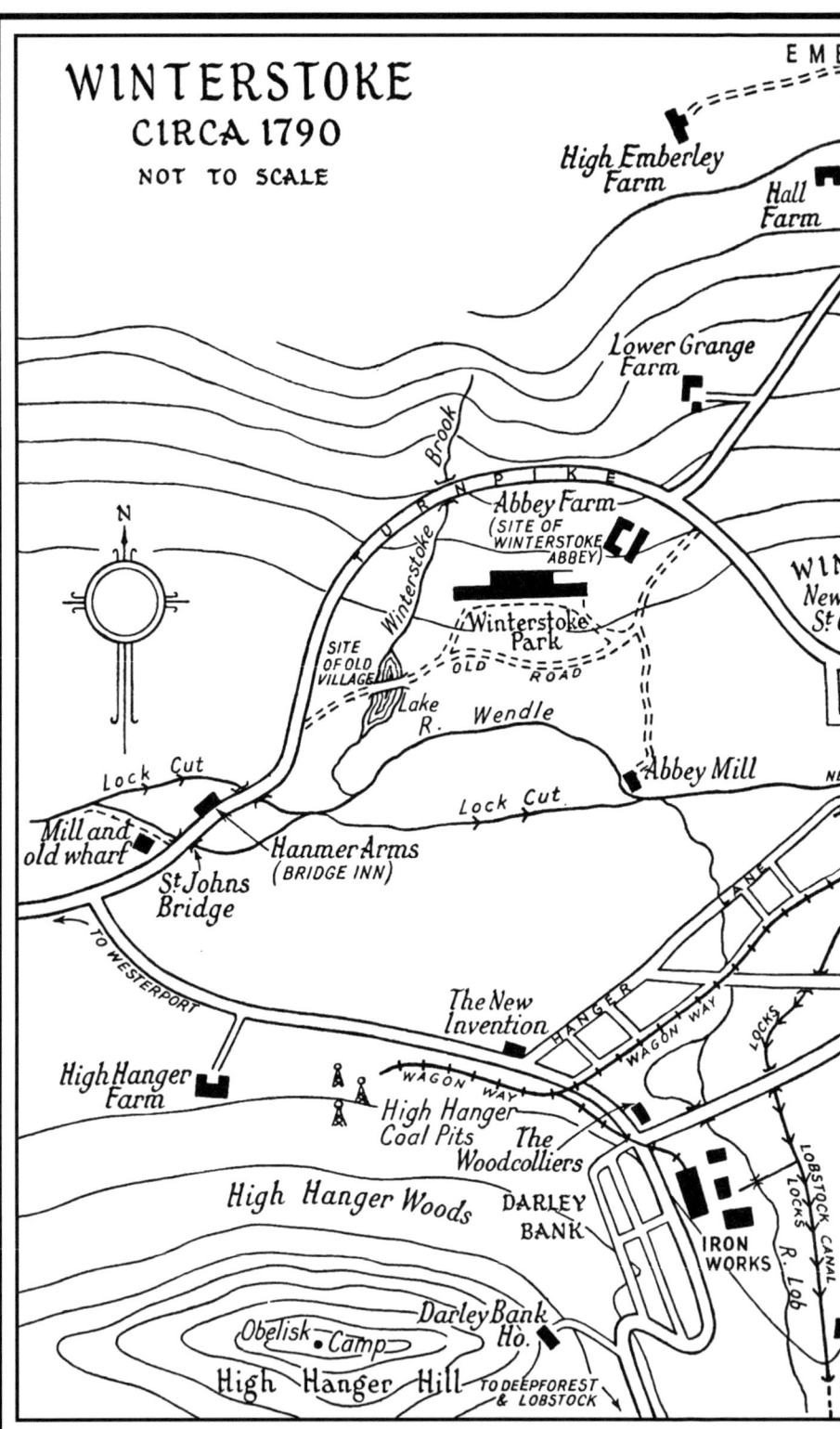

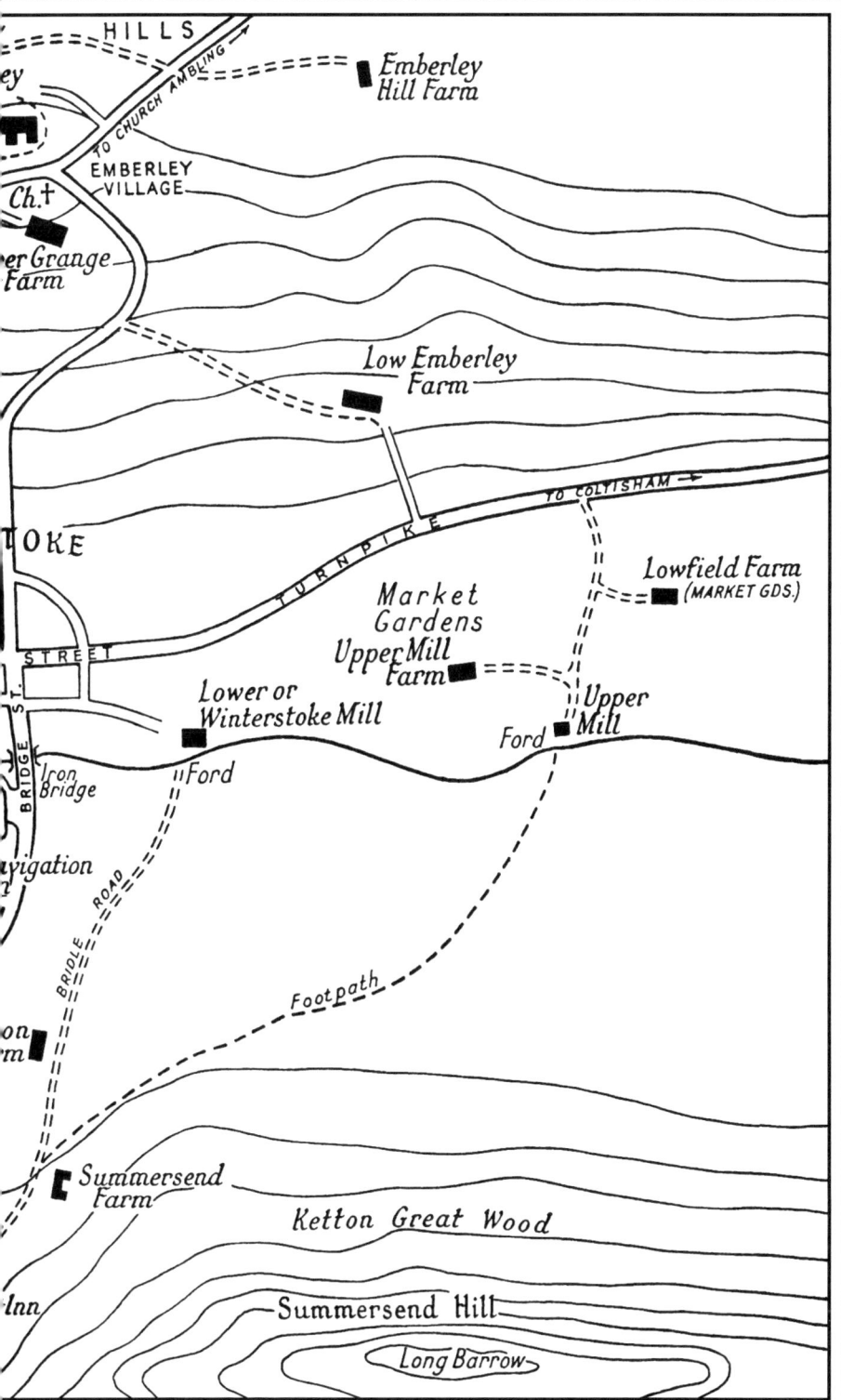

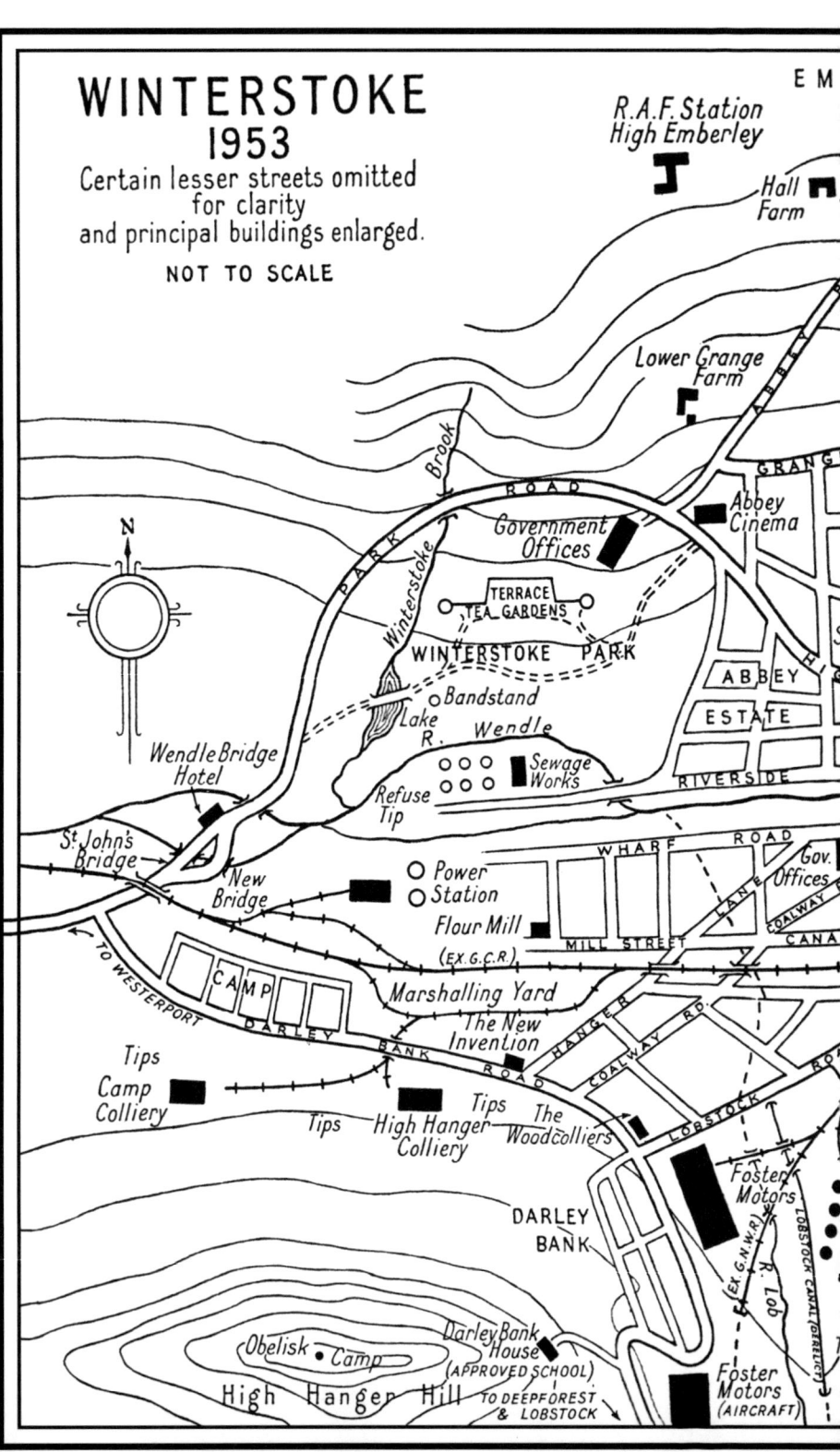

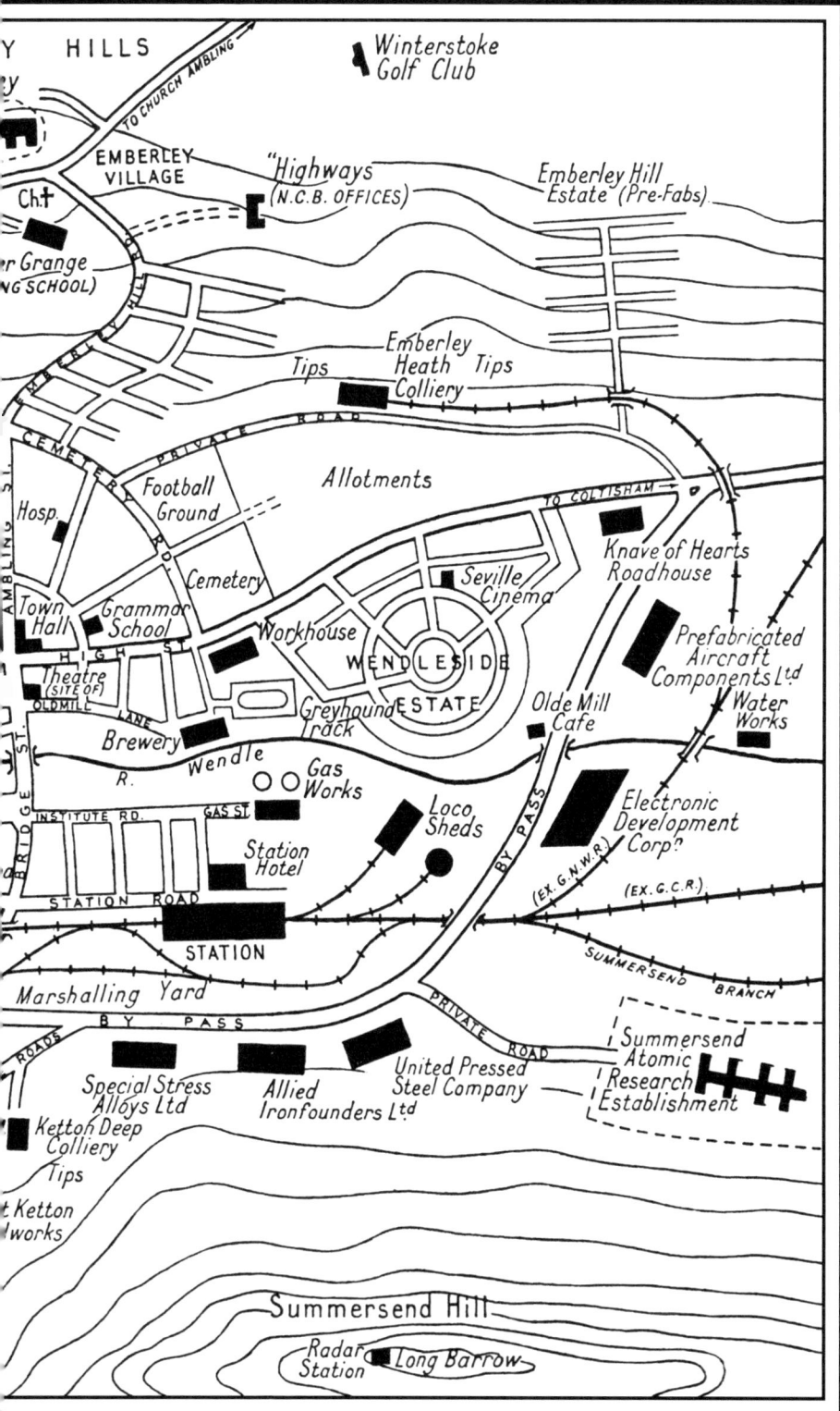

Foreword

TWENTY-THREE years ago, with the boundless optimism of youth, I sat down to write in a large exercise book a first novel which I confidently hoped would turn out to be a masterpiece. *Strange Vista*, as it was called, was nothing if not ambitious, one of those interminable family sagas beginning in the mid-eighteenth century and continuing through many generations. A naïve and romantic plot, partly auto-biographical in the tradition of first novels, was set against the background of a developing industrial town. Not content with past and present, the story finally wandered off into a 'Scientifiction' future where aeroplanes and cars were driven by electricity broadcast from a series of enormous Power Stations, one of which was situated in my imaginary town. No more refuelling; another shilling in the meter was all that was required. There was a swift and dramatic denouement when the amount of high voltage current floating about in the atmosphere suddenly caused a mysterious and fatal brain disease. The Power Stations failed, all road traffic came to a standstill, and huge airliners tumbled pell-mell from the skies. Only my hero and heroine had had the wit to foresee this disastrous end to the industrial era and lived happily ever after in their remote arcadian refuge.

Alas, the execution was by no means equal to the grandiose conception and *Strange Vista* never got beyond the covers of the exercise book. The plot was thin and irrelevant, but the basic idea—the growth of an imaginary industrial town—continued to haunt my imagination. So the 'Wolvercroft' of *Strange Vista* has become the 'Winterstoke' of this book with the difference that the town itself is now the main character and there is no superimposed plot or journey into the future. The object has been simply to paint a word

FOREWORD

picture of the period of industrial revolution, not forgetting the changes in thought and opinion which inspired and accompanied it. There are obvious reasons why it would be at once impracticable and highly undesirable to use the history of any actual town, even under a disguise, for such a purpose. The town of Winterstoke does not exist, and readers who seek to identify it with any actual town in the English Midlands will search in vain for clues. The quotation of the pronouncement by local justices in Chapter 2 and the criminal statistics quoted in Chapter 7 both, in fact, apply to Worcestershire, but they are merely taken as being typical of conditions in the Midlands at that time and in no respect, topographical or otherwise, does Midshire resemble that county.

Many incidents, such as the drowning of the old village church in the lake in Winterstoke Park, are based on historical occurrences in different parts of the Midlands, while I have introduced a few real figures of national importance, such as James Brindley, into the story. Also, but to a very limited extent, the earlier industrial achievements of my Leeds family are based on those of the famous Darbys of Coalbrookdale. In their lives and thought, however, there is no resemblance. All the other local characters, the Winters, Hanmers, Blenkinsops and Fosters, are entirely imaginary and do not bear any relation whatsoever to any actual persons, living or dead.

For certain details of the early iron industry I am indebted to Dr. Raistrick's book on the Darby family, *A Dynasty of Ironfounders*, and to the quite invaluable *Transactions* of the Newcomen Society.

L.T.C.R.
1954

Chapter One

THE CISTERCIAN ABBEY of Winterstoke is to-day remembered only by scholars. Its cloisters were once the scene of the labours of that indefatigable medieval historian Ambrosius, but parchment has outlived stone, for of this great church no trace remains.

In the earlier pages of the celebrated Chronicles of Ambrosius history and legend are inextricably mixed. His only sources were those heroic tales and ballads told or sung in the smoky firelight by generations of itinerant storytellers and musicians. And when the cups went round, when the harp sounded, the veil between substance and shadow, between mortals and immortals, wavered and shifted like the leaping reflections of the firelight. Gods became men and men like Gods; chieftains and petty kings became identified with heroes and magicians as old as time. So it is that Ambrosius can add little to our knowledge of those men who once dug the vallum of High Hanger Camp and who now sleep their eternal sleep in the long barrow on Summersend Hill. They were hidden from him by the mists of two thousand years, whereas a mere six centuries separate us from Ambrosius. Yet the world of this monastic historian, working in his small stone cell or pacing on sandalled feet from shadow to shafted sunlight in his quiet cloister seems to us remote indeed. In our world we effect greater changes in a decade than occurred in any one century of the Middle Ages. If Ambrosius returned to Winterstoke to-day he would find his familiar valley changed beyond recognition, yet the men of the ages of Bronze and Iron would have had no difficulty in recognizing the Winterstoke of the Cistercians.

From his fortified settlement at High Hanger, from his lofty burial place on Summersend or from the ancient trackway which followed the contours of the Emberley Hills,

WINTERSTOKE

iron age man looked down over the treetops of the wooded hill slopes into a deep valley which was impassable except in times of summer drought. For through it the river Wendle looped its way lazily seawards in a wild wilderness of marshlands and shallow, reedy meres of brackish water. Although Winterstoke is over thirty miles from the sea at Westerport, high spring tides then flowed unimpeded far inland, and if they happened to coincide with a land flood, then the opposing waters drowned the whole valley until it resembled a long arm of the sea. No wonder the first men of Winterstoke kept to the high ground. This does not mean to say that they never frequented the valley. It was a source of food far too valuable to be neglected. We may guess that they developed the skill of the fowler, for mere and marsh teemed with duck of many species, with wild swans and migrant geese, with piping curlew and innumerable snipe flickering and glancing overhead in drumming flight. From their eyries in the hills the peregrine falcon took their toll, stooping out of the high air with the speed and precision of avenging furies upon the arrow flights of widgeon or greylag. Bitterns boomed in the deep reed beds, herons stood sentinel by the shallow pools, while the swift 'fish hawk', the grey osprey, nested upon the inaccessible islands of the marsh. For fish there were in abundance, including the noble salmon which came up the Wendle in great numbers to spawn in tributary streams such as the Lob which has carved the narrow valley between Summersend and High Hanger hills. While early man's skill as a fowler can only be conjectured, we know for certain that he was an accomplished fisherman, because dredging operations on the Wendle have discovered his net weight rings of stone and bronze. Thus the abundant wild life of the Wendle valley provided the first men of Winterstoke with an unfailing food reservoir; a welcome addition to the resources of their flocks and herds and of those first tentative experiments in cultivation which we may still trace in the close turf of the hills.

Even in Saxon England, where life begins to emerge from

WINTERSTOKE

the shadows of myth and conjecture, the primitive landscape of the Wendle valley had changed scarcely at all. Those changes which the men of the Iron Age would remark, had they returned in the lifetime of the monk Ambrosius, began when the Norman, Hugh Fitzwinter, built his castle keep on the higher slopes of the Emberley Hills facing the mouth of the little valley of the Lob. Hugh Fitzwinter had been a staunch supporter of the Conqueror and his master had rewarded him with great estates. Except for the fact that the source of his worldly power was the strength of his sword arm and not a cheque-book, Hugh might be described as the Norman equivalent of the commercial tycoons with whom we are familiar. To us, therefore, his story sounds scarcely credible.

A little distance to the west of the castle where what we now call the Winterstoke brook formed a small and sheltered valley before becoming lost in the Wendle marshes, there stood at this time a ruin. A small and roofless rectangle of unbonded stone, it was reputed to have been the cell of the Celtic Saint Cenodoc in the days of the Saxon Kingdoms. What happened on that bright, far-distant morning when Hugh Fitzwinter chanced to ride past this ruined cell in the course of a hunting expedition no one will ever know. Doubtless even Hugh himself would have been at a loss to explain what occurred to him in that moment. Naturally the occasion became the subject of legend. Some said that Hugh saw the Saint at prayer in his ruined cell; others that a vision of Our Lady appeared before him and that at sight of her his impatient charger stopped in its tracks and bowed its head. But whether we believe or disbelieve these old stories really matters little; for the consequences are a sufficiently miraculous measure of the significance of the spiritual event. For at this one stroke the proud and hard-bitten Norman warrior renounced all temporal power, surrendered his estates to his son and became for the remainder of his days a contemplative recluse. With the help of his chaplain he rebuilt the Saint's cell, and this was the origin of the little Norman church of Saint Cenodoc. As he laboured at his building or sat in silent meditation in the solitude of the woodland glade, the grizzled old knight must have appeared a figure wild and strange indeed. For it is said that he never put off his suit of chain mail. As the links, once so bravely burnished, rusted away, they became a symbol of the transience and vanity of the life he had foresworn.

Hugh Fitzwinter's dramatic renunciation (which was by no means unique in his time) is sometimes described as 'giving up the world'. The description is misleading unless we define more exactly the nature of the sacrifice. It is true in so far as this great Norman gave up the world of men, of material wealth, of principalities and jealous powers. It is not true to say that he turned his back upon the natural world, upon those beauties created by God for man's enjoyment. Although we cannot fathom his mind at this distance of time, we may be sure that he would have regarded such a rejection as blasphemous in its ingratitude. It would also have been highly illogical, for we cannot doubt that the beauty of the natural world was an instrument of his conversion. Indeed there may have come to him no vision in mortal shape; only a sudden overwhelming realization that this sunlit woodland glade, bright with new leaf and loud with birdsong, was man's lost Eden. But he did not fall into the fatal primitive (and neo-primitive) error of identifying the creator with his creation, and so it is not as a pantheist that we should see the builder of Winterstoke's first church.

Hugh Fitzwinter's vision was destined to have far-reaching results. Influenced by his father's example, William Fitzwinter made a substantial grant of lands in the valley of the Wendle to the reformed Benedictines of Citeaux. To our eyes this gift might have appeared somewhat backhanded, for although it represented a considerable acreage, the greater part of it, as we have seen, consisted merely of salt marsh and shallow mere. But, disregarding any motive of piety and judging William's grant solely from the practical aspect of land reclamation and development, it is clear that his action was a very wise one. For these monks were dedicated by their rule not only to poverty and prayer but also

WINTERSTOKE

to labour which was, according to their founder, a form of prayer if rightly carried out in humility of spirit. This rule of labour had made them, as William Fitzwinter probably realized, the most accomplished husbandmen and craftsmen in Europe, men who devoted themselves to making fruitful such waste places.

From the day that the followers of the rule of St. Bernard and Stephen Harding established themselves in comfortless temporary huts a little to the east of Hugh Fitzwinter's oratory and laid the foundations of their first church the primeval landscape of the Wendle valley began to change. We, with all our powers of steam, electricity and internal combustion to command would have felt daunted by the magnitude of the task which these men set themselves. That they were quite undaunted was due to an attitude towards the work in hand so utterly different from our own that it is difficult for us to comprehend. Sometimes we regard work as an end in itself; much more commonly it is merely a means, frequently uncongenial, to a material end; to secure a larger profit or a heavier wage packet; to gratify personal vanity or ambition in the acquisition of power, influence or reputation. The members of this first humble but stalwart community at Winterstoke looked for no such rewards. Their work was neither a means to a material end nor an end in itself since they believed that to labour truly was a form of prayer, and true prayer seeks no reward. Prayer is the means whereby the created acknowledge and praise the creator; it is not directed towards, neither does it either foresee or presuppose any finite end. Similarly, by equating work with prayer, this first religious community of Winterstoke cheerfully embarked upon an immense task whose end they could not foresee and whose fruits they knew they would not live to enjoy. It occupied them for centuries, and in this brief epitome of their labours we who have changed the face of the earth in a hundred years, must bear this spacious time-scale in mind.

The first task before these monastic husbandmen was to control the river Wendle. Only then would it be possible to reclaim and improve the valley lands. For several winding miles the banks of the river were raised by from three to five feet, the necessary earth being the spoil from the drainage dykes which were cut behind them. When this work was finished and the latest length of embankment had been consolidated by time, a weir was built across the river at the downstream end of the embanked reach. This naturally raised the level in the reach, but it also slowed down the rate of flow and therefore reduced the rate of bank damage by erosion. But the greatest advantage of the new weir and the real reason for its construction was that its height had been nicely calculated from the experience of long observation to exclude the highest of spring tides. It was essential that the reclaimed lands should be thus protected from the menace of brackish water. Although these monastic engineers (for such they undoubtedly were) were concerned to exclude tidal waters, they did not attempt altogether to prevent fresh water flooding. Experience had taught them that the fertility of their fields was improved by periodic flooding provided the waters were checked so that they could deposit their rich silts and not tear uncontrolled over the land when they would inflict great damage. The method by which the marshes and meres were drained was by cutting dykes and protecting their outfalls through the heightened river banks by means of wooden sluices or 'clows'. But when after many years had passed fertile fields replaced marsh and mere it was realized that these old dykes could serve a new purpose. Fresh dykes were cut and flood banks thrown up between field and field to form an elaborate system of flood control. As the Chronicles of Ambrosius and other ancient records reveal, there were, periodically, great floods on the Wendle which no man-made banks could withstand. But in the case of the average winter or spring flood, or the sudden spates after summer storm the system worked well. By means of the sluices the floodwaters could be turned at will into this embanked field or that, to be released again when the river level fell to normal. Not only did these fields gain fertility from such controlled flooding; they acted as

WINTERSTOKE

valuable 'wash lands', safety valves, in other words, which by relieving the pressure of the waters, prevented or lessened unwelcome flooding elsewhere.

This matter of the control of the river Wendle has been mentioned first and at some length because it was quite literally the material foundation upon which the community of Winterstoke built and prospered. But once again the time factor must be stressed. The work described covered a long period; it was a process which did not so much precede as accompany the growth of the Abbey. The work of drainage had other results besides transforming a wilderness of marshland into fertile fields. When the Cistercians came to Winterstoke the valley was still almost entirely without communications. Travellers on foot or horseback moving from east to west across the country avoided it, using either the prehistoric trackway which wound along the contours of the Emberley Hills or the straight Roman way which skirted Deepforest to the south on the further side of High Hanger and Summersend hills. There was, it is true, an ill-defined track along the valley, but it was passable only in high summer. The same is true of the north to south track which branched away down the hillslopes from the ancient road in the neighbourhood of Emberley Castle, forded the Wendle near St. Cenodoc's cell and then climbed away towards Deepforest up the western flank of the Lob valley. But with the progress of the drainage works and the growth of the Abbey the ancient ridgeway to the north became at first unfrequented and later disused as the easier valley roads became more passable and more important. The effect of the new weir was to deepen the water over the old ford and necessitate the construction of an underwater causeway, but at the beginning of the thirteenth century St. John's Bridge was completed to replace the ford. This beautiful many-arched bridge of stone has been fated by history to be the only substantial work of the monks of Winterstoke to survive practically intact in our own century. To-day, after nine hundred years, the massive cut-waters, each shaped like the prow of a ship, still cleave the waters of the Wendle. Close

WINTERSTOKE

beside this bridge was the Abbey gatehouse and the hospice for wayfarers which was later to become the Bridge Inn. Opposite, on the downstream side adjacent to the weir, stood a corn mill whose great breast-shot water-wheel harnessed the power of the pent-up river to drive three sets of stones. A little distance below this mill's tailrace was St. John's Wharf.

It was not only upon the valley floor that the work of land reclamation went on. Along the lower slopes of the hills the woodlands were cleared and more fertile fields created. Thus in the days of Ambrosius an Iron Age man looking down into the valley from his old hilltop eyries would have seen a fertile garden in place of the wilderness of marsh and mere and forest. He would have seen rich pastures, some dotted with flocks and herds and others ripening to haysel; fields of standing corn rippling like wind-dappled water when a light breeze brushed the heavy ears; orchards heavy with fruit, and, along the sheltered southward facing slopes of Emberley, vineyards. But what would first catch and hold his eye would be the Abbey itself which had been the cause of this transformation and the heart of all its activity.

In imagination we can reconstruct with fair accuracy the Abbey as it was in the lifetime of Ambrosius. Its foundations were plotted by members of the Midshire Archæological Society before the site was finally built over, and an admirable plan appears in their *Transactions*. Moreover, under Cistercian rule, the disposition of the various monastic buildings in relation to the church was almost invariably the same. Only the menial buildings, in other words those wholly connected with the practical and lay activities of the community, were arranged according to local convenience. The heart of the Abbey was, of course, the great church whose scale was such that it would seem to brood over all other buildings like a hen over a clutch of day-old chicks. Like the rest of the monastery it was built by the community, using local stone which they obtained from two quarries not far from the site; one on the eastern flank of Summersend

WINTERSTOKE

Hill and the other further down the valley in the direction of Westerport. Stone from the Summersend quarry was in all probability floated down the Wendle on rafts whenever a freshet provided sufficient depth. Stone from downstream was brought up to St. John's Wharf on the tides by the small, shallow draft barges or 'snakers', which were the descendants of the long boats of the Vikings.

The nobility and calm majesty of Tintern and Fountains abides with them even in their ruin. Seeing them we realize with how perfect a fitness and beauty this Abbey church of Winterstoke must have crowned its setting of winding river, verdant fields and wooded hills. It was a symbol in stone of the fruitful partnership between God, man and nature which had been made manifest in ripening wheat and laden vine. Despite the immense scale of aisled nave, choir and transepts, the eye was neither overwhelmed by sheer size nor wearied or distracted by any elaboration of detail decoration. The Cistercians deliberately eschewed such decoration so that the beauty of Winterstoke lay in its simplicity and in a perfection of line and proportion which has never been surpassed in Early English architecture.

On the south side of the Abbey nave was the Great Cloister which was enclosed by the following buildings: on the west the dormitory of the conversi or lay brethren was built over a long range of cellars and storehouses; on the south was the refectory flanked by kitchen and buttery. Its length extended from north to south and at its entrance from the cloister was the lavabo. On the east side were ranged the parlour, where lay business was transacted and the rule of silence relaxed; the calefactory or day room, a chamber having hot flues under the floor where the brothers could warm themselves after night offices, and the Chapter House. Over this eastern range of buildings was the monks' dormitory from which the night stairs gave direct access to the south transept of the Abbey Church. Beside the Chapter House ran a vaulted passage which led to the Library and Little Cloister with its cells for study. Here it was that the monk Ambrosius laboured so diligently. The water supply

WINTERSTOKE

and drainage of the domestic buildings was provided by leats taken from the Winterstoke brook which flowed through the kitchen, the lavabo, and the necessariums adjoining the two dormitories.

Besides this main block there were a great number of detached buildings, most of them ranged about what was called the Base Court. The largest of these was the infirmary and, most probably, the Abbot's Lodging in the time of Ambrosius. Many other smaller buildings could not be precisely identified by the antiquaries but were obviously connected with the manifold secular activities of a completely self-supporting community; stables and lodgings for labourers; brewery, winepress and stillroom: granary, slaughter house and farmery; workshops of carpenters, stonemasons, smiths, weavers and curriers. Where a monastery has not, as in this case, completely disappeared, it is usually the sacred buildings which survive because of their sheer size and because they were not readily adaptable to serve any other purpose than that for which they were built. Consequently, seeing only the ruins of church or cloister we tend to underestimate the extent, the diversity and the importance of the secular activities of the great monastic houses, particularly those of the Cistercians. Some of us are inclined to look upon a monastery as the human equivalent of a beehive with the Abbot and his monks, ostensibly devoting themselves to prayer and contemplation but in reality living off the fat of the land, representing the queen bee and the drones, while secular activities consisted simply of servile workers slaving solely to support this idle elite. In fact the monastic system was far more complex than this, nor was there any such arbitrary dichotomy between sacred and secular activity. It was a hierarchical organization which attempted to express in temporal and finite terms the medieval conception of an eternal order in which God, man and nature were interfused in a hierarchy of infinite degree. The sacred, represented by the great church and, in human terms, by the Abbot and his monks, was certainly the apex of this organization, but between them and the meanest and

WINTERSTOKE

most mundane activity of the community no gulf was fixed. There were no broken rungs in the ladder which led from the Abbot through the monks and the conversi down to the humblest of lay labourers.

In its sacred activities the Abbey of Winterstoke represented not only the faith of Christendom but the storehouse of a European tradition of wisdom and learning which the church had nursed through the dark ages. It was by virtue of this heritage that the Abbey became, in its secular capacity, the mother of all our institutions and our crafts. The conception of our schools, our hospitals, our agricultural methods and the majority of our crafts and trades can all be traced back to this most fertile monastic womb. In agriculture the Cistercians were the pioneers of rotational cropping while their improved methods of stock breeding and raising laid the foundation of England's first source of mercantile wealth—her wool trade. But the monks of Winterstoke also brought to birth a later and much greater source of wealth. Even the wisest among them could never have foreseen that the first small iron smelting bloomeries which they set up beside the Wendle would one day grow into so prodigious a giant.

The improvements and innovations for which the Cistercians were responsible did not only benefit the monastic community and their lay brethren. The Abbey acted as an agricultural and technical college to the increasing number of lay labourers who were drawn into the prosperous orbit of its many-sided activities. In the neighbourhood of the little church of St. Cenodoc between the Abbey and St. John's Bridge a village community established itself. In return for their services to the Abbey in craft or agriculture, these peasant cottagers were allotted grazing rights and cultivated strips on certain of the improved lands which thus became the common fields of the village.

The ultimate downfall of the Abbey of Winterstoke was a tragedy brought about by its own success. Not only did the prosperity of the Abbey itself prove too great a temptation to its all too human and fallible community, causing them

WINTERSTOKE

gradually to relax their early rule of poverty, but the Abbey's children, the crafts and the laymen who practised them, grew too strong for their mother. They 'came of age', demanded freedom and chafed against the discipline and control of a parent who had grown lax in her old age. Even in the lifetime of Ambrosius this weakness, these stresses and strains, were beginning to appear in the fabric of monastic life, but about the time of his death they were greatly aggravated by the tragic visitation of the Black Death.

During the two years, 1348–49, that this frightful scourge raged in England it is estimated that more than half the population of the Winterstoke area died. The immediate effect of this disaster was to impoverish both the Abbey and the lay community of the village. Within the great church the sonorous cadences of Gregorian chant sounded less strongly and so symbolized the life which had ebbed away to leave fields untilled and crafts languishing for lack of labour. This critical situation enforced changes which had a far-reaching effect upon the whole monastic economy.

Hitherto the great majority of those who worked on the monastic estate had done so upon what we would now call a part-time basis. For the rest of the time they laboured on their own lands which had been allotted to them in return for these services to the Abbey. Some modern historians still hold the view that this system of land tenure was a form of slavery and that when the peasant either avoided these due services by paying rent for his land, or insisted upon monetary payment for work done, he made a vital step towards freedom. No doubt, like every form of human contract, the old system of 'boon work' was open to abuse, but when we compare the profoundly unstable value of money with the absolute and unshakeable value of land, the contract appears less one-sided.

As the village community prospered so they became increasingly reluctant to carry out their prescribed services on the monastic demesne. They were doing well and so preferred to work full time on their own account, and pay the fines levied from them for their failure to fulfil their

WINTERSTOKE

contract. Although in effect these fines were a form of rent, until the Black Death struck they were not officially recognized as such at Winterstoke where Cistercian rule forbade the taking of rent. They were still a payment in default of services due and not a land rent. But after the plague had passed the surviving villagers found themselves in so strong a position that for a time they were able to impose their own conditions on their monastic parents. They contracted with the Abbey to take up on payment of rent the strips in the common fields which had fallen vacant owing to the death of their fellows. Deprived almost entirely of the customary services of its landed tenants, the Abbey demesne now faced an acute labour shortage. Some of the Abbey workshops were leased to craftsmen, others were eventually manned by the landless labourers who, taking advantage of this nationwide situation, had defied the law which had hitherto bound them *adscripti glebæ* to their home manors, and roamed the country to sell their services to the highest bidder. Yet despite this influx the labour shortage remained, nor were the new tenant farmers able to take up all the neglected fields. To meet this situation a considerable acreage of the Abbey lands was laid down to permanent pasture and devoted exclusively to sheep raising. Like their sister communities elsewhere, the Cistercians of Winterstoke thus became great flockmasters. It is one of the ironies of history that both the factors which caused the downfall of the Abbey, the breaking away of its lay children and great material wealth, should have stemmed from the impoverishment caused by the Black Death and the steps taken to meet that crisis. For although it took much less labour to shepherd sheep than to till the fields, wool was at this period by far the most profitable commodity in England. Whereas in earlier days the English had been a self-sufficient island race whose exports were negligible and whose imports were confined to the luxuries enjoyed by the court and the nobility, the wool trade fathered a new race of merchant princes who made the English a force to be reckoned with in the markets of Europe. The trade had developed long before the Black

WINTERSTOKE

Death, but after 1350 it expanded rapidly, and whereas in its first phase exports had consisted almost exclusively of raw wool destined to be woven on Flemish and Italian looms, now, more and more, England exported the finished cloth. A certain amount of cloth was manufactured at Winterstoke, and a fulling mill was built on the Winterstoke brook. But most of the local wool crop was exported in the raw state either by water to Westerport or by pack-horse to Coltisham and Church Ambling, both townships having become important centres of the cloth trade.

The effect of this mercantile prosperity upon the Abbey of Winterstoke is graphically illustrated by the changes which took place during the long reign of Abbot Thomas Luttrell which occupied the middle years of the fifteenth century. In the figure of Thomas Luttrell we see how far the community of Winterstoke had strayed from the rule of poverty, humility and industry which its enlightened founders had so steadfastly followed. For this proud spiritual lord wielded as much power and commanded as much wealth as the greatest of the medieval nobility. Like them he lived and moved with great pomp and circumstance. With the fourteenth-century drift of the wealth of the woollen trade away from East Anglia into the West Country and the south-west Midlands, Winterstoke Abbey had become a favoured port of call for the rich merchants of the Staple and other influential travellers. Thomas Luttrell decided that his predecessors' modest quarters in the infirmary range were no longer fit for the reception and entertainment of such distinguished company. So the old lodging became, in all probability, an additional Guest House, while Abbot Luttrell built for himself, a little to the west of the Abbey and on slightly higher ground, a magnificent new house. With its spacious apartments, its immense kitchen of the cavernous ovens and hearths and, above all, its great pillared hall, 150 feet long by 50 feet wide, aside from the castles of a few great nobles, no subject in England was more sumptuously housed than Abbot Thomas. Only his brother Abbot of Fountains in the North could boast a larger hall.

WINTERSTOKE

In justice it must be said that the material wealth of the Abbey was by no means wholly devoted to the comfort of the Abbot and his guests. The monastic buildings were considerably enlarged, enriched and beautified during Luttrell's reign at Winterstoke. It was he who initiated the building of the beautiful perpendicular tower, which is referred to in the contemporary records as the 'great tower' or the 'Luttrell Tower', and which was not finally completed until shortly before the dissolution. Yet even here it is difficult to resist the suspicion that this lofty tower may have been conceived, not so much as a tribute to the glory of God as a memorial to the greatness of Thomas Luttrell. In any case it represented another departure from the strict Cistercian rule which decreed that the houses of this reformed order should not feature lofty towers or spires. Perhaps St. Bernard saw in such aspiring shafts of stone a danger of spiritual pride, and in the case of the Luttrell Tower such a view was probably justified. If pride built the tower, then assuredly it symbolized pride's speedy and inevitable fall for it did not long outlive its builder.

By Abbot Luttrell's day the monastic community had greatly changed. The number of conversi had dwindled considerably, while of the monks in choir, few now con- concerned themselves with any practical secular activity. The practice of leasing lands which had been introduced by *force majeure* after the Black Death had been much extended with the consequence that the larger proportion of the Abbey lands was now farmed by tenants. Thus the greater part of the Abbey's wealth was now derived from rents and dues, and Chapter and Parlour which had once been as full of talk of crops and stock as a farm kitchen had now become the administrative offices of a great estate.

After the dissolution the extent of monastic corruption was frequently exaggerated in order to justify the event, thus creating a misleading picture which has survived down to our own day. Where so many autonomous communities were concerned no generalization can be valid, but where, as at Winterstoke, some records survive, they usually reveal

WINTERSTOKE

that conditions on monastic estates were generally better than on those of the great lay landlords. Rents were in some cases higher, but tenants and even sub-tenants enjoyed security of tenure, freedom from rack-renting which gave them an incentive to improve their holdings, and the material benefits of the example and instruction provided by the greatest agriculturists of the age. The home farm which supplied the needs of the Abbey continued to be a model of good husbandry for the tenants, while the Abbey kept a 'poor purse' for the relief of those in trouble. Nevertheless, because the Cistercians of Winterstoke had so far relaxed their rule as to become wealthy landlords instead of poor husbandmen they became the object of a growing pressure of resentment and envy; the more so since they were members, not of an English, but of a European order which was represented, in this instance, by the mother house of Citeaux.

Agriculture and the export of wool was not the only source of the Abbey's wealth during this last period of its history. The flat-bottomed 'snakers' with their square sails which traded to St. John's Wharf in increasing numbers whenever tide or freshet served now bore away with them not only wool and cloth bales but increasing quantities of iron and surface coal. For this development of the iron trade the conditions created by the Black Death were once again responsible. Indeed, the far-reaching effects of this disaster are very commonly underrated by historians. Because no other major epidemic followed it, England again became more populous so that by the time of the death of Abbot Luttrell the population in the Winterstoke area was approximately the same as it had been a century and a half before when the plague had struck. But the agricultural policy which had been adopted in a time of acute labour shortage had become so commercially successful that it was not to be abandoned to provide land for the landless. Prosperous tenant yeomen who were the descendants of the humble cottars who had been lucky enough to survive the plague were unwilling to subdivide their holdings or to con-

WINTERSTOKE

vert the pastures of the 'golden hoof' back to common fields for strip cultivation. There were thus an increasing number of landless labourers in the district and it was this circumstance which led to the expansion of the iron and coal trades. The number of bloomeries in work in Winterstoke increased steadily throughout the fifteenth century. At first established by the monks themselves, a number of tenants now followed the monastic example by setting up bloomeries on their lands. Such yeomen did not abandon farming, neither did the ironworkers themselves turn their backs on the land. The trade was looked upon as complementary to the primary occupation of agriculture. Some of the ironworkers might have holdings of their own, while those who did not worked in the fields of the yeoman owner of the bloomery when required. In this way the iron trade absorbed the additional labour which became available and at the same time solved the problem of the fluctuating seasonal demand of agriculture for labour. From the outset the Cistercians had solved this problem in the same way by developing both husbandry and the trades in partnership and thus preserving a balance between them.

Iron ore, mined in Deepforest, was brought to the Winterstoke bloomeries by pack-horses which picked their way down the rough trackway which wound across the flank of the Lob valley. Although the labour involved was considerable, the tonnage produced by this centre of the medieval iron trade, even at its height, was infinitesimal judged by our standards. Each bloomery consisted of a small furnace blown by treadle bellows like a blacksmith's forge in which ore and fuel were mixed. By such means it took nine men working for from twelve to fourteen hours to produce two hundredweight of wrought iron 'blooms'. It was to facilitate this laborious process that the Cistercians of Winterstoke undertook what was destined to be the last extension of their secular activities. A second shallow weir was thrown across the Wendle at a point almost directly opposite the Abbey, the fall thus provided being sufficient to drive the under-shot wheel of a new mill. Here the power of the wheel was harnessed to work two sets of bellows which supplied blast to two bloomery furnaces. This new iron mill soon became known as a 'water bloomery', as distinct from the older 'foot bloomeries' where the bellows were worked by treadle.

It was when the lower slopes of High Hanger hill were being cleared for cultivation in the twelfth century that there had been found in the shallow depression left by an uprooted tree, the first of those 'black diamonds' whose presence was destined to have so profound an effect upon the future of Winterstoke. The outcropping seams may have been noticed previously, but the value of this black substance as a fuel was not realized until, in this process of clearance, a fire of roots and tree butts was lit in this convenient hollow. From that time forward coal formed a useful addition to winter firing for those tenants on whose lands the seams could be found, but it was not until this later period that coal getting, like iron working, became a regular part-time occupation and coal began to be exported beyond the immediate district.

Although these latter-day developments of Cistercian Winterstoke are of great significance in the light of future events, they were of small extent and had far less effect upon the landscape of the Wendle valley than Abbot Luttrell's Tower; here or there a heat shimmer in the air above the flue of a bloomery; here or there in the hanging woods the thin blue smokedrift of some charcoal burner's fire; now and again the distant creak and sigh of bellows or the thud and ring of a hammer. But that was all. The great tower, with its newly completed upper courses and pinnacles of unweathered stone glowing in the sunlight like a crown of gold, commanded a fair prospect. The partnership between man and nature was still a happy and a fruitful one. Though there were now many more pastures, sewn with sheep as thickly as the sky with stars, there were still orchards and vineyards and fields ripening to harvest. How far the Cistercians of Winterstoke fell short of their first high and selfless ideals can never be determined, but this much is

WINTERSTOKE

certain: after their tenure of four hundred years they left the valley an infinitely richer and more beautiful place than they found it. That they had been true husbandmen to the valley lands was proved by the rich consummation of that marriage. Moreover, it had been a love match and not a ruthless subjugation; the wilderness had been ordered but not destroyed as though it were some implacable foe or a thing of no account. Marshes and meres below St. John's Wharf were still a paradise for the wild-fowler. Rivers and streams still teemed with fish, to be netted after the ancient fashion for the griddle or trapped in the putcheons of the weirs to stock the monastic fish-ponds.

One bright morning in the summer of 1539 a small group of horsemen clattered over St. John's Bridge and drew rein at the Abbey gateway. If any villagers watched them pass it is unlikely that they would suspect that such a visitation presaged anything unusual, for among such simple country folk the news of momentous political changes travelled slowly. They probably concluded that the richly clad figure at the centre of the group was some wealthy merchant who had come to discuss business with the new Abbot Waldegrave and to enjoy his liberal hospitality. The stranger, who looked about him with such shrewd appraisal was certainly on business bent, and as certainly he was a figure of national significance. This arrogant man with the cold eyes and the thin-lipped mouth was Master of the Rolls to His Majesty Henry VIII, Chancellor of Cambridge University and Visitor General of Monasteries. Although a commoner, the son of a rascally and fraudulent brewer in Putney, at this particular moment in history no man in England under the king wielded greater power. Even the greatest of nobles had found it expedient to curry the favour of Thomas Cromwell however much they might privately detest him. Two characteristics had enabled Cromwell to achieve this position: an overweening ambition as great as that which had caused the downfall of his late master Wolsey, and a machiavellian worship of State power incarnate in the person of his new royal master whom he served without conscience, heart or religious scruple. Only two years later, when his head was struck off on Tower Hill, he was to meet the fate which inevitably overtakes such ambitious agents of unbridled power, but that story does not concern us here.

Needless to say it was upon no merchant's business that Cromwell came to Winterstoke that fateful day. He was playing a much richer game and had come to demand the surrender of the Abbey to the king. It was a tribute to the value set upon this particular prize that the Visitor General had chosen to come in person. Usually he remained in London and left such jackal's work to his four Commissioners. Sometimes the Commissioners met with resistance, and there were occasions where stubborn abbots or priors who had refused to surrender their properties had been hanged in their own precincts. But the momentous meeting in the Chapter which sealed the fate of this Abbey was marked by no such high drama. The end of medieval Winterstoke was in fact singularly inglorious, for the recently installed Abbot Waldegrave proved to be a cipher of the King's party who, having been promised a rich chaplaincy in return for his compliance, yielded up the Abbey without scruple. Of the monks, some followed their Abbot's example, while those who refused to acknowledge the King as the spiritual head of the Church eventually made their way to the Continent. The lay brothers who remained continued to work on the estate as labourers or craftsmen, some of them assisting in the work of pillage and demolition which was not long delayed.

One might have supposed that at least a part of the monastic estate would be granted by the Crown to the descendant of that William Fitzwinter who had originally bequeathed it to the Church in pious memory of his father. For the family had not only maintained a direct male succession through the troubled centuries but had remained firmly rooted in the place allotted to them by the Conqueror. Its sixteenth-century representative was Sir John Winter, Lord of the manor of Emberley. There is a fine, proud ring about the title 'Lord of the manor' which is in this case

WINTERSTOKE

somewhat misleading. It suggests the autocratic ruler of great estates whereas in fact the Fitzwinter lands had gradually shrunk as a result of church grants and forfeits until, despite their ancient title and noble blood, the family had become little more than prosperous yeomen. Sir John's lordship consisted merely of a draughty fourteenth-century hall, built on the moated site of the original Norman keep by his more prosperous ancestor Robert Fitzwinter (the last to use the ancient prefix), a home farmery, the small village of Emberley with its church and its common fields, and a few outlying farms which were in the hands of yeoman tenants. The Winters had fought for the cause of York throughout the Wars of the Roses, that protracted and unprofitable struggle in which so many representatives of the ancient aristocracy of the age of chivalry either destroyed each other or emerged impoverished and exhausted. Those who, like the Winters, had faithfully followed the white rose of Plantagenet from the triumph of Mortimer's Cross to the final disaster on Bosworth Field did not find much favour in the Tudor court, nor did they seek it. About that court had grown a new aristocracy who measured their strength in money rather than in the number of armed retainers they could muster. Sir John Winter, even had he been in a position to do so, was not fitted by nature to play the poker game of power politics with Henry and his creature Cromwell. The Norman blood ran strong in the Winters, and in Sir John's portrait—the long, proud but melancholy face, the high-bridged, aquiline nose and dark eyes brooding under heavy lids—we recognize a different species of man from those shrewd, square-faced merchant princes who had risen to power by replenishing Henry's exchequer and who were now angling for their pound of flesh in the shape of a share of the monastic spoils.

Typical of these new men of power was Sir Richard Hanmer, Groom of the Bedchamber to Henry VIII. The Hanmers were a family of East Anglian yeomen stock who had ridden to power and prosperity on a woolsack. Amongst the merchants of the Staple, Hanmer had become a name

WINTERSTOKE

to conjure with, not only in England but in the markets of Europe, and their gold had done much to consolidate the Tudor Throne. Now, Sir Richard Hanmer sought the reward of his family's fealty and was not disappointed. He was created Earl of Winterstoke and received the rich prize of the monastic estates.

The Abbot's house had seemed the last word in luxury and grandeur in the days of Abbot Luttrell, but to the new Earl, accustomed to the splendours and the ease of life in the Tudor court it appeared a dark and gloomy warren ill fitted to be the palace of a noble of such wealth and power. So the house was extensively rebuilt and enlarged, the Abbey buildings being used as a convenient quarry for material. In this connection it is a tribute to the esteem which this great church still enjoyed in the neighbourhood that the local inhabitants, led by Sir John Winter, had combined in an attempt to save at least a part of the Abbey from destruction. Elsewhere, similar attempts were sometimes successful. At Tewkesbury, for example, the whole Abbey church was saved, while at Pershore and Abbeydore the choir and transepts were spared while the naves were destroyed. But Abbeydore, as a Cistercian house, was an exception. The very fact that the Cistercians chose to build their abbeys in lonely and waste places sealed their fate in the sixteenth century, and so it was with Winterstoke. The local population was too small to raise the necessary ransom, while it could be argued that they already possessed places of worship adequate to their needs in the church of St. Cenodoc, which had continued to serve the villagers of Winterstoke, and in its near neighbour St. Peter's at Emberley. So Richard Hanmer had a free hand.

When we walk through the lofty nave and aisles of one of our great cathedrals it may seem incredible that anyone should set to work to demolish them so completely that not one stone remained on another. Quite apart from any considerations of impiety or vandalism it seems too formidable a task to undertake for a purely destructive and unfruitful purpose. We are so accustomed to seeing the far less sub-

WINTERSTOKE

stantial buildings of our own age: derelict factories which the industrial revolution has outpaced, casualties of war or the detritus of military encampments, surviving for years in ugly ruin because it is worth no one's while to pull them down and clear their sites. Many monastic ruins have, of course, survived, and it is this survival which should be the source of wonder, not the fact of demolition. For wherever, as at Winterstoke, any considerable new building was contemplated in the vicinity, the labour involved in demolishing the most massive of buildings was at that time considerably less than that of quarrying and dressing virgin stone and transporting it to the site. Thus the destruction of Winterstoke Abbey by Richard Hanmer was no deliberate and costly act of desecration but merely a practical expedient which put to good use a building which no longer served any purpose in the new age which he represented.

It was the purely sacred buildings, the Abbey church and its cloisters which became his quarry because of their inutility. Chapter, Refectory and Dormitories became the barns, storehouses and granaries of the Earl's home farm, while the infirmary and guest house was rebuilt to house his steward. So, to the greater glory of the first Earl of Winterstoke the destruction of the splendid church which generations of tireless hands had raised to the glory of God, went forward relentlessly. The long, empty aisles echoed the clink of chisel, pick and crowbar, the crack of hammers, the shouts of the workmen and the intermittent crash of masonry falling from the high vault to the floor of nave or choir in a smother of dust. And as this great symbol of the medieval world fell, so Winterstoke Place, symbol of the new world of the Renaissance, arose beside it.

There was as much difference between Richard Hanmer's new palace and Sir John Winter's dark and damp abode on Emberley Hill as there was between the latter and the grim Norman keep which it had replaced. Great new windows flooded hall, parlour and long gallery alike with light. Applying the lesson of the perpendicular style to secular purpose, the narrow lancets of Abbot Luttrell's hall

WINTERSTOKE

were replaced by windows more than twice their width, massive external buttresses being thrown up between them to reinforce the weakened walls. The new house, for such it could be called so drastic were the alterations, was E-shaped in plan, presenting a frontage of three projecting gabled wings, their façades almost entirely occupied by great oriel windows whose stone mullions extended through both storeys. A more striking contrast to the austere, meticulously proportioned beauty of Cistercian architecture than the interior of Winterstoke Place it would be difficult to conceive. For Richard Hanmer was what a later age would call a *nouveau riche*. Great wealth and the desire for ostentation were not yet governed or restrained by that sensibility and good taste which is only acquired by time and experience. Winterstoke Place was a work of fine craftsmanship, but it was an example of craftsmanship run riot for the lack of any controlling hand or any guiding purpose save the desire for display. Consequently the armorial bearings of the proud owner which were set in the new leaded windows glanced their jewel lights of ruby, sapphire and gold upon apartments whose spaciousness was spoiled by the vulgar profusion of their ornament. The effect was restless, so bewildering and distracting to the eye was the intricate lozenge moulding of the plaster ceilings, and the over-heavy woodwork of panelling, stairways, doorcases and overmantels all elaborately and minutely carved without regard for the proportions of the whole. Even the furniture was treated in the same fashion, the legs and feet of table, chair or tallboy swelling out into meaningless dropsical globes for no better reason than to provide a greater area for the indefatigable carver. Yet here, as in the Palace of the great Cardinal at Hampton, there could be distinguished amid this brash display a crude entablature, an ill-proportioned column, a top-heavy pediment, which were the primitive portents of a new architectural style. With the completion of this great house which was at once a caricature of the age which had passed and of the new age which was to come, a great chapter in the history of Winterstoke drew to its close and a new era began.

Chapter Two

IF ANY of the smaller tenants of the Winterstoke estate had imagined that they would benefit by the change from monastic to secular rule they were doomed to disappointment. Richard Hanmer duly installed his family in their new and palatial home, but he was frequently absent himself either at the Court or on mercantile and political business abroad. He therefore delegated responsibility for the day to day administration of his great estate to his steward, Stephen Folliot. From the few estate papers which survive it would seem that this Folliot was a hard-working, conscientious and, on the whole, a just man. But, as the tenants soon found, Stephen Folliot's brand of justice was not so generously tempered with charity as that of his monastic predecessors. Indeed, it could not be otherwise when the high sense of duty of this steward was exclusively devoted to serving the best interests of his absent master. Whether the master would have acted more generously than the man had he concerned himself more directly with the affairs of his estate we cannot know, but it seems unlikely. For Richard Hanmer was one of England's first great men of business, and as such he regarded his estate in a light different from that of his predecessors and different also from that of the older lay landlords such as Sir John Winter. His sense of ownership was much more absolute. The lands of Winterstoke were his; he was no steward, holding them in trust either for God or for the King. He could not command the allegiance of his tenants, nor were they under obligation to him except for the payment of rents. Yet perhaps some of the tenants who had chafed against the medieval obligations and clamoured for this freedom now realized that the old responsibilities had been mutual. For there was now no hostilarius to receive the weary traveller, no almoner to

WINTERSTOKE

help the poor and the sick with the aid of the herbs which were rendered to him by the community; nor did Stephen Folliot hold any 'poor purse' with which to help those in trouble even if he had a mind to do so. The old monastic estate could be likened to a wagon wheel in which the hub of the Abbey was linked to the felloes of tenants and village community by many spokes of mutual obligation to form a strong, self-sufficient and highly-organized whole. When the hub was suddenly knocked away, every spoke either split or fell out. The estate retained the shape of the wheel because felloe was still held to felloe by the iron strakes of external authority, but it possessed much less internal strength as a structure. Winterstoke Place might form a new centre, but it did little to stiffen it. An attempt was soon made to remedy this fatal weakness from within by a system of voluntary contributions by the more prosperous within the parish towards a fund to help the poor and the sick. This failed and the next effort to remedy a worsening situation came from without in the form of Elizabethan legislation which levied a Poor Rate from each property holder and person of estate and made each parish responsible for its poor. This was the first step upon that long legislative road whereon the warm spirit of Christian charity was destined to fall by the wayside and to be replaced by cold ethics enforced by the compulsion of remote authority.

Charity is one of the greatest of virtues, but charity exercised by force of law is not charity at all for, like all goodness, the source of charity is the spirit. This is aptly illustrated by the new attitude towards the poor in the parish of Winterstoke. The Cistercians had regarded an opportunity to exercise charity as an occasion for thankfulness and for this reason the porter at the Abbey gate acknowledged a knock with the words 'Deo Gratias' before greeting the arrival with the blessing 'Benedicite'. Now, however, the homeless, the needy and the sick were brusquely turned away; indeed, the more desperate and pitiable their plight the more unseemly the haste with which they were hustled beyond the parish boundary for fear that they

WINTERSTOKE

would become a charge upon the Poor Rate. Circumstances beyond their control forced the villagers of Winterstoke to adopt this callous attitude; to harden their hearts and 'pass by on the other side'. For the increase in the number of dispossessed who became vagrants upon the roads of England was so great in the period which followed the dissolution that no small community like that at Winterstoke could possibly afford to play the good Samaritan. To do so would have been to risk an inundation of immigrants far beyond the capacity of any country parish to support.

It is easy for us to imagine the splendours and the mannered graces of the Tudor and Elizabethan worlds in which Richard Hanmer and his son Henry moved on their successful and flamboyant way. We have been made familiar with that romantic aspect of sixteenth century England but not with the miseries upon which much of that splendour was based. It is more difficult for us to picture the ragged, motley crew of so-called 'sturdy beggars' who could each day be seen plodding over St. John's Bridge, and who, like the gypsies of to-day, were forever being ordered to move on. This nomadic army was the consequence of the agrarian policy adopted by the great Tudor landlords which was tersely but eloquently summed up in the contemporary couplet:

> *Commons to close and kepe*
> *Poor for bred to cry and wepe.*

The changes which occurred on the Winterstoke estate compose a typical illustration of this policy and its effects.

Of all people, Richard Hanmer was the last to underestimate the value of the 'golden hoof'. To provide him with additional sheep-walks, a greater acreage of arable land was laid down to pasture than had ever been the case in monastic days, while his larger tenants followed their landlord's example. In consequence, at a time when there was no lack of labour, much less labour was required. In addition to this laying down of arable, much rough grazing

WINTERSTOKE

land on which the villagers had enjoyed rights of common pasturage was enclosed and reserved for Hanmer's privileged flocks. That the villagers were not deprived of their common land altogether was not so much due to their landlord's scruples as to the good counsel of Stephen Folliot. Aware of the intransigent temper of the tenantry, this shrewd steward advised his arrogant master that it would not be wise for a new broom to sweep too clean. So the villagers retained an acreage of common pasture and, like the larger tenants, they continued to enjoy the right of estover in the woods of High Hanger and Great Ketton. But this loss of common pasture impoverished the villagers in two ways. It necessarily reduced the stint of livestock which each could carry on the reduced area of grazing, and this in turn affected the fertility of their arable strips which they manured by stock folding. In this way both the landless and the landed labourers on the Winterstoke estate were impoverished, while there was no longer any 'land room' in which the community could expand. Landless labourers were forced by the all-conquering sheep to seek other employment; small freeholders and copyholders could only secure an adequate livelihood if they could find some supplementary occupation. Their plight was aggravated by a great increase in the price of corn and other basic commodities for which the break down of the old medieval organization was responsible.

Early in the fourteenth century, Winterstoke had been granted by royal charter a weekly market and an annual three-day fair on the feast of the Nativity of St. John the Baptist (June 24th). These fairs and markets were held in and about the churchyard of St. Cenodoc and were, until the dissolution, governed and regulated by the jurisdiction of the Abbey. This government had two main concerns: to maintain the 'Assize', that is to say, the quality of all that was offered for sale, and to fix prices at a just level. To this end prices were posted in the market and Officers of Assize appointed—Searchers of Leather, Tasters of Bread and of Ale—to guard against deceitful workmanship or adultery,

WINTERSTOKE

and those who broke the Assize or took 'excess of gain' were fined. The worst sin of the medieval market had been that of 'engrossing', of seeking to profit by buying up a commodity to create a scarcity and then selling out at a high price. Hence the practice of buying to sell again was forbidden unless the buyer performed some work upon it before reselling. For example, a man who bought corn could sell it again as flour but not as corn. After the destruction of the Abbey, the Winterstoke market continued to be held as before, but under conditions of commercial anarchy in which sorely-needed supplies either never reached the market at all or soared to prices beyond the reach of the poor. For Richard Hanmer, a man whose power lay in 'excess of gain', was unlikely to apply those spiritual sanctions in restraint of trade which, in his view, would represent the restrictive and reactionary shackles of a bygone age. Yet things came to such a pass that the local justices did make an attempt to preserve the old order by regulating prices and preventing engrossing. We find them complaining that: 'A nomber of wycked people in condicions more lyke to wolves or cormorants than to naturall men did most covetusly seeke to holde up the late great pryces of corne and all other victualls by ingrossinge the same into their private hands, berganynge beforehand for corn and in some parts for grayne growinge and for barlie before yt be made mawlte and for butter and cheese before yt be brought to ordynarie markettes for to be bought for the poorer sort.' But such strictures proved vain. Although the attempts of the justices to regulate the corn trade and to prevent the laying down of too much arable to pasture were backed by the force of laws, secular authority was unable to prevent this disintegration of the old economy. It was to prove equally powerless to regulate the growth of the new commercial and industrial England which was coming to birth. It was a painful birth, occasioned by the irresistible pressure of necessity.

The villagers of Winterstoke were more fortunate than many of their fellows elsewhere. They were not forced to join the ragged throng upon the roads because there were

WINTERSTOKE

other sources of employment to which they could turn. They had long been accustomed to make up cloth for their own use, and now necessity drove them to make up cloth for sale. This soon plunged them into bitter conflict with the long established Guilds of Weavers in Coltisham and Church Ambling, the first of many similar clashes between the new economy and the old which could not be reconciled. The organization of the Guilds was medieval. They endeavoured to equate supply with demand by regulating entry into the trade. They maintained a standard of quality by laying down rules and terms for apprentices and journeymen so that a man might not become a master weaver until he was in very truth the master of his trade. They saw in the cheap country-made cloth which began to flow into their towns from Winterstoke and other rural parishes a grave threat to their time-honoured and carefully-ordered system. They were right. The weavers of Winterstoke, on the other hand, saw in the Guilds a restrictive monopoly whose concern it was to prevent poor and honest men from obtaining a livelihood in the best way they could. They were right also. The real wrong lay in the new landlordism and the new agrarian policy as represented by the first Earl of Winterstoke, but even if the contestants realized this, such august merchant princes were above attack.

Some of the cloth produced at Winterstoke may well have been up to the high standard of the Guild weavers, but whatever its quality its price had to be cut. For whereas the Guilds produced according to demand, the village weavers produced from necessity and a demand had to be created. Markets had to be found, but the villagers were not in a position to find them, nor would the Guilds help them. Some intermediary was needed. He came in the shape of the very character that all medieval economists had fought against: the engrosser, the 'middle-man', the man who bought cheap to sell dear. So hard a bargain could he drive with the hard-pressed country weavers that he could sell their cloth in the towns at prices well below those fixed by the Guilds and still clear a handsome profit. An Act

WINTERSTOKE

passed by the government of Henry VIII prohibited the making of cloth for sale except in certain specified towns where the industry was under Guild control, but it became a dead letter. Pressure was too strong. In this, as in other trades, the Guilds were ultimately defeated and forced out of existence, but the fruits of victory did not go to the new producers. As the cost of living soared, as fewer and fewer families could afford to live on and by the land, so more and more turned to this trade or to that, impelled by the stern necessity to produce or to starve. The more overcrowded a trade became, the more the astute merchant was able to profit by the abject buyer's market which was thus created, always provided—and this is the vital point—that he could find a market for the goods he bought. In an England which was soon to abandon as impossible any attempt to regulate local supply in accordance with local demand, the scapegoat of the old world would become the key figure of the new. The economy of Winterstoke was no longer that of a self-sufficient community trading in its surpluses. It was becoming more and more expansive and of that expansion the merchant, operating at first in a steadily widening orbit at home and in Europe, and later in every corner of the globe, was the agent and the arbiter.

Although the opposition of the Weaving Guilds was ineffective, it was sufficient to cause many of the domestic workers in Winterstoke to turn from weaving to iron-working and coal-getting, trades which, in middle England, were free from Guild control. Although they did not know it, these men had the future on their side. For the cloth trade eventually melted away to the North of England to leave Coltisham and Church Ambling quiet country towns, rich in the substantial memorials of past prosperity, but playing little part in this story of industrial revolution.

It was in the narrow valley of the tributary Lob that the Winterstoke iron trade became concentrated, for when Richard Hanmer built his great house he had banished the small bloomeries and forges from its vicinity, including the 'water bloomery' on the Wendle. The latter had been

WINTERSTOKE

converted to a corn-grinding mill as an adjunct to the home farm which occupied the site of the Abbey. It is unlikely that a visitor to Winterstoke in the last years of the reign of the first Elizabeth would attach any particular significance to the contrast already apparent between the north and the south banks of the river. But we who in spirit may now journey back there through time, burdened with the knowledge of things past or passing or to come may savour the drama of that contrast.

It is a golden June evening after a day of great heat and the river slides smoothly and soundlessly between the massive piers of St. John's Bridge. In this clear water the salmon lie, lazily breasting the slow current with effortless, sinuous movement as though swayed like the trails of waterweed by the eddies of the stream. Occasional ripple-rings flaw the surface as a fish sucks down a fly. The mill beside the bridge which has churned its tall wheel all day is silent now; nor is there any sign of life on the wharf beyond where two bluff-bowed barges lie at rest with their unbleached square sails furled. But there is a deep-throated murmur of voices from the Inn opposite, and a belated hay wain rumbles over the bridge. A smocked wagoner walks at the head of his straining team as the wagon creaks and sways along the dusty, rutted road past the medieval gatehouse of Winterstoke Place, past the cottages of wattle and thatch and the squat Norman tower of St. Cenodoc's until it disappears round a bend in the road.

On the upper terrace of Winterstoke Place the second Earl is strolling with a mixed company of guests, enjoying the coolness and fragrance of the evening air, the men no less than the women as colourful as the peacocks that pace and flaunt upon the lawns. Time has already begun to mellow this great house. Looking at the long, gabled façade of sun-warmed stone it is no longer easy to distinguish by texture the first Earl's work from that of his predecessor, Abbot Luttrell. Its appearance has been enhanced and dignified, also, by its setting of formal gardens which are

WINTERSTOKE

now approaching the zenith of full maturity. These descend in a series of broad terraces from the south front: pleached alley and arbour; lawn of fine turf or camomile; beds of June flowers so strictly ordered by close-clipped box into intricate geometrical patterns of massed colour that they resemble the leaded lights in a window of stained glass. They look their best in this level, golden light of evening which lengthens the shadows of the yews and draws colour from the flowers even as the first dew fall draws out their scent. This, no less than the village street beyond the gates, is Shakespeare's England as we have always imagined it; that street could be the home of the village players in *The Dream*, this garden the perfect setting for the courtship of Beatrice and Benedict or the pathetic antics of Malvolio. There is a ripple of laughter on the terrace and, listen! someone, the Lady Hanmer perhaps, is playing upon the virginals. Sounding softly through an open casement, the music is quickly dissolved and lost in the wide silence. The lady is playing a piece by William Bird, a simple, plaintive little tune strangely at variance with the vivid colour and richness, the abounding vitality and self-confidence of this Elizabethan world. For us this thin and melancholy music is prophetic. It is as though it sounded a lament for an age whose bright splendours were so soon to pass away. It is across the river, in the narrow valley of the Lob and in the woods of High Hanger and Great Ketton, that we must look for the birthplace of the more sombre world which was to come.

In woodland clearings and on the steeply-tilted common lands of the narrow valley, in crazy shacks or in more substantial cabins of timber and thatch a new population is establishing itself in defiance of the law prohibiting new building without an allotted acreage of ground. This new immigrant population have found new trades for themselves in and about the woods, but the living is hard and so long as the light lasts the work goes on. The outlines of both wooded hills are blurred by the blue smoke of many charcoal fires which hangs like strands of mist on the windless evening

WINTERSTOKE

air. Beside each turf-covered pyre stands the burner's shack, and throughout the short summer's night the colliers will be watchful, ready, should a wind spring up, to move their wattled screens to shelter the windward air-vent from a draught which would cause the heap to flame and so destroy the charge. Although in the depths of these leaf-laden woods it is already twilight, the chock of the axe still echoes through the glades. The more sizeable felled timber will be reserved for building, but the smaller loppings are being cut into cordwood for the charcoal fires. Women and children are at work with barking knives, stripping the bark from felled oak for use in the tanner's steeping pits.

From clearings along the lower slopes of High Hanger woods an increasing tonnage of coal is being drawn. It cannot be used for smelting iron, but the smiths use it on their hearths, while although the rich still prefer wood or charcoal there is a growing domestic demand for coal in the district which is supplied by water down the Wendle or by packhorse over the hills. The old flat mines or footrills are partially worked out and no longer able to meet this demand so the miners of Winterstoke have followed the seams underground. Tunnels have been driven into the hillside, each spewing out an unsightly trickle of waste spoil down the cleared slope. At one point at the hill foot a vertical shaft sixty feet deep has been sunk to meet the fall or 'dip' of the seam. Here a patient horse, urged on by a ragged small boy, is plodding round and round the narrow hoof-churned circle of a gin hauling up chaldrons of coal from the depths. The same chaldrons are used to raise or lower the miners or for drawing water from the drainage sump at the shaft bottom.

Picking its way down the steep, winding trackway that descends the flank of the Lob valley comes the last packtrain of the day, each horse carrying on its crucks a burden of three hundredweight of iron ore or limestone from the mines and quarries of Deepforest and Lobstock. Like most of the charcoal that is being produced in the woods it is bound for the ironworks beside the Lob.

Here in this narrow valley lies the heart of this new

WINTERSTOKE

Winterstoke, a heart of glowing metal ceaselessly active, and beating to the rhythm of many hammers, smith's hammer ringing on anvil, the clang of the oliver, or the metronomic thud of the heavy tilt hammer at the forge. This last is silent now, but the others still sound from the 'outshuts' of the cottages which are scattered like bricks down the steep slopes. Here, as can be seen by the glow from their open doorways, the smiths have their hearths, their wives and families sharing the work by blowing the fire or treadling the oliver. This last is a heavy hammer whose helve is pivoted so that it strikes upon the anvil when the treadle is depressed and is raised again by the spring of an ash pole slung under the roof.

There are still some small bloomeries of medieval pattern in work, one or two 'foot bloomeries' where the bellows are worked by a treadle and ash pole like the olivers, but the remainder 'water bloomeries' where a small water-wheel, turned by the Lob or its tributary streams, works the bellows. But this old bloomery method is no longer capable of meeting the smiths' demand for iron. Already they have become obsolete and within fifty years the last of the Winterstoke bloomeries will go cold. The real centre of this little world of iron is now the charcoal blast furnace with its loom house and its adjacent forge which was set up at the expense of Henry Hanmer, second Earl of Winterstoke, and leased to his yeoman tenant, Alfred Darley. It is the vital link between the miners and charcoal burners on the one hand and the smiths on the other.

This blast furnace is encased in a square of masonry built into the slope of the valley so that proportioned quantities of charcoal, ore and burnt lime may conveniently be fed from the flat top or 'bridge' above into the decanter-shaped upper part of the furnace which holds the charge. In the base of the furnace is the firestone crucible, six feet deep and tapering from six feet in diameter at the top to four at the bottom. At the top of it is the blast hole and at the bottom the tapping hole. The blast is supplied to the furnace from the ponderous double-acting bellows driven by the waters

WINTERSTOKE

of the Lob, the air being led to the blast hole through an annular space in the brickwork where it is to some extent pre-heated. The lime, the virtue of which as a flux in the furnace has already been recognized, is burnt with coal in nearby kilns built into the hillside in the same manner as the blast furnace. The men who tend this new furnace may no longer observe the ancient daily rhythm of labour and of sleep. For six months or more it has been fired continuously to produce an average of twenty tons of iron a week, the flare from its open throat lighting up the silent woods at night or throwing a false sunset glow on the skirts of low-flying clouds. But the limiting factor is the flow of the River Lob. Already the great bellows creak and sigh with painful slowness and the output of the furnace has fallen in both quantity and quality as a result of the weakening blast. Soon it will be blown out and then relined and repaired in readiness for the autumn rains.

In front of the furnace is the 'loom house' where the molten metal is run into moulds shaped for it in the clay floor. Occasionally simple castings such as hearth backs are cast in this way, but most of the metal is run into 'pigs'. Unlike the blooms produced by the older method, these pigs are brittle and useless to the smith until they have been treated in the forge. There they are reheated in an air furnace and pounded under the heavy tilt hammer to disperse the excess carbon and make the metal ductile. The bars of wrought iron thus produced are then slit by hand into rods of sizes suitable for the smiths. In this 'finery', as it is sometimes called, a small quantity of steel is also produced by cementation for the use of the edge toolmakers. The great head of the tilt hammer is mounted on a stout helve of ash pivoted at a point about two-thirds of its length away from the head. The other end of this helve is shod with an iron pane which engages the cogs of a massive wheel mounted on the axle tree of the water-wheel outside the forge. As each cog of the slowly revolving wheel strikes the pane it depresses it and so lifts the hammer head from the anvil, letting it fall again as cog and pane move out of engagement.

WINTERSTOKE

Water power is thus used to raise the hammer only; its own weight delivers the blow, while its rate of strike can be varied by altering the number of cogs on the driving wheel. The smith sits before the hammer in a swinging chair suspended from the roof, flexing his knees against the base of the anvil as he works the hot metal to and fro under the hammer. A chain, hanging beside him, is connected to the sluice on the headrace of the water-wheel, so that he is able to start and stop the hammer at will.

As in the case of the nearby blast furnace, the limiting factor of this forge is the water supply, although here the problem is not so acute because the demand is intermittent. Now, with the forge dark and silent in the summer dusk, the hammer pond above is slowly filling up. This means that even in the droughts of midsummer a certain amount of work can be done before the pool is exhausted. In time of winter rains or melting snows when the blast furnace roars its loudest, the output of raw iron exceeds the capacity of the forge so that a stock of pig-iron can be built up which will serve to keep the forge in work during the period when the furnace must be blown out. Moreover, the fact that iron-working must perforce slack off in summer for lack of water suits well the majority of the workers involved. For these miners, charcoal and lime burners, furnacemen, finers, slitters and smiths of Winterstoke are not yet an exclusively industrial community entirely divorced from the land. Their new activities and their new skills have, as it were, grown up in those cracks in the old rural economy of medieval England which appeared after the dissolution. But although these cracks continue to widen, the older structure has not yet fallen apart. Many still have land of their own and many more work seasonally as farm labourers. Even the far-seeing and ambitious Alfred Darley at whose instigation blast furnace and forge were built is no man of iron but an active and prosperous yeoman farmer. So life is still governed by a seasonal rhythm, the drought-enforced idleness of furnace and forge coinciding with the season of haysel and harvest when most labour is needed in the fields.

WINTERSTOKE

What of the smiths for whom most of the iron produced in the old bloomeries and in the new furnace and forge is destined? What are they forging on the hearths in their cottage outshuts? Some are skilled tradesmen: scythe-smiths, making scythes and other edge tools; locksmiths; loriners and spurriers forging bits, spurs, harness buckles and other horse tackle. But an overwhelming majority are nailers. Because nail-making is the least skilled of all the metal trades it is the one to which the hard-pressed small holder or landless labourer and common-squatting immigrant most readily turns in an effort to better his condition. Therefore, even at this early date, it is already tending to become an overcrowded trade, displaying that instability and those chronic conditions of acute poverty and sweated labour which result from overcrowding and which would disfigure the whole history of the hand-made nail industry.

When we delve down through centuries of English history in search of the seed from which the Industrial Revolution sprang we find that the roots go much deeper than we had imagined; that they form a complex web in which there is no distinguishing cause from effect, so subtle is the interplay of the forces involved. Yet it is tempting to isolate the figure of the Winterstoke nailer, forced into this precarious trade by worsening agricultural conditions, and labouring long hours with his family at his cottage hearth, as an unwitting architect of industrial England. It was his insatiable demand for iron which created Darley's blast furnace and forge and, through them, the increasing demand for charcoal, for ore, for limestone and for coal. It was the need to create a market for his nails which brought to power the merchants, the prosperous ironmongers who ranged ever further afield. So, at this turn of the century, we see the Winterstoke nailer already sandwiched between two layers of capitalistic enterprise, soon to join forces over his head and ultimately to crush him out of existence.

The more skilled of the Winterstoke smiths, the makers of edge tools, the loriners and locksmiths, some of whom inherited a tradition of craftsmanship which had originated

WINTERSTOKE

under monastic tutelage, are in a much stronger position than the nailers. Yet in this 'free' trade even the most skilled craftsman may be threatened by unwelcome competition from aspiring newcomers. For the greater the influx of new recruits at the bottom of the nail trade, the greater the tendency for those at the top to graduate into some other craft more skilled, more lucrative and more secure.

Those who still imagine that industrial England sprang into instantaneous life towards the end of the eighteenth century when James Watt 'invented' the steam engine may find this picture of Winterstoke at the beginning of the previous century scarcely credible. Nostalgic pictures of a simple rural 'merry England' as exemplified by the old villages of Winterstoke and Emberley, and of the courtly England of Winterstoke Place have so captured the fancy to the exclusion of all else that it is difficult to believe that blast furnaces and mechanical hammers could ever have had their place in the England of Shakespeare. Surely, they will say, this picture of the Lob valley is an anachronism in the England of the players and the well-turned sonnet, in an age whose signature tune is the music of lute and virginals, not the clangour of hammers. Surely if Alfred Darley's furnace and forge had really existed in this England it would have been regarded as the marvel of the age and we should have discovered many more references to ironworking in contemporary literature. There are various reasons why these developments, so pregnant with significance for us, occasioned so little contemporary remark that their history is extremely difficult to trace. In the first place, like most of the early centres of ironworking, the Lob Valley was remote and, owing to the appalling state of the roads, seldom or never visited by the literate minority. Secondly, the Elizabethan and the Jacobean looked out upon his world through eyes very different from ours; eyes which, despite the effects of the Reformation and the Renaissance of learning, still retained the shadow of the medieval vision as in a glass darkly. Consequently, while they accepted and might actively exemplify the new mercantile spirit of their age, they did not regard such activity as the be-all and end-all of life. The Hanmers may have violated most of the medieval canons during their rise to power and wealth, but the beauties which soon mellowed Winterstoke Place revealed that they regarded neither as an end in itself. The pursuit of wealth and power for its own sake, the idolatrous worship of man's handiwork as instruments of power and evidence of man's mastery of the world, such aberrations of pride were not yet. Thus the Hanmers of Winterstoke regarded the noisy activities in the Lob Valley merely as a profitable offshoot of the primary industry of agriculture. The second Earl had financed the building of the blast furnace and forge for his progressive yeoman tenants and now drew rent from them in the same manner as he might cause new barns and bartons to be constructed. From the time of the Black Death onwards the chief crop from the Winterstoke estate had been wool, but now iron was taking its place. Such a simple statement would sum up the contemporary attitude to the new trade. It had grown up in a framework which was still in many respects medieval; no one could know that the hammers of Darley's Bank, as it was now called, were forging a new world and a new school of thought which would soon shatter that framework forever.

Throughout the first half of the seventeenth century progress was slow. The old bloomeries either vanished or became fineries and a second charcoal furnace took their place, but otherwise, apart from one significant development which will be mentioned later, our picture of the Winterstoke iron trade does not alter technically until after the civil war. Limited water power and transport facilities combined with a knowledge of iron-smelting which was still primitive effectually prevented any considerable expansion. Moreover, although the trade was free in the sense that there was no local Guild of Ironworkers, medieval conceptions of trade regulation and control continued to influence legislation and to limit the expansion of the Winterstoke iron industry. Thus when the ironmongers from the Midland shires began to invade the London market,

WINTERSTOKE

they came into conflict with the powerful Ironmongers' Company with the result that there was fought a similar battle to that between the free weavers of Winterstoke and the weaving guilds of Coltisham and Church Ambling. The arguments on both sides and the results were precisely the same. The only significant difference was that this battle of iron was fought at much longer range than the older wool fight with the result that the Winterstoke smiths, whose livelihood depended on the outcome, knew little or nothing of the distant struggle which was going on between merchant and merchant. But they suffered from its repercussions when they were forced to accept a sacrificial price for their nails or buckles or locks. This was the first stage in a process of expansion which would one day make Winterstoke dependent upon the fluctuations of an unstable and bitterly competitive world market.

The State, through the local justices of the peace, continued its efforts to control trade by means of enactments such as that which forbade any man to practise a trade unless he had served a proper apprenticeship. But attempts at control, whether they were made by the Guilds or by the State, could only check and not prevent the growth of free iron-producing centres such as Winterstoke. They failed for the same reasons that had caused the failure of the weaving guilds. They were unable to resist the overwhelming pressure of necessity which was behind production and their regulations were only enforceable in an organized urban community. Winterstoke was not such a community; it was a rural area whose inhabitants were combining ironworking with agriculture, and here no urban writ could run effectually.

So, in spite of restrictions and difficulties the Winterstoke iron trade continued slowly to expand. The trade map of England was changing. By a great northward movement the trades were assuming the geographical pattern which they were destined to retain until the twentieth century. The textile trade was moving away from the midland counties to the north of England and to fill the void the

WINTERSTOKE

iron trade was moving into the midlands from the south. Although the story of the Winterstoke iron trade in the sixteenth century was not unique in the shires of the western midlands, until the end of that century Sussex retained its position as the great iron-producing county of England. It was the Wealden men who cast the cannon of the little ships which challenged the galleons of Spain, and in the minds of most Elizabethans the name of Sussex was synonymous with iron. But with the new century a decline set in, slow at first, but quickening to a collapse after the civil war. Furnace after furnace went cold, forge after forge fell silent. In an area which was mostly in Sussex but which included parts of Surrey and Kent there were still thirty-five furnaces and forty-five forges in 1653, but by 1667 there were only eleven furnaces still in blast and eighteen forges at work. This rate of decline was almost exactly counterbalanced by the rate of growth of the Midland iron trade. There were various good reasons for this. In the west midlands there were still great areas of woodland to feed the furnaces with charcoal; in the south the Government became alarmed at the inroads which the insatiable furnaces had made into the Wealden woods and feared that a failure of timber supplies to the naval shipyards would result. Having a lower average annual rainfall than the Midlands, the Wealden furnaces had to be blown out for lack of water power for a proportionately longer period. Thirdly, the south country ironmasters suffered more from the lack of transport facilities than the midlands. Though a good market in London was comparatively close at hand, it could not be reached except over-land through the heavy Wealden clay, and attempts to solve this problem by canalizing the Wey, the Medway and the Sussex Ouse came too late to save the trade. Winterstoke, on the other hand, was not unique in the midlands in being able from the outset to export by water down the Wendle to Westerport. Difficult though the navigation of the Wendle was in these early days, it nevertheless possessed an immense advantage over land carriage by pack-horse. But perhaps the most cogent reason for the rise

WINTERSTOKE

of the midland iron trade and its conquest of the south is to be found in the vacuum left by the loss of the textile trade combined with acute land hunger. These were the circumstances which created the army of domestic ironworkers for which there was no parallel in the south of England.

The rate at which domestic ironworking in general and the nail trade in particular continued to grow at Winterstoke may be judged by the fact that the smiths' demand for material was sufficient to justify the erection of a slitting mill at Darley's Bank in 1636. This, like the two furnaces and the forge, used the power of the River Lob, a fourth pool and dam being constructed directly below the forge, the rapid fall of the Lob down its narrow valley being peculiarly favourable to such development. This was the one important technical innovation which took place at Winterstoke between 1600 and the outbreak of civil war. Once again the Darley family, represented by Alfred Darley II, were the instigators, the capital being furnished jointly by him and by Charles, third Earl of Winterstoke, who seems to have displayed a keener interest than his father in the activities of his enterprising tenants. Of the mechanical arrangement of such early slitting mills no detailed information has so far been discovered, but we may guess that the erection of the mill was the outcome of a visit paid by Alfred Darley to the Hyde House at Kinver in Staffordshire where the pioneer ironmaster, Richard Foley, had installed the first slitting mill in the Midlands seven years before. It is not without significance that this Richard Foley was himself the son of a sixteenth-century nailer. It is safe to assume that Darley's mill followed closely the pattern of Foley's, but whether rotating cutters or reciprocating shear blades were used to slit the bars wrought under the helve hammer in the forge is not known. Whichever the method, it is fairly certain that, after slitting, the rods were reheated and then evened and trimmed by passing them through water-driven rolls. This slitting mill is noteworthy as the first machine in the iron trade to provoke the long and often bitter

WINTERSTOKE

struggle of machines versus men which was to accompany the whole course of the industrial revolution and in which the machine was always the ultimate victor. Though there is no record of any attempt having been made to destroy the new mill, the iron slitters of Winterstoke complained bitterly against the machine which had robbed them of their arduous and tedious livelihood. Their protests soon died down. Doubtless they were quickly absorbed elsewhere in the industry.

The civil war between King and Parliament which broke out in 1642 and spread an untold amount of destruction and misery over England until 1649 can scarcely be compared with the previous civil struggle of the rival roses. The average commoner of the fifteenth century wearied of the seemingly interminable struggle between opposing nobles and few were strongly partisan. But in the war of the seventeenth century a whole people were involved, neighbour found himself opposed to neighbour and a position of impartial neutrality was difficult to sustain. One of the causes of the conflict which is often overlooked yet is of the greatest significance was the fact that both the first Stuart kings endeavoured to exercise control over commerce. This principle they inherited from the Tudors as part of the medieval legacy which the latter had wrested from the church. Although their efforts to apply this principle were not conspicuously successful, they provoked bitter resentment in the areas of recent trade expansion. What brought the constitutional struggle between king and parliament to a head was, in fact, the very same issue over which so many local skirmishes had already been fought between the old craft guilds of the medieval towns and the new free traders. The arguments on both sides were still the same and remained as irreconcilable as ever. So it came about that Parliament drew its staunchest supporters from the new industrial districts, while the king's forces were recruited mainly from the landed gentry, from rural areas untouched by the new trades and from towns where the guild system still held sway. This explains why Winterstoke was sharply

WINTERSTOKE

divided by the civil war. From Alfred Darley downwards, the ironworking community and its associated miners and wood colliers were solid for Parliament. The forges and furnaces of Darley's Bank made a great contribution to the equipment of Cromwell's forces which were aptly named 'Ironsides', so loyally did the men of iron support them. The sympathies of rural Winterstoke, on the other hand, lay with the king's party and this sharp cleavage contributed greatly towards the breakdown of the ancient association of industry and agriculture which had hitherto prevailed. Henceforward the two worlds would drift ever further apart.

The war placed Charles Hanmer in a peculiarly difficult and invidious position, for he had a foot in both camps. As a great landowner and the head of a family who, since the time of Henry VII, had maintained close and cordial relations with the Court, he would feel himself under obligation to support the king. At the same time, the rents the Earl received from mining and ironworking already represented a substantial part of his estate revenue. He was also financially involved with his most influential tenant, Alfred Darley, than whom there was no more active and outspoken supporter of Parliament. But Charles inherited the astuteness which had carried his grandfather to power and he doubtless argued that to take active, and if necessary forceful, measures to prevent the ironworks from becoming a Parliamentary armoury would be straining his loyalty too far and that, in any case, such an effort would prove not only self-destructive but in all probability futile. In the event he seems to have emulated the celebrated vicar of Bray with considerable success. It was a difficult and dangerous role to play at this time, but thanks to his considerable power and wealth allied to his own statecraft he was able to carry it off. By making substantial contributions to the king's hard-pressed exchequer he was able to retain the Royal favour and to secure freedom from molestation by the Royalist forces. At the same time his influential association with Alfred Darley seems to have won him a

WINTERSTOKE

similar immunity from the Roundheads. It is true that on one occasion a contingent of Royalist troops, sent to break down an arch of St. John's Bridge as a strategic move, continued up the Lob valley and inflicted some damage to the ironworks before they were beaten off by an undisciplined but formidable army of ironworkers armed with weapons as assorted as sledge hammers, pick-axes and scythes. But reprisals, when they came, were directed, not against Winterstoke Place, but at Emberley Hall which was pillaged with characteristic thoroughness by a small Parliamentarian force. Happily, before Sir Hugh Winter rode to join the King's standard he had commended his wife and family to the care of a kinsman so that the only victims of this wanton encounter were his elderly steward and his wife who escaped with a beating and found asylum at the home farm. Emberley Hall remained an untenanted ruin until the Restoration, for Sir Hugh paid as dearly for his loyalty to the house of Stuart as his ancestors had done in the cause of Plantagenet. Escaping to France after the final wreck of the king's fortunes, he returned with the young Prince only to meet his death at Worcester, one of the many victims of that slaughter which Cromwell called his Crowning Mercy. So it was not until the Restoration that a grateful king restored the small estate to his son Sir Stephen who rebuilt and reoccupied the Hall.

While Charles II was thus mindful of those who had remained steadfastly loyal to the house of Stuart, he could not afford to be too rigorous in condemning or penalizing the waverers especially when they were families of great wealth and power. So we find Henry Hanmer, the fourth earl, enjoying the royal favour no less than his poorer neighbour, and becoming an influential figure at the court of St. James. This was not so unnatural as it may sound. Like many other revolutionaries before and after them, the Parliamentary Party, by their extremism, had forfeited the sympathies of their more liberal-minded supporters. Charles Hanmer was one of the many who had felt the need for reform but who was deeply shocked by the action of the

WINTERSTOKE

Regicides which he regarded as murder. Profoundly mistrusting the rule of the Lord Protector he had devoted the remainder of his days to urging that restoration of the monarchy which he did not live to see, and to instilling his heir with a devotion to the king over the water.

The return of the king was an occasion of great rejoicing and relief for a people who had grown heartily sick of a despotic régime whose grey, humourless and repressive character had proved so foreign to their nature. To many ardent Royalists it must have seemed that life was beginning again where it had ended in 1649 and that the years of civil war and Commonwealth would soon be seen to possess little historical significance. They were wrong. Not only did Charles II make no attempt to exercise the royal prerogative in the way that his father had done, but Government no longer concerned itself with commerce except in the role of arbitrator. The principle of *laissez-faire* had been accepted. The ironworkers of Winterstoke and the 'people of the middle sort' who supplied their material and marketed their finished goods had won a decisive victory. Although no victory in history was destined to have more momentous consequences, the actual protagonists remained unaware of its full significance. For it was no less than the triumph of a new philosophy and a new attitude to life. Although its revolutionary effects did not immediately become obvious, they proceeded, slowly at first, but with an increasing weight and momentum, to change the world and to invade every department of life.

Claiming to rule by divine authority, Charles I had attempted with small success to exercise those powers which Henry VIII had wrested from the church. He was the last frail and ineffectual instrument of that doctrine of a natural law based upon an eternal law which had built medieval Winterstoke out of an uninhabited wilderness. It had already lost its hold over the minds of men and it perished with him. It was extinguished by the belief that the unfettered exercise of self-interest was a natural human right. With a religion which no longer saw the temporal

WINTERSTOKE

and the eternal worlds as parts of a single whole but drew a sharp distinction between them, such a belief was easily reconciled. That this was so is evident from the fact that Josiah Leeds and his son, the second Josiah, who, more than any other men, were responsible for the immense changes which took place at Winterstoke during the eighteenth century, were both religious men. They were, after their lights, as deeply religious as the Norman, Hugh Fitzwinter, yet the difference in outlook between these men of the eleventh and eighteenth centuries was profound.

When, with his own hands, Hugh Fitzwinter had built his little oratory in the woodland glade beside the Winterstoke brook, he renounced the fallen world of men but accepted the natural world as the glass of eternity, an earnest of the paradise of God. It was because he did so that his action set in motion that train of events which transformed the valley of the Wendle from a wilderness to a fruitful garden. Josiah Leeds also believed in an eternal world, but it was a world remote and apart from the temporal world in which he had his being and in no way were the two interfused. The natural world and the world of men were one, a vale of tears and tribulation, a hard proving-ground through which Christian must fight his way in the hope of salvation hereafter. On earth men are free to create their own heaven or their own hell according to their thought. Josiah Leeds created the ironworks of the Darley Bank Company with the result that the garden of Cistercian Winterstoke became a wilderness once more. But it was to be a very different wilderness from that lonely, natural solitude of marsh and mere which the Saxon had known. It was to be a man-made desert of blackened bricks and mortar, of smouldering spoil and slag heaps, of flame and smoke and thick, polluted streams. Pious, honourable, infinitely conscientious, scorning alike the riches, the vanities and the beauties of the world, the Leeds family succeeded by a prodigious outpouring of energy, ingenuity and resource in building about them a world which was the exact embodiment of their desolate and sombre vision.

Chapter Three

JOSIAH LEEDS was a connection by marriage of the Darleys. The son of a Staffordshire maltster, he was brought up in his father's trade but was soon attracted away from it by the iron industry in which Josiah saw much greater scope for his ability. That ability and energy was such that he became a valued associate of the Foley family in their ironworking enterprises with the result that he was already a man of substance with a considerable experience of the trade when he made his first recorded visit to Winterstoke in the year 1704. He came at the request of his sister-in-law, Hannah Darley. The death of her husband, Alfred Darley III had left her sadly in need of advice and help, for their children had died in infancy and she had been left to manage Alfred's affairs as best she could. For three years the conscientious Josiah continued to guide his sister-in-law in the control of her late husband's estate and to make periodical visits to Winterstoke. In the course of these visits he became so impressed by the possibilities of trade development at Darley Bank that he disposed of his Staffordshire interests, built a modest house for himself on the slopes of the Lob valley, and moved his family thither in the autumn of 1707. In the spring of the following year the Darley Bank Company was formed, the capital being held in equal shares by Hannah Darley, Josiah Leeds and the trustees of George, the young Fifth Earl of Winterstoke, who was still a minor.

For the first important development at Winterstoke in the eighteenth century this new company was not directly responsible although Josiah Leeds was actively concerned in it. This was the improvement of navigation on the river Wendle. During the previous century the steadily growing tonnage of coal and of raw and finished iron which was shipped

WINTERSTOKE

downstream from St. John's Wharf had made the defects of the river as a navigable waterway increasingly obvious. But the river had been the scene of perpetual conflict between opposing interests since medieval times and previous attempts to improve the navigation had been defeated. That Josiah Leeds succeeded where his predecessors had failed is an interesting illustration of the effect of the constitutional changes which the civil war had brought about.

At the time the Cistercians built their mill and wharf the Wendle was a tidal river between St. John's and the sea. As such it was an open or free river so far as navigation was concerned, the watery equivalent, as it were, of unenclosed common land. But just as much of the land which was common in the eleventh century was subsequently cleared and enclosed, so the Wendle was enclosed during the Middle Ages by the construction of a number of fish weirs and mill weirs between Winterstoke and Westerport. Above these weirs the river was no longer held to be free but was considered to be the property of those who owned the land upon its banks. If the river formed a boundary between properties, then that boundary was not the river bank but the centre of its bed. St. John's Wharf had remained the upper limit of navigation although the continuance of traffic thus far had not been maintained without conflict. The weirs below St. John's were of two kinds. Those nearer the sea at Westerport, where the river was subject to most tidal influence, were half tidal, that is to say they were of such a height that vessels could float over them at high water. There was a constant fight to maintain a sufficient draught of water over the sills of these weirs. When, as frequently happened, a vessel struck a weir, often sustaining serious damage in the process, the bargemaster accused the weir owner of raising the weir in order to hold back more water for his mill. The weir owner would deny this and either blame the level of the river or accuse the bargemaster of damaging his weir through being too deeply laden.

On the higher reaches of the Wendle the weirs were constructed with a removable portion which consisted of a series

WINTERSTOKE

of wooden sections called 'paddles' which were held by water pressure against stout posts or 'rimers'. Both paddles and rimers could be withdrawn to make a narrow passage for boats through which the current flowed like a mill race. Downstream traffic had to ride this current, while craft proceeding upstream had to be hauled against the torrent either by a fixed winch mounted on the bank or by a forrard mounted deck winch. In either direction the passage was a hazardous proceeding. Here again there were endless disputes between bargemasters and weir owners especially in seasons of low water. A considerable loss of water to the mill was involved each time the weir paddles were drawn and weir owners either demanded an exorbitant toll before they would agree to draw or else flatly refused to do so. Often in summer droughts some luckless vessel, deep laden with coal or iron, would run fast aground in midstream upon some shoal and remain there for days or even weeks until the owner of the weir above could be prevailed upon to draw his paddles and so send down a welcome 'flush' or 'flash' to float off the stranded boat and send her on her way. It is not surprising that these 'flash weirs', as they were called, were often the scene of bloody free-for-alls between the millworkers and the navigators. When it came to brute force the navigators usually won the argument, for the single square sails of the barges were very seldom sufficient to propel them unaided, and they were therefore accompanied by gangs of bow-hauliers. Whereas the navigation of the Wendle became a highly skilled hereditary craft, son succeeding father as bargemaster for generations, bow hauling merely called for unwearying brute strength. The job attracted the roughest and toughest of men who were not only more than a match for any force a millowner could recruit to protect his weir, but became the terror of the whole riverside neighbourhood.

This protracted battle of the Wendle was not merely a simple issue of navigators versus weir owners. The landowners joined in the fray to make it a complicated three-sided contest in which the odd man out would find his interests ranged now on this side, now on that. Landowners

WINTERSTOKE

resented the passage of bow hauliers through their property and would attempt either to close the 'haling way' or to levy tolls for its use. At several points between Winterstoke and Westerport the Wendle haling way switched from bank to bank of the river to avoid the more recalcitrant of these landowners. This caused further delays to navigation, for where there was no bridge or flash weir, the hauliers must needs be ferried over or walk to and from the nearest crossing. In most cases ferries became established at the tow path crossings, but the ferry owners levied a toll for their use. In their resistance to the bow hauliers the land and weir owners were allied against the navigators, but upon another issue they were in conflict. This was the landowners' contention that, by holding up the waters, the weirs increased the risk of flooding. In this particular dispute the position of the navigators was equivocal. They welcomed any attack upon an obstructive weir owner, and on a claim that a half-tide weir should be lowered or removed they might support the landowners. But a campaign for the removal of a flash weir did not have their support. However obstructive its owner might be, they knew full well that, by holding up the water in the reach above, it enabled them to trade at times and seasons when navigation would otherwise be impossible.

In this chaos of conflicting interests the only controlling authority was the local Commissioners of Sewers headed by the Earls of Winterstoke, but as arbitrators they were singularly ineffective, certainly so far as the bargemasters were concerned. They were the local branch of a Royal Commission set up to improve land drainage and prevent flooding. To this end they could, and did, order the bed of the Wendle to be 'scoured', make drainage cuts or insist that a weir be altered or removed if it unduly restricted the river's outfall. But they were not empowered to further the interests of navigation in any way, and the fact that the scouring of the channel assisted the bargemasters was purely coincidental. It was this impotence, combined with the increasing tonnage shipped from his estate which induced Charles Hanmer to apply to the king for powers to improve the

WINTERSTOKE

navigation. These were granted by Charles I in the form of a Patent dated 1635 which authorized the Earl to make the river navigable for boats of convenient burthen by 'casting down weirs and erecting or making fludgates, sluces or other engins or devises'. This Patent left to Charles Hanmer the task of reaching agreement with property-holders and other interested parties along the course of the river, although it made provision for a Commission to be set up to arbitrate in the event of dispute. Dispute there certainly was. Both weir and landowners held that the king could not grant any exclusive rights over a private river and that the Patent was an abuse of the Royal prerogative over the rights of the subject. So nothing was done and the age-old dispute dragged on until the greater matter of the civil war put a stop to it.

When Josiah Leeds and his supporters reopened the question they encountered the same bitter opposition but the constitution now provided a different means of ventilating and settling such disputes. They applied, not to the Queen but to Parliament for an Act which would empower them to carry out the necessary work, and in this case the battle was joined and the opposition overcome before the Lower Wendle Navigation Act passed into law and the Company of Proprietors of the Lower Wendle Navigation was formally incorporated in 1710. The long overdue work of improvement then proceeded rapidly. The last of the old fishweirs dating back to medieval times were soon demolished, their owners being paid agreed sums in compensation by the Company. Two of the half-tide weirs were also demolished on the same basis while the third was raised and a pound lock constructed beside it. Pound locks were also constructed on short cuts beside each of the three old flash weirs, Pigeons Mill, Abel's Gullet and Fingerlow, the millowners being compensated by the Company for the loss of their right to levy tolls. In addition, two new cuts and pound locks were built at St. John's and Winterstoke Abbey Mill to enable craft to ply to a new wharf within easier reach of the ironworks in the Lob valley. The Company had originally sought powers to make the river navigable as far as Coltisham another ten miles up-

WINTERSTOKE

stream, but the opposition of the numerous millowners and the expense which would have been involved in compensation and in constructing the many locks led the proprietors to drop this part of their project. So Darley Bank Wharf, as it soon came to be called, became the upper limit of the navigable Wendle and so it remained.

Compared with the river locks with which we are familiar to-day, the first locks on the Wendle were very crude affairs indeed. The 'pounds' or 'pens' between the gates were not masonry chambers but simply an enclosed portion of the lock cut with sloping turf-covered sides. Only at the upper and lower ends where the gates were hung was there vertical timber piling consolidated at the back with clay and earth. The gates themselves did not swing in hollow quoins but were merely hung on massive hooks and rides like any farm gate, with the result that they were far from water-tight. The sluices in these gates which admitted water to or released it from the pound exactly resembled the old paddles of the flash weirs and were, indeed, so called. The paddle itself, a stout rectangle of elm planking which covered the orifice in the gate, was attached to a long wooden bar having a number of holes at its upper end so that it could be levered up with the aid of a handspike. The lock gates had no counterbalance beams but were opened and closed by means of chains and winches.

The most difficult problem which the Wendle Navigation Company had to solve was how to overcome the chronic lack of navigable draught in the two long reaches above and below the lock at Abel's Gullet where, in dry seasons, loaded boats had often been stranded for weeks at a time. The position here was now likely to be even worse than before because one of the conditions of the agreement which had been reached between the Company and the millowners was that the former should only be entitled to draw sufficient water to fill the locks. This meant that the old practice of 'flashing' which had so often been employed to lift a boat off the shallows was now prohibited by the Act. Nor was it possible to increase the depth of water in these two reaches

WINTERSTOKE

by building intermediate weirs and pound locks. The opposition of the mill- and landowners had resulted in a clause in the Company's Act which forbade the construction of any new weirs and pound locks in these reaches. The mill-owners had alleged that by restricting their headwaters and at the same time causing the water at their tailraces to back up, such new weirs would seriously interfere with the working of their mills. The landowners had produced the old argument that new weirs would increase the risk of flooding. In the face of all these difficulties the Company had to resort to a compromise which, though far from satisfactory, was the only one possible. At a carefully chosen position in each of the two reaches they erected a 'navigation weir'. This consisted of a masonry weir having a wide gap in midstream which could be sealed at will by a gate. This, like the lock gates, carried paddles and could be opened and closed by a winch on the bank. As the gate normally stood open, this arrangement satisfied the objectors. But in times of low water the bargemasters could close the gate behind them when moving upstream with the result that the reach above would make up enough to allow them to proceed on their way. Moreover, because the prohibition of 'flashing' did not apply to these navigation weirs, they could be judiciously used to help craft in difficulties on their downstream side.

In spite of all these works the navigation of the Wendle was still a hazardous proceeding, especially in times of flood or drought, while by modern standards it was painfully slow. Moreover, it would be a mistake to suppose that the passing of the Wendle Navigation Act silenced the centuries old disputes for ever. The countrymen of the English midlands at this time had little respect for the rule of law, and on many occasions the Company and the bargemasters had to resort to physical violence to maintain their legal rights. When the carpenters came to install the gates of the new lock at Fingerlow Mill they were savagely attacked by a party of thugs hired by the miller. The terrified carpenters fled for their lives across the water meadows while their assailants hacked their half-finished work to pieces and then threw their

WINTERSTOKE

tools into the river. The carpenters returned and completed their work under the protection of a strong posse recruited from the ranks of the bow hauliers. There were subsequent battles over the Company's legal right to the use of the haling way, while scarcely a season of drought would pass without some skirmish between millers and bargemasters. A bargemaster would complain that the miller's men had forcibly attempted to prevent him using a lock. The miller would argue, rightly or wrongly, that the bargemen had been trying to draw the paddles to send down a 'flash' and that in obstructing them he had been acting within his rights. Thanks to the tough constitution of their bow-hauliers, the bargemasters usually had the better of these encounters.

Although they did not know it, these millers and landowners of the Wendle valley who continued so stubbornly to assert their rights represented a bygone age and might as well have tried to stop the flow of the river as resist the relentless pressure of the new world that was now building at Winterstoke. In spite of the primitive works, in spite of all the hazards and conflicts, the importance of the Wendle Navigation to the Darley Bank Ironworks was as great as that of a main artery to the heart. As slowly but as purposefully and ceaselessly as the current upon which they moved, the low-laden barges swung away from Darley Bank Wharf and slid silently downstream, their hulls hidden between the banks from all but the staring cattle but their tall masts and sails visible by the hour, now near, now far off, as they followed the Wendle's windings through the wide water meadows. As the years of the eighteenth century rolled by they carried an increasing volume and variety of cargoes on the first stage of journeys which became ever longer as the trading orbit of the Darley Bank Company widened like the ripples from a stone flung into a pond. Cargoes of coal and of iron in every form and shape; pig and sow iron, iron blooms, bundles of nailer's rods and bar iron, nails, edge tools and finished smith's work of every kind; domestic cast-iron ware, pots, 'coppers', grates, hearths and hearth backs in increasing volume and variety. The most difficult and

WINTERSTOKE

precious cargoes of all were heavy castings and forgings whose function was often a mystery to the bargemaster who contracted for their freight. These were the vital organs of new machines which were soon to supersede those powers of wind and water, hand and horseflesh, which had prevailed since time out of mind. Before long the Wendle barges would be bearing down-river huge cylinder castings, six feet or more in diameter, bound for the pumping engines of the deepening coal pits in the midlands and the north or the tin mines of the far south-west.

For the increased output of domestic cast-iron ware by the Darley Bank Company, Josiah Leeds was responsible. In place of the old practice of running the molten iron into crude clay moulds formed in the 'loom floor' he introduced the technique of using moulds and cores of pure dry sand formed in boxes. These moulds were still run direct from the blast furnace. So great did the output of iron castings become that one of the blast furnaces, both of which were rebuilt, enlarged and improved by Josiah, was soon exclusively devoted to this work while the other specialized in the production of pig iron for the use of the finery and forge.

One of the problems confronting Josiah Leeds, and one which was by no means peculiar to Winterstoke, was the growing shortage of charcoal. Although the Darleys had made a practice of planting coppice wood, the rate of regeneration of the depleted woodlands could not keep pace with the insatiable demands of the two blast furnaces. The bare hillsides of High Hanger and Great Ketton, once so richly clothed with noble stands of timber but now a waste of scrub and saplings, told their own tale. Something must be done if the Darley Bank Ironworks was to escape the fate which had overtaken so many Sussex furnaces. Josiah already had experience of the making and use of coke fuel in his father's maltings so, with coal almost literally at his door, he began to experiment. Coal drawn from the High Hanger pits was coked in the open and tried in the pot-casting furnace. So far as the casting trade was concerned the experiment proved an immediate and complete success, the higher temperature melt of the iron producing castings of much finer quality than did charcoal iron. But experiments at the forge with coke-smelted pigs showed that the material was quite unsuitable for the production of wrought iron. His son, Josiah II, would eventually solve the problem of producing 'pit coal pig', as it was called, of a quality acceptable in the forges. Meanwhile the use of coke in the 'loom' furnace ensured a saving of precious timber, while the furnace producing forge pig continued in blast on charcoal.

A higher output of iron from both blast furnaces was achieved, not only by the improvement of the furnaces themselves, but by Josiah's efforts to overcome the old difficulty of water shortage in summer. He installed pumps worked by horse gins which returned the waters of the Lob from the lowest level to the upper furnace pool through iron pipes of his own casting. This reduced the length of the summer period during which the furnaces had to be blown out, although the pumps could not counteract the effect of a prolonged drought. Nor could any pumps prevail against extreme frost. The laconic and cryptic phrase 'To treading ye upper wheel' which appears against a substantial wages item in the Company's accounts for the month of January 1712 suggests that an effort was made to keep the upper furnace in blast during a spell of frost by manning the water-wheel like a treadmill.

While Josiah Leeds was making these experiments and improvements at Darley Bank the domestic iron trade in the Winterstoke district continued to expand and the smiths' demand for rod and bar iron became so great that the Darley Bank Company built a second forge and slitting mill in 1720. Because the Company found themselves unable to smelt enough charcoal iron to satisfy their two forges, they began to buy supplies of charcoal pig from other furnaces in more favoured districts to the south and west. These water-borne imports of raw iron to Winterstoke continued until the middle of the century.

While the Company's production of forge iron was thus restricted, the output of castings from Darley Bank increased

WINTERSTOKE

apace. At first the foundry had produced almost exclusively domestic cast-iron goods which were sold in the Midland markets, but thanks to Josiah's improvements in technique the moulders were soon engaged upon much heavier and more ambitious work. Already, the tireless and indomitable hand of Josiah Leeds had wrought greater changes upon the face of Winterstoke in two decades than had occurred during the whole of the preceding century. The windows of his house, like those of the cottages he had built for his ironworkers which now terraced both flanks of the Lob valley, surveyed a scene such as no mortal eye had ever beheld before. Beside the succession of still, sky-reflecting pools in which the waters of the river had been pent, there now ranged a long line of buildings, furnace and loom house, forge, rolling and slitting mills, each making to the whole its particular contribution of smoke and flame or mechanical din of heavy tilt hammers and rolls. Between the buildings and beside the margins of the pools the valley's green floor had already been buried beneath the arid, death-dealing excreta of ironworking: black sand, coal dust, mounds of pot- and tap-cinder. Dominating all was Josiah's coke furnace, 'Bedlam Furnace' as the men of Winterstoke had aptly christened it. The sulphurous fume from the heaps of coal coking on the level space near its bridge made the furnace a column of smoke by day. At night it became a pillar of fire, the skyward glare from its white-hot heart outshining the ruddier glow of the charcoal furnace below. When Josiah and his son, who was already becoming active in the works, looked down upon this creation of theirs, did they find it good? Did they ever question whither it was heading, or were they too absorbed by the fascinating problems of technical mastery to consider the future? We shall never know.

Although no history book has recorded it, February 15, 1722, was a date of momentous significance in the history of Winterstoke. For this day saw the successful birth, out of the molten womb of 'Bedlam Furnace', of the first cylinder for a Newcomen engine to be cast in iron. Never was birth more carefully prepared for or more anxiously awaited. The two

WINTERSTOKE

Josiahs, father and son, were themselves the midwives. Nothing must be left to chance, for the big cylinder, over three feet in diameter, eight feet long and an inch thick, would tax the capacity of the furnace further than any casting so far made. The mould, fashioned and perfected, checked and rechecked with infinite labour and care, had been completed some time before but had been awaiting a moment when they could be assured of a strong and unfailing blast. Now that moment had come. For the past four days the February rains, sluicing down from curtains of cloud which hung low over Deepforest, had sent such a roaring spate of waters down the Lob that with all the wheels at work the ponds were still running weir. Old Josiah himself superintended the boys who, with their laden baskets or 'boxes', had stocked the furnace bridge with the exact proportions of coke, calcined limestone and ore. And later, standing below on the loom floor, it was he who, with no word spoken but only an impassive and scarcely perceptible nod of the head, signalled the furnaceman to broach the tapping hole. How vivid is the picture of that far-off dramatic moment. The furnaceman couching his tapping rod like a lance; the sudden scintillating sizzle of sparks as he breaks through the fireclay, and then the molten iron gushing out, its glare lighting up the circle of intently watchful faces. Even when the pouring had been satisfactorily completed there could be no assurance of success. That was only confirmed later when the big casting had cooled and when, after being cleared from the mould, it rang true under the fettling hammer.

To the Devonian, Thomas Newcomen, belongs the distinction of being the first man in the world to master and command a power other than that of wind or water. His first successful engine, erected near Dudley Castle in 1712, was the fruit of ten years' labour and experiment. In the erection of this and many subsequent engines his name was linked with that of another Devonian, Thomas Savery. The latter had previously invented a machine for drawing water from mines by the vacuum produced by condensing steam. This machine had no moving parts and was never satisfactory in

WINTERSTOKE

working, but Savery's patent was so worded as to cover any possible method for 'Raiseing of Water and occassioning Motion to all Sorts of Mill Work by the Impellent Force of Fire'. Therefore, until 1733, when the patent lapsed, Newcomen's engines could only be built under licence from Savery and his successors who received royalties from them.

Although contemporaries called Newcomen's invention a 'fire engine' and we would call it a steam engine, it was really neither. It was a vacuum or atmospheric engine. The most characteristic and noteworthy feature of the Newcomen engine was its ponderous wooden regulating beam. Poised on its central trunnions overhead, its ends formed segments of a circle over which rode the chains which connected them to piston and pump buckets respectively. When steam was admitted from the copper boiler to the lower, enclosed end of the vertical cylinder its pressure was so little above that of the atmosphere that the power it exerted on the piston was negligible. Rather was it the weight of the descending pump buckets which raised the piston to the top of its stroke. At this moment of the cycle the steam admission valve was closed and a jet of cold water was sprayed into the steam-filled cylinder. By condensing the steam, this created a vacuum below the piston which was therefore driven downwards through the cylinder by the pressure of the atmosphere acting on its upper surface. Thus did the engine perform its power stroke. Remarkably ingenious though it was, Newcomen's working cycle involved the alternate heating and cooling of the cylinder and this continual heat loss made the engine uneconomical in fuel by the standards of a later day. It is not surprising that the first engines were installed to pump out the coal mines where plentiful supplies of fuel were at hand. In an attempt to minimize this defect, the cylinders of the earliest Newcomen engines were cast in brass, a metal which absorbed and lost heat rapidly. The thicker cylinders of cast iron were naturally less efficient, but improved foundry methods produced them so much more cheaply that iron replaced brass on all the larger engines.

The successful casting of their first Newcomen cylinder

WINTERSTOKE

brought the Darley Bank Company a small but steady flow of orders, not only for further cylinders but for other engine parts: cylinder bottoms, pistons, pump barrels, valves and pipework. Whereas we think of an engine as a unit supplied and erected by a single manufacturer, the Newcomen engine was very different. Only the more vital parts whose production involved special equipment and skill were supplied by manufacturers such as the Darley Bank Company. Local labour erected the engines and carried out much of the work such as the construction of the regulating beam. Before 1733 only a few industrial undertakings were working upon a scale large enough to afford the cost of installing a Newcomen engine and paying the rental demanded by 'The Proprietors of the Invention for Raising Water by Fire' who held Thomas Savery's patent after his death in 1715. But when the patent lapsed in 1733, the fact that rents were no longer payable combined with the improvement which had taken place in production methods led to a great increase in the number of engines built and therefore to an increased demand for castings from Darley Bank. For the same reason, although the first cylinder had been cast at Darley Bank in 1722, it was not until 1734 that Winterstoke could boast its first 'Fire Engine'. This, a 'bastard machine', as the men called it, was erected at High Hanger coal pit to pump water from the deepening workings. Its introduction is indicative of the changes which were taking place in the Winterstoke coal industry.

At the beginning of the seventeenth century, the coal industry, if such it could then be called, was still governed by the customary laws of the court of the manor of Winterstoke. The few who were digging coal at this time combined their coal getting with agriculture and in their eyes, as in those of the manor court, their black harvest was regarded in the same way as any other crop from their fields. Most of them were copyholders, their holdings being retained by copy of court roll, subject to the custom of the manor, and passing by surrender and admission in the court. As such they enjoyed the right freely to get coal both for their own use and

WINTERSTOKE

for sale. It was, perhaps, the number of new immigrants to the district and the increase in coal working which resulted that led to the appearance in the manorial records of the 1630's of a new distinction between 'Free' and 'Customary' copyholders. The free copyholders enjoyed the old rights, but the customary copyholders might only get coal for their own use and were prohibited from selling coal except under licence from the lord of the manor. This subject of mineral rights is a complex one because the position varied from manor to manor, but in the case of Winterstoke the distinction between two classes of copyholder no longer appears after the Restoration. It may safely be assumed that at this time Henry Hanmer succeeded in extinguishing altogether the rights of tenants freely to work minerals other than for their own use and reserved to himself and his heirs the exclusive right to the minerals under his estate. This step is important for it brought the Hanmer family greater wealth than ever the wool trade had done.

The Earl's mineral rights brought no immediate enrichment, for although the output of coal continued to increase, the workings were still on a small scale and carried on upon a basis which was still semi-domestic, the tenant of a working, or 'adventurer' as he was sometimes called, having the status of a yeoman farmer employing, perhaps, a dozen hands. It was Josiah Leed's 'Bedlam Furnace' combined with the fact that the more easily accessible coal measures were rapidly being worked out, which changed the character of the Winterstoke coal industry. The success of Josiah's coke smelting experiment made the delivery of a large and assured supply of coal to the furnace essential, and it was obvious to him that the present coal getters of High Hanger could not be depended upon to maintain that supply. Most of the coal he was using was drawn from that vertical shaft below High Hanger wood which had first been sunk over a century ago. The workings of this mine had since been considerably deepened and extended, and the lessee of the working rights was a certain Jacob Folliot, a descendant, no doubt, of the first Earl's steward. By the standards of the time, Folliot and

WINTERSTOKE

his twenty miners were drawing a considerable tonnage of coal from this pit, but he lacked capital and was fighting a losing battle against water in the bottom levels.

Soon after Josiah Leeds had come to Darley Bank, Hannah Darley died and her share in the Darley Bank Company was taken up by Josiah and the Winterstoke Trustees in equal portions. So far, the ironworks and the works of the Wendle Navigation Company were the only examples of heavy capital investment in the area. But now, as Josiah explained to George Hanmer, further capital must be expended in the development of the mines if the ironworks were to continue to prosper and expand. Young George was no industrialist but a landowner whose interests remained rural, and in matters of this kind he had an implicit faith in Josiah's judgment which, from a pecuniary point of view, was certainly not misplaced. So the High Hanger Pit, together with several smaller workings, was brought within the orbit of the Darley Bank Company, Jacob Folliot being appointed the Company's mining manager. This marked the beginning of coal mining as a large-scale capital enterprise at Winterstoke, and within fifty years practically the entire output of coal from the High Hanger seams was being drawn from the Company's mines.

Josiah Leeds' energy transformed High Hanger as rapidly as he had changed the face of Darley Bank. Cottages were built for the miners close to the pits at what later became known as Hanger Lane. Great stables were built to meet the increased demand for horse-power. The coal-drawing 'whims' and Josiah's pumps in the new drainage shafts, each called for a pair of horses working continuously in four-hour shifts; ponies were now used in the pit to drag the corves of coal from the working face to the pit bottom on sleds; more horses were needed to draw the chaldrons of coal from the pithead to 'Bedlam Furnace' or to the new wharf on the Wendle for shipment. Increasing traffic soon made these ways so rutted and miry that they threatened to become impassable. So Josiah ordered precious timber to be felled, squared, and laid down for the wagon wheels to run upon,

WINTERSTOKE

the longitudinals being braced at intervals by cross ties or 'sleepers'. The pits, the ironworks and the wharf were thus soon linked by continuous wooden wagon ways or 'ginny rails'.

It was the miners of Winterstoke and not the ironworkers who were the first to sever their links with their rural past. Could we but meet the men who laboured at the furnaces, forges and foundries of Darley Bank in the first half of the eighteenth century we should realize that they were far from being 'industrial workers' in our sense of the term. Many were still part-time countrymen, while of those who were not, very few were more than one generation removed from the soil and revealed the ties of blood in a habit of mind and in figures of speech wherein the technical terms of their new trade were curiously mixed with country usages immemorially ancient. Such a mixture was natural so long as the iron harvest was dependent upon water power and the strength of men and horses. The furnaces might impose a new discipline, but despite Josiah's horse-pumps, it was not yet a discipline impervious to seasonal change. Summer droughts and autumn rains still set the time for the blowing out and blowing in of the furnaces, while there could be no clearer proof of the vigour with which ancient rural custom survived in this alien environment of flame and smoke than that these occasions, especially the blowing out, should become the subject of celebration. Entries in the accounts of the Darley Bank Company for Blowing Out Beef and Blowing Out Beer show that a kind of fiery 'harvest home' supper took place at the Company's expense when a furnace was extinguished. Perhaps our vulgar reference to an ample meal as 'a good blow out' may refer, not to any abnormal distention of the stomach, but to this forgotten festival. This customary blowing out supper is only one indication of a relationship between employer and employed at Darley Bank very different from that which obtains to-day and which makes it easier for us to understand how naturally, for those concerned in it, industrialism grew out of a rural environment. The leading hands at the furnace and in foundry, forge and slitting mill were contractors to the Company rather than employees and they employed, and were solely responsible for, their own labour. Except for the fact that they did not own the heavy plant and buildings, they were thus master men and as such they possessed a far higher status than any foreman or works manager to-day. Helped by a common nonconformist faith which recognized no distinctions, they met Josiah Leeds as equals.

The organization of labour at the High Hanger pits was similar. The miners were of the same country stock as the ironworkers, were men of similar habits of mind and independent temper. It was the nature of their trade which divorced them so speedily and so completely from their old environment that Hanger Lane became a place apart, the home of a community whose life was ordered, governed and knit together by the perils, the exacting labour and the special knowledge of a world unknown to outsiders. Even the language of the men who squatted on their hams before the doorsteps of Hanger Lane was often unintelligible to the laymen with its talk of 'sides of work' or 'benches' or 'slippers' and 'fire stink'. For they were among the first to invade that lost land of semi-tropical forests which had flourished century after century in the swamps left by the ebb of the Silurian sea only to be submerged finally like Atlantis and petrified in that great tomb of the ten-yard seam which stretches across middle England. So that the furnaces of Darley Bank might feed upon the stored energies of primordial summers, the plodding ginny horses lowered the men of Hanger Lane down to catacombs where life and work was no longer effected, sweetened or varied by any natural rhythm of time or season, of daylight or darkness, of summer's heat or winter's cold. The invariable temperature of the pit was that of the earth itself; its reverberating sounds: clink of picks, rumble of sleds, or the sudden crash of undercut coal, only seemed to accentuate its sinister silences just as the feeble flicker of a miner's candle emphasized the immanence of a darkness so unnatural in its totality as to be almost palpable.

High Hanger pit was worked upon what became known as the pillar and stall system. Its galleries led to the 'sides of

WINTERSTOKE

work' which consisted of a series of symmetrical chambers in which the roof was supported by four massive columns of coal and by a series of smaller pillars whose number varied according to the miners' estimation of the safety of the roof. Upon that judgment their lives depended. Added to the risk of roof fall was the other ever-present peril of fire damp, a deadly mixture of air and finely suspended coal dust which could ignite and 'flash' spontaneously and which, in spite of the fact that the miners called it a 'stink', was quite odourless. Such a flash brought either death by burning or by suffocation from the equally deadly after-damp, but it was found that the 'pillar and stall' system tended to confine the danger to the particular chamber where the flash occurred.

The method of working was to undercut the 'benches', as the lower part of the seam was called, and then, having cleared away the coal and waste to be carried through the galleries to the 'pit eye', to dislodge the overhanging coal in the upper seam or 'slipper' with wedges and hammers. This work was hard and hazardous enough, but when the chamber had been excavated to the maximum customary size, which was usually about fifty yards square, there still remained the task which involved the greatest danger of falls and fire-damp explosion. This was known as working 'at twice' and consisted of weakening the supporting pillars so as to encourage the roof to fall in. When it had fallen, some of the coal in the pillars could be recovered although a great deal was inevitably wasted. Because fire-damp is a mixture of air and fine coal dust, the danger of explosion is greatest in a dry pit, so that in this respect the extreme wetness of the High Hanger workings was an advantage. But the miners paid heavily for their comparative safety when they lay or crouched half-submerged in coal-blackened water, squinting upwards through narrowed eyes as they hacked away at the benches. It had been possible to drain the shallower workings on the hill slopes by driving tunnels to their lowest point, but as the deep pit followed the inclination of the seam to ever deeper levels, so water was encountered in greater volume, water which could not be drained by natural means and which

WINTERSTOKE

began to tax the horse gins to the utmost. This was the situation which, in 1734, led to the erection of the Newcomen engine at the head of High Hanger pit.

No wonder the miners christened this engine a 'bastard machine'. Not only was its appearance strange beyond all precedent, but to ears hitherto accustomed only to the creak of horse gins it spoke with a strange voice. Enclosed in a brick engine house, the protruding pump end of its regulator beam with its dependent chains resembled the head and beak of some enormous bird, pecking into the depths of the pit with a motion so lifelike and yet, in its unvarying and unwearied monotony, so unlike life that it might provoke that same disquiet which the nodding head of a mannikin inspires; a disquiet that is no less than the ancient fear of all questionable shapes which, being dead, assume the semblance of life. It would not be surprising if this automaton of Thomas Newcomen's awoke such sleeping terrors in those who for the first time watched the slow but unfaltering precision of its motion or heard, coming from within the tall engine house, the laboured breathing of the new power sigh and sob ceaselessly with each repetitive effort. In familiarity, fear of the new machines would soon be forgotten. To-day, the memory of this first engine is only preserved in the name of the 'New Invention' Inn at Hanger Lane.

The livelihood of those below ground depended entirely upon the tireless exertions of this automaton, but as the price of its efforts it subordinated its attendants to its own mechanical rhythm which, like the life in the black depths of pit into which its pump rods fell, was arbitrary and in no way related to any natural rhythm set by sun or moon.

The installation of this new power at High Hanger pit inaugurated at Winterstoke the first of those great cycles of expansion which gave the industrial revolution a gathering momentum like that of a great flywheel. The fact that it enabled the pits to be driven deeper into the coal seams meant more and cheaper coal. More and cheaper coal meant more and cheaper iron, which in turn produced larger and more powerful engines which could bring about another repetition of the same cycle of cause and effect. With the coming of this engine and the death of Josiah Leeds I, which occurred five years later, the first vital period of industrial expansion may be said to have come to an end. During the long reign of Josiah II at Darley Bank that expansion would proceed yet more rapidly upon its triumphal way.

Chapter Four

'EVERYTHING THAT GROWS holds in perfection but a little moment'. Ripeness is all, yet the fruit is no sooner ripe than it is rotten; the flower no sooner full than overblown, faded and fallen. Should we savour the beauties of the world so keenly were it not for the knowledge of this transience? Certainly we esteem most exquisite a loveliness which we know is doomed soon to pass away or which, in retrospect, may be seen to carry within it the seeds of its own mortality. This is as true of the works of man as it is of natural things. The century following the Restoration witnessed the development of industrial techniques which, judged by any valid moral or aesthetic standard, were destined to become the most desolating and destructive force which the world has ever known. Yet this development was accompanied by a flowering of craftsmanship of a perfection never seen before in England and, as we know now, never to be seen again. With the swift decay and fall of that flower in the nineteenth century we are familiar, for the evidence, as remote from our time as the monuments of the ancient world, lies all about us. Much more mysterious are the circumstances which produced so sudden and so prodigious a blossoming at that very same moment in history when there were sewn the tares which would destroy it. For although only a few great names survive in popular esteem, the genius which created this all too brief golden age of the visual arts was not the monopoly of a small minority but was in widest commonalty spread. Unknown country craftsmen could execute work which was little, if at all, inferior to that of the great masters and which makes the task of attribution difficult for those who treasure these past riches. An infallible and instinctive sense of fitness and proportion which is at other times either wholly lacking

WINTERSTOKE

or vouchsafed only to a chosen few, suddenly inspired the vision and informed the hands of a whole people. Certainly for a time, but for a time only, it seemed that they were incapable of making any ugly thing, and by what other or better standard than this are we to judge the achievement of a civilization?

To appreciate to the full this tragic paradox of flower and tare growing in the same soil there is no need for us to travel far from the flare and fume of Bedlam Furnace or from the close darkness of High Hanger Pit. We have only to cross the Wendle, stroll through the formal gardens of Winterstoke Place, and then wander in imagination through the splendid apartments of the house itself. Wrought iron gates screen but do not conceal terrace from terrace of the garden, superimposing upon their background of sky, green tree and flower a spider web of metal as delicate in its complexity of loop and scroll and slender vertical as silver filigree work. Surely, we might say, only the hammer of Jean Tijou could transform so intractable and unpromising a material into a screen of such lightness and grace. But we should be wrong. The gates were forged by an unnamed local smith from rods that had been wrought and slit in Alfred Darley's mill. The same is true of the house. To the order of Henry Hanmer it was much altered, and its interior completely replanned and redecorated. Who was the architect? Certainly it was not Wren although it would seem to be the work of some outstanding genius. Could William Talman or Robert Hooke be the author? Possibly, but more likely it was the work of some architect quite unknown. Though classical in conception, the execution could only belong to the English tradition. We know from surviving records that it was not the Italian Antonio Verrio but his English peer, Sir James Thornhill, who painted ceiling and fresco, fancifully including a portrait of his noble patron, heavily periwigged, being escorted through his garden by lightly-clad muses who seek to entwine him in their garlands. But of the other masters who helped to create the rococo splendour of Winterstoke, who wrought those ceilings with their heavy yet perfectly-

WINTERSTOKE

proportioned mouldings of fruit and flowers, of twined oak and acanthus leaf, we know nothing. If we should suspect the hand of Gabriel Cibber or Gibbons in the carving of marble fireplace, or of pine panel or doorcase, again we do but honour the unknown dead. Most probably these carvers, too, were local men, for even such details as doorlocks and furniture or hearthgrates are exquisite in workmanship and design but would certainly have been made locally. As we wander, visitants from a twilit future, from beauty to beauty in these now vanished rooms, furniture, china, silverware, clocks by Quare or Tompion, books in superb bindings of tooled morocco, everything however small or mundane that the eye rests upon displays the same virtuosity, a prodigality of craftsmanship which can never be either overwhelming or individually ostentatious because its natural exuberance is perfectly controlled and disciplined.

One wonders what old Josiah Leeds thought of the magnificence of Winterstoke Place after the austerity of his own modest four-square house of brick at Darley Bank on the rare occasions when he called to confer with the Earl on some financial matter. For the two men moved in different worlds which met only upon the ground of a common business interest. George Hanmer, despite the wealth which coal and iron were bringing him, still the great landowner who thinks in the aristocratic language of the past; Josiah Leeds the industrialist, the man who thinks only of the present in terms of the hard realities of furnace or machine, but who may have guessed by a kind of sub-conscious awareness, that it is in his capable hands that the future lies. 'Vanity, vanity, all is vanity . . .' perhaps Josiah's thought echoed Ecclesiastes, for although he was himself a craftsman who maintained an exacting standard of workmanship in his ironworks, the exercise of human skill to create so lavish a display had no place in his philosophy. To labour truly and earnestly was a good in itself which must result in the betterment of mankind. Its fruits would be enjoyed hereafter. It should be the purpose of wealth to oil the wheels of progressive commerce, not to be wasted in sensuous satisfactions

WINTERSTOKE

and the pleasures of the eye. So might he have thought, and in so thinking, the current of the age was moving with him.

Unlike his father, George Hanmer was no great patron of the arts. He was an outdoor man, a typical hard-riding, hard-drinking country squire of the period who, despite his great wealth, had as little to do with current fashionable fopperies as with the new commerce. We may admire in the Winterstoke Municipal Art Gallery to-day a painting by George Stubbs which was most probably the fifth Earl's only substantial contribution to the treasures of Winterstoke Place. Painted at some time shortly before his death in 1770 it depicts the old man, a stocky, grizzled, bullnecked figure, mounted on a cob appropriate to his weight and attended by a bewhiskered henchman and a favourite hound. The group in the foreground, the gentle slope of the park, the noble house in the distance, the trees heavy with yellowing autumn leaves which can never stir nor fall, all seem bathed in a gentle golden light which, under repeated varnishings, seems almost sub-aqueous, holding this tranquil moment of the past in perpetual suspension like a fly in amber.

But if George Hanmer made no other positive contribution to the beauty of Winterstoke he neither neglected nor marred it, having a simple but profound respect for his father's good taste. Thus, when his nephew, Ernest Hanmer, succeeded to the Earldom (for George had remained a bachelor) we might suppose that he, likewise, would prize so rich and so mature an inheritance. But that young man had other ideas.

Whereas the fifth Earl in his later years was often referred to with affection behind his back as 'Old George', his successor was invariably known as 'His Lordship' or even, with bitterness, as 'His Majesty'. Nothing could more effectively illustrate the contrast between the two men. Ernest, sixth Earl of Winterstoke, was the issue of his father's marriage, eminently successful in the worldly sense, to the Lady Arabella Sargent who was richly endowed in both senses of the term. Not only had her beauty and wit made

WINTERSTOKE

her a toast of the town but she had inherited a considerable fortune and brought to her husband a magnificent house in Berkeley Square. Here young Ernest grew up. By the time he left England to make the Grand Tour he had, despite his youth, already become a figure in polite society. When Ernest arrived at Winterstoke in a mud-bespattered scarlet wheeled curricle to view his inheritance, the impression created by this languid young man with his foppish clothes, mincing walk and affected manners upon retainers accustomed to the bluff and forthright provincialism of 'Old George' may well be imagined. But, as Winterstoke would soon discover, appearances were never more deceptive. As his uncle's major-domo rendered an account of his stewardship, Lord Ernest seemed to be more interested in the process of snuffing himself from a minute box of gold-mounted enamel. Yet his air of boredom was no more than a fashionable veneer. The new Earl was certainly vain, but he was also ambitious, strongly self-willed and remarkably shrewd. As he flicked imaginary specks from his immaculate cravat with a beringed hand and studied the motifs on the plaster ceiling above his head, he did not miss a word of what his steward had to say. That worthy realized this when, with cold precision, his new master gave his orders. When Lord Ernest returned to London the staff breathed a heartfelt sigh of relief, but the respite was short-lived. The visitation was the prelude to changes on the right bank of the Wendle greater than any which had taken place since the dissolution of the Abbey.

The splendours of Henry Hanmer's Winterstoke were by now nearly a century old. Taste had changed during 'Old George's' long reign, and what had well satisfied his conservative tastes no longer appealed to a young man who had but lately made the Italian pilgrimage and who now regarded himself as a leader of fashion. To the eye of this aspiring young exquisite, schooled in the architectural ideas of the new Palladians and the refinements of the brothers Adam, the craftsmanship which we should admire, the richly-carved woodwork, the heavily-moulded coffered

WINTERSTOKE

ceilings and Thornhill's flamboyant murals, appeared as ostentatious and vulgar as an overdressed doxy. All must be changed. Thanks to a combination of his mother's fortune, his late Uncle's frugal habits and the revenue which coal and iron were now bringing to the estate, Ernest Hanmer could command immense wealth, and he proceeded to change Winterstoke Place in no uncertain manner.

Although the work carried out by Henry Hanmer's unknown architect had considerably altered the appearance of the house, involving as it did the rebuilding of the entire west façade with new fenestration as well as considerable changes in the interior layout, the original E-shaped ground plan of Richard Hanmer's Tudor mansion had remained. If we compare contemporary engravings of the house in the two periods, their affinity is obvious. The rebuilding undertaken by Ernest Hanmer between 1773 and 1776 was far more drastic and transformed Winterstoke Place beyond recognition. That the young Earl should have employed James Wyatt rather than Adam as his architect was to be expected. For Wyatt's completion of the Pantheon in Oxford Street in 1772 had made him the most fashionable architect of the moment, and the star of Robert Adam was beginning to set. Under Wyatt's direction the central projecting wing of the three was completely demolished to make room for a great hall of Roman magnificence with a floor of inlaid stone and colonnades of scagliola pillars painted in imitation of yellow Sienna marble. This hall occupied the whole of the space between the east and west wings and extended to the full height of the building. Instead of presenting the gable ends of three projecting wings, the south front thus became a single block, but to match the shallow cupola which gave top light to the great hall Wyatt diversified his new façade by building out a central semi-circular bay with columns extending to the eaves. Moreover, to break the height of this central block and to make the composition the more imposing, colonnades were thrown out east and west which terminated in two identical octagonal pavilions. It is impossible to deny that

WINTERSTOKE

this severe but impeccably proportioned façade of Wyatt's possessed both dignity and grandeur. Yet compared with the three previous incarnations of Winterstoke Place, the Gothic, the Tudor and the Rococo, this, its final Palladian metamorphosis, seems to lack warmth and humanity. We feel that it is monumental rather than domestic in conception. And what, we may ask, as we survey this long façade of honey-coloured stone which the sulphurous exhalations of Darley Bank would so soon blacken, or stand in the cold, echoing magnificence of the pillared hall, does this monument celebrate? Pride and self-worship, the pride of its owner and the genius of its architect? Or is it a mausoleum, a portent of that twilight which was so soon to fall, unconsciously celebrating the fact that a brief golden age has reached an apogee whence there can be no advance and no return? Although, by contrast, they reveal the architect's lightest and most delicate vein, when we pass through the lofty mahogany doors from the great hall into the superb range of ground-floor apartments, there is no escaping from the conviction that this house represents the end of an age. Gone is the old robust and vigorous craftsmanship, so self-confident and assured that it seemed incapable of admitting the possibility of error. Here now are interiors made magical and unsubstantial by workmanship so ethereal in its refinement that we feel it may dissolve at a touch. Here, against backgrounds of pale colours are plaster and stucco mouldings of ribbon, scroll and classic vase so slight that they look as impermanent and fragile as the sugar decorations on a wedding cake. Here, instead of Thornhill's bold murals, are faint, calligraphic arabesques and, in small roundels and lunettes above mantel or doorcase, formalized paintings of nymph, shepherd, and flying cupid from the hand of the Italian, Biagio Rebecca. And yet in this supremely sophisticated craftsmanship do we not detect, for all its high competence, a reticence almost amounting to infirmity of purpose? It is a suspicion which the grandiloquence of great hall and exterior façade cannot dispel. It is as though they enshrined a tradition of craftsman-

WINTERSTOKE

ship which, having put off its healthy flesh to become all intellect and spirit, is now about to die. From such attenuated elegance it proved to be but a short step to that meaningless and mechanical ornamentation of the next century which possessed neither spirit, intellect, grace nor even honesty, but was merely a medium of ostentation to be purchased by the yard. James Wyatt himself, for all his undoubted genius, belongs not to the golden age but to its decadence. Soon after his work at Winterstoke was finished he cast off the great English classical tradition as though it had become an old and unfashionable coat and began building in sham Gothic at Ashridge and Fonthill. His defection marked the beginning of an age when style, like ornament, would become a debased veneer supplied to order and applied to the façade of any given building with as much facility as a layer of stucco.

Ernest Hanmer's transformation of Winterstoke by no means stopped short at the house itself. Indeed, from the point of view of the social historian, the rebuilding of Winterstoke Place was the least important of his undertakings. The old formal gardens which had remained substantially unchanged since Tudor times were not at all in keeping with the young Earl's ideas of Romantic Landscape. While Wyatt was busily engaged upon the new house, who better than Lancelot 'Capability' Brown to advise him upon the improvement of the prospect? It was quite obvious that the comparatively small extent of the gardens and park would allow Brown's talents little scope. He must be given a more ample canvas to work upon, and since money was no object, this was soon provided. The first step was to promote a Bill of Enclosure. This provoked strong opposition from the villagers of Winterstoke, but, here as elsewhere, this last desperate defence of their ancient rights was of no avail. Common fields and rights of common pasture which, notwithstanding the encroachments of the first Earl, had survived since 'time out of mind' must now be ruthlessly filched away. The fact that the Winterstoke Enclosure Act marked the final stage in that process whereby the people of

WINTERSTOKE

Winterstoke lost their age old roots in their own soil mattered nothing. They were at the mercy of a generation of landowners to whom the old conception of stewardship had become utterly foreign and who believed that each man possessed an almost sacred right to do what he would with his own. Where such a philosophy flourishes and there is no recognition of mutual rights and responsibilities, power must always prevail and never before had the landowners of England possessed greater power in their wealth and in their influence upon Government. If Ernest Hanmer wished to replan his estate in the contemporary mode, who should stop him? Who, indeed? The Enclosure Commissioners were corrupted, the Committee of the Commons which debated the Bill was packed and the Petition of the villagers against the Bill lay unopened on the table. It was a sorry, tragic story which was to be repeated many times throughout the length and breadth of England. So the sixth Earl of Winterstoke had his way and the commoners of Winterstoke became 'the labouring poor' or, as a later age would call them, a 'proletariat'.

Needless to say, the arguments advanced in favour of enclosure at Winterstoke made no mention of the projects with which the name of Lancelot Brown was associated. Rather did they stress the agricultural improvements which would result. The great virtue of the old system of common field agriculture had been that the common grazing enabled a small farmer to carry more stock than he could otherwise support and so keep his arable strips in better heart when lying fallow. Again, the flocks and herds on the common pasture could be communally tended which meant a great saving in labour. The seizure of common pastures made the lot of most small farmers impossible even if they were lucky enough to obtain an award from the Enclosure Commissioners. But the enclosure arguments dwelt only upon the faults of a system of agriculture which was now condemned out of hand as 'barbarous' and 'primitive'. The yield from the arable strips was too low and the system of free-ranging stock made selective breeding of livestock impossible. If the

WINTERSTOKE

growing population of Darley Bank was to be adequately fed it was high time that the new 'high farming' methods were introduced at Winterstoke.

That the old system of agriculture was open to valid criticism there can be no doubt. To see that a ruthless policy of confiscation was not the only way of solving the problem we need go no further than the neighbouring village of Emberley where we find the Winters still firmly rooted in the moated manor house of their ancestors; Lords of the Manor still, though now no longer titled. There was never an Enclosure Act for Emberley. The process of enclosure had taken place gradually through the years by the mutual consent of landlord and tenant. As a result we find many small farms on the Winters' modest estate: Emberley Hill farm, High and Low Emberley, Upper and Lower Grange, Church, and the Hall farm. In addition, each householder in the village has a small holding sufficient for his needs.

By contrast, on Ernest Hanmer's much larger estate there were after enclosure only four farms: Abbey Farm, High Hanger, Ketton and Summersend. All had existed before enclosure but were rebuilt and enlarged by the Earl, for they now embraced between them all the land which was not either emparked or occupied by the Darley Bank Company. Whereas the activities of the Winter family occasioned no remark, the high farming methods practised on the Winterstoke Estate called forth pæans of praise from the agricultural experts of the day. Never were there fat beasts of such size as the Earl's sleek Herefords, such sheep as his flocks of Leicesters, such pigs as his Tamworths. Yet it is a significant fact that the arable acreage of the estate declined as a result of enclosure, a circumstance which shows how specious was the advancement of the needs of the coal and iron-working community as a pretext for enclosure. For the great need of the poor smiths and miners of Darley Bank and High Hanger was cheap bread; the price of prime beef and mutton was far beyond their reach, while for bacon they looked, not to the Earl's Tamworths but to the pig in their own sty

WINTERSTOKE

which, for most of them, was now their only link with their rural past.

The decline of arable acreage was not only due to a preoccupation with stock breeding. To a much greater extent it was due to the size of the area which was emparked. When we consider the work which Lancelot Brown carried out at Winterstoke on behalf of his patron we realize that few oriental despots ever wielded great wealth with less scruple or to more fantastic purpose than did Ernest, sixth Earl of Winterstoke. Altogether, Brown and his associates expended four hundred thousand pounds on his behalf, much of which had been won by the flames of the Darley Bank Furnaces or in the dark galleries of the High Hanger pits. To begin with, the area emparked included the whole of the old village of Winterstoke which, with the exception of the church, was so completely demolished that no trace remained. Its inhabitants were rehoused in a new and larger settlement of exemplary design but somewhat arbitrary planning which was sited some distance east of Winterstoke Place at the point where the way from Church Ambling and Emberley village met the valley road almost directly opposite Darley Bank Wharf. Here a new bridge over the river was planned to connect this transplanted Winterstoke with the growing industrial community at Darley Bank and Hanger Lane. Consisting of great spans of black iron cast under the direction of Daniel Leeds at Darley Bank and set in massive stone abutments, this bridge was completed and opened in 1779. With the old village went the old road leading to St. John's Bridge, and the medieval gatehouse to Winterstoke Place which, apart from the bridge and some remnants of fabric still to be seen at Abbey Farm, had been the only substantial memorial of Cistercian Winterstoke. Part of the original road became a driveway through the park. The road which replaced it swung to the north at the new drive gates and lodge just beyond the Bridge Inn, and followed the imperious sweep of the high park wall in a great semi-circle until it rejoined the old route near Abbey Farm.

That the church of St. Cenodoc was not razed completely

WINTERSTOKE

like the rest of the village was not due to any religious scruples but to reasons romantic and aesthetic. The church stood in a shallow depression which the indefatigable Brown proposed to transform into a lake by diverting and damming up the waters of the Winterstoke brook. He suggested that the tower should be demolished, and the nave arcades re-erected on an elevated site at the end of one of his vistas where, as he pointed out to his patron, they would make a delightfully picturesque and romantic ruin. Meanwhile what was left of the church should, he proposed, remain to be submerged beneath the clear waters of his lake like a miniature Atlantis. The Earl called this plan a pretty conceit and commended Brown for his admirable sensibility and taste. Meanwhile James Wyatt was commissioned to build a church for the new village. The result was a lofty and imposing structure of cruciform plan with a dome at the crossing, built in that early Italian Renaissance style which the architect subsequently used to similar purpose in the chapel of Dodington in neighbouring Gloucestershire. The most striking interior feature of this new church of St. Cenodoc was the huge black marble catafalque surmounted by a spectral group of mourning figures, larger than life in white marble, which covered the entrance to the Hanmer vault in the chancel. So effectually did this phantasmagoria dominate the altar that an uninitiated visitor of heathen faith could be forgiven for supposing that this was a temple dedicated to the worship of the bygone Earls of Winterstoke.

Besides the Norman arcades of the old church, Lancelot Brown embellished his skilfully contrived vistas in the new park with many other features. A Palladian bridge carried the main drive across the newly-filled lake. There was also a Temple of Theseus, a rotunda, and a Grove of Virgil with a Grotto, not to mention various statues, urns, arbours and other minor objects skilfully disposed. The old gardens with their rigid, formal patterns of borders, of box and yew and pleached alley had no place whatever in the romantic landscape picture of Brown's fashionable conception, and they were ruthlessly swept away. In their place a

WINTERSTOKE

series of smooth balustraded terraces and broad stone steps led, on the lowest level, to a fountain of truly heroic proportions. Here the horses of Neptune's chariot plunged in a great stone basin, sporting dolphins spouted and Mermen blew from their conches jets which soared ninety feet into the air. To provide the necessary head of water for this display a reservoir pent up the headwaters of the Winterstoke brook on Emberley hill and a Darley Bank beam engine, discreetly concealed, patiently pumped back the water to this reservoir from an underground culvert.

Although the River Wendle formed the southern boundary of the home park, Brown's activities extended well beyond the river as far as the slopes of High Hanger Hill. Fortunately for his plans, standing on the terrace before Wyatt's great façade, the colliery workings and the new building at Hanger Lane lay somewhat to the east of south. He was therefore able to plan a long vista between avenues of trees which would mask this evidence of vulgar activity and lead the eye over the river and onwards yet again to the very skyline of High Hanger where an obelisk one hundred feet high provided a dramatic full stop. From the top of this column the stone effigy of Ernest, sixth Earl of Winterstoke, wearing the wreath and toga of a Roman Emperor, gazed down over his domain. A tablet on the plinth of the column bore his name and title, the date in Roman numerals, and the singularly appropriate family motto, 'What I have I hold'.

Chapter Five

THE FIRST important development at the Darley Bank Ironworks after the death of Josiah Leeds I in 1739 was the installation in 1742 of a Newcomen engine in place of the horse-pumps to return the waters of the Lob from the lowest level to the upper furnace pool. The pumping engine at High Hanger Pit had by then been in work for seven years, and Josiah II had been encouraged to take this step by its reliable working and by the practical experience which had been gained. From this time onwards the 'fire engines' employed by the Darley Bank Company in their ironworks and mines increased steadily in number, in power and in efficiency, and this development was accompanied by a corresponding increase in the manufacture of cylinders and other engine parts for customers.

By 1745 another of the pits at High Hanger which the Company now controlled had reached depths which could no longer be effectually drained by horse pumps, and here another Newcomen pump was built at the pithead. Ten years later, Josiah again rebuilt and heightened Bedlam Furnace, installing there an engine with a cylinder 5 feet in diameter and a stroke of 10 feet, a labouring giant which made the original High Hanger engine seem a puny thing. Its function was to circulate a constant flow of water to the wheel which, driving box bellows of improved design, supplied the blast to the furnace. This marked another significant stage in the process whereby the regularity of the beam engine made ironworking increasingly independent of the seasonal vagaries of water power. But this independence was purchased at a price. In the ironworks, as in the pits, for the old seasonal rhythm with enforced spells of labour and of rest such as the natural world orders for all other living things, the new unflagging mechanical power substituted its own

WINTERSTOKE

relentless discipline. It could be said that man, of his own will, was making himself the slave of his own genius.

It was not Josiah II but his son Daniel who, in 1780, severed the last link between iron smelting and water-power at Darley Bank. For in that year he blew in for the first time the New Bank Furnace whose blast was provided, not by water-wheel and bellows, but by a blowing engine which, pumping air as previous engines had pumped water, delivered it to the furnace through a regulator which ensured an even blast. But by that time several other important changes had taken place. It is very unlikely that the Company would ever have built their New Bank Furnace had not the problem of producing a good bar iron from coke-smelted pig at last been solved.

With a few exceptions who were regarded as eccentric, the aristocratic rulers of eighteenth-century England who delighted to patronize the arts were not interested in the activities of horny-handed ironmasters. Fashionable society rang with the praises of architect, actor, or reigning wit, but of the much more significant work of the new industrialists we hear little or nothing despite the immense contributions which they were making to the revenues of great estates. Improvements in iron-smelting technique were not the subject of eager debate in salon, club or coffee-house. In this we may approve the standard of values of our ancestors but not their foresight. From the standpoint of history, the successful production of wrought iron by coke-smelting was an achievement of far greater moment that any work of eighteenth-century artist or craftsman. For the ironmaster's blast furnace was the womb of industrial revolution, and each improvement in furnace technique meant that the machine could take another and more confident stride forward. True, the furnaces must have fuel, but that fuel could not be won without the aid of the engines which the furnaces begot. True that the expansion of trade depended on improving transport, but once again that improvement depended on iron. Without iron shoes no pack-horse could move; without iron fastenings no boat could be built. The

WINTERSTOKE

Pennine valleys are sometimes considered the cradle of the new age, but without iron the inventions of Lombe, of Hargreaves, Arkwright and Crompton would have been still-born and the great mills never built. Cast iron and wrought iron were the sinews of the new world. If the production of wrought iron had continued to depend any longer on charcoal fuel, technical development in other directions would have ceased for England's woodland resources were practically exhausted.

Until 1766 it had been considered quite impossible to smelt iron for the forge with coal or coke. It was argued that the alkaline vegetable salts in charcoal absorbed the sulphur in the iron which made it 'short' whereas neither coal nor coke could do this because these fuels themselves contained sulphur. But two ironworkers of Shropshire, Thomas and George Cranage, proved that if the coke-smelted pig iron was reheated in what was called a reverbertory furnace which kept the metal out of contact with the fuel, a perfectly satisfactory wrought iron could be produced without the aid of charcoal. Although their method was soon superseded by the improved puddling process which is in use to-day and which was developed by Peter Onions and Henry Cort, it was the Cranage brothers who, by a comparatively simple discovery, first made the iron trade independent of the charcoal burner. Not that the prejudice of the smiths in favour of charcoal iron was easily overcome. It was only by artfully mixing coke iron in with consignments of charcoal iron unknown to the buyers that Josiah Leeds II was able to prove its suitability and secure its acceptance.

The effect of the new process at Darley Bank was immediate. Charcoal smelting in the old furnace ceased and it was soon rebuilt and blown in on coke fuel. Imports of charcoal pig iron to Darley Bank Wharf also ceased. Hitherto there had been little development in the forge since the second forge and slitting mill had been opened in 1720, and the Company's output of bar iron had barely kept pace with the demand of the local smiths. It was the expansion of the Darley Bank casting trade which had marked the reign of

WINTERSTOKE

Josiah Leeds I. But now the distinguishing feature of the Darley Bank works under Josiah II and Daniel was increasing activity in the forge. So far as ironmasters such as the Leeds family were concerned, the invention which made the expansion of wrought iron production possible could scarcely have come at a more opportune moment. For as Enclosure Act followed Enclosure Act from 1760 onwards, so the demand for bar iron and nailers' rods soared. It was simply a repetition on a far greater scale of the social process which had accompanied the less radical enclosures of Tudor times. All over the country commoners and small freeholders who had hitherto subsisted either wholly or partly upon a share of the soil of England found themselves robbed of this unfailing source of livelihood. Except for the minority who could obtain work as labourers on the new enclosed farms, all must turn to some industrial employment. In Winterstoke and throughout the Midlands the trades which absorbed the majority were coal mining, ironworking and, above all, because it need not be so strictly localized, the domestic metal industry. The pack-trains of the powerful ironmongers and their agents—the 'foggers' as they were called—delivered rod and bar iron and collected finished goods in villages which had never before known the glare of the forge and the thud of the oliver in cottage outshuts. As a result this domestic iron industry in general and the nail trade in particular became appallingly overcrowded, a situation which was grossly exploited by the foggers. The old life of these countrymen had never been an easy one; it was never the rustic idyll which some romantic writers on rural England would have us suppose. But the life had been bred in the bone for generations and the seasons dictated its rhythm and its periods of rest. And so long as a man possessed land he possessed a sense of security which nothing else could give and could look the world in the face. But now in order to earn the barest necessities of life doled out to them by the foggers under the truck system, whole families of dispossessed countrymen, men, women and children must needs work at the forge from dawn until midnight. Thus,

WINTERSTOKE

stubbornly, they fought to preserve their independence, to hold the family together and to avoid the ultimate degradation of 'going on the Parish'. What were their opinions on the high park walls, the arbours, grottoes, temples and obelisks of Ernest Hanmer and Lancelot Brown? Perhaps, to use a countryman's term, the sheer magnitude of their tragedy and its wantonness left them dumbstruck.

For Daniel Leeds and the Darley Bank Company these changes meant only one thing—more wrought iron. The ironmongers' insatiable demand for rod and bar iron became too much for the old water-driven forges and slitting mills to satisfy and so the next important technical developments at Winterstoke took place. In 1782, two years after the New Bank Furnace with its direct blast engine had been blown in, a Watt rotative beam engine was built and installed by the Company to drive the helve hammers of a new forge. In 1788 a second Watt engine of similar type was driving a new and improved rolling and slitting mill. Hitherto the steam engines of High Hanger and Darley Bank had all been reciprocating pumps, but now Winterstoke saw for the first time an engine which was not only more efficient in its working but which had been endowed with rotative motion. It was thus a machine far more versatile in application which made obsolete the intermediary water-wheel. Once again the tempo of work on Darley Bank quickened in obedience to a pace set by these new machines. Could we but hear a series of sound recordings of the voice of the ironworks made in each decade of the eighteenth century, their cumulative effect, in quickening rhythm and gathering volume, would be reminiscent of Prokofief's *L'Apprentice Sorcière*; the first muted rhythms of water-wheel, helve hammer, leathern bellows and horse-gin yielding, in mounting crescendo, to the surge and thunder of full orchestra and percussion in steam rolling mill and heavy forge.

James Watt's particular contribution to this industrial overture was not rotative motion but an engine of vastly improved efficiency. The crank, the simplest form of deriving rotary from reciprocating motion, had been patented by

WINTERSTOKE

James Pickard of Birmingham, and to circumvent this patent the two Watt engines at Darley Bank employed the more cumbersome method of sun-and-planet gearing which was soon to be discarded. The problem which Watt had set himself to solve was how to obviate the besetting fault of the Newcomen engine—that alternate heating and cooling of the cylinder which made the engine so inefficient. Watt's solution was to exhaust the steam from the cylinder into a separate receiver and condense it there instead of in the cylinder itself. Although the working pressure was still low, Watts' machine was a true steam engine, deriving its power from steam pressure aided to a limited extent by the vacuum created in his condenser and not, as in the Newcomen engine, from atmospheric pressure alone. At this time the efficiency of an engine was judged by its 'duty', which represented the number of gallons of water which could be raised one foot for each bushel of coal consumed. It is a measure of Watt's achievement that the 'duty' of his first engine was nearly twenty-three million gallons as compared with the figure of 4.3 for the Newcomen. In a little over fifty years this 'duty' figure would rise to one hundred and fifty million gallons.

Because Watt's design demanded much greater accuracy in construction and finish, for some years the inventor had been frustrated by a manufacturing technique unable to fulfil the demands he made upon it. One of the greatest difficulties was the machining of his cylinders. The old Newcomen cylinders had been bored at Darley Bank by means of a rotating boring bar which produced a bore that was perfectly circular but seldom truly parallel throughout its length. It was the great ironmaster, John Wilkinson of Berstham, who first succeeded in producing a machine capable of boring a cylinder to satisfy Watt's more exacting standards. It was upon such a machine, whereon the cylinder revolved about a stationary boring bar, that the cylinders for these Watt engines were finished at Darley Bank.

The new engines with their demand for steam at higher pressure called for better boilers, but here the engines themselves helped to solve the problem by driving machines which

WINTERSTOKE

revolutionized the art of the boiler makers. The first spherical iron boilers to supersede the copper boilers of the earliest Newcomen engines had to be made from small plates forged under the helve or 'plating' hammer, but now the steam-driven mill could roll plates four feet long, eight inches wide and half an inch thick. There was thus set in motion another of those cycles of expansion by which the revolution proceeded: more powerful engines, larger rolling mills, larger boiler plates, stronger boilers with fewer seams, higher steam pressures, more powerful engines. Within two decades the pioneer, Richard Trevithick, was using steam at a pressure of 145 pounds to the square inch, and demonstrating that a small direct-acting high pressure engine could deliver as much power as a ponderous beam engine many times its weight. But for the moment let us admire the engine of James Watt by contrast with the earlier Newcomen.

The Newcomen pump which delivers water back to the upper furnace pool has been made more efficient by the addition of what is known as a 'pickle pot' condenser to adapt it to the Watt cycle. Yet with the elimination of water power in sight, its days are numbered and already it looks archaic. The massive but crude workmanship of the wooden regulating beam and the piston and pump chains with their wooden links and iron pins is so obviously that of millwrights versed in the medieval tradition of wind and water mill or horse gin. Its method of working is, as Samuel Smiles described, 'a very painful process, accompanied by an extraordinary amount of wheezing, sighing, creaking, and bumping.' But so soon as we enter the tall engine house beside the new rolling mill we realize that the age of wood is almost over; that this is the iron age and that the millwright is fast becoming a mechanical engineer. But he is still a great and proud craftsman. The engine is more cohesive in form, and the proportion of each part is more nicely adjusted to its purpose. And by contrast to the old Newcomen with what smooth precision do these parts move; the tireless swing of that long connecting rod to the planet wheel; the centrifugal governor wheeling round; the exact geometry of the parallel motion between beam and piston rod; the delicate levers of the gab valve gear rising and falling. Long after the architects had abandoned the classic tradition, the engineers, by a strange irony, would embody the proportions and symmetry of a vanished style in beam engines of monumental scale; engines in which graceful fluted columns of cast iron supported the great beam high overhead and where the shape of each part was determined not only by function but by classic form.

On the technicalities of the many different engines of Newcomen and Watt types which were built by the Darley Bank Company during the eighteenth century there is no need to dwell, but one engine, which was really a combination of both types, must be mentioned because of the important part which it played in the expansion of the High Hanger coalfield. This was the small two cylinder beam engine patented by Adam Heslop. Heslop's steam or 'hot' cylinder was powered by steam pressure as on the Watt engine, but instead of exhausting into a condenser, the steam passed to the second 'cold' cylinder which actuated the other end of the beam and which produced additional power on the Newcomen 'atmospheric' principle when the steam was condensed. A connecting rod and crank on the atmospheric side of the beam produced rotary motion. Because the engine was neat and compact compared with its contemporaries, and because its two cylinders made it unusually smooth and flexible in operation, there was one particular duty for which it was ideally suited—it could replace the old horse gins for colliery winding. This little engine of Heslop's, therefore, completed the conquest of steam at Winterstoke. It banished horse power from the pitheads just as the Watt engine had made the ironworks independent of water power. The new winding engines made a bizarre addition to the already sombre landscape of High Hanger for, unlike the earlier Newcomen pumps, they were not enclosed in engine houses but stood in the open beside their cupola-shaped boilers and tall smoke stacks. With their gaunt framework and nodding beams they might have been

WINTERSTOKE

the animated skeletons of the armoured monsters which had once stalked through the tropical forests of the coal measures.

By the end of the century it was no longer possible for a visitor to Winterstoke Park (as it was now called) to remain unaware of the activity beyond the river despite all the skill of Lancelot Brown. Vista and avenue could not shut out the fierce glare of Bedlam and New Bank furnaces which painted the night skies over Darley Bank with the lurid colours of a false, apocalyptic sunset. Like roll of drums and distant gunfire, the tumult of rolling mill and heavy forge brought to the silence of terrace and temple a faint but threatening undercurrent of sound. The installation of each new steam engine meant that another chimney stack added its quota to the fume from furnaces, from lime kilns, from heaps of coking coal and from perpetually burning gob fires which at night seamed the black spoil heaps of High Hanger with veins of scarlet. In still weather the smoke hung over the valley like a thundercloud or tarnished the mists which rose from the river meadows. When the winds blew southerly the sulphur could be tasted as well as smelt. Each raindrop carried its kernel of soot to stain the stonework of Wyatt's long façade with sad streaks of grime. Even the colours of Brown's carefully-planned landscape seemed to lose lustre as though seen through a darkened glass.

Perhaps it was this omnipresence which led the sinth Earl and his lady to spend so many months of each year at their town house. Because the enclosures had contributed so much to the growth of the Darley Bank Company it could be said that the Earl was responsible for fouling his own costly nest. But this poetic justice did nothing to compensate those who, robbed of their land, their ancient rights and their liberties, now laboured in the fierce heat of forge, foundry and mill or in the perilous darkness of the deepening mines.

Chapter Six

As the Darley Bank Company's consumption of coal and its output of iron increased, so the traffic over the wooden wagon ways to the pits and to the Company's wharf on the Wendle grew heavier. To keep them in repair, more and more money had to be expended on scarce timber. In an attempt to reduce this excessive wear and tear, Daniel Leeds tried the experiment of sheathing part of the High Hanger wagon way, which suffered most, with flat plates of iron. In 1766, however, a particular combination of circumstances persuaded Daniel to make a bolder experiment.

Already the iron trade had expanded to such an extent that its ramifications had become sensitive not merely to national but to international events. Though never the overt cause of war, the new fiercely competitive industrial economy acted as an international irritant, while the stature of a nation and its capacity to wage war was coming to depend more and more upon its resources of coal and iron rather than upon the wisdom of its statesmen or the size of its armies. Of all this the miners and iron workers of Winterstoke knew nothing. All they knew was that the old stability of their rural past had gone; that they had become the helpless dependents of an industry which offered them no security at all, so wild and unpredictable were its fluctuations of fortune and so bewildering the changes in food prices which accompanied these alternating booms and slumps. Thus the Seven Years War was a boom period for Darley Bank, but after the Peace of Paris the iron trade slumped and there was a spell of acute depression. To give him his due, Daniel Leeds did what he could to combat a state of affairs which, though he may have understood it more clearly than his men, he was equally powerless to control. But by 1766 the position was so bad

WINTERSTOKE

that he was forced to consider blowing out Bedlam Furnace. It was at this juncture that it occurred to him to replace the wooden wagon ways with rails of cast iron. This work would keep the furnace in blast for some time and, he argued, the Company could not lose by it. If the experiment was a success its advantages would be great; if it failed the new rails would represent a stock of iron to be drawn upon when trade improved. In the event, however, when war broke out once more in 1775 and the iron trade boomed, the rails were not drawn upon for they had proved themselves far too useful.

In four years over a thousand tons of rails were cast from Bedlam Furnace. The whole of the system which linked the collieries, the ironworks and the wharf was relaid, and numerous short connections were laid in to pits, engine houses and workshops so that in all there were nearly ten miles of the new track. Each rail was a yard long, over an inch thick, and cast with a flange on the inside which guided the unflanged wheels of the wagons. This enabled the existing stock of wagons to be used and also meant that while the work of relaying went slowly but steadily forward, the same wagons could run on either the new track or the old. Besides the rails, thousands of iron chairs were cast which were spiked down to the old wooden cross ties or sleepers to support and locate the rails.

So surely were the wagons guided by the flanges of this iron way and so much more smoothly did they run that a single horse could not only draw a much greater load, but it was only on the route between the collieries and the ironworks that horse haulage had to be used in both directions. Down the gently falling gradients of the lines which led to the Wendle wharf the loaded wagons of coal or iron could run by gravity. Perched on the long arm of a crude wooden brake, the wagoner controlled the speed of his rumbling load while the horse, which would draw the empty wagons back again, trotted behind or, at a later stage, was carried down in a special wagon called a dandy cart.

A tradition lingers at Darley Bank to this day that at some

WINTERSTOKE

unspecified time at the beginning of the nineteenth century a locomotive designed by Richard Trevithick was built at the works and hauled coals along the tramway from High Hanger to the ironworks. The Company certainly carried out work for Trevithick, but if a locomotive was built on the lines of that engineer's famous Pennydarran engine it vanished without leaving a trace in the firm's records. Perhaps its weight destroyed the cast-iron rails. Perhaps an engine which combined the power of locomotion with a boiler pressure so high for those days as to seem positively lethal was considered too fantastic and too dangerous for everyday use. That great Cornish engineer was too far ahead of his time. Over forty years would pass before Winterstoke saw the first practical realization of his dream.

The new iron tramways solved the Company's internal transport problem for many years, but there still remained the problem of improving transport over greater distances. Here the immediate question was how to improve and cheapen the supply of iron ore and limestone from the mines and quarries of Deepforest and Lobstock beyond the hills which hemmed in the Lob valley. This traffic had increased enormously but it was still handled by pack-horses as in medieval times. A well-used pack-horse track soon wore down until it became a mud-filled ditch on level ground or a stony, rapidly eroding watercourse on the hills. The pack-trains would then leave it and repeat the process nearby. As a result, by the middle of the eighteenth century this route over the hills looked, in a bird's-eye view, like a series of slug trails which crawled and meandered haphazard across the green. Landowners along the route not unnaturally protested against this state of affairs and the Darley Bank Company became involved in many disputes over wayleaves. Yet this was only the most pressing part of the general problem of handling the imports and exports of a growing industry. The Wendle Navigation and the coastal shipping trade from Westerport had provided a partial solution, but the problem of transport to or from any area far from the sea or from a navigable river remained. For an overland haul of

WINTERSTOKE

more than fifteen miles the cost of pack-horse transport became almost prohibitive, while over most of the so-called roads of Middle England reliable transport by wagon was usually impossible for at least eight months out of the twelve. The only road worthy of the name at Winterstoke was that from Westerport to Coltisham which crossed the Wendle at St. John's. Its upkeep was the responsibility of the parish, but the method of repair consisted of tipping a load of ungraded stone into the ruts when they became axle deep. In 1772, at the instigation of Ernest Hanmer, a Turnpike Act was passed and the road became the responsibility of a Turnpike Trust who were empowered to erect gates and houses in order to levy tolls for maintenance. This provoked almost as much resentment as the Enclosure Acts. The new gates at St. John's were several times torn down or damaged in the night, for the villagers looked upon them as an encroachment upon their freedom of movement and alleged that the tolls were merely enriching the Trust. Certainly it was some years before there was any marked improvement in the condition of the road, and until the end of the century its value for goods transport remained extremely limited.

It was one bitter winter's morning in January of the same year that was to see the start of his successful wagonway experiment, that Daniel Leeds mounted his cob and rode over the snow-powdered hills to Lobstock to attend a meeting of mine proprietors and landowners which would have a vital effect on the history of Winterstoke. Present at this meeting at the 'Angel' in Lobstock was James Brindley, the Derbyshire millwright who had just successfully completed the canal from Worsley to Manchester for the Duke of Bridgwater. It was known that a second and much longer canal was now projected, and had already been surveyed by Brindley, which would unite the eastern and western coasts of England and pass a few miles to the south of Lobstock. The meeting had been organized to discuss the possibility of constructing a navigable waterway from a junction with this proposed coast to coast canal, through Lobstock and the Deepforest district to join the Wendle Navigation. Finger-

WINTERSTOKE

low Mill in the flat lands of the lower valley had been suggested as the obvious point of junction with the river, but Daniel Leeds was concerned to urge that, despite the greater physical difficulties, the canal should join the head of the navigation at Winterstoke. He foresaw that the canal would then connect directly with the ironworks, whereas for the purpose of his traffic the other route would be very circuitous. This view had brought Daniel into conflict with the Wendle bargemasters and, with the exception of Lord Winterstoke, with his fellow proprietors of the Navigation Company. At a stormy meeting in Westerport they had argued that they would enjoy a share in all the traffic which the new canal might bring to Fingerlow whereas if it joined the river at Winterstoke they were as likely to lose traffic as to gain it. Even in Lobstock and Deepforest opinions were sharply divided. Those who did most business with the Darley Bank Company supported Daniel; others maintained that the Winterstoke scheme would either prove impracticable or extravagantly costly and that the Fingerlow route would not only be cheaper to construct but would give Lobstock a more direct outlet to the sea at Westerport.

Now, over glasses of port or pots of mulled ale, the protagonists argued afresh and submitted their rival schemes to the arbitrament of the engineer. That unlettered genius refused to commit himself until he had made a survey of the suggested routes, although he shocked into silence the spokesman of the Wendle Navigation Company with the gruff remark, made in a dialect so broad that some of those present could scarcely follow it, that if he had his way he would build a canal down the Wendle valley and be done with the river. It was upon Brindley's assurance that he would examine and report upon the proposed canal that the meeting came to an end.

Two months later, Brindley completed what he described in his diary as 'an ochilor survey' of the country between Lobstock and the Wendle. Forcing his way by mazy, ill-defined trackways through the brakes and spinneys which hid the Deepforest mines; striking across country over fields

WINTERSTOKE

sodden by February rains, where his horse floundered in the heavy Midland clay; standing at last at gaze like some eighteenth-century Cortez on the crest of the camp on High Hanger Down, the first of the great civil engineers mapped out his route with little to aid him except his two eyes and his own self-taught gifts. As the windy dusk was falling he walked his tired horse into the stableyard of Darley Bank House and was hospitably received by the Leeds family. Having done excellent justice to the substantial meal which was quickly provided, he surprised his host and hostess by promptly retiring to bed and not reappearing until noon on the following day. They did not realize that this was their strange guest's invariable method of working out his problems.

Although Daniel Leeds had stubbornly promoted the Winterstoke scheme in public, in private he had felt by no means certain that the physical difficulties of the route could be overcome. But in his writing-room that afternoon the engineer reassured him. True, the idea of tunnelling through the watershed at the head of the Lob valley which Brindley proposed so calmly daunted even his adventurous mind. Yet it was precisely the matter-of-fact way in which Brindley outlined his scheme which inspired confidence and, as events proved, that confidence was not misplaced.

The Lobstock Canal Bill was bitterly but unsuccessfully opposed by those who had favoured the Fingerlow route and by landowners who objected to the passage of a canal through their property. But the Company of Proprietors of the Lobstock Canal Navigation finally won the day and in the spring of 1768 their Bill received the Royal Assent.

It was the construction of the canals which first made the people of England aware of the achievements of the men of the new age and conscious of the revolution which was taking place in their midst. Travellers were rare in eighteenth-century England; observant and inquiring travellers who recorded their experiences like Defoe and Arthur Young were even rarer. The small black patches in the Midlands and the North which marked the new industrial areas on a

WINTERSTOKE

map of England still predominantly green were as yet *terra incognita* to the majority. Even those in their immediate vicinity saw only the outward shape of things and knew nothing of the technical miracles which were being performed within the new mills, ironworks and mines. But to build the canals the engineer left the dark obscurity of his workshop and invaded the country, weaving, like some industrious spider, a web of silver threads over the green map. Fine as gossamer though these narrow water lanes might appear on the map, they nevertheless knit together as strongly and surely as links of steel those dark areas which had hitherto been isolated one from another.

Whereas the improvement for navigation of natural channels such as the Wendle had occasioned little remark, these wholly artificial waterways which strode over rivers on aqueducts, climbed ladders of locks or burrowed under the hills, were hailed as the wonder of the age. In an area extending for several miles round Winterstoke there were few people who did not at one time or another drive, ride or walk, according to their station, to gaze in awe and amazement at the works of the celebrated James Brindley. It was the task of driving the great Ketton Tunnel, over a mile in length, which occasioned most wonder, and speculation was rife as to whether the work would succeed or fail. A few expressed confidence; many more scoffed and dismissed the enterprise as fantastic folly. But in spite of these doubters the work went steadily on.

No sooner had construction been authorized than the 'navigators' invaded Winterstoke like a dense flock of chattering, brawling starlings swooping on stubble in autumn. A ragged army of Irishmen, gipsies and dispossessed countrymen from every county in the Midlands and the North, they encamped in a meadow below Ketton Farm, building themselves rough huts from whatever materials they could lay hands on. The scenes of drunkenness and brawling and the babel of dialects when their overseers paid them their wages at the 'Woodcollier' defied description. But when landlord Blenkinsop contemplated the trampled compost of clay, beer

WINTERSTOKE

slops, spittle, blood and broken glass which they left on his sanded floors and then tallied his takings, he reflected that it was worth it.

It was the 'navigators' who dug the deep trench which followed the winding contours of the hills and who made its bed watertight with Brindley's infallible specific of puddled clay. Then there were the horse-keepers whose pack-trains were the supply lines of the construction gangs, and finally the aristocrats of the labour force, the skilled masons and carpenters who built culverts and bridges, lock chambers and lock gates. The whole of this army was under the command of Brindley's able pupil Robert Whitworth who made his headquarters at Darley Bank House while the northern end of the canal was building.

Brindley had planned the Lobstock Canal on the characteristic lines which he always favoured: concentrations of locks at Lobstock and Winterstoke leading up to a long, devious summit level which included Ketton Tunnel and which tapped the headwaters of numerous small streams and springs. In dry seasons this long summit would itself hold a great store of lockage water but, to provide additional reserves, reservoirs would be formed on the watershed, feeding the summit through open leats. With the exception of Ketton Tunnel the works presented no particular difficulty and proceeded with remarkable speed. To form the northern terminal a great rectangular basin was dug beside the Wendle at Darley Bank Wharf. Because the engineer heartily mistrusted and disliked the vagaries of rivers, the basin was situated well above the level of the highest flood, access to it from the Wendle being provided by a lock large enough to admit the river barges. From this basin the invading army left behind them a gash of raw earth and muddy water, stopped at regular intervals by the flight of twenty new narrow locks, which looped away southwards up the Lob valley. With their curving wing walls, their deep chambers of brick and stone seventy feet long but little more than seven feet wide and their gates with outspread balance beams and rack and pinion paddle gear, these new locks looked very

WINTERSTOKE

different from their predecessors on the Wendle. From one of the 'pounds' between these locks a short branch canal crossed the Lob on a culverted embankment to bring the new transport into the heart of the ironworks.

The completion of this section of the canal was a gesture of confidence on the part of Brindley and Whitworth which the sceptics considered foolhardy. For until the tunnel was completed it could not be used nor even supplied with water. As a temporary measure, so that its puddled bed should not dry out, water was pumped into the pounds from the Lob.

South of the tunnel, the work of cutting the long summit level from Lobstock proceeded even more rapidly. No sooner was a section completed than water was admitted to it up to a temporary dam or 'stank' so that boats could aid the construction work by bringing up loads of gravel, clay or bricks. Owing to Brindley's practice of following the natural contours, in all the twelve winding miles of canal between Lobstock and Ketton there was no embankment or cutting of note so that the amount of spoil to be moved was negligible. Within two years of the passing of the Act, the canal to the north and south of Ketton had been completed, but the cutting of the great tunnel itself was quite a different proposition.

Because of their special skill and their knowledge of the local strata, Daniel Leeds reinforced Whitworth's tunnel construction gangs with miners from his High Hanger pits. Work began on the hilltop where, along the line of the canal, a series of vertical shafts were sunk down to canal level. From the bottom of these shafts headings were then driven north and south towards each other. Above each shaft horse gins kept the workings clear of water, lowered the men to their work and drew up the excavated spoil. Grassgrown spoil mounds, looking not unlike the work of the men of the first Iron Age on High Hanger Down and Summersend, remain to mark to this day the site of these shafts. In one of the headings a spring was struck of a volume which proved quite beyond the power of all the horse pumps which could be mustered. To the chagrin of the construction gang and the delight of the sceptics, the heading had to be abandoned

WINTERSTOKE

to the victorious waters which rose until the level stood some distance up the shaft. In response to an urgent appeal for help and advice from Whitworth, Brindley himself rode over to inspect the drowned shaft, which appeared to cause him more pleasure than dismay. The engineer welcomed the spring as an additional supply to his canal, indeed he had been counting upon such a discovery. As for the immediate difficulty, a 'fire engine' would solve that, he said. So as soon as the weather served a thirty-hundredweight cylinder, a cylinder bottom, pump barrel, bucket, pipes and all the necessary parts and materials to erect a Newcomen pump were dragged from Darley Bank up on to the hills by sweating, struggling horse-teams. Wheezing and clanking, trailing its banners of smoke and steam in the windy upland air, the labouring Newcomen slowly but surely conquered the waters in the drowned heading, and so the work went on. For four years the miners and navigators toiled in the narrow headings, pitting muscles and wits against rock and water, against treacherous shales and heavy, stubborn clays. Then the last two headings met. But the work was by no means over. The completed heading was so narrow that two men could hardly pass in it; so low that it was not possible to stand upright. Three more years went by before the work of opening out the heading and lining walls, roof and invert with millions of bricks was finished. The stop-planks which had for so long stanked off the waters of the summit level at South Ketton Bridge were then lifted. A wavelet of water surged over the new brickwork of the invert and advanced into the darkness of the tunnel. Soon it was lapping against the gates of Winterstoke top lock. The Lobstock Canal had been completed. The sceptics were compelled to eat their words in the general chorus of praise, but James Brindley, the architect of the canal, had not lived to celebrate his victory.

The official opening of the canal on June 26, 1775, was declared a day of public holiday in Lobstock and Winterstoke and was an occasion destined to live long in memory. The sun shone out of a cloudless sky; hardships and antagon-

WINTERSTOKE

isms were forgotten in a carefree spirit of excited optimism, which seemed to infect everyone from the visiting noblemen to the poorest nailer, who shut his nailshop for the day and tramped with his wife and children to join the cheering throng which lined the towpath. Perhaps this wonderful achievement would indeed mean better times for all. In readiness for the great day a number of the long, narrow canal craft had been assembled at Lobstock Wharf. Here, at 8 a.m. precisely, the canal proprietors, Daniel Leeds, Robert Whitworth, Lord Winterstoke and other local noblemen and gentry with their families stepped aboard the boats *Heart of Oak* and *Britannia*, while lesser notables and crowds of 'navigators' and other canal workmen packed the craft which were to follow them. The procession then moved away, headed by the *Pride* which bore in her hold the combined church bands of Winterstoke and Lobstock who scraped their fiddles and viols with a will. The highly polished brasswork on the tackle of the towing horses flashed in the June sunlight and from the procession of boats banners floated which bore such inscriptions as: 'A Health to the Proprietors', 'Success to Navigation' and 'Long Live the King'. It was a brave sight, and all along the route, even in the lonely coppices of Deepforest, there were countryfolk to line the banks and cheer the procession on its way. The passage of Ketton tunnel took some time, for here the towing path ended and the towing horses must be detached and led over the hilltop. But in the boatloads of 'navigators' there was no lack of willing 'leggers' to propel the boats through and at one o'clock precisely the *Pride*, the *Heart of Oak* and the *Britannia* were greeted with a deafening ovation from the assembled crowd of ironworkers and miners, as one by one they emerged from the last lock and sailed into Winterstoke basin. Here the gentry adjourned to a marquee for luncheon while, for the benefit of the crowd, an ox had been roasted and free beer was now liberally distributed at the expense of the Proprietors. In the afternoon the flotilla returned to Lobstock, to be greeted by similar scenes of enthusiasm and the distribution of more beer and beef, while the more select

WINTERSTOKE

company dined and drank many toasts at the 'Angel' in the very same room where the first tentative meeting had been held on that winter's morning nine years before.

It was surprising how soon the nine days' wonder became as much a part of the life of Winterstoke as the river. The 'navigators' disappeared as suddenly as they had come and the raw wounds they had made soon healed. Water plants quickly established themselves to soften the margins of the still water, and the hedge which had been planted along the towpath side thickened and grew up. The hollow thud of closing gates and the rattle of falling paddle racks became familiar sounds as the long boats locked down the Winterstoke flight, low loaded with their burdens of ore, limestone or moulding sand for the ironworks, or rose slowly upward, step by step, with return freights of coal or pig and bar iron. The canal became the life of a new community which established itself either on its waters or about its banks, a community of boatmen, horsekeepers, boatbuilders, publicans, farriers, maintenance men and lock keepers who were a world unto themselves.

The Canal Company did not operate their own boats but were merely toll takers like the Wendle Navigation Company or the Turnpike Trusts. At first the traffic was purely local and consisted of boats operated by or for the Darley Bank Company. Shuttling to and fro between the works and the Deepforest mines, they were worked by the men who had once had charge of the pack-horse trains. But the Lobstock Canal was only one strand of the network of waterways which was spreading across the Midlands to make possible a steadily widening orbit of trade, to break down old local monopolies, to generate new industries upon its banks and to create a more fiercely competitive commerce. Just as the Winterstoke boats began to range farther and farther afield with their freights of coal and iron, so strange boats from parts of England which had hitherto seemed as remote as some foreign country began to appear in the Winterstoke canal basin. With cabins fitted up after the pattern of a gipsy caravan, these far-travelled boats were the homes of

WINTERSTOKE

that strange nomadic people who had come from who knows where to roam the new water roads wherever the trade took them. Some of them carried cargoes of cloth, foodstuffs or other merchandise which had hitherto been almost unobtainable in Winterstoke but was now being imported by enterprising merchants. The task of working this increasing traffic through the dank, dripping cavern of Ketton tunnel became the monopoly of professional 'leggers' who lay, two to a boat, on each end of a plank athwart the gunwales to push with their feet against the tunnel walls. Their headquarters were the two alehouses, 'The Boat' and 'Tunnel House', which stood at each end of the tunnel.

Surrounded by warehouses, by the slipways of a boatbuilding dock and by the great stables of 'The Navigation' inn, whither landlord Amos Blenkinsop had transported himself with an astute eye to further business, the new basin at Darley Bank Wharf soon became a flourishing inland port. Boats and barges jostled each other in the basin as they waited their turn to move under the hoists of the warehouses or within range of the massive wooden jib of the crane which swung the corves of coal out of the tramway wagons from High Hanger. There was an almost continuous procession of horses to or from the stables as boats arrived or moved off, and the Inn had a brisk trade in fodder as well as beer. Increasing traffic made business in the boatyard equally brisk. Caulking mallets clattered continuously, the pungent smell of hot tar was always in the air, and every now and again another long black hull slid sideways down the slipway into her element. Row after row of new buildings ringed this busy nucleus and these were soon linked by Daniel Leeds' great iron bridge with the Earl's new Winterstoke across the river.

Between canal and river there was little love lost at any level. The Wendle bargemen and their bow-hauliers despised and disliked the new 'dry land sailors', the former because canal navigation seemed to them an unskilled job and the latter because they feared that the canal system of horse towage threatened their livelihood. The Wendle barges were

WINTERSTOKE

too broad of beam to pass through the canal locks, and the canal boats too long for those on the river even if their captains had been willing to face hazards of current and shoal of which they knew nothing. So the two worlds only met, frequently with violence, at Darley Bank basin and in the tap room of the 'Navigation'.

The relations between the Proprietors of the two Navigations were no better. The forebodings of those who had opposed the Winterstoke canal scheme and argued in favour of the junction at Fingerlow proved well founded. The canal did not bring any immediate increase of trade on the Wendle, and in some cases trade was lost. To some areas where the Darley Bank Company had previously consigned goods by Wendle barge and coasting vessel, Daniel Leeds now found it cheaper and quicker to consign by the new canal system which was far less subject to delays by drought, flood or storm. Nevertheless the Wendle remained Winterstoke's vital trade route to the sea, and Daniel repeatedly urged upon the Company the necessity of improving their river works if they would retain and expand their trade. Their navigation must, he argued, be brought up to the new standard of efficiency which the canals had set. Let them rebuild and improve the locks to a size which would enable the canal boats to work on to the river and so avoid the necessity for transhipment. Let them dredge the shoals and replace the old Navigation weirs by locks to save delays. Let them provide a horse-towing path throughout. But Daniel's arguments were in vain. The proposal to make the river suitable for canal craft was furiously assailed by the bargemasters who saw it as a threat to their monopoly, while the idea of a horse towing path nearly caused a riot among the bow hauliers with the result that the alarmed Company dropped it like a hot coal.

This conflict was still proceeding when the success of the new water transport led to a speculative boom in canal projects. All over the country canal schemes were promoted, many of them quite worthless and conceived without regard either for engineering difficulties or for the traffic they would

WINTERSTOKE

yield. Of these paper schemes Winterstoke had its share. A canal which involved a tunnel two miles long under the Emberley hills was even proposed for the sole purpose of linking Winterstoke with Church Ambling, a sleepy market town which had long ago forgotten its bygone wool trade. Needless to say the scheme collapsed. The only local promotion of this period for which an Act was obtained and construction actually started was the Winterstoke & Coltisham Canal, but in the unsettled period of the Napoleonic war the undertakers came to grief. All that remains of their scheme to-day is a few miles of grass-grown earthwork which winds along through the watermeadows of the upper Wendle like some prehistoric dyke.

By this time old Daniel Leeds had ended his long career at Darley Bank, but his son Jonathan Leeds was carrying on his father's struggle against the inertia of the Wendle Navigation Company, and when a canal was proposed which would run parallel with the old river navigation down to Westerport he seized upon it as a useful weapon. Resigning his seat on the river Company's board he lent his full weight to the canal scheme, not because he had any faith in it but because he hoped by this means to force the Company to put its house in order. To a limited extent he succeeded. The river was dredged, locks were repaired, and freight charges were reduced, so in consideration for these measures, all of which were of great benefit to the Darley Bank Company, the canal project was dropped. Yet the bargemasters and bow hauliers still held their monopoly. Nor was the Lobstock Canal Company innocent of abusing its comfortable monopoly, for as the time went on there were frequent protests by carriers and merchants against its high toll charges. For the present, however, the two navigation Companies held the whip hand and they knew it. They only settled their long-standing differences, reduced their charges and carried out long overdue improvements when it was too late and when they were threatened by a common enemy. But that is another story.

Chapter Seven

IN 1700 WINTERSTOKE was still a village, or rather it was two villages: the old medieval settlement by St. John's Bridge, and the community of common-squatting iron-workers and coal-getters which had sprung up haphazard and mushroom-like across the river and which, like a cuckoo in a small bird's nest was rapidly outgrowing its ancient neighbour. Its growth was such that by the mid-century the population of Winterstoke was equal to that of the old town of Church Ambling, while between 1760 and 1830 it more than doubled itself. Such was the tremendous impetus which enclosure, steam power and canal transport gave to the pace of industrial revolution. Lord Winterstoke's new village, the settlement about the canal basin, the iron and coal communities of Darley Bank and Hanger Lane all grew until they formed one dense warren of bricks and mortar lining both banks of the Wendle and crawling up the lower slopes of the hills. Like a blot of ink spilled on to virgin blotting paper, each year the black of slate roof and spoil tip spread further over the valley's green floor. Yet this stain became deeper as it spread. In the early years of the nineteenth century speculators began to take advantage of the insatiable demand for house-room by building the maximum number of houses in the minimum of space. The green oases of garden, orchard or paddock disappeared and the old detached cottages of earlier immigrants were either overwhelmed or swept away. In their place grew back-to-back houses, terrace by terrace and court beyond narrow court. Yet even these squalid rookeries could not satisfy the demand. Whole families occupied single rooms worse than prison cells, so cabined and confined were they and so cut off from every green and living thing. Most of them were denied even the benefit of the wan sunlight which filtered through the pall of smoke which overhung the valley. For their windows looked out upon enclosed courts scarcely wide enough to provide space for stinking communal privies and garbage heaps.

The population of this new Winterstoke soon exceeded that of any town in the county and yet it could not be called a town in any hitherto accepted sense of the word. Its neighbours, the ancient medieval towns of Church Ambling and Coltisham, like the old village of Winterstoke, possessed a traditional corporate life which had been the fruit of a slow process of organic growth intimately associated with their rural environment. They were self-governing communities proud of their customary civic rights and responsibilities and practising those arts and crafts which are, or should be, the particular contribution of the town, not only to its immediate neighbourhood but to the history of civilized living. A vital part of the corporate life of Church Ambling and Coltisham throughout the Middle Ages had been the trade guilds whose function it had been to preserve by regulation the balance of trade between the husbandman of the country and the craftsman of the town. We have already seen how, after the dissolution, these guilds and the balance of trade which they had for so long maintained were gradually destroyed. The new Winterstoke of the early eighteen hundreds represented the consummation, the ultimate victory, of the new *laissez faire* philosophy which had been two centuries agrowing. It was not so much a town as what modern planners, in their ugly jargon, would call a 'conurbation'; an amorphous mass of uprooted humanity struggling to win a livelihood from coal and iron under appalling conditions of hardship, squalor and grinding poverty. Here there was no corporate life, no communal pride, no civic rights or responsibilities, no attempt at regulation of any kind, only the remorseless whip of economic necessity. Except for the fact that coal seams, iron lodes and water power had originally determined its location, the fierce activity of this new town and the inexorable economic forces which drove it were in no way related to its environment. Its inhabitants

WINTERSTOKE

were wholly dependent on the world market which the new philosophy had won and were the helpless victims of the vagaries of a bitterly competitive trade. By 1800, two-thirds of the army of nailers and other domestic smiths in Winterstoke parish were working for the American market alone, and the decline of that trade after 1810, competition from Belgium and the introduction of machine-made nails brought untold misery to this overcrowded industry. Yet these hard-pressed domestic workers did at least succeed in preserving some shreds of their old rural independence. They still worked at hours of their own choosing in the familiar surroundings of their own homes, while in many cases they still possessed patches of garden which had not yet been engulfed by the rising tide of bricks and mortar.

Not so the miners and ironworkers in the back-to-back terraces of Hanger Lane and Darley Bank. As the slump which followed the Peace of Paris had first shown, their livelihood was little more secure than that of their fellows whereas the claim of the Darley Bank Company over their lives had become absolute. So far from lightening their labours or shortening their hours of work each new machine, each technical innovation meant a more fiercely competitive and therefore more unstable economy, a more relentless pace, a more exacting and rigid discipline. Working hours grew longer and wages lower. The old 'butty' system, as it was sometimes called, whereby a foreman or 'overhand' contracted with the Company and employed his own labour still survived. But as the scope of the Company's activities widened so it became the more impersonal and the old paternal relationship which had once existed between the Leeds family and their skilled workmen became less intimate. A system which had originally preserved the virtues of independence and individual responsibility was now sadly abused. The bargains struck between Daniel and Jonathan Leeds and their 'overhands' were generally hard; those made between the overhands and their employees were even harder, but their terms were not the concern of the ironmasters. Most of the overhands ran 'tommy shops' and paid their men, not in money but in goods of inferior quality at prices which were often far above those prevailing in the open market. In spite of prohibitory Acts of Parliament, this truck system of payment continued to flourish and employers refused to interfere with the 'overhands'' freedom of contract. Wages, which were already little above starvation level, could never under this system command their true purchasing power. In the attempt to make ends meet under these dire circumstances, the children of the new Winterstoke were put to work almost as soon as they could walk. For centuries children had been accustomed to labour with their parents in the fields, but the work demanded by this industrial age was of a very different order. For twelve and fourteen hours a day boys toiled as stockers in the stifling heat and fumes of the furnace bridges at Darley Bank, or loaded and dragged the corves of coal through the dark galleries of the High Hanger Pits. Through equally interminable hours children only five or six years old acted as trappers in the pits, crouching alone and in total darkness in some inaccessible corner of the mine where they controlled the 'traps' or air-lock doors which governed the ventilation system. A boy of fourteen was judged sufficiently responsible to control a Heslop winding engine when it lowered a human freight down the mine's dark shaft.

Where labour was so cheap and so plentiful, human life was of little account, especially in the underground world beneath High Hanger. Here the safety lamp, one of the very few humanitarian inventions of the day, brought no safety. Any virtue it possessed was offset by the working of deeper levels where inadequate ventilation increased the threat of spontaneous explosion in the stagnant, stifling air and where the peril of roof falls became much graver. Accidents in the pits were seldom or never the subject of inquest or inquiry so that their toll of human life cannot be assessed. We do not know how many crushed or blasted victims were hauled to the surface; nor how many forgotten dead may still lie entombed in old, abandoned workings. But if we add to the toll of these unrecorded tragedies the men blinded by

WINTERSTOKE

nystagmus or riddled with consumption and the victims of the recurrent epidemics of cholera, typhus and smallpox which swept through the overcrowded back-to-backs like forest fires, then we can begin to form some idea of the weight of human misery which hung over Winterstoke as heavily as the smoke tainted fogs that rose from the polluted river.

When we remember that the majority of those whom the new philosophy had condemned to a life sentence under conditions so degrading and brutalizing were countrymen bred in a long tradition of sturdy independence it may seem surprising that they acted with such moderation and that the population of Winterstoke did not rise in organized revolt. There were two reasons why they did not do so, the strength of a bygone conservative tradition and the savage repression of authority.

Nowadays every demagogue who claims that he fights on behalf of the working man likes to call himself a 'progressive', but at this time the roles were reversed. It was the working men who remembered lost lands, lost rights and lost liberties who were the conservatives. The 'progressives' were the new class of industrialists who, intoxicated by the power of their machines, prophesied that, provided they were allowed complete freedom to pursue their great undertakings, progress towards a better and more prosperous world would follow automatically. Great landowners, such as the Earls of Winterstoke, who were the rulers of England, stood apart from these contending forces. They understood neither and did nothing to mitigate the clash between them. The new industry had brought them immense wealth in rents and mineral royalties and, as the enclosure movement showed, they also exemplified the philosophy of self-interest. But they did not recognize the fact that their enclosures, combined with the new industrial power and the new transport had created a unique and revolutionary social situation calling for drastic treatment and reform. When their attention was inevitably drawn to the new black areas on the map of England it was not attracted by a desire for reform or because they shared the industrialists' messianic faith in his machines but because they saw in these areas, rife with misery and discontent, a menace to their security and power. For the bloody and terrible lesson of the French Revolution was fresh in their minds, while the threat of Napoleonic invasion now hung over England. In that event, could the Crown depend upon the loyalty of the teeming population of the new towns? No emotion can more readily unleash the evils of tyranny, injustice, violence and false witness than fear, and the rulers of England became mortally afraid of the new black Winterstoke which sprawled and fumed and flamed in the valley of the Wendle. Any expression of discontent on the part of miners or ironworkers was looked upon as seditious, as an incipient revolution which threatened to overthrow the Constitution. Protests against the price of bread or the abuses of the 'tommy shops', concerted efforts to obtain a better wage or more humane hours of work were met, not by any promise of reform but by more rigorous repression and punishment. So that they should not outbid each other for labour, manufacturers could, in defiance of the Combination Laws, associate freely for the purpose of regulating wages, whereas the ringleaders of any attempt among the workmen to combine were prosecuted, indicted by the perjured evidence of spies, and sentenced to imprisonment, to transportation or even to death.

The old traditional machinery of local government in Winterstoke was unfitted to deal with the problems of the new town for it had become quite unrepresentative. Yet it was the very fact that it had ceased to represent the corporate will of the governed which now made a time-honoured system so corrupt and so effective an instrument of tyranny. Until 1832 the town was still governed, as in medieval times, by the jury of the Court Leet of the Manor of Winterstoke which met at Easter and Michaelmas and which was nominated by Lord Winterstoke's steward. His steward also empanelled the jury which elected annually the three chief officers of Government, the Reeve and two Constables.

WINTERSTOKE

These holders of ancient feudal office wielded power and authority such as their humble rural predecessors never dreamed of, reigning as petty dictators over the new town and, like every dictator in history, using spies and informers to make every man suspicious of his neighbour and so strengthen the rule of fear and force. Any miner or ironworker who roused the suspicions of the constables could be prosecuted on a variety of trumped-up charges, for sedition, for conspiracy, for a breach of the Combination Laws or even under the Vagrancy Acts. And once he had fallen into their clutches he knew there was no hope of impartial justice and that a committal to Assizes was almost certain to follow. For the local magistrates consisted of two members of the Leeds family and a Deepforest mine owner.

Under such a system of government the great landowner and the industrialist, as represented by the two families of Hanmer and Leeds, held absolute power in Winterstoke and that power was backed by all the forces of the Crown. In 1812 a new barracks was built at Church Ambling where four regiments of foot soldiers and two cavalry regiments were quartered in case of need. It was Government policy to dispose their forces in this way within striking distance of an industrial town but not in the town itself. For it was argued that if, for example, troops were quartered in Winterstoke they might themselves become disaffected and either refuse to act in the event of revolt or even take the part of the insurgents. Although on one occasion there was a quite needless display of military force when a peaceable and orderly meeting of miners took place on High Hanger Down, Winterstoke was never the scene of a Peterloo tragedy. The reason for this was probably the domestic organization of the manufacturing section of the iron trade which survived until the period of reform and thus spared Winterstoke the worst rigours of a factory system which drove the cotton workers of Lancashire to so desperate a pitch of misery and resentment.

Besides Church Ambling Barracks, two other forbidding buildings, one at Church Ambling and one in Winterstoke

WINTERSTOKE

itself, remain to this day as grim reminders of this chapter in our social history. The first of these was the new county gaol which was built in 1812, equipped with a treadmill ten years later and enlarged by the addition of a further sixty cells. The second was the Poor House, or 'House of Industry' as it was called, which was built at Winterstoke by the Board of Guardians appointed by the local magistrates under the powers of Gilbert's Act of 1782. Hitherto, vicar and churchwardens had been responsible for the poor of the parish. When we survey these buildings to-day it is impossible to deny that the architects of this period of artistic decadence, whatever Gothic follies they might perpetrate for private clients, served very well the ends of the Crown. Nothing could be better calculated to strike terror and despair to the hearts of its hapless guests than the cold, massive, meticulously proportioned façade of Church Ambling Gaol. 'Abandon hope all ye who enter here' is the clear statement, not only of the threatening prison gate but of each great block of rusticated stone. The effect is reminiscent of George Dance's Old Newgate prison and we feel that its unknown architect must either have been inspired, like Dance, by the *Carceri* of Piranesi, or haunted, like Vanbrugh, by a claustrophobic terror of confinement. Certainly, like other prison buildings of this period, it is a masterpiece of the sadistic and the macabre. That the building fulfilled an urgent need is revealed by the criminal statistics of committals and sentences to Assizes and Courts of Quarter Session in Midshire. Before 1821 no figures are available, but during the thirty years immediately following no less than 376 persons, including many women and young children, were sentenced to death at Church Ambling, many for offences as trivial as the theft of a loaf of bread, 1,333 were sentenced to transportation, a fate from which few ever returned, and 5,813 received terms of imprisonment, so that the new treadmill was put to good use. Comment upon these terrible figures is at once impossible and needless. They reveal more eloquently than any pages of impassioned prose by what means the spirit of the erstwhile

WINTERSTOKE

commoners of Winterstoke was broken by their new masters and harnessed to the discipline of new machines and new economics.

The 'Union', as it is now called, in Winterstoke has not the same architectural pretensions as Church Ambling Gaol, but its long frontage of soot-blackened brick and narrow barred windows looks as cold and as pitiless as the prison. We cannot believe that its builders were moved by any spark of charity or compassion; or that they regarded it as anything other than a place of shame and degradation. This building fulfilled an urgent need also, for by the first decade of the nineteenth century one out of every seven inhabitants of Winterstoke was a pauper. Looking at this building, we can understand why, quite apart from any feeling of pride and self-respect, a man would work himself to death rather than go 'on the Parish'. Here the overseer, like a slave master, organized the paupers in labour gangs to earn their keep. Here the parish children were loaded and despatched like livestock in packed wagons to provide cheap labour for the Lancashire cotton mills where the demand for children was much greater than in the iron trade.

The reeking, overcrowded courts of industrial Winterstoke, the new barracks, gaols and poorhouses, may appear to us to constitute an indictment of the new order too monstrous to be ignored by any contemporary. Surely those who built these new buildings must have realized that there was something terribly wrong with their society of poverty and punishment. Surely, too, the families of Hanmer and Leeds who ruled Winterstoke must have been monsters of wickedness, rapacity and inhumanity. Yet in fact contemporaries, with a very few exceptions, did not see these evils as we do, nor were William Hanmer, the seventh Earl, and Jonathan Leeds or his brother Peter arch-villains. Indeed, if both these old-established Winterstoke families had suddenly and simultaneously produced unscrupulous and heartless rogues it would have been a very remarkable coincidence. William Hanmer and the Leeds brothers were neither better nor worse than their predecessors. The Earl

WINTERSTOKE

supported the campaign for the abolition of the slave trade in the Lords and was regarded by his associates as a man of remarkable intelligence, sincerity and humanity. Like his forebears, Jonathan Leeds was a deeply religious man who lived simply and without ostentation and devoted his life to the affairs of the Darley Bank Company. But they were typical men of their age in their different spheres, and in order to appreciate why they did not realize the evil that they did nor see in the new Winterstoke a catastrophe of civilization, it is necessary to understand the prevailing mentality of the age. It is customary to say of men that they are known and judged by their works. So, when we come to assess the corporate achievement of a civilization we pass judgment upon its animating faith and philosophy. The horrors of Winterstoke do not indict any individual man or any particular class of men; they condemn as inadequate and false, as an affront to God, to nature and to man, the philosophy of industrial revolution.

There is no neat contemporary exposition of this philosophy. We do not find it in the economic or social theories of Adam Smith, Malthus, Ricardo, Bentham, James Mill or Joseph Hume; nor do we find it if we travel back to the writings of Hobbes or Descartes for, although all these writers influenced it, the faith and philosophy of a civilized society at any given period in its history consists of certain implicit assumptions. They are of immense importance as the starting-point of thought and action, but for this reason they are extremely difficult to analyse. They may change unpredictably, sometimes slowly, sometimes rapidly. Social and economic circumstances and the interpretations of theologians, mystics, philosophers and artists are the perpetual ferment of such changes, being influenced by the assumptions of the day but at the same time modifying them in ways which are often very different from the intention of the philosopher concerned. When we look back to pass judgment upon the men of the first industrial age, the fact that we do so with a reasoning biased by the assumptions of our own age makes it the more difficult for us truly to

WINTERSTOKE

read their minds. But seeing the misery, the havoc and the lasting harm which they wrought we can at least say with certainty that they were woefully misguided and wrong, and in that certainty, attempt to discover where their error lay.

By contrasting the minds of the Norman Hugh Fitzwinter and Josiah Leeds I, we have already seen how the medieval conception of the natural world as revealing a divine order and law whose sanctions should govern human society was rejected. So far as human consciousness was concerned, this rejection consisted of the withdrawal of God from the world. For Josiah Leeds God was transcendent but no longer immanent. Josiah Leeds sincerely believed that by worship he could submit his soul to the guidance of the divine will on its troubled journey through the world and that in accordance with his conduct on that journey, divine justice would mete out reward or punishment hereafter. But that the world itself was a revelation of divine order and therefore itself one aspect of Godhead was a conception that never entered his head. Hence it became perfectly possible to reconcile such a profession of religious belief with the materialistic Cartesian view of the world as the product of mindless, mechanical forces where the only order is that imposed by the light of human reason. In this way, without any awareness of impiety, man usurped the office of God in the conduct of human society and an Age of Faith was succeeded by an Age of Reason. With human reason thus securely enthroned, its free exercise became the only natural law and the old medieval checks and restraints which had sought to control human appetite, pride and frailty were gradually swept away as infringing upon the sacred rights of individual freedom and self-interest. It was the enthronement of human reason and the policy of *laissez-faire* in commercial affairs that inspired the great era of technical invention which man in his arrogance chose to call the 'conquest of nature'.

By the time the era of steam power and canal transport had been reached, these fundamental assumptions upon which the revolution was based had become much too firmly entrenched in men's minds to be disturbed by any catastrophic social consequences. The suffering and degradation to which they condemned humanity in their new town of Winterstoke in no way troubled the consciences of William Hanmer, Jonathan Leeds or their contemporaries. By piecing together convenient extracts from the work of contemporary philosophers and economists they were able to evolve theories which squared with their assumptions and which proved to their own satisfaction that such social conditions were not the result of any flaws in the social order, nor of any inhumanity or injustice on their part but were simply due to the operation of immutable economic laws. From Adam Smith they took the theory that for government to intervene in matters of trade could do nothing but harm because it interfered with 'the obvious and simple system of natural liberty' whereby unfettered individual enterprise could not fail to enrich society. From Burke they took the view that employer and employed were so dependent on each other that no free contract between them could fail to be other than just to both parties any more than the employer's profit could fail to benefit his workmen. Conditions in Winterstoke and its overcrowded Poor House scarcely bore out this theory, but here the doctrines of Malthus came to the rescue. The reward of labour was fixed by unalterable law and any coercive attempt to interfere with that law would injure employer and workman alike. Moreover, since population inevitably tended to exceed the means of subsistence the reward of labour must necessarily always remain below the level of subsistence. Hence the consoling conclusion that poverty is an inescapable condition of man. Finally, they accepted from Ricardo the idea that profits and wages were determined inexorably, like commodity prices, by the laws of supply and demand.

Underlying and enforcing all these particular economic and social theories was another basic assumption which the machines of the new age helped to foster. This was the belief in automatic progress. Eighteenth-century man was dazzled

WINTERSTOKE

by his own inventions. He did not see them as the outcome of a particular philosophy whose validity was open to question. Because man had never before harnessed the power of steam, not even in the great civilizations of Greece and Rome, he assumed that he stood upon the topmost pinnacle of human progress. That previous civilizations might have held different views on the relationship between man and his world; that material conquest and civilization might not necessarily mean the same thing—these were doubts which never occurred to him. As invention succeeded invention, each more ingenious than the last, the story of man appeared to him as a continuous forward march from the primeval slime towards some unimaginable goal of peace and prosperity. Because earlier generations of men had not possessed the wit to invent the steam engine, it followed that they were 'primitive' and that he was both wiser and better than they were. Later, the Darwinian theory of evolution would be accepted without question as the natural sanction of this belief. The new machines thus represented irrefutable evidence of human progress and 'natural' laws could be invented to explain away any awkward facts which seemed to point to the contrary.

It is only when we look at industrial Winterstoke through these contemporary spectacles that we begin to understand it aright and to realize that its rulers were not evil but misguided. A poverty and desperation-driven revolt by the poor must be savagely repressed, not only because it threatened the stability of the state but because their betters, in their superior wisdom, knew that it was contrary to their own interest as well as to that of their employers to run counter to natural economic laws. Jonathan Leeds found nothing in the condition of the employees of his Darley Bank Company to conflict with his religious beliefs or to cause him a single qualm of conscience. He convinced himself, and did his best to convince those recalcitrant workmen of his whom he confronted from time to time from his seat on the magistrate's bench, that the prospects of the poor were, in the light of eternity, better than his own.

WINTERSTOKE

It was easier, he would remind them, for the poor than for the rich to enter into the kingdom of Heaven and they should therefore be duly grateful and accept with suitable humility and thankfulness that state of life to which it had pleased Almighty God to call them. To rebel, he would add sternly, against this divine dispensation was an offence against God and man which was punishable by both. He must have found some of the offenders singularly stubborn and deaf to his Christian teaching. For they only knew that they had once possessed freedom and a share in the soil of England and they failed to understand why they should thank their Maker for the fact that both liberty and land had been taken away.

There was no lack of religious activity in the new Winterstoke. The female members of the Leeds family and many other supporters both of dissenting sects and of the established church busied themselves in the work of charity and Bible teaching. These devoted souls were frequently shocked by the scenes of abject poverty and misery which confronted them in the course of their errands of mercy, but they regarded them as we should regard the after-effects of an earthquake and not as symptoms of any social sickness. And if they made gifts of food or clothing they were at pains to make the recipients of their charity realize that they received such gifts by favour and not by any right. Like Jonathan they impressed upon the new poor the importance of resignation if they would enjoy their due reward hereafter, and explained that for this reason Bible reading, by teaching them the virtue of humility, was of much greater value than any earthly reward such as a full belly.

For the murder of 'Merry England' the seventeenth-century Puritans are commonly held responsible. To a certain extent this is true. Yet more truly it is to the zeal of these earnest and joyless busybodies of the nineteenth century that we owe, not merely the unrelieved gloom of the English Sunday, but a much darker legacy of rejection and negation. That grim faith which squared so readily with the prevailing commercial philosophy has lost its power

WINTERSTOKE

to-day, but its blasphemous rejection of the beauties, the joys and the sweetness of life remains. The church music, the church ales of the religious festivals, the trade guild processions, ceremonies and plays of the medieval villages and towns all fulfilled a primary human need to express the savour of life and satisfaction in creative work well done. But in the new Winterstoke of work and want the reformers saw to it that this elemental need was denied and that no stubbornly perpetuated spark of traditional sport, festival or custom should survive to lighten the grey monotony of days. They insisted that Sunday, the one day of the week on which the poor of Winterstoke were free from the iron discipline of mine, rolling mill, forge or furnace, should be exclusively devoted to religious observance, reading or instruction. They even invaded the last strongholds of the public houses to suppress music and singing so that the 'New Invention' or the 'Woodcollier' became gloomy drink shops where a man could no longer find good fellowship in self-expression but only the solace of liquor in which to drown his sorrows.

Thanks to the untiring efforts of these reformers many did find a consolation in religion which they could find nowhere else. But many more lost all faith in a religion which could so tacitly condone wrongs of which they were most passionately aware. These wrongs were too grievous and too pressing to be withstood. They created a new order of working-class champions who, in the face of every kind of persecution and oppression which their masters could invoke in the name of law and order, advanced the necessity for reform with growing vehemence and authority. Confronted by this increasing and sustained pressure their opponents were forced to yield ground and the philosophy of *laissez-faire* was gradually modified.

From this time forward to the present day this story of Winterstoke must be read against the background of what came to be called 'the Class war', a war in which both sides changed their ground as was only to be expected in a campaign which was carried on for a hundred and fifty years. As they lost their faith in the philosophy of 'enlightened self-

WINTERSTOKE

interest' it was the forces of the Right who ultimately became the reactionaries, the defenders of individual liberties. Finally, the horrors revealed by the second world war and its aftermath caused many of them to doubt even their cherished belief in automatic progress. It became apparent to them that science and technology were not, after all, synonyms for civilization but were compatible with a barbarism far more inhuman that any which existed in the past. The old confidence of the Victorian era gave way to bewilderment and doubt. Meanwhile it was the labour movement which, as it grew in strength, succeeded its rival as the champion of material progress. It ceased to look back to liberties lost; it accepted the industrial machine and fought on only over the question of who should control it. By the same method that the early industrialists used to justify their belief that the self-interest of the individual would automatically benefit the community, the labour movement, from the writings of Karl Marx and others, justified its 'gospel' that the self-interest of the community would automatically benefit the individual. Let the State, representing the community, take over the control of the industrial machine and all would be well. Thus the Utopian dream of the Socialist State came into being as the new religion of the poor of Winterstoke.

What appeared to prove beyond question the truth of this political theory was the progressive decline in the value of money which accompanied the whole course of this social war. No matter how hard the workers of Winterstoke fought for increased wages, prices forever moved up ahead of them with the result that they found themselves little or no better off. Hard-won gains were persistently nullified in this way so that they must perforce join battle with their employers again. It was easy to believe that the sinister and insatiable figure of the Capitalist was solely responsible for this state of affairs and that as soon as he was removed, the gap between wages and prices would close. Over a hundred years were to pass before the labour movement would achieve the power and the opportunity to translate theory

WINTERSTOKE

into practice by making this experiment. Meanwhile there were many immediate wrongs to be righted.

The first victory was won in 1825 when the right of workmen to combine was at last reluctantly conceded by the repeal of the Combination Laws and the Winterstoke Mechanics Union was officially recognized. Two years later the Winterstoke Mechanics Institute was opened and became the headquarters of Union activity. Even more momentous was the struggle for Parliamentary reform which culminated in the Reform Bill of 1832. This was the first decisive blow struck by the new industrial England against an ancient régime which had refused to acknowledge its existence. It sealed the fate of the great landowners just as surely as it curbed their power. With the passing of the Bill, the fact that Winterstoke was no longer a village but a large town was belatedly accepted. Winterstoke became a borough, governed by Mayor, Aldermen and Counsellors and returning a member to Parliament. As the criminal statistics show, this new form of local government was little less harsh and repressive than the old. Nor was it much more representative for it was controlled by a narrow oligarchy of burgesses and freemen who allowed the majority of the inhabitants of Winterstoke no say in local affairs. Nevertheless it was an improvement upon its predecessor and paved the way for further reform. Under the Municipal Corporations Act which followed three years later, all the ratepayers of Winterstoke were enfranchised. The inhabitants of the new town began to acquire a civic consciousness and its administration a civic dignity which gradually mitigated the old corruption and oppression. The last important step in this process was made during the Victorian era when the Local Government Act of 1888 established the present form of local administration under which Winterstoke became a County Borough free from the Midshire County Rate, its population by that time being well in excess of the minimum of 50,000 stipulated by the Act.

In a society which accepts technical and scientific developments as indisputable evidence of human progress and therefore intrinsically good, men must necessarily struggle along in the wake of an implacable machine, adjusting their lives, their social order and their philosophy as best they may to the pace which its giant strides dictate. Hence the fact that the technician and the scientist have between them dominated the history of Winterstoke for two hundred years. Hardly had the first reforms of the eighteen-thirties been achieved than Winterstoke began to hear rumours of a new invention which was destined to inaugurate another and much greater wave of industrial and social expansion. Away to the north, men said, an engineer named George Stephenson had given the steam engine wings and sent it hurtling down an iron road.

Chapter Eight

IT WAS THE TIDINGS of the new railways in the north and the rumours of further railway schemes which roused the Proprietors of the Wendle Navigation and the Lobstock Canal from their lethargy. In the face of this threat to the monopoly which they had enjoyed and abused for so long the old feud between the two Companies was forgotten and they set to work belatedly to put their respective waterways in order. New and larger locks were built on the river and the two old navigation weirs which had proved such a hindrance to traffic in the reaches above and below Abel's Gullet, were demolished. Despite the protests of the bow hauliers, the Company obtained powers to construct a horse towing-path from Darley Bank Wharf to Westerport and completed the work in twelve months. Meanwhile a great deal of overdue dredging was done on the river.

On the improvement of their canal the Lobstock Company consulted the last of the great canal engineers—Thomas Telford. After he had carried out a survey, Telford made two proposals; first, the construction of a second parallel tunnel at Ketton to relieve the congestion and traffic delays due to the restricted size of Brindley's original bore; second, new cuts to reduce the length of the tortuous summit level between Ketton and Lobstock. The Company rejected the first proposal as too costly, but they directed Telford to proceed with the second with the result that the canal distance between Lobstock and the south end of Ketton Tunnel was reduced by three miles.

With the original work of James Brindley, these new cuts planned by Thomas Telford present a striking contrast; they show how much progress the civil engineer had already made in the campaign against nature. They also reveal that the canal engineers were responsible for developing those con-

WINTERSTOKE

structional techniques which would presently be employed by the railway builders to such great effect. With the exception of his Ketton tunnel, Brindley had bowed to nature and his canal had, so to speak, followed the grain of the country. As a result, when the scars of construction had healed, his winding summit level looked more like a natural watercourse than a man-made channel. For example, at one point near the village of Bowford Priors his canal made a wayward loop, over a mile long, round the flanks of a modest promontory of high ground which at this place thrusts eastwards into the Deepforest country. Telford beheaded this loop by means of a short but deep cutting through the high ground. At Barnby Moors where the canal encounters the valley of the little river Dargle there is another similar contrast. Brindley carried his canal up to the head of the valley where it tapped the source of the river, made an acute turn, and then followed the contours of the opposite side until it could resume its true direction. Telford's new cut, on the other hand, marched boldly across the valley on a high embankment, spanning the Dargle by a cast iron aqueduct.

In his Dargle aqueduct, in his road bridges which bestride the deep canyons of his cuttings, even in the light, elegant spans by which he carried his towing-path over the old discarded loops of Brindley's canal, Thomas Telford shows us that he was not only a great engineer but the architectural master of a new medium. Like the great beam engines of the early nineteenth century, these cast-iron bridges of Telford's are classic in their form and proportion. While the last of the architects abandoned their birthright for a mess of Gothic pottage, the first great engineers, Telford, the Stephensons, Isambard Brunel, became the last heirs to the tradition and craftsmanship of the golden age. Using new materials in new forms for new purposes, their achievements were daring architectural adventures monumental in conception. But this marriage between architecture and engineering was dissolved all too soon by an unbridled commercialism that could see no profit in the graces of a previous age.

WINTERSTOKE

The reforms carried out by the proprietors of inland navigations were too belated. Traders had suffered too long from their high toll charges and from their failure to improve their waterways. An expanding commerce demanded some reliable, nation-wide system of transport whereas the outlook of the navigation companies had remained parochial. If they had not abused their monopoly, if they had co-operated one with another instead of being divided by petty rivalries and jealousies such as had marred the relationship between the Lobstock Canal Company and the proprietors of the Wendle Navigation, then the victory of the new railways would not have been so swift and absolute and England might have possessed an inland waterway system of more lasting value. As it was, the country was ripe for the new railways, and once proud canal companies soon found themselves suing their rivals for a mercy they did not receive in an age when all the spoils went to the strong.

Winterstoke's interest in the new railways was first actively aroused by the proposal to build a great trunk line from Earlspool in the north-east to London. In these early days when engineers doubted the adhesive powers of the new locomotives on smooth rails, a level road was considered all-important and in spite of the size and industrial stature of the new town, it had been suggested that the line should leave Winterstoke to the west, running by way of Lobstock and Coltisham. The advocates of this proposal pointed out that it was not only the most direct but also the easiest route between the two cities. Winterstoke, they argued, could most conveniently be served by a branch line down the Wendle valley from Coltisham. In the heated railway debate which developed, the two great families of Hanmer and Leeds found themselves in opposition to one another. Jonathan Leeds died shortly before the argument began, but his brother Peter and Peter's son Thomas played the same part in it as their ancestor Daniel had done when the Lobstock Canal scheme was mooted and with the same interest in mind—that of the Darley Bank Company. Peter Leeds, the far-sighted industrialist, realized that the new transport possessed unlimited possibilities. It was of the utmost importance, in his view, that the Company should be served directly by a great trunk line of railway. If Winterstoke was relegated to the backwater of a branch line, the new town might suffer and its trade begin to ebb away to Lobstock or to Coltisham. The Company's trade with Deepforest, Lobstock and districts to the north-east and northwest was now well enough served by the Lobstock Canal and its connections, thanks to the recent improvements. In any case, a proposal that the new railway should follow the course of the canal would not only be fiercely opposed by the Canal Company, but rejected on the score of construction cost. The Darley Bank Company's greatest need was for better longdistance communications with the north and south of England than the canal system could offer, and that was precisely what this new railway promised. Peter Leeds therefore urged upon the promoters his view that the line should turn west into the Wendle valley at Coltisham, pass through Winterstoke and then resume its due southerly course at Westerport. The increase in mileage over the Lobstock-Coltisham route would not be great and the cost of construction would be lower along the easy levels of the valley. Moreover, Peter argued that this route promised greater traffic revenue.

By a campaign of intensive lobbying, Peter Leeds secured powerful support and set up a rival committee to press his proposal. Moreover, although the Lobstock Canal Company were opposed in principle to any railway scheme, he pointed out to them that the adoption of the Winterstoke route would mean that Lobstock would remain a canal stronghold. Privately, so great was his faith in the new system of transport, Peter Leeds believed that before many years every town in the country would be connected by rail, but he kept this thought to himself and by astute argument he was able to reach an understanding with the Lobstock Company whereby they agreed to confine their opposition to the proposed Lobstock and Coltisham route. But Peter Leeds and his supporters did not have the field to themselves

WINTERSTOKE

by any means. They soon became involved in a legal and parliamentary battle far more protracted, more bitter and more costly than that which old Daniel Leeds and his party had waged over the route of the Lobstock Canal. Ranged against them were the Wendle Navigation Company and the Wendle bargemasters, the proprietors of the Westerport, Winterstoke and Coltisham Turnpike, the coach owners who used that much improved highway, and many traders in the town of Lobstock which would be excluded from rail communication if the Winterstoke line was adopted. Added to these who found their special interests threatened were the many landowners and farmers who were prepared to fight the coming of any railway and firmly believed the canal owners and the coach proprietors who prophesied that the new invention would destroy the crops and stock on any lands through which it passed. One of the most powerful members of this opposition, fighting the issue with all the considerable forces he could still command both locally and in the House of Lords, was old Lord Winterstoke. He fought as a proprietor of the Wendle Navigation and of the Turnpike Trust. He also fought as a great landowner who foresaw that this new monster would not only ruin his lands but intrude, belching steam and smoke, upon the landscape which his father had so expensively contrived with the aid of Lancelot Brown. Railways were a menace to the country and threatened to throw thousands of honest men out of their traditional employments. They were wild and impracticable schemes foisted upon a gullible public by unprincipled speculators. He declared open war on the railway and hired a number of unemployed Wendle bow-hauliers to police his estate and remove, by force if need be, any suspicious loiterer who could not satisfactorily explain his business. 'I would rather,' the Earl declared, 'see a highwayman or a burglar on my property than an engineer,' and when the first party of engineers set foot on the Winterstoke estate for the purpose of making a preliminary survey they were promptly and resolutely attacked by the Earl's posse who drove them off and smashed their apparatus. The survey was finally made with the greatest difficulty under the cover of moonless nights by engineers working as stealthily and furtively as poachers by the glimmer of dark lanterns. To-day, when the long expresses thunder through the Wendle valley it is interesting to recall this night-shrouded and conspiratorial scene, more suggestive of gunpowder, treason and plot than of any commercial undertaking, which was the first presage of their coming.

Just as James Brindley had judged the claims of the rival canal factions, so it was the great George Stephenson who was called in to settle the issue between the two railway committees. He decided in favour of the Winterstoke route, and the plan was adopted by the subscribers who appointed George and his son Robert engineers of the London & Earlspool Railway. The new Company ultimately won their long parliamentary battle against the opposition but at a terrible price, not only in legal costs but in monies paid to landowners such as Lord Winterstoke for the property they must needs acquire. No sooner had the London & Earlspool Railway Act received the Royal Assent than construction began, the works being let to different contractors along the route. The major engineering works were attacked by a great force of 'navvies' and labourers under the command of Robert Stephenson himself, but the line along the levels of the Wendle valley presented no constructional difficulty and the work was carried out by many small contractors who each, like the 'overmen' in the Darley Bank Company, employed their own 'butty' gangs.

The meadow below Ketton Farm where the 'navigators' of the Lobstock Canal had encamped seventy years before had long since disappeared under bricks and mortar, but west and east of the town, on the waste land between Hanger Lane and the river and near the ford below Summersend Farm, the railway gangs built their crude thatched huts of unbonded stone like two detachments of some invading army preparing for a long siege of the town. Though the contractors recruited much local labour, even the inhabitants of the Hanger Lane back-to-backs regarded the neigh-

WINTERSTOKE

bouring shanty town with some suspicion, and as on the previous occasion, those who profited most by the invasion were the local innkeepers. The Bridge Inn at St. John's had by this time been transformed into a large and prosperous posting house known as the 'Hanmer Arms', and here the thirsty hordes were actively discouraged. But in the bars of the 'New Invention', the 'Woodcolliers' and, in particular, 'The Navigation' where the Blenkinsop family still presided, trade quite literally roared, for the railway gangs were well paid by the standards of the day. Working with tireless energy they assuredly earned their pay however recklessly they might consume it, for the long low embankment of raw earth advanced down the south side of the valley with astonishing speed, crossing over Bridge Street (as the road over the new river bridge was now called) and the turnpike east of St. John's by spans of cast iron set in massive stone abutments.

A branch connection was laid into the Darley Bank Works, for that Company had undertaken several large contracts for the railway. A great quantity of the wrought iron rails for this revolutionary road came from Peter Leeds' furnaces and rolling mills, while on many of the spans of the bridges we may read to this day the cast inscription: 'DARLEY BANK IRONWORKS 1837.' But of far greater importance in the story of Winterstoke than these contributions, which might be termed part of the regular stock-in-trade of the ironworks, was the building of six locomotives at Darley Bank to the design of Robert Stephenson. Stephenson's own locomotive works at Newcastle was so overloaded with orders for the new railways that contracts for the London & Earlspool engines were placed with a number of manufacturers among whom the Darley Bank Company, a firm on the line of route with a long experience of steam engine building, was an obvious choice. The contract marked the beginning of an important new chapter in the history of the Company.

When these engines left the works they carried no numbers, but each bore on the polished mahogany lagging of their boiler barrels a brass name-plate. *Hurricane, Sirocco, Mistral,*

WINTERSTOKE

Whirlwind, Tornado and *Typhoon* they were called, and no machines could have been more aptly named. For in them the craftsmanship which had hitherto embodied the new steam power in stationary beam engines of massive scale, had now harnessed it to a new, fleet purpose which gave to steam the wings of the wind. Fluted brass dome and flared chimney cap, slender safety valve casing and burnished steel railings on the driving platform, all displayed the classic proportions of the older beam engine fined down to a lightness and elegance no longer monumental but befitting the function of the new machine. Robert Adam would surely have approved, for beside their cumbersome predecessors these early locomotives are comparable in their grace and refinement of detail with the workmanship of Adam. And just as Robert Adam stood at the end of the golden age of architecture, so in these steam locomotives the association of art with engineering expressed itself for the last time.

The first of the six engines to be completed and the first to give the people of Winterstoke a glimpse of the steam locomotive in action was the *Hurricane*. At a speed which belied her name and did not betray her capabilities she rumbled cautiously to and fro over the new embankment on a single temporary line of rails hauling wagon loads of spoil, ballast and, later, sleepers and rails. It was not until the Wendle valley section of the L. & E.R. was officially opened to the usual accompaniment of speeches, luncheons, ox roastings and the liberal distribution of free liquor by the Company that the steam locomotive really displayed its powers. The inaugural train consisted of no less than thirty four-wheeled vehicles; first there was a line of open 'thirds' which scarcely merited the name of coaches and were packed to suffocation by a standing crowd of swaying and shouting humanity; then came a rake of second-class coaches, roofed but open-sided above the waistline; next, like a row of stagecoaches, followed the exclusive closed 'firsts', and finally, well out of range of smoke and smuts, there came flat wagons bearing the open carriages of the gentry who, mollified by the blood money they had extorted from the Company, had

WINTERSTOKE

consented to grace the occasion. At the head of this long, packed caravan of assorted vehicles, their brass domes and boiler lagging bands flashing in the sunlight, were the two engines *Tornado* and *Typhoon*, their engine-men, immaculate in the dignity of white cord suits and beaver hats, each standing proudly on his driving platform, hand on burnished regulator, like a captain on the bridge of his ship. This was the power and the glory, the new marvel of the age. No wonder the people who thronged the line-side all along the route cheered themselves hoarse as the great train, its flying pennants of steam lifting and dissolving into the blue sky, rumbled down the long perspective of rails that stretched straight as a sword blade down the valley. Although the train did not exceed thirty-five miles an hour, it appeared to travel at a rate fantastic to eyes that had seen nothing faster than a galloping horse. It must have been an anxious occasion for the two drivers, for the crowds along the line were quite incapable of estimating the speed of their approach, and although the day was not marred by any tragedy, there were many near misses.

That during the early years of its operation there were no serious accidents on the L. & E.R. was remarkable. For we must appreciate how absolutely unique and unprecedented a development this iron road was. In the safe control of trains of a hundred tons or more moving at high speed on a rail prescribed course over hundreds of miles of country, no experience gained on turnpike roads, canals, or even on the old tramways which were the railways' ancestors was of any value. Semaphore signals, interlocking, the electrical block system, continuous brakes, track circuiting, all those developments which contributed so much to railway safety, were gradually evolved by experience of trial and error, but for the first few years of its existence, the L. & E.R. trains worked by guess and by God, and incidents which would have made a latter day traffic superintendent's hair stand erect were accepted as part of the normal routine. 'Policemen' armed with flags or with signal lamps at night dispatched and controlled trains on the time interval system.

WINTERSTOKE

The first locomotives were prone to suffer from a variety of teething troubles. Hence if a train failed to appear after the time interval had elapsed it would be assumed that it was in difficulties and any engine that happened to be available would be sent to its assistance along the wrong road. This meant that if the driver who had been sent to the rescue suddenly encountered the belated train speeding towards him he had to do some very rapid thinking—and equally rapid reversing. An engineer might decide to take out a locomotive for purposes of test or to examine part of the permanent way, while for some time an eminent scientist of the day who rejoiced in the name of Dionysius Lardner lurked about the line in the Wendle valley with a special train with which he was carrying out certain tests the exact purpose of which only he ever understood. Consequently there was always the possibility of encountering a train where no train had any right to be.

Although the L. & E.R. brought to the people of Winterstoke possibilities of long-distance travel which had never existed before except in the form of the stage-wagon or the stage-coach which few could afford, for some years it remained only a possibility for the majority. For the Company showed themselves singularly disinclined to cater for the third-class passenger until Parliament stepped in by compelling them to provide third-class accommodation on at least one train per day in each direction. Like so many cattle wagons, the third-class stock was marshalled in the two night goods trains which, before the advent of the 'Parliamentaries', spent the long night hours alternately stopping, shunting and crawling as they made their seemingly interminable way across England.

One of the most important features of the railway's uniqueness was the fact that the Company who built and owned the new iron road also owned and worked all the traffic upon it. Hitherto river navigations, canals, turnpikes and tramways alike had been open to any carrier who cared to use them provided he paid the prescribed tolls to the proprietors. It was accepted as a first principle of inland transport that for an owner of any highway to act also as a carrier upon it would be to establish an unjust monopoly by enabling him to compete unfairly against the private trader. It was upon this principle that the canal companies had been prohibited by Parliament from acting as carriers. When the Liverpool & Manchester Railway Act was passed the same principle was recognized, and in theory private traders were at liberty to run their own trains on the line on payment of tolls. But it was realized at once by the railwaymen, and much more belatedly by Parliament, that the old system was not applicable to the new road; that it would be fraught with every kind of peril and reduce any attempt at order to chaos. Nevertheless, the old idea of a free highway died hard. Dr. Dionysius Lardner's experimental train, and the special trains kept for their exclusive use by some members of the aristocracy were legacies of it. Another much longer-lived legacy were the fleets of privately owned goods wagons which made their appearance.

In the competitive battle with the canals which rapidly developed, the ability of the railways to operate their own traffic proved an invincible weapon. A system which was controlled by a great number of small companies with no common policy, which lacked uniformity of draught and lock gauge and whereon traffic was handled almost exclusively by a great number of small local traders could not hope to compete successfully for long-distance traffic against the railways. With the sole exception of the adoption by the Great Western Railway and its far western protégés of Brunel's 7-foot gauge, the railway engineers recognized the importance of gauge uniformity. George Stephenson, the father of railways, believed implicitly from the moment of birth that his child would one day become a giant, straddling the world. In the more parochial and self-sufficient England of the eighteenth century, James Brindley, the father of canals, had looked upon his waterways as children of their region only. Long-distance rail traffic was soon aided, not only by uniformity of gauge but by the establishment of a Railway Clearing House to handle and apportion the revenue

WINTERSTOKE

from traffic consigned over several companies' lines. The canals never provided any such facility but they did make an attempt to fight back.

While the London & Earlspool Railway was still building, the proprietors of the Lobstock Canal and those of the coast-to-coast waterway with which the Lobstock connected agreed to join forces in face of the common enemy. They applied to Parliament for powers, not only to amalgamate but also to become carriers, and as a result the Midshire Union Canal Company and the Midshire Union Canal Carrying Company were formed. For the quicker handling of general merchandise, the new Carrying Company launched a fleet of light 'fly boats', worked by all-male crews as opposed to the family boat system, and these plied day and night throughout the system. With this introduction the local canal proprietors must have felt more confident for a while, but, as Peter Leeds had suspected, Lobstock was not destined to remain for very long a canal stronghold.

Although the railway companies avoided many of the mistakes of their predecessors, in their relations with each other it took them a long time to learn that co-operation paid better dividends than a state of more or less open warfare. The old conflict between the Lobstock Canal Company and the proprietors of the Wendle Navigation was a trivial brawl compared with the scale and ferocity of the attacks launched upon each other by rival railways. In view of the prevailing commercial philosophy this was only to be expected. Winterstoke became a strategic point in one of these battles. Sometimes the town benefited as a result, more often it did not; as for the contending companies they never benefited at all.

That the immediate success of the new railways led to an orgy of wild speculation in which fortunes were won and many more fortunes lost on worthless schemes is well known. The speculative boom in canals of the early 1790's pales into insignificance beside the follies of the so-called 'Railway Mania'. Winterstoke had its share of rowdy public meetings, of proposal and counter-proposal, but when all the speculative bubbles had burst, one important railway scheme

WINTERSTOKE

remained and succeeded in obtaining the necessary public support despite the temporary slump which followed the exposure of George Hudson, the 'Railway King'. This was the Great North-Western Railway which was to provide a more direct central route between London and the North. So far as our immediate district is concerned, the new line was planned to pass through Church Ambling, Winterstoke and Lobstock. This was a far more difficult line of country than the promoters of the London & Earlspool had ever envisaged, but railway engineers had rapidly gained confidence, both in their own ability to overcome natural obstacles, and in the power of the steam locomotive to surmount gradients.

Landowners were now taking a more favourable view of railways, thanks to the immense sums they succeeded in extracting from the Companies, but the Great North-Western encountered intense opposition from its rivals in the field, notably the Midshire Union Canal and the London & Earlspool Railway. Railway Companies liked to regard the shires of England which they served as theirs by proprietorial right, and in the sombre mahogany splendour of their London boardroom the Directors of the L. & E.R. met in council of war to decide how they might repel so insolent an invasion of their territory. It was well known that the Great North-Western scheme had been fathered by an ambitious Company in the north-west which wanted its own direct route to London. The L. & E.R. had recently changed its hitherto high-handed attitude to that Company in the hope of persuading it to see reason and drop the project. But the Company had declined to succumb to these blandishments. Very well then, let it be war. The L. & E.R. Directors decided to form an alliance with that intransigent Company's deadliest rival in the North, and before the Great North-Western Railway Bill was presented to Parliament the two Companies had obtained powers to amalgamate and declared war together under the name of the Grand Central Railway. But the Great North-Western faction refused to be deterred by this show of strength. Nor

WINTERSTOKE

had they been idle as the Directors of the Grand Central discovered. When they tried to woo the Midshire Union Canal Company with the idea of using them as a pawn in their game they found to their intense chagrin that the Great North-Western had been there before them. The upstart had struck a bargain with the Canal Company's shareholders whereby it had secured a controlling interest in return for the offer of a guaranteed dividend. So the Canal Company withdrew its opposition and the Grand Central Directors found themselves fighting almost alone. Fight they did at prodigious expense but to no avail. To add to the ignominy of their defeat, Parliament granted the new Company joint use of Winterstoke Station and running powers over the Grand Central from Summersend Junction, where the new line from the North would join it, to Ketton Junction where it would curve away southwards up the Lob valley.

So it was that for the third time in its history the construction gangs descended upon Winterstoke but with the difference, as the local inhabitants soon saw for themselves, that since the London & Earlspool had been built, railway construction had become a very efficient and highly organized undertaking. Railway contracting was a ruthless and pitiless business which only the fittest survived. It had bankrupted hundreds of small contractors to leave only a very few powerful men of whom one of the greatest was Brassey, contractor to the Great North-Western. Like his predecessors, Brassey recruited a great army of local labour along the line of construction, but these were everywhere leavened by his own picked force of 'navvies' which represented what was probably the most efficient human machine which the world has ever seen. Wherever works of magnitude were involved, there the contractor concentrated this elite in the greatest number. Winterstoke was invaded in strength, for there was not only a tunnel to be driven under the headwaters of the Lob parallel with the old canal tunnel, but a great embankment and cutting to be constructed where the line would climb out of the flat fields of the Wendle valley and scale the escarpment of the Emberley Hills.

WINTERSTOKE

These descendants of the old 'navigators' did not this time build themselves huts of stone and thatch. They were housed in two camps of wooden huts provided by Brassey, one established in a field near Emberley Hill Farm and the other near the grass-grown spoil mounds left by the builders of Ketton Tunnel. Amongst these picked men of Brassey's there was a tremendous pride and *esprit de corps*. They could be recognized anywhere, not only by their stature and their muscled strength but by their invariable self-chosen uniform: a wide-awake white felt hat with upturned brim, square-tailed velveteen jacket, waistcoat of spotted scarlet plush, corduroy breeches buckled at the knee and high laced boots. They ate and drank prodigiously of red meat and whisky as well they might for they worked for anything up to sixteen hours a day with a speed and energy which seemed tireless. They organized themselves in 'butty gangs' of ten to twelve men, each of which contracted to shift so much 'dirt' or 'stuff' within a specified time. But they were more than highly skilled labourers with immense resources of strength and endurance; as the heirs to the experience of generations of 'navigators' they possessed considerable practical knowledge of geology, soil-mechanics and all the problems of natural drainage. Whereas it had taken the canal navigators seven years to complete the narrow bore of Ketton Tunnel, these men, working on the opposite side of the Lob, drove the double-line bore of Darley Bank Tunnel in under two years. The work of their fellows in the deep Emberley cutting was no less remarkable and in some ways more hazardous. Much of the soil excavated was used in forming the approach embankment below, but much more had to be drawn out of the deep defile by means of 'barrow runs'. These consisted of a series of plankways laid down the precipitous sides of the cutting. A navvy would push his enormous barrow, loaded with anything from three to four hundredweight of spoil to the foot of a run, and attach it to a rope which ran over a pulley at the top and thence to the traces of a horse. He would then guide the barrow up the run as the horse pulled it—a most perilous proceeding.

WINTERSTOKE

Wild and lawless though they were, and not seldom drunken and brutal, nevertheless the old proud independence and indomitable character of the English commoners found its last vigorous expression in the navigators. From what ranks they sprang no man can say. Perhaps their first parents were those 'adventurers' who, in the seventeenth century, embanked the fens under the direction of Sir Cornelius Vermuyden. When the Great North-Western Railway was completed they vanished from Winterstoke never to return. Their Thermopylæ was fought some years later on the bleak Pennine moorlands where, by Blea Moor and Hawes, they carved the Midland route to Carlisle—the last of the great main lines. Then they melted away as mysteriously as they had come and England has never seen their like again. They were the giants of those days and the work of their hands stands for all time as surely as pyramid or Roman wall.

Local labour and local initiative was responsible for the only remaining work of railway construction which Winterstoke was to see. This was the six miles of single line from Summersend Junction to the small town of that name round the flank of the hill. Although this Summersend Branch was built by a locally formed Company it was worked from the outset by the Grand Central and ultimately absorbed into its system.

When the Great North-Western was opened with the usual festivities it may have appeared to many that their victory was complete. But bloody though the heads of the Grand Central's Directors might be they were by no means bowed as the unfortunate newcomer very soon discovered. In the joint station at Winterstoke the Grand Central recognized the Achilles heel of the new route and proceeded to wound it by every means in their power. Because they had secured a majority on the joint board which was set up to control the station, their unhappy rival was for a time almost powerless to mend matters except by countering force and guile with the same coin. Their locomotives were denied the right to take water at Winterstoke. Grand Central locomotives be-

WINTERSTOKE

came mysteriously derailed in such a way that while they left their own running lines clear they effectually fouled the North-Western junctions at Ketton or Summersend. Pitched battles sometimes accompanied their removal by the aggrieved company. Even when these extreme measures were abandoned under the threat of legal proceedings it was always possible to arrange for the joint section to be occupied by a heavy goods or a dilatory 'local' whenever a North-Western express happened to be due. It always afforded the loyal staff of the Grand Central the highest delight to watch one of the proud eight-foot single 'highflyers' of the North-Western come to a grinding standstill at Ketton Junction home signal and wait there, safety valves roaring impatient wrath, while a goods guard checked his train at his leisure or a locomotive crew took on water from a standpipe with the stopcock shut down to a trickle. On the station itself the North-Western staff lived in a perpetual state of siege. Timetables were torn down as fast as they could post them up, and on one occasion their booking office was raided and its stock of tickets scattered broadcast over the platform. In the goods yard it was only with the greatest difficulty that North-Western freight could be loaded or discharged. The North-Western countered this campaign by progressively cutting its fares and accelerating the times of its trains between London and the North, but the Grand Central took up the challenge. The ensuing battle was hard fought, for although the newcomer possessed the shorter route to London, it was heavily graded compared with the old straight levels of the Grand Central. When the North-Western cut the time of their best train between London and Winterstoke from three-and-a-quarter to three hours, the rival line replied by reducing their time by another fifteen minutes. It is doubtful whether the passengers by these flyers really appreciated such historic feats when they were hustled unceremoniously along the platforms and packed into the comfortless six-wheelers of these short, featherweight racing trains. Many, we may be sure, would gladly have accepted fifteen minutes or more of extra travelling time in

WINTERSTOKE

exchange for a little more elbow room. Finally, when the journey time had been reduced to two and a half hours, tragedy intervened. The down 'Comet' of the North-Western, flying down the grade from Darley Bank Tunnel, became derailed on Ketton curve. Fortunately the coupling between tender and first coach broke and the train remained upright, but the locomotive *Tubal* carried its unfortunate crew to their death. Plunging down the embankment, it came to rest, enveloped by a great cloud of steam, in the waters of the Lobstock Canal. The Grand Central greeted this calamity with ill-concealed jubilation, but it was short-lived. Only a fortnight later their up 'Eclipse' was derailed at excessive speed on the curve near Coltisham Station with much more serious results, fourteen passengers losing their lives.

It was these two disasters and the public outcry they provoked which finally brought the two Companies to their senses and to agreement. Fares were stabilized and the journey time for the fastest trains between London and Winterstoke was fixed at two and three-quarter hours. The Grand Central ceased to dominate the joint board of control with the result that the bleak, ill-protected station which had been totally inadequate for the increased traffic was at last replaced. The new commodious joint station of six platforms with an all-over glass roof supported on slender trusses and pillars of cast iron was esteemed the architectural wonder of Winterstoke—as indeed it was. The old embargo on water supplies was lifted, and the Great North-Western built its own locomotive depot at Winterstoke adjacent to the Grand Central shed. So the two railways settled down fairly amicably as neighbours in Winterstoke although traces of the old rivalry survived for many years.

The fierce loyalty of their respective staffs helped to keep it alive and so did the Companies' timetables as those unfortunate passengers who were rash enough to change at Winterstoke from one Company's line to the other usually discovered. A traveller from Lobstock for Westerport generally found that the Grand Central train for Westerport

WINTERSTOKE

was booked to leave five minutes before his train from Lobstock was due in, or vice versa. Even where a connection was grudgingly made, neither Company would ever hold a train for the other in the event of late running, and its staff seemed to derive much smug satisfaction from informing stranded passengers that *their* trains ran on time.

This story of the railways of Winterstoke, despite its tragic conclusion, is amusing to recall in retrospect, but the railway travellers of the time did not find it so funny. Nor is it so amusing when we realize that it was only one much publicized encounter in a bitter and completely unprincipled economic war which was going on all over the new commercial England. The battles between rival railways have been recorded in history because they were played on the open stage where the public were the pawns in the game. The stories of similar battles waged between rival factories, mills or ironworks in the markets of the world and the untold damage and suffering which they caused have never been recorded. We can only judge their cumulative effect by the legacy of bloody and exhausting international conflicts which they provoked. And, as the eventual agreement on fares between the rival railway companies shows, there can be only one conclusion to the anarchy of a trading policy dictated by the philosophy of complete individual freedom ungoverned by any moral sanctions. This is a process of agreement on terms dictatedby the strongest, which ultimately leads to a trade monopoly. Thus the nineteenth-century philosophy ensured its own defeat from the outset. For when such a monpoly is complete, that freedom, which was as earnestly argued and fought for by our ancestors as any article of religious faith, ceases to exist at all.

Looking down upon Winterstoke from the height of High Hanger Down we can distinguish the stages of growth for which the canal and the railways were responsible as clearly as the growth rings on the sawn butt of a tree. Like the canal basin, the black, steaming bulk of the railway station soon produced its satellite growth: the locomotive sheds, the old roundhouse of the Grand Central and the saw-toothed,

WINTERSTOKE

many chimneyed roof-line of the North-Western shed; the block of Blenkinsop's new Railway Hotel, its square stucco façade and over-pretentious pillared portico confronting the station entrance; new streets, Station Road and Institute Road with their cross connections, all lined with new terrace cottages, pubs and chapels in variegated brickwork whose raw blues and reds and yellows were soon toned down by the all-pervading grime. And of course the marshalling yards extending their metal-meshed ash ballast where before there were still green fields: Central Yard where the two Companies interchanged traffic; Ketton Junction Yard which handled the Ironworks traffic; Hanger Lane Yard whence there came a continuous clash of buffers as tireless shunting engines, weaving this way and that like dogs harrying sheep, shuffled and reshuffled the rakes of empty and loaded coal wagons.

But the coming of the railways which so changed the face of the town and inaugurated a fresh wave of expansion, spelt decline for some and disaster for others. So rapid now was the speed of industrial revolution that a man might think he was riding the crest of a wave of prosperity only to find himself outpaced and faced with ruin in a few years. Thus, despite the new flyboats, the canal basin was no longer so thronged with traffic as of old. There were vacant stalls in the stables of the 'Navigation' and the clatter of caulking mallets from the boatyard was no longer so insistent. Below the basin, a line of barges, some half sunken and dismasted, lay by the Wendle bank. On the turnpike it was not so much a case of decline as of swift extinction. In the yard of the 'Hanmer Arms' weeds began to sprout between cobbles where no weeds had grown before. The shrill whistle of *Typhoon* had silenced the fanfare of the Westerport and Coltisham coach forever. Old John Foster who had held the ribbons for twenty years was forced to acknowledge defeat. For a time he plied between Winterstoke station and Church Ambling, but the opening of the Great North-Western robbed him of even this traffic. So the old man opened a livery stables close to the station and, with a

WINTERSTOKE

station bus and a small fleet of growlers, resigned himself to picking up such crumbs of traffic as his proud conqueror chose to let fall. The triumph of steam was complete.

Chapter Nine

WITHIN FIFTY YEARS of the coming of railways, the population of Winterstoke had again doubled itself. Many social historians have endeavoured to explain this phenomenal increase in population which marked the progress of industrial revolution. Enforced migration from the country to the iron and coal working area brought about the original growth of the town, but although this influx continued throughout the nineteenth century, the population figures for the whole country show that it could have accounted for only a small proportion of Winterstoke's new population. The explanation favoured by most modern historians is a fall in the death rate due to improved medical knowledge, but there can be little doubt that the older theory of a higher birth-rate played a significant part in the growth of the new Winterstoke. Greater medical knowledge there might be, but it was many years before anything was done to improve living conditions in the fever-ridden courts of Hanger Lane or Darley Bank or to sweep away their noisome midden heaps and privies which the night-soil carts visited so infrequently. Few medieval villages could have had an infantile mortality rate higher than that of the mining colony at Hanger Lane, whereas its fecundity was unbounded. The demands of the industrial system and the efforts of the religious zealots had between them ensured that the poor had only two pleasures left to them, drink and copulation. The reformers would no doubt have robbed them of the first along with the rest had they been able, and in any case drink had to be paid for. But the pleasures of the bed were free and no reformer could interfere with them nor government tax them. Moreover, whereas we now regard children as an economic liability, in the Winterstoke of the early nineteenth century they were

WINTERSTOKE

looked upon as an asset. The child of a smith or nailer began his education in the domestic smithy by blowing the forge or treadling the oliver almost as soon as he could walk and so made a contribution to the family revenue which was worth more than his keep. The same applies to the employees of the Darley Bank Company whose children were put to work in the mines or in the ironworks. Historians may say what they will about the effect of a falling death-rate; the fact remains that the growth of Winterstoke was most rapid during the period when living conditions were at their worst and when child labour was most freely exploited.

So far this word-picture of Winterstoke has been comparatively simple in its structure because its life and growth has been almost exclusively dictated and determined by two great ruling families and the little worlds, so different in character, which they created: the great house of the Earls of Winterstoke which sapped and finally destroyed the old medieval economy; the furnaces, mills and mines of the Leeds family which attracted the new town and its tentacles of water and rail transport as a magnet attracts iron filings. But now, when we come to the great, sprawling town of the mid-nineteenth century, the old simple structure disintegrates and the picture becomes far more complex and chaotic in its form. Out of that ruthlessly competitive scramble which pauperized so many, new men of power emerge to challenge and, in some cases, to break the old ascendencies.

The defeat of the Earls of Winterstoke by the precocious and powerful forces of the town whose growth they had done so much, indirectly, to promote could equally well be described as poetic justice, a process of long overdue reform or a tragedy. That the sins of proud and acquisitive fathers were visited upon their children could be called the Nemesis of divine justice. The tragedy lies in the fact that the process involved not merely the downfall of a ruling caste who had abused their power but the ruin of English agriculture.

Until the end of the eighteenth century the interests of the two great families of Hanmer and Leeds had marched amicably side by side. But despite their revenues from coal and iron, the Hanmers remained landowners, and after the turn of the century the landowners and the new industrialists found themselves involved in an increasingly bitter conflict as the interests of the old green and the new black Englands diverged. The landowners fought a stubborn rear-guard action but their days of power were over. The Reform Bill gave the black a voice in the Government of England which became increasingly powerful and authoritative as the years passed. This first decisive victory was followed by the skirmish over the railways in which the black again carried the day, and by the most significant of all these trials of strength, the struggle over the Corn Laws. Expressed in local terms this was a battle waged by a united Winterstoke against the entire agricultural community of the county, a protracted encounter in which the Leeds family were at one with their workmen for the cause of the black, while Lord Winterstoke fought for the green in alliance with yeomen farmers such as Thomas Winter of Emberley Hall.

The Corn Laws were the last surviving expression of the old conception of trade protection. They were designed to control by price regulation the importation of foreign wheat, admitting it in time of scarcity, excluding it in time of plenty in order to safeguard the interests of the English farmer. That such an anomaly should have survived so long in an age which preached that any such interference with freely-competitive trade was a violation of natural law was due to two things: to the power of the great 'high farming' landlords such as the Earls of Winterstoke and to the fact that, despite enclosure and industrial expansion, agriculture was still England's greatest industry and the occupation of the majority of Englishmen. But now the supremacy of the old order was challenged. As we have seen, there was no longer any connection between the economics controlling the trade and the wages of Winterstoke and those of its rural environment. The two had drifted poles apart. Thomas Leeds could see no reason why his farming neighbours should not

WINTERSTOKE

accept his own economic doctrine of freedom. The Corn Laws should be repealed so that wheat, like his iron and coal, could find its natural price level. Discontent was rife in Winterstoke owing to the high cost of bread. The workmen of Darley Bank and High Hanger supported the agitation for repeal to a man, and local farmers such as Thomas Winter became the victims of ugly demonstrations and wanton damage. No one questioned whether the cause of the trouble might not be that industrial wages were too low and that the price of wheat might in fact be a just price, although this would have been the first consideration to occur to a 'primitive' medieval economist.

English agriculture was inevitably affected by the wars, the booms and the slumps of trade by which the industrial revolution proceeded on its headlong way. Agriculture shared in the trade boom which accompanied the Napoleonic war and in the immediate slump which followed the peace after Waterloo when the price of wheat fell by fifty per cent. in a matter of months and thousands of farmers were bankrupted. Thereafter, under the protection of the Corn Laws, the sick trade gradually recovered and the accession of Victoria appeared to mark the beginning of a new era of prosperous high farming. Even when the campaign against the Corn Laws was won the effect was not immediate so that few if any farmers can have realized the implications of the black victory: that it marked the end of an agricultural England which had endured for two thousand years, and that in future the country's fortunes would be irrevocably bound up with the new and chronically unstable industrial economy. The repeal of 1842 did not take effect for seven years, while it was not until the 'seventies that the influence of the new economics in world markets really made itself felt. From that time onwards the divorce of the black from the green became complete and Winterstoke became almost entirely dependent upon the 'cheap' foods which she imported from overseas in exchange for her manufactures. In reality these foods were purchased at a terrible price: the wholesale exploitation of overseas producers and the rapid

WINTERSTOKE

exhaustion of the fertility of virgin soils which new mechanized techniques of 'conquest' made possible. It may seem a far cry from our Wendle valley to the leached soils and dust bowls of the Americas yet they were only a part of the trail of destruction which the new town spread across the world. It is only by keeping this far-distant tragedy in mind that we can understand how it was that Winterstoke could continue to expand its population when just beyond its black periphery farm after farm fell to rack and ruin and field after field where once the good corn had waved fell back to derelict pasture amid a wilderness of unbrushed hedgerows and broken-down gates. To this tale of ruin the railways contributed their share for they preferred to handle bulk shipments of foodstuffs from the expanding docks at Westerport rather than the small, short hauls of local produce and therefore granted the former more favourable rates. At first, when imports were mainly confined to grains, the local farmers turned from corn to the hoof, but the perfection of refrigeration methods eventually made meat importation possible and soon ruined this market also. As a last resort, most of them ultimately became cow-keepers, exporting the fertility of their cow-sick pastures in the churns that their floats carried daily to the nearest station. Only the most deep-rooted of yeomen farmers such as the Winters of Emberley, husbandmen in the true sense of the word who looked upon their land as an almost sacred trust, contrived by every desperate expedient and self-sacrifice to ride the storm and keep their own lands and those of their tenants in good heart. With the lands of the Winterstoke estate it was an altogether different story. The town had already encroached considerably upon the farms of High Hanger, Ketton and Summersend, and when the great agricultural landslide set in there was no longer any incentive to check the growth of so profitable a crop as bricks and mortar. They were completely engulfed by the town and by the end of the nineteenth century only a part of Summersend and of the Abbey home farm which adjoined the Park remained under cultivation.

WINTERSTOKE

A people whom the industrial revolution had cut off from the soil of England now lightly broke their faith with it and accepted with equanimity this rural catastrophe. The voice of the industrialist had silenced that of the landowner, and his view of England as the workshop of the world, exclusively dedicated to producing manufactures in exchange for the food provided by a grateful planet, was accepted without question. Each year the industrial revolution produced fresh wonders and so intoxicating were these fruits of technical ingenuity that no one stopped to ask what would happen to this system of exchange when other countries followed England's example.

To us, looking back over the years, it may seem astonishing that such an uncomfortable question was not asked, for already there were signs that England could not hope to retain for long an unchallenged monopoly in the new manufactures. Already many of the Winterstoke nailers were faced with ruin as a result of the importation of Belgian nails. The old system of domestic industry in the iron trade with its lack of capital resources could no longer survive in the savage jungle of commercial competition. It died slowly (there were still domestic forges to be found in Winterstoke in the twentieth century) but none the less surely. Capital, which had been confined to the basic industries of coal and iron production and to heavy engineering, now began to invade the field of light manufacture. The first step in this process was made when the smith abandoned his domestic forge and went to work, with six or a dozen of his fellows, in a forging shop built and equipped by the 'fogger' who had previously supplied him with material and marketed his finished goods. He continued to work for the fogger on the same basis as before but with the difference that he no longer owned shop, tools or equipment. His skill was his only remaining asset, and that was soon challenged by mechanical competitors. In the production of a wide range of light metal goods and components the fly-press, the power press or the drop hammer with its dies rapidly ousted the anvil and the oliver from many of the foggers' forges. As a result,

WINTERSTOKE

numerous small factories, forges and foundries sprang up to provide employment for the swollen population. Many of these small businesses were little better able to withstand competitive stresses than the domestic forges they replaced. A few managed to carve a small but secure niche for themselves in the commercial world and remain, dingy but undefeated, to this day. A few by judicious amalgamation and trade agreement grew into large and powerful companies with ramifications extending far beyond the boundaries of Winterstoke. Many more have either disappeared or survive to-day as lorry garages, as laundries, as scrap-yards or warehouses for their more fortunate competitors, or simply as blackened ruins where slates have slipped and every soot-darkened pane of glass has long ago disappeared from its iron casement.

None of these small concerns threatened the supremacy of the Darley Bank Company; they merely replaced the domestic smiths as customers for its coal and iron. The Company appeared to grow from strength to strength. Each year its output of coal from the High Hanger field increased. Tall pithead gear and winding house transformed the appearance of the old High Hanger pit, while further to the west a new and deeper pit known as Camp Colliery was sunk on the remaining lands of High Hanger Farm. The farmhouse itself became the colliery office and its buildings were converted into pony stables, lamp room, and fodder stores. This new colliery meant more housing, and in the low-lying fields west of the colliery marshalling yards a new suburb of terrace cottages no better than their predecessors at Hanger Lane was added to the town. This was tersely known as Camp. The name was apt, for living conditions in the new terrace were comparable with those in the shanty town of the railway builders which had once occupied the same fields.

In the ironworks of Darley Bank, Bedlam and New Bank furnaces had been replaced by hot-blast furnaces of greater capacity and in 1856 the Company achieved a record output of raw iron. No one in that year could have guessed that

WINTERSTOKE

this would stand as a record for all time; that the days of the Darley Bank Company as a great iron producer were nearly over. For this very same year when the furnaces roared and flamed as never before was marked by the introduction of the Bessemer Converter in place of the crucible process of steel-making. This revolutionized the industry in a few years by substituting mild steel for wrought iron and by moving the centre of the basic trade away from the Midlands to the North-east where the ores were more suitable for steel production. The Bessemer Converter was followed ten years later by the Siemens-Martin open-hearth process which transformed the boiler-making and ship-building trades by producing mild steel plate at a price far lower than that of the wrought iron equivalent.

Why did not the Darley Bank Company adopt these new processes? The question is difficult to answer. The local ores might not be so suitable as the northern lodes, but that steel production at Winterstoke was perfectly feasible events were soon to prove. Perhaps Thomas Leeds, the last of his line to be actively connected with the Company, was not of the same adventurous metal as his forebears; or, more probably, he was too absorbed in the engineering side of the business, particularly locomotive building, which had greatly expanded. However it came about, for the first time in its history the Darley Bank Company allowed the initiative to pass into other hands. If they were not prepared to produce steel at Winterstoke there were others who would, for the demand was insatiable, and even if the ores were not of the most suitable quality there was an abundance of coal still untapped. Again, the vast extension of banking and credit, 'the funding system' as Cobbett called it, which was the foundation of industrial expansion, and, finally, the passing of the Companies Act which limited liability in the event of failure, all favoured the promotion of new and ambitious commercial enterprise. These were the circumstances which, in the 'sixties, brought the Great Ketton Steelworks to birth.

The idea of forming a steel company at Winterstoke

WINTERSTOKE

originated with a number of small manufacturers in the metal trade who used an increasing quantity of steel which they must needs import by rail from the North. They had for long looked jealously at the Darley Bank Company's monopoly and now that Company's failure to hold the initiative and to supply their needs was their opportunity. Yet the moving spirit, the financial genius of the new enterprise was a man with no previous experience in the industry whatever, a new man of power who had emerged head and shoulders above the commercial free-for-all to challenge the hitherto undisputed sway of the families of Hanmer and Leeds. This was Sir Richard Blenkinsop, Whig Member of Parliament for Winterstoke, twice mayor of the town, director of the Great North-Western Railway, owner of the brewery known as 'Blenkinsop's Entire' and of the Winterstoke Steam Milling Company.

Whereas the Hanmer family had ridden to power on a woolsack and the Leeds on a fiery juggernaut of coal and iron, the vehicle which had brought the Blenkinsops to prosperity was the beer barrel whose contents had helped to drown the sorrows of several generations of Winterstoke's poor. Sir Richard's ancestors had kept the little alehouse on Darley Bank known as the 'Woodcolliers', making their beer in a brewery behind the house which resembled the 'outshut' forges of the adjoining cottagers. It was the coming of the Lobstock Canal which had founded the family fortunes by encouraging old Amos Blenkinsop to gamble the whole of that thrifty family's accumulated savings on the 'Navigation' at Darley Bank Basin with most profitable results. It was the demand of the canal traders for corn and fodder for their boat horses which had encouraged the Blenkinsops to branch out into that trade with a success which had been crowned by the building of the steam mill. What matter that the fortunes of the canal were now in eclipse? The Blenkinsops had followed the trade. The brewery and the Railway Hotel were built out of the profits derived from slaking the thirst of the railway builders. Sir Richard never tired of telling this family success story as proof of the doctrine of self-help of

WINTERSTOKE

which he was a great exponent, but his heirs were much more reticent.

The new Company purchased Ketton and Summersend farms from the Winterstoke Estate and it was on this site where the lower slopes of Summersend Hill fell away into the Lob valley that the steel plant grew up, its tall blast furnaces and stacks, coke ovens, slag heaps and rolling mills dominating the old works of the Darley Bank Company strung along the floor of the valley below. To supply the furnaces of 'Ketton Bar', as the new works was called locally, the Company opened its own colliery a little to the East of the steelworks. This became known as Ketton Deep and was in its day the most up-to-date pit in the country. Reared high on their gaunt gantries above the twin shafts of the pit, the upcast and the downcast, the spinning wheels of the headgears plunged the cages like plummets to a depth of a thousand yards. No wooden props but hoops of steel which frequently buckled under their immense burden supported the roof of the main haulage ways where pit ponies were replaced by compressed air haulage engines. Strung like beads on the whipping steel thread of their head and tail ropes, trains of coal tubs rumbled along these ways with a roar and rattle deafening in the confined darkness. Working at such great depths was only made possible by an improved ventilation system. Air was forced into the mine from the surface through the downcast shaft and was eventually exhausted through the upcast, its circulation throughout the mine being ensured by a system of air-lock doors so laid out that they required no 'trappers' to mind them.

The organization of the Great Ketton Steel Company was typical of the new and powerful public companies which grew up during the latter half of the nineteenth century following the Companies Act; an organization completely different from that of the old Darley Bank Company with its family control and its association of semi-independent 'overmen'. Each presiding member of the Leeds family had, during their successive reigns, exercised a degree of personal control over the destinies of their great undertaking which is quite

WINTERSTOKE

unknown to-day. Not for nothing were they called ironmasters. Each generation served a long apprenticeship, learning the hard way under his father's strict eye to become a master of his trade, and had by that mastery guided not only the financial but the technical development of the Company. Thus each member of the family, the two Josiahs, Daniel, Jonathan, Peter and Thomas had been personally responsible for improvements in foundry, furnace and forge, in the application of power, in transport, in the machine shop, and finally in locomotive building. To the last, old Thomas Leeds remained the 'gaffer', a man whose decision in any dispute or technical problem was the ultimate law from which there was no appeal; an iron autocrat whose life was dedicated to the great responsibilities which he accepted and wielded by inherited right. But in the case of Sir Richard Blenkinsop who, as chairman of directors, was the presiding genius of the Great Ketton Steelworks, the position was quite otherwise. Whereas the figure of Thomas Leeds, like that of Abbot Luttrell or Ernest Hanmer belongs to a historic past, that of Sir Richard is recognizably modern. He was what we now call a 'tycoon' or a 'V.I.P.', a financier who concerned himself not at all with the technicalities of the various businesses he owned or controlled but was master of one craft only—the making of money. While the Leeds family had lived for their business, Sir Richard lived for himself and for the advancement of the name of Blenkinsop. His aim was success, and success for him spelt two things: money and power. To their acquisition he devoted his great abilities with complete singleness of mind and purpose. That every undertaking he touched prospered was due to two remarkable gifts: an almost infallible commercial flair which he exercised with the unperturbable and ruthless skill of an expert gambler; and a remarkable capacity for assessing the character and ability of his fellowmen. He possessed the instinct to find and the means to buy the best brains for whatever job he sought to fill and this was the secret of the success of the Great Ketton Steel Company. For practical purposes, responsibility was

WINTERSTOKE

delegated at Great Ketton to an elaborate, highly-organized human machine of key men; a hierarchy of managers, under-managers, works engineers, superintendents, foremen and charge-hands which took the place of the old 'overmen'. There was no sub-contracting at Great Ketton. Every man was an employee of the Company. Although Sir Richard Blenkinsop occupied the apex of this pyramid of responsibility, only a matter of the highest policy could scale that exalted height and whereas at Darley Bank a man never knew when he might not find old Thomas Leeds standing at his elbow regarding his activity with a critical and practised eye, he might work for years at Great Ketton without setting eyes on the chairman. Only the 'high-ups' of the hierarchy had access to the heavy mahogany holy of holies of the chairman's office, and even amongst that exalted company a summons thither usually occasioned considerable trepidation. The relationship between employer and employed which had inevitably weakened at Darley Bank as the Company grew in stature was broken altogether at Great Ketton. In fact, the organization of the new works was as recognizably modern in character as its author.

Despite his responsibilities at Great Ketton, Sir Richard did not relax his control over the affairs of his brewery where expanded buildings, new vats and new maltings were the tangible evidence of success. But he placed his son Henry in charge of the Winterstoke Steam Milling Company, and this confidence was not misplaced. Sir Richard was inordinately proud of Henry. He had been able to give him the polish of an expensive education which he himself had lacked, but Henry was an apt pupil, and beneath this smooth surface finish was a character as hard and calculating as his father's. 'A chip of the old block' Sir Richard called him and the derelict water mills along the Wendle were the measure of young Blenkinsop's first business success. Admittedly it was not a particularly hard-won victory. When wheat disappeared from the fields of the Wendle valley and the truck-loads of imported grain waited their

WINTERSTOKE

turn to be shunted under the hoists of the steam mill, it was a walk-over for Henry. Winterstoke Lower Mill had already disappeared for it had been the scene of old Amos Blenkinsop's first essay in the milling trade and the Brewery now occupied its site. But the Upper Mill and the Mill at St. John's both fell silent as a result of Henry's enterprise. Soon all along the Wendle and its tributaries broken-down weirs, rotting wheels and races choked with reeds and mud told the same tale as derelict pastures and ruined barns. Only the Abbey Mill, grinding grist for the Winterstoke estate, survived until the first world war. With the passing of these water mills, the life of the river came to an end for the last of the Wendle barges furled its sail in 1870. Even its wild life deserted it, for the river had become Winterstoke's sewer and in water so polluted that even the vegetation shrank from its margins neither fish nor fowl could survive.

Sir Richard Blenkinsop looked upon the running of the Steam Mill as mere 'prentice work for the career he had planned for Henry. With no more competition than a bunch of illiterate country millers could provide, success was too easy. The lad was made for sterner stuff and an excellent opportunity to try his metal soon occurred. In 1875 at the age of eighty-two, but hale and hearty to the last, old Thomas Leeds died and his passing marked the end of a long era in the history of Winterstoke. He left no heir and his chief executor, his younger brother John Leeds, was the only surviving male representative of the family. John had been a prominent nonconformist minister in the Midshire circuit for many years. He had never played any active part in the affairs of the Darley Bank Company and was not prepared, at his advanced age, to step into his brother's shoes. But he had inherited his share of the family's shrewdness and it did not take him long to discover that all was not well with the affairs of the Company. The autocratic old man had held the reins of the business in his hands to the last, but even had those hands been younger and more sensitive to the demands of the hour, the Company had grown too big and

WINTERSTOKE

unwieldy to be handled in the old fashion by a single pilot. There is always a risk that in such a position a practical man will neglect the wood for the trees in the guise of particular technical problems. This had proved true in the case of Thomas Leeds. Ever since the days of his youth when the Company had built the *Hurricane*, the steam locomotive had absorbed his whole interest until in old age its perfection had become almost an obsession with him. That each locomotive which the Company built should be better than the last was a principle to which every other consideration was sacrificed and that some of the splendid machines turned out at Darley Bank during his régime should be still at work is tribute enough to the achievements of old Thomas and his craftsmen. But, alas, while these locomotives undoubtedly enhanced the reputation of the Company, the profit and loss accounts on which Thomas turned his blind eye coldly revealed that they were too costly a form of advertising. The Company had been gradually falling behind in the hard commercial and technical race with the result that its methods and much of its equipment had already become out-of-date. For while Thomas had been absorbed with his locomotives the new steels, combined with the new standards of precision made possible by the work of Maudslay and Joseph Whitworth, were revolutionizing industry. Moreover, as John Leeds and his co-executors soon discovered, the managers and 'overmen' of mines, furnaces, rolling and slitting mills had taken advantage of their independence and lack of supervision by feathering their own nests rather than that of the Company. It was a serious situation which must obviously be fully discussed with the surviving proprietor, George, eighth Earl of Winterstoke.

So it came about that a bleak winter's morning found old John Leeds, an incongruous and lonely figure in his suit of sombre black amid the cold magnificence of Wyatt's pillared hall, awaiting an audience with his Lordship. It was destined to be the last meeting between the two great families, although its significance could not be realized by either party at the time. Declining the offer of a glass of Madeira, the

WINTERSTOKE

minister went straight to business whereupon it speedily became apparent that Lord George, the man of property, was no more capable of setting the Company's house in order than the man of God, indeed rather less so. Perhaps both recognized that they represented an ancient régime, that this brazen new world was beyond them and that they had become as much a part of history as the splendid room in which they sat. At all events, these two proud men reached a decision which must have been hard for them and which must surely have made old Thomas Leeds turn in his grave. Sir Richard Blenkinsop should be consulted forthwith.

Now Sir Richard was flattered but not in the least surprised when he was invited to a meeting with the Earl in the presence of John Leeds at Winterstoke Park. He had been keeping a sure but discreet finger on the pulse of the Darley Bank Company for some time, so he had his answers ready and prescribed his infallible specific for ailing businesses—an injection of new capital and new blood. He suggested that the coal-mining and the engineering and iron-founding activities of the Company should be separated and that two new public companies should be floated for the purpose of taking over these assets, and providing the necessary capital for their proper development. As for the Company's furnaces and rolling mill, developments in the steel industry would render them obsolete in a few years' time if they were not so already, and he regarded them as liabilities. It would pay a new engineering company better to buy in the raw material it required for its forge and foundry from more specialized producers than to keep its own furnaces in blast for the purpose. Lord Winterstoke and the legatees of Thomas Leeds could either sell their holdings *in toto* or in part to the new companies or take up shares in one or both of them to the extent of such holdings at a valuation which must in any event be made. In such cold and prosaic terms as these, the old Darley Bank Company received sentence of death. For in Sir Richard's philosophy there was no room for sentiment in business; it was a ruthless game in which no holds were barred and

WINTERSTOKE

in which money was either made or lost according to the proficiency and strength of the player.

In the event, Lord Winterstoke and the Leeds legatees decided to retain holdings in the newly-formed High Hanger & Camp Colliery Company but to sell out their interests in the works at Darley Bank. This suited Sir Richard's book admirably for it enabled him, in the name of his son, to obtain a controlling interest in the Darley Bank Forge & Engineering Company and to install Henry as its first managing director. To the discomfiture of many of the older hands, the new broom lost no time in sweeping clean and the whole internal organization of the works was remodelled by Henry on the lines laid down by his father at Great Ketton. New Bank and Bedlam furnaces were blown out and dismantled. Beam blowing engines, rotative mill engines, rolling mill and forge machinery, all the plant which had been the pride of old Daniel Leeds' eye and the last word in technical development fifty years before had become obsolete by the standards of Great Ketton. All were ruthlessly broken up and in the new cupolas of the Darley Bank foundry or the furnaces of Ketton returned to the molten womb whence they had come. Soon all that remained of the old ironworks was a few broken brick ends, a few obstinate, half-buried hulks of rusting metal and the great mounds of pot and tap cinder which resembled the vomit of some extinct volcano and where, in green mosses and occasional clumps of tenacious willow-herb, nature was struggling to reassert herself. In place of the old, new machines appeared in strange shapes and with new voices. The metronomic rhythm of the tilt hammer which, whether water or steam driven, had been the heart-beat of the Darley Bank forge ever since the days of Alfred Darley was heard no more.

In the new forge the beat of each heavy drop stamp, of each one of the battery of Nasmyth steam hammers that stooped like bow-legged titans over the glowing forgings made its own individual and variable contribution to a confused and earth-shaking thunder of percussion. From the

WINTERSTOKE

machine-shop, too, came strange voices, the urgent rasp and chatter of new tools which the steels of Great Ketton had made possible and which would in their turn beget their still more accurate and efficient successors. Wheel lathes, boring lathes, turret and capstan lathes; radial drilling machines, planing machines, shaping machines, all less cumbrous in form and motion than their predecessors, but more complex and more formidable in their speed and deft precision of movement. All these were powered by a steam engine of entirely different form. Gone was the old beam engine which had towered vertically in a tall and narrow engine house. The new giant, a mighty horizontal, tandem-compound mill engine with a fifteen-foot flywheel, reclined behind altar rails of polished steel like some recumbent god in an immaculately tiled and whitewashed temple incensed with the acrid odour of hot cylinder oil. No harsh or discordant sounds of mechanical effort disturbed the almost cloistral quiet of this new engine house where even the engine men seemed to speak in lowered voices and to move soft-footed over the polished floor. With so perfect a poise and balance was the power of this engine now harnessed that its great wheel revolved and the long burnished arm of its connecting rod rose and fell with no tremor of vibration, while the massive crosshead slid through its well-oiled guides with little more sound than that of heavy breathing.

These new and smoothly efficient machines which populated the workshops of Darley Bank represented the mechanical incarnation of the mind which now controlled the destinies of the undertaking. Not that Henry Blenkinsop had any share in their design or installation for he was no more of an engineer than his father was but used his inherited ability to find and pay the best men for the job. He was no progressive idealist dreaming of mechanical Utopias nor did he, like the Leeds dynasty, regard the development of the Darley Bank Forge as an end in itself, as an absorbing succession of technical problems to be wrestled with and overcome. But to a far greater degree than his father, Henry Blenkinsop was obsessed by the desire for

WINTERSTOKE

power in all its manifestations: the power of money which gave him dominion over men; the power of efficient machinery which enabled him to subdue intractable materials and conquer his commercial rivals. The whole elaborate and impersonal organization which he succeeded in building up over the years at Darley Bank was the fruit of his relentless and insatiable pursuit of power.

Henry more than fulfilled his father's hopes. A knight baronet, Member of Parliament, head of a great engineering firm with a world-wide reputation, director of many public companies; successor to his father on the boards of the Great Ketton Steel Company and the Great North-Western Railway, his career was a model of success as success was measured in Victorian England. Unfortunately, old Sir Richard did not live to see his son set the final seal on the family aspirations when, comparatively late in life, he married Letitia Hanmer, sole heiress of Winterstoke, and was subsequently rewarded for his many services to industry with the title of Baron Winterstoke, first of the new creation. Yet despite this glittering record, of all the characters who have so far played a part in this story of Winterstoke, that of Henry Blenkinsop is the most unsympathetic and the least enviable. The Hanmers were ambitious and pursued wealth and power in ways which were sometimes as ruthless and as unscrupulous as those of any commercial magnate. But for them the pursuit was never an end in itself. It was a means which enabled them to create a long tradition of gracious living, to patronize the arts of the golden age and so to surround themselves with a store of beauty for the enrichment of their posterity. The Leeds family set no store by the beauties of the world, but neither did they seek wealth and power. They were content to live simply and to derive a craftsman's satisfaction from the work of their hands and brains, enhanced by the misguided but none the less sincere belief that they worked for the lasting benefit of mankind. But Henry Blenkinsop sacrificed all such rewards and satisfactions to the indulgence of the most barren and fatal appetite that can afflict the human mind. He also sacrificed the warmth of human friendship and sympathy, for there is no one so lonely and unloved as the man who makes himself the incarnate symbol of material power. Like his father before him he enriched his native town by his enterprise and by various benefactions and endowments but they did not make his name beloved. For these contributions were never wholly disinterested, being calculated either to yield a dividend or to promote the name of Blenkinsop with an eye to further honours. Moreover, the town accepted his gifts in the spirit in which they were given, for they expected such crumbs to fall from his table, knowing very well that they were but crumbs when measured by the scale of his fortune. Although the first Baron Winterstoke died full of wealth and honours and although a statue of him was to be seen in Winterstoke until 1941, his name is now forgotten where those of the Hanmers and the Leeds have become part of a remembered tradition. Neither practising nor patronizing any art, he created nothing of lasting worth or beauty and left behind him no memorials other than the great organizations of the Darley Bank Forge and the Ketton Steelworks. But they were machines far too efficient to falter when their designer's hand dropped from the controls.

Chapter Ten

WHILE THE INDUSTRIES of Winterstoke were undergoing their nineteenth-century transformation, the town itself began to change its shape, or rather a recognizable shape began to emerge out of chaos as one by one there arrived the amenities and institutions with which we are familiar. In the dusty files of the *Winterstoke Sentinel* which made its first appearance in 1840 we may read, for example, the pæans of praise which accompanied the paving of the streets, the opening of gas and water works and of new town and market halls. Each in turn was described as a remarkable combination of art and industry and a milestone along the road of human progress. But to-day the inhabitants of Winterstoke have grown so accustomed to these monuments of the Victorian age that if they were asked to describe their appearance in any detail they would be quite unable to do so. Like the clock on the domestic mantelpiece they have become so familiar that they never consciously *see* them and would only become aware of them if they disappeared or ceased to tick. The basket and bag laden throng which packs the market hall every Saturday afternoon never notices the quite astonishing neo-Gothic elaboration of the ironwork with which the painstaking moulders of the Darley Bank foundry enriched each pillar and truss of this lofty shed which lurks, filled with echoes and the smell of bad fish, behind an imposing false façade of stone in Bridge Street. Not one among the thousands who hurry past the Town Hall every day looks up at its prickly Gothic pinnacles, at the grime-laden intricacies of variegated brickwork, Purbeck stone mouldings and columns of coloured marble, or pauses to ponder over the incongruous absurdity of its romantic balcony where a succession of portly mayors or town clerks have announced election results or other important events to an expectant populace.

WINTERSTOKE

When Sir Richard Blenkinsop built 'Cedar Lodge', an imposing stucco villa standing in spacious grounds off the Coltisham Road, he chose a kind of debased Italianate style. Was it because Sir Richard also founded the Winterstoke Gas Light & Coke Company, that this same style reappears in the Gaswork's retort house? We may think it inappropriate in a building which, hemmed in by dropsical gasometers, belches smoke from every cranny at not infrequent intervals. Similarly we may wonder why the municipal pumping station by the upper Wendle should present the appearance of an elaborate fortification, and why it was necessary to provide even the top of its chimney stack with a crenellated parapet. Was the architect an enthusiastic reader of the novels of Sir Walter Scott or did he dream of building a tower for the Lady of Shallot instead of a flue for a Lancashire boiler? With the passing of the years, some of us begin to see these Victorian buildings once again, but perhaps only a visitor from some other planet or from a remote past could ever appreciate them to the full. It requires that unclouded eye of wonder and surmise which we, alas, have lost. The only nineteenth-century public building in Winterstoke which has never aspired to resemble anything but its own mundane self is the sewage works, which, with its odorous outfalls and filter beds, was established on the island formed by the lock cut and the old channel of the river.

It was a long time before these new amenities brought about any marked improvement in living conditions for the majority of the inhabitants of Winterstoke. The Wendle, which divided the town into two halves, had become a boundary line of very great social and economic importance. Although the southern part of the town accounted for by far the greater proportion of its population, the northern was the more exclusive and enjoyed a monopoly of its amenities. For the site of Ernest Hanmer's model village on the north bank had become the town's centre, and the old Westerport to Coltisham road ('High Street'), Bridge Street and Ambling Street were its main thoroughfares. Along these streets

WINTERSTOKE

stretched the principal shops, the discreet bow-fronted windows of old-established tradesmen and the more blatant plate-glass emporiums of later arrivals, while at the point of their intersection stood the Town Hall, facing St. Cenodoc's parish church. Here towards the end of the century a considerable group of Georgian buildings which adjoined the Town Hall was demolished to make way for a free library, museum and art gallery. This great dour block of brick, encased by a thin shell of ashlar stonework, exhibited an odd confusion of Doric and Roman orders which contrasted strangely with the variegated Gothic of its near neighbour. Its appearance was hardly calculated to provoke a thirst for the arts, and its most popular department proved to be the public reading room which provided a welcome refuge for the old, the homeless, and the unwanted. Few visited the cases of geological specimens and local finds of stone implements in the museum or lingered long before the pictures in the gallery. These, before the Hanmer collection was acquired, consisted of some very large romantic landscapes by artists with high-sounding but unfamiliar names, a few scrupulously detailed works by lesser-known followers of the Pre-Raphaelite school, and a number of portraits of bygone mayors and counsellors in full regalia. Altogether it cannot be said that this example of Victorian cultural enterprise brought back to the grey lives of the people any of the colour, warmth or beauty of which they had for so long been deprived. A far greater boon to them was the Winterstoke Theatre Royal which, in the face of bitter opposition from every religious denomination in the town, opened its unholy doors at the corner of Bridge Street and Old Mill Lane in 1872. This was indisputably the happiest of all the Victorian contributions to Winterstoke, although a passer-by would hardly appreciate the fact from its somewhat drab façade. Perhaps its unknown architect deliberately set out to placate and mislead the puritans by designing an inscrutable exterior which would betray no inkling of the rococo splendours of plush and gilded stucco which it harboured. That the cold light of day could strip the magic from this interior could reveal that it was no more than a tawdry caricature of the rococo of the Golden Age, was of small moment. Even if the flesh was weak the old spirit which the joyless economists, politicians and theologians of the new age had so strenuously denied was here defiantly and unashamedly alive in the plump, naked cupids who trailed their garlands and spilled their brimming cornucopias over the proscenium arch, in the lightly draped nymphs and caryatids who upheld the hissing gas lights or the canopies of the stage boxes. This 'temple of concupiscence', as one dissenting minister called it (though few of his flock understood what he meant), was for the poor of Winterstoke a place of pure and unalloyed magic, bringing to the eye and ear pleasures they had been utterly denied for a hundred years. They packed the gods to welcome on the gaslit boards of this Theatre Royal the descendants of those strolling players who had delighted their ancestors in the far-off days when Wendle flowed clear and corn grew on Darley Bank.

Even on this north side of the river, different parts of the town revealed subtle social and economic distinctions. Thus only the most prosperous and eminently respectable tradespeople dared to settle in the region to the west towards Winterstoke Park, where the doctors, solicitors, bankers and successful business men had their detached villas in the neighbourhood of Butterfield's new Gothic Church of St. Mary. For shopkeepers and clerks there were the more modest stucco terraces in the north-east angle of the cross formed by the intersection of the main streets; an area bounded by the arc of Cemetery Road, where a dense crop of white marble in what had once been a meadow called Lower Leasowes showed that space in Winterstoke was as strictly rationed for the dead as for the living. Also in this quarter was the hospital founded by Sir Richard Blenkinsop and the new Grammar School founded by his son. The poorest quarter north of the river, though still considered respectable, was that to the east of Bridge Street. It was bounded, in the direction of Coltisham, by the high wall of the workhouse and by the tall buildings of 'Blenkinsop's

WINTERSTOKE

Entire' beside the river at the bottom of Old Mill Lane. These last looked in the distance like the roof-line of some French château and bathed the area in the sweet, cloying aroma of malt.

Once across Daniel Leeds' great iron bridge all pretence of civic dignity was soon lost. Only in Station Road had the Railway Hotel and Foster Brothers Livery Stables between them succeeded in preserving the tone of the north side. Elsewhere the locomotive depots, the gasworks and the canal basin were the only notable landmarks in a desert where terraced cottages, pubs, chapels, pawnshops and small factories jostled each other in a labyrinth of narrow streets. The meanest of these were about the canal basin and reflected the decay of the Lobstock Canal. Here in Canal Street and Wharf Road, houses originally better built and more spacious than their successors of the railway age had become decaying slum tenements, stubbornly refusing to die amid the desolation of empty warehouses, silent quays and evil-smelling docks where the swollen corpses of unwanted dogs floated in a scum of garbage on the stagnant water.

Yet in spite of such evidences of poverty, this district bordering the south bank of the Wendle did contrive against almost overwhelming odds to preserve a certain air of shabby self-respect, a refusal to be defeated by the black blight which had eliminated from it every living thing except man. The inhabitants of the north side did not disown this part of the town; they deigned to acknowledge its existence and were not averse to visiting it if the occasion arose. It was a relationship which resembled that of master and servant in which each knew their place. The really unmentionable Winterstoke, the Winterstoke that most of those who dwelt north of the river contrived to forget, lay beyond the railway. Indeed the line of the Grand Central with its long embankment and its acres of marshalling yards formed a very convenient and substantial pale which kept this wild and savage territory out of sight and out of mind. For life in the crowded courts of Ketton, Darley Bank, Hanger Lane and Camp left no room for any of the niceties of civilized living. Intrepid explorers forced by necessity to enter this dreadful region returned with horrific tales of gory combats on spoil tips between fighting cocks, bull terriers and, not infrequently, their owners; of dead-drunken men clogging the gutters outside the 'Woodcolliers'; of screaming, half-naked viragoes who tore out each other's hair in handfuls before an audience of amused menfolk and scared, pale-faced children; of adolescents sleeping four in a bed with their parents, and of houses in which even the lower treads of the stairs had been torn out and chopped up for fuel. Such tales were inexpressibly shocking to polite Victorian ears and were usually reserved for male audiences. But they were not looked upon as evidence of the degradation to which the industrial order had reduced their fellow men, but as the natural behaviour of a barbarous and alien race. So far as the respectable townsmen were concerned it was as natural for a Hanger Lane miner to commit incest, to beat his wife insensible or to spend his Saturday night lying in a pool of his own vomit as it was for an African savage to walk naked or to wear a ring in his nose. To the ladies of north Winterstoke the whole area south of the railway was a *terra incognita* definitely out of bounds. Nursemaids were forbidden on pain of instant dismissal ever to trespass beyond the pale, while no mistress of an elegant villa in Park Road would dream of engaging domestic staff from such a quarter.

Pavements and metalled roads, main drainage, gas and water mains spread rapidly through north Winterstoke and more slowly but surely through the hinterland between the railway and the south bank of the Wendle. But here they stopped short. Only the roads over which clerks and managers walked or drove to the great works were metalled and adequately lit. For the rest, until the end of the century the night-soil carts continued to creak and jolt over unmade, miry ways as they went about their noisome business; whole courts continued to depend for water on a single well or stand-pipe, and only a few rare gas lamps, provided more for the benefit of the police than for the inhabitants, hissed and flickered in the draughts of narrow alley ways.

WINTERSTOKE

Yet some progress had been made although there might seem to be little evidence of it. Though labour in the mines and in the works of Darley Bank and Great Ketton was no less, and in many cases more, exacting, hours were not so intolerably long and there was no longer child labour. Such sweated conditions were now confined to the obscurity of some of the small factories which lurked in the back streets and they would not survive there for many more years. The fight for reform had gone steadily forward and was beginning to bear fruit. But, alas, in the course of the hard century which was now passing the true aim had been lost to sight. The battle was no longer against a system which had enslaved, degraded and deluded mankind; the demand was for a larger share in its spoils and a voice in its control.

What changes there have been since, thin ghosts from an atomic age, we visited Winterstoke at the end of the reign of the first Elizabeth, to watch the salmon lying in the clear eddies of the river under St. John's Bridge, to see the charcoal burners at their work in High Hanger Wood, and in the Lob valley the glow of Alfred Darley's first furnace. How many worlds away now seem those bright, brave figures who strolled on that still summer evening through vanished gardens; how thin and faint the tinkle of the virginals. We come again now as an autumn dusk falls over Winterstoke to stand on the bare hilltop of High Hanger Down. It is the end of Victoria's long reign; the end, too, of the age of 'unconquered steam'. Looking southwards over Deepforest, the landscape has scarcely altered. The scars of distant mines are lost in the long perspectives of tree and copse and softly folded landscape. A far-off plume of steam from a North-Western train; a reach of the Lobstock Canal reflecting a glint of sunset light between the trees; these are the only evidence of change. But when we look west and north, what a dour, fierce world of sound and fury do we see. Dusk and drifting smoke are beginning to blur the outlines of the town, but the gas lighters with their long poles are already going their rounds, pin-pointing with light one after another of the maze of streets. Closely and clearly beyond the river

WINTERSTOKE

march the twinkling lights, but towards the foreground they begin to straggle and falter, to leave pools of mysterious darkness, to be dimmed by the flare from some unseen furnace, or to be momentarily lost in an eddy of steam like a moon in cloudwrack. We can hear the distant rumble of cartwheels over cobbles and from the railway marshalling yards the clash of buffers and creak of snatched chain couplings. The red eye of Ketton Junction down-distant flicks to green as we watch, and in the necklace of warning lights over the junction itself other green lights appear. An expectant lull seems to fall over the activities of the yards in the few moments which elapse before the down 'Comet' bursts out of the mouth of Darley Bank Tunnel in a sudden flurry of smoke and sound and flies down the bank towards Ketton curve. A very different train this from that earlier 'Comet' which, drawn by the ill-fated *Tubal* in the old racing days, met disaster on the canal bridge; a shining serpent of bogie corridor coaches headed by a sleek high-boilered 'Atlantic' locomotive, her coupled wheels a blur of flailing side rods, yet holding her train securely under the power of the vacuum brake.

No trees grow now on this side of High Hanger Hill, only a close turf more grey than green and pitted and pocked like some gigantic rabbit warren by the scars of old workings. The gentle contours of its lower slopes have been altogether obliterated, buried deep beneath a miniature mountain range of sullenly smouldering pit mounds from whose sharp summits the tram rail ends jut skywards like slipways for a space ship. Between the mounds we can see the winding wheels of High Hanger Pit spinning in a drift of gaslit steam. Directly below us in the Lob valley the hammers and stamps of the Darley Bank Forge are pounding with a sound like muffled gun-fire and here again there is the inevitable drift of white steam, steam jetting from the hammer exhausts to mingle with the smoke of the forge furnaces.

The Cistercian Abbey, Richard Hanmer's great house, the Darley Bank Ironworks, we have seen each in turn dominate Winterstoke, become the centre about which its

WINTERSTOKE

life has revolved. But now, as we stand here in the dusk, we are left in no doubt that the mastery has passed from Darley Bank to the Great Ketton Steel Works. The furnaces of Great Ketton no longer flare continuously as did the open throats of New Bank and Bedlam, and no longer are they backed by smoking heaps of coking coal. Conical caps have stopped their throats and they are fed by lifts which crawl up their pitiless steel sides. Only when a cone is lowered to admit a charge does the familiar glare light up the sky. Yet if the crude drama of old Darley Bank is lacking, Great Ketton conveys an impression of concentrated heat and power, of a vast plutonic energy which is the more menacing for being partly concealed. We may feel that the name of Bedlam is far more apt for Great Ketton Steelworks than it was for Darley Bank. Not here the blatant, white-hot simplicity and easily explicable rhythms of the old ironworks. The steelworks confounds the eye and ear with a perpetual pandemonium of lights and sounds whose origins can only be guessed at. There is a steady torrent of sound which might be the furnace blast or the rolling mill and is most probably a common chord struck by both. But over and above this ground bass come sudden metallic detonations which reverberate like the clash of cymbals; or a crash like that of a falling tree from the direction of the coking plant where a cloud of steam billows up. Mysterious lights gleam and vanish about the feet of the furnaces; some spontaneous internal eruption of white-hot metal momentarily reveals a row of roof-lights in dazzling outline; wheeling arcs of fire from unknown and invisible sources play upon drifting smoke. Then high on the side of the slag tip a ladle spills its contents and for an instant the whole sky seems to flower in flame as the thin cooled shell of the slag bursts as it falls and its molten yolk streams down the steep slope. The lights of the town look pale as we turn away.

Once out of range of Great Ketton and Darley Bank, it is quieter and more peaceful down in the town than it is upon the slopes of High Hanger Hill. The cobbles and gaslit pavements of Station Road are almost deserted for the station has

WINTERSTOKE

already dispatched its evening spate of local traffic and the late trains from London and the North are still to come. From behind the high wall come the usual sounds of railway activity: the squeal and grunt of protesting wheel flanges as a shunting engine runs over points; the inevitable clash of buffers and, of course, that ubiquitous sight and sound of escaping steam as a locomotive safety valve lifts and sends a white cloud billowing overhead on the wind. 'Unconquered steam'—steam driving locomotives, blowing furnaces, wielding enormous hammers, pumping water, lifting coal, driving sails from the sea and turning a thousand machines; everywhere steam. But listen! There is a new and quite unfamiliar sound in the air, faint but growing louder as we approach the entry to Foster Brothers stable yard. It is repetitive yet occasionally hesitant, part cough, part sneeze; an asthmatic wheezing now feeble, now loud. It could be a machine of some kind, though no self-respecting steam engine since the days of Thomas Newcomen has ever laboured in such travail. Undoubtedly the sound comes from Fosters' yard. Looking down the entry we can see its source standing under a gas lamp. It looks at first sight like one of Fosters' high dog-carts, yet the whole vehicle is enveloped in a haze of blue smoke and is being wracked and shaken to and fro by some invisible force. Two men seem to be wrestling with this mystery, one with his head and shoulders buried in the open boot at the rear of the vehicle, and another lying prone on the cobbles. With a final gasp and splutter the noise stops, the smoke dissolves and the man with his head in the boot straightens his back. We have had an unexpected glimpse of Winterstoke's first horseless carriage and heard the first feeble pulings of a newborn power.

Chapter Eleven

UNTIL THE AUTUMN of 1896 very few people were aware that one of the new-fangled horseless carriages was lurking in their midst. Young Bob and Peter Foster spent most of their time tinkering with their strange contraption in the privacy of the family mews, often to the annoyance of their father's cabmen and the alarm of the horses. Stablemen complained bitterly of the machine's poisonous breath and of the treacherous pools of dark oil which it persistently excreted on to their swept cobbles. To soothe these ruffled tempers, George Foster would make a show of reprimanding his boys, but secretly he was proud of their pioneering efforts. As for grandfather William, who had accompanied his father on the old *Eclipse* and still cherished his long, polished post-horn, he found the horseless carriage a great joke, little dreaming, as he chuckled over its strange antics, that it would one day avenge John Foster's defeat. Occasionally, after nightfall, the carriage would furtively emerge to make a brief, hesitant sortie through unfrequented back streets, its candle-lamp eyes blinking with the vibration, its exhaust tuff-tuffing manfully and its automatic inlet valve sneezing, to the astonishment of stray drunks and belated pavement loungers. For the law saw no distinction between such carriages and the lumbering traction engines which hauled the farmer's threshing drum, and refused to concede them the freedom of the road. As soon as that freedom was grudgingly acknowledged in November, 1896, however, the Foster brothers' horseless carriage appeared boldly in the light of day before a wider audience. Bob and Peter could not join the triumphant procession of cars from London to Brighton on 'Emancipation Day' but they celebrated the occasion as best they could by driving up Bridge Street and along the length of the High

WINTERSTOKE

Street, an exploit which won them a somewhat facetious and patronizing paragraph in the columns of the *Winterstoke Sentinel*. To the youth of the town the brothers were heroes, but by the older generation they were generally regarded with disfavour. Anyone who owned or drove horses hated the sight of them. Horses were certainly terrified by the machine, and more than once an angry driver struck out at Bob with his whip as he struggled to control his rearing and plunging team. Again, when the best method of starting the engine was to create a petrol fire so as to encourage the surface carburettor to vaporize its fuel, it was difficult to persuade the perturbed onlookers that the machine was not about to explode and that the services of the fire brigade were not required. The opposition made no attempt to conceal its delight when, growing more venturesome, the brothers attempted to scale Emberley Hill with mechanical results so disastrous that they had to be towed back to the Mews behind 'Rosie', the oldest and most staid member of the Foster brothers' stud. But in spite of the enmity and the setbacks the young Fosters persevered, for they dreamed, not only of larger and faster cars, but of motor omnibuses which would replace the horsedrawn 'knifeboards' which their father ran between the High Street and the railway station. In the event these dreams proved a little premature, for steam and the rail had still one more card to play before the motor bus could come into its own and they played it through the medium of another new agent—electricity.

The Tramways Act of 1870 had empowered Town Councils to build tramways, and in 1901 the Winterstoke Council applied for and obtained an order from the Board of Trade authorizing the construction of the Winterstoke District Tramway system. The lines and overhead cables were laid through the High Street, Ambling Street, Bridge Street and Station Road. Subsequently they even penetrated the hinterland of the Lobstock Road as far as the 'Woodcolliers'. The moaning, clattering monsters which lumbered along the new tracks flashing blue fire struck far more terror to the hearts of the horse traffic than the little horseless carriage

WINTERSTOKE

had done and they soon drove George Foster's knifeboards off the road. The source of their power was a new building at the end of Wharf Road beside the Wendle. It was Winterstoke's first electric generating station and it housed five of the very latest examples of steam engine design, Willans high-speed compound engines, each direct coupled to a Crompton dynamo. Here there were none of the moving rods and links or the majestically-wheeling cranks which had made earlier engines machines of such hypnotic fascination. These engines were totally enclosed and even their disc flywheels spun so swiftly and so truly that their highly-polished rims scarcely betrayed a flicker of motion. Their cylinders, teak-lagged and brass-banded, rose one above the other like the tiers of a wedding cake. No extraneous detail marred the smooth immobile symmetry of their outline, for steam was admitted to the cylinders internally through their hollow piston rods. By contrast to the slow, heavy sighing of the big horizontal mill engine at Darley Bank, the voice of these machines was an urgent throbbing, a steady pulsation of power which was the last word of the reciprocating steam engine to the demand of the age for speed and yet more speed. 'More revolutions' called the new race of electrical engineers, 'whooo—whooo—whooo' sang the spinning armatures of the dynamos, power flashing from their gleaming copper commutators, and the great heart of the old power replied, holding the load so steadily hour by hour that on the switchboards of polished slate the needles of the voltmeters scarcely wavered from their appointed mark.

Two of these new generating sets were exclusively dedicated to the tramways, one running and one standby, but the remaining three supplied other users with current. One set ran continuously, a second was brought in to share the evening overload, and the third was spare. For the demand for this product of steam's latest partnership grew steadily. The wealthier householders and the smarter and more enterprising shopkeepers preferred the new carbon filament bulbs to their old gas mantles; the Theatre Royal was re-

WINTERSTOKE

equipped with electric foot and house lights and carbon arc floods; one by one the manufacturers replaced their steam engines by electric motors. It was not many years before the first steam turbines came to Winterstoke power house and the reciprocating engines, except those powering the trams, became standbys.

The power station down Wharf Road was not the only new temple of magic in the town. The exchange of the National Telephone Company in Church Street was filled with technical mysteries even less intelligible to the layman. A new and enthusiastic generation of young men could talk as much as they liked about sound waves and carbon particles; it was miraculous, and at the same time rather frightening, to pick up the telephonic instrument by its slender handpiece of fluted brass and hear the disembodied voice of your friend, familiar and yet somehow strangely thin and unfamiliar, speaking to you over miles of wire. The telephone system did not spread rapidly in Winterstoke and it was some years before its subscribers could be connected to any town in the country. For the Company's right to lay underground cables was disputed and there was a long drawn out argument over the control of the new system before a vacillating Government finally decided to make the post office responsible for it and to pay the Company an agreable sum in compensation. Whereas the power cables from the generating station were laid underground like the gas mains, the telephone system at once changed the landscape as its poles marched out along the roads. Soon the elaborate but invisible root system of sewers, of gas, water and electricity mains which was making Winterstoke one complex organism, one enormous living machine, would have its overhead counterpart in an intricate cat's cradle of wires and cables.

It is a paradox that the coming of electricity helped to bring about the extinction of the electric tram by making the horseless carriage respectable, yet this was the case in Winterstoke. So soon as battery charging facilities became available in the town the enterprising but eminently respectable Doctor Harald of Abbey Road invested in a smart electric

WINTERSTOKE

brougham. The sight of this prosperous physician bowling round the town in his gleaming vehicle with its smart black leather mudguards driven by his familiar coachman in top hat and white cockade, did much more to reconcile the population to the horseless carriage than the efforts of the Foster brothers. Yet their dreams were coming true. Cars were beginning to appear with increasing frequency in the streets of Winterstoke. Though not so silent as the doctor's sedate and decorous brougham, they moved far more swiftly and purposefully than the Fosters' old horseless carriage, and with less mechanical protest. Their wheels travelled more easily and lightly over the cobbles for instead of solid bands of rubber they were shod with pneumatic tyres. Admittedly their great-coated and begoggled drivers were often to be seen wrestling with these new tyres by the roadside to the accompaniment of a great deal of blasphemy, but these new vehicles could no longer be dismissed by even the most confirmed champion of the horse as a mere mechanical extravaganza. Whether they liked it or no, the new power had arrived.

Despite the outraged mutterings of his cabmen, George Foster was persuaded to invest in two motor cabs with towering landaulette bodies which duly joined the old growlers on the rank outside the railway station. So popular did they prove that two more, and then a further two, each pair an improvement on their predecessors, were added to the fleet which was housed in a new garage at the Coltisham end of the High Street with Bob Foster in charge. Bob insisted that the services of the new garage should be available to any motorist and so the Winterstoke Autocarists' Depot came into being. 'Everything for the Autocar' was Bob's enterprising slogan, and motorists were glad to find somebody so willing to struggle with obstinate tyres, to cure the unfathomable maladies of new-fangled electrical ignition systems, to sell them cans of petroleum spirit or to replenish with carbide the generators of their acetylene headlamps. Meanwhile, Winterstoke's first motor bus appeared, plying between the railway station and Emberley village with Peter Foster at

WINTERSTOKE

the wheel. It was a crude vehicle: steeply ascending tiers of seats behind the driver with only a simple canopy on stanchions for protection; wooden wheels fitted with solid rubber tyres and a final drive by two grumbling, exposed chains covered with a mixture of oil and road grit. Yet like the taxies it proved popular and, so far as the trams were concerned, it represented the thin end of a very formidable wedge.

By 1914 Winterstoke had learnt to accept the new power which had appeared on its roads as part of the normal. No machine could be more docile and well-bred than the 'Silver Ghost' Rolls-Royce for which Doctor Harald had just exchanged his electric brougham, and the intransigent past of the horseless carriage was quite forgotten. Even the despised horses themselves were rapidly growing accustomed to the sight and sound of the cars which now began to invade the streets; long, low 'torpedo' touring cars equipped with the electric lamps which the tungsten filament bulb had made possible. Only the roaring solid tyred buses and lorries, the trams or the snorting steam wagons still caused panic amongst the horse-drawn traffic. But the powers of internal combustion and electricity were still in their infancy. Upon a society which, during a century of precocious development, had endeavoured to adjust itself to the pace dictated by steam power, the technicians of the revolution had launched these new mechanical forces which dictated a much faster rhythm, developed far more rapidly and so produced another bewildering cycle of social change. Each year brought something new to wonder at so hot was the pace. A sound of angry buzzing, like that of some enormous wasp which seemed to fill the sky over Winterstoke, brought people running from their doors to point and shield their eyes as they gazed upwards at their first aeroplane. They could see the intrepid aeronaut, a small figure slung like some black spider in the slender web of struts strung between the wings which was all that served for fuselage. They watched the strange and wonderful machine, pitching and swaying dizzily through the uncharted currents of the air at seventy miles an hour,

WINTERSTOKE

until it disappeared over the brow of High Hanger Down and its droning faded in the distance.

A strange and garish new frontage in Bridge Street harboured another new and more exotic marvel. A fantastic erection of white pierced woodwork and stucco, red plush curtains and mirrors, it resembled the entrance to an oriental mosque except that the whole of its bizarre outline was pricked out by hundreds of dazzling electric lamps. This was a palace, indeed, the Winterstoke Electric Theatre, and what an inexhaustible store of wonders peopled the hot darkness within! Here, while a tireless pianist tinkled and strummed, you could sit, for less than the price of a seat in the gods at the Theatre Royal, and watch a shadow pageant of restless figures: pompous gentlemen in flyaway collars, correct frock coats and striped trousers, who slipped on banana skins, fell down flights of stairs, bombarded each other with custard pies or were found, hiding behind the potted palms, in the boudoirs of outraged ladies; grim-faced cowboys, hopelessly outnumbered by hostile Comanche and Cherokee, defending the stage-wagon to the last bullet; romantic heroines with long, curling tresses and kohl-darkened eyes being kidnapped by handsome sheiks or facing a fate worse than death in the old log cabin. What a Nirvana to be able to relax and allow the mind to lose itself in this fairyland; to forget for a while the hard and unromantic realities of life in twentieth century Winterstoke, the thin rain falling on the cobbles outside, the raw smoke-laden wind in the alleyway, the never-ending drudgery of cramped kitchens and back-yards, and the brazen voices of the steam bulls of Darley Bank and Great Ketton which would bellow their peremptory summons through the cold darkness of winter mornings.

The progress of internal combustion and electricity might have continued even more rapidly had the brittle fabric of European society been able any longer to withstand the titanic stresses and strains imposed upon it by a competitive world economy driven by such prodigious mechanical powers. It could not. In August, 1914, chaos was loosed upon the world. It took the people of Winterstoke some time

WINTERSTOKE

to discover that this was not like other wars; that it was not merely a bloody trial of strength played out according to old-established rules of war by professional armies marching and counter-marching over remote battlefields. The Crimea and the South African campaign were the only wars they had known. They began to realize that this war was different: when every able-bodied man was conscripted to join the shambles in the Flanders mud; when new machines at Great Ketton began to hatch in their thousands the wicked steel shells; when, instead of locomotives, the first tanks crawled like amphibious monsters from primeval slime out of the forge at Darley Bank; when windows were darkened and the wheeling arc of a searchlight on High Hanger Down picked out the sinister silver cigar shape of a Zeppelin; when they heard its bombs crump down on the courts of Hanger Lane and in the morning saw the pointless and poignant havoc, the utterly meaningless misery which was all that so prodigal a display of aeronautical bravado had achieved. This was indeed a new kind of war; the first inevitable and gigantic clash between rival industrial machines which involved, not armies alone, but whole peoples and where the potency of the weapon made the hand that held it seem a puny and a pitiful thing.

Chapter Twelve

IT WAS PROBABLY just as well that the first Baron Winterstoke did not live to see his only son and heir grow to manhood. Who knows by what strange freak of genetics the union of Henry Blenkinsop and Letitia Hanmer produced so strange an issue. Though he was the apple of his mother's eye, his father could scarcely have approved of this tall, willowy young man, of his extravagant clothes and mannered gestures, of the sweet disorder of his long dark hair which hung over the collar of his velvet jacket. Bernard Blenkinsop seemed a very languid youth; his slow, graceful movements and slightly stooping shoulders, the large heavy lidded eyes which looked as though at any moment they might close in sleep, even the gesture with which he brushed back the long curling lock of hair which strayed persistently over his forehead, all implied that the business of living was a wearisome burden almost too heavy to be borne. It is doubtful whether he would ever have graced Winterstoke with his presence at all had it not been for the fact that his mother continued to live on there in solitary state. He had inherited none of that fierce material ambition which had driven his father and grandfather and which still drove the thundering workshops of Darley Bank and Great Ketton. Never in his life did Bernard go nearer to these fuming and flaming sources of his wealth than the Park, for he was not merely disinterested; he actively loathed them and the town which had grown up about them for their overwhelming ugliness and what he regarded as a blatant vulgarity. This revulsion did not inspire in him any reforming zeal because he did not see Winterstoke as a black affront to God, to nature and to man. There was no such dichotomy in his view of the world. For Bernard's god was Art, and all life and nature was so much crude and vulgar raw material that had not been hallowed

WINTERSTOKE

by this deity. Just as we accept the bitter weather of a winter's night by drawing the curtains close and stirring the fire, so Bernard's unquestioning acceptance of life was implicit in his rejection of it. The *Marius* of Walter Pater was his model and, like his fellow æsthetes, he believed that the Artist was a kind of high priest, a man unlike other men whose life should burn 'with a hard gem-like flame', refining in the crucible of his exquisite sensibility the crude dross of the world. Because the industrial revolution was utterly inimicable to any form of artistic activity it had begun by forcing the artist to become a lonely individualist and had produced passionate rebels such as Percy Bysshe Shelley. But by the 'nineties that passion was spent; the artists of the Decadence had grown aweary of the world. So the new Lord Winterstoke rarely visited his family seat, preferring to burn his gem-like flame in London and Paris, and in debating with the chosen few the finer points of æsthetic doctrine at his rooms in Chelsea or on the plush-covered benches of the Café Royal. A contemporary might have said that he contributed a very ineffectual last chapter to the long history of the Hanmers and to the aspirations of the Blenkinsops. But we who stand in the future should not look too hardly on Bernard, for never was there a society more worldly and more implacably hostile to a man of his temperament. His literary output was very small but of some quality—an occasional contribution to *The Yellow Book*, one slim volume of poems, no more. Yet it could truly be said that he achieved more in these few pieces than ever his father or grandfather had done notwithstanding all their drive and ambition. Not that Bernard was by any means a major poet. Yet some of his verses are still memorable, and especially is this true of the last poem which he wrote. A sonnet, untitled, but generally believed to be an elegy on the death of his mother, its simplicity is in striking contrast to the acutely self-conscious and somewhat overcharged verbal felicity of the rest of his work. We could more readily believe it to be by the hand of some minor Elizabethan than by a writer of the Decadence:

WINTERSTOKE

'*Who then should mourn this passing of bright day,*
Or fear to follow you to Lethean shades?
Night shrouded splendour of lost summer's noon,
Where you are gone, there shall I seek you soon.'

These closing lines of Bernard's sonnet could well stand as an epitaph to the poet himself and to that great house of which he was the last representative. After his mother's death, Bernard closed Winterstoke Park. It was not that he lacked the means to keep it up but that he could no longer tolerate its melancholy, and who should blame him? For melancholy indeed it was; as elegaic as its owner's valediction. A pervasive atmosphere of slow but certain decay and dissolution everywhere emphasized mortality. What could be more likely than that Bernard should have conceived his poem when, after seeing his mother's coffin borne into that monstrous marble catafalque in St. Cenodoc's, he wandered alone upon the moss-covered terraces. For no churchyard could be so evocative a symbol of transience as Winterstoke Park in its decline.

The corrosive fumes of Darley Bank and Great Ketton had not only stained Wyatt's façade and Brown's temples, pavilions and balustrades a uniform, funereal black, but had begun to eat away the smoothly chiselled surface of their stone. Though lawns were still shaven and unused walks trimmed, the conceits of Brown had long ago been abandoned to this slow insidious rot. Stone urns had burst asunder; goddess and nymph had fallen from their pedestals in dripping shrubberies to cover their nakedness in a years-old blanket of leaf-mould; over the unswept paving of the Temple of Theseus rusty drifts of dry leaves whispered as a raw air stirred them. The fountain had not played since Bernard's father died. Sprouting weeds had split the parched floor of its stone basin, and its blackened figures had grown hoary headed from the droppings of bedraggled sparrows: Neptune grasping a broken shafted trident; his attendant Mermans with distended cheeks sounding continually upon empty air what forlorn and unimaginable fanfare? The sur-

WINTERSTOKE

face of the lake was now so flawed with reeds and water weeds that it could no longer mirror the symmetry of the Palladian bridge, and autumn gales had taken toll in the long avenues. But it was not only wind-torn gaps which betrayed the imminence of the town. In the middle distance the railway, the black tips of Camp Colliery and the brick and slate terraces of the mining community had trespassed impudently upon that Grand Vista which stretched to the obelisk on High Hanger Down.

Upon this desolation the great house, looking more like a mausoleum than ever in its funeral scarf of grime, stared down with blank and witless incomprehension from rows of shuttered windows whose whiteness contrasted as sharply with the stone as the teeth of a grinning blackamoor. It entombed the treasures of an age that had become as dead and as remote as that of the Pharaohs: cavernous rooms where candelabra which once flashed prismatic fire from their lustres now hung like stalactites in the darkness; where riches of inlay, ormolu and gilt lay shrouded in ghostly sheets. So the house remained in the silence of death until the early spring of 1916 when it was re-peopled by the maimed and blinded, the shell-shocked and gas-poisoned victims of the first war of science and machines. For Bernard bought Ambling Park in 1915, moved most of the family treasures thither, and reopened Winterstoke as an Emergency Hospital. Had it not been for this precautionary move the Hanmer portraits would not be in the Winterstoke Art Gallery to-day. In 1920, when the last patient had been discharged but the hospital equipment had not yet been removed, fire broke out one night in the room which had been used as an operating theatre. The cause of the outbreak was never established, for exploding bottles of ether soon created a raging inferno which spread rapidly through the adjoining wards and burst into the pillared hall. Old Bedlam furnace never flared so fiercely as did Winterstoke House when the glass in Wyatt's dome melted and through this great circular flue long tongues of flame and flying sparks roared into the sky. Although they practically pumped the lake dry, all

WINTERSTOKE

that the combined forces of Winterstoke, Westerport and Church Ambling fire brigades could do was to prevent the blaze from spreading to the two octagonal pavilions at the end of the long colonnades. The central block was completely gutted. Just as dawn broke there were urgent warning shouts from the firemen, followed first by ominous cracking and rending sounds and then by a tremendous crash as amid a fountain of sparks the entire roof collapsed. By noon, all that was left of Wyatt's work, apart from the pavilions, was a ruined shell of calcined stone and a black tangle of smouldering beams and rafters. So perished Winterstoke House.

Shortly before he died, unmarried, in 1923, Bernard presented the Park to the town, and to-day all traces of the fire have vanished. On any fine Saturday afternoon you may, provided you can grab yourself a seat at one of the crowded tables, enjoy your ice cream sundae, or a cup of municipally brewed tea, in the terrace tea gardens where the house once stood. From the park below float the strains of the scarlet-coated Ketton Colliery Band, a colourful centrepiece to a cloth of deck-chairs. The band is only one of several pleasures which you may indulge when you have finished your tea. You may hire a hand-operated paddle boat on the lake or travel by miniature railway to Virgil's Grove and pay your sixpence to see the Grotto which the Council have embellished for your edification. Signposts point the way to further delights: 'To Clock Golf', 'To the Lido', 'To Kiddies' Paddling Pool'. Even if the weather is unkind you can still enjoy your tea in the East Pavilion where pottery masks of women's faces decorate the walls and where you can enjoy a continuous programme of swing music by putting your pennies in a chromium plated radio gramophone with coloured lights inside. And on any Saturday night throughout the year you can dance in the other Pavilion to the music of Joe Luke and his Jive Jugglers. But we cannot yet indulge in these truly democratic pleasures for we have not journeyed so far. England is still in the throes of the First World War. The time is 1917, the scene Emberley Old Hall.

WINTERSTOKE

There was no new Hall at Emberley. The word 'old' had simply attached itself to the original Hall as naturally as to an ageing man. For this house which had outlived all the vicissitudes of its proud neighbour had indeed grown very old. It was a retiring house. In summer when the tall elms were in heavy leaf it was quite hidden from the casual gaze of a passer-by in the village street. Even in winter, all that could be seen through the trellis work of bare branches hung with ruined rooks' nests was a vague grey shape from which protruded a confusion of gables and tall chimney stacks. It was as though the belt of elm trees and the inner ring of the moat together formed some charmed circle which had sheltered and protected the Hall from the tempest which had swept through the Wendle valley. The gables of the old house had pondered their reflections in the still surface of the moat for so many centuries that they appeared to lean, Narcissus-like, over the water, and only to be prevented from falling by massive buttresses which propped its ancient bulk as poles support the branches of an overladen apple tree. Dark panelling and undulating floors of elm planking made the interior seem twilit even in high summer, as if the rooms had grown too old to tolerate bright light. Moreover the personality of the house seemed to have become so strong that it was able to impress itself upon anything that was brought into it, imposing upon refectory table, eighteenth-century wine-cooler or Victorian arm-chair the same patina of age. Round the panelled walls of the dining-room (which was only used on state occasions) hung the Winter portraits: Sir Guy, the staunch Plantagenet whose funeral helm and gauntlets hung over his tomb in Emberley Church, Tudor Sir John with his proud, sad face; Sir Hugh the Cavalier who died at Worcester fight, with his lace and lovelocks. His son Sir Stephen was the last of the gallery, for later generations of Winters could spare neither the time nor the money to sit for their portraits.

To this beleaguered fortress and its lands generations of Winters had remained faithful through every change of fortune. Wars continued to take their toll of them. The reigning representative of the family, Thomas Winter, had lost a brother at Spion Kop and two of his three sons in Flanders. There was not much incentive, one could say, to go on fighting and farming for a country that had turned its back on its own soil, but tradition ran strong in the Winters.

It was in this year of 1917 that Thomas Winter and his fellow farmers suddenly found themselves blinking in an unaccustomed limelight, hailed by Government and Press as the hope and pride of the nation. The reason for this sudden *volte-face* was the success of Germany's submarine blockade. Confronted with this danger, England realized how fatally vulnerable she had become. Belatedly the word went out to speed the plough.

A country which had once led the world in agriculture had become so completely divorced from the soil by its fatal industrial obsession that few if any of those who issued the order to plough realized the practical difficulties involved for farmers who, for a generation or more, had been compelled to become stock breeders and cow keepers and were in no way equipped for arable farming. Had they asked a builder of locomotives suddenly to produce cotton cloth, or a maker of buttons to build aeroplanes, they would have appreciated the difficulty. Nevertheless, Thomas Winter and his fellows responded nobly to the call. But in return for their efforts to change the whole economy of their agriculture almost overnight they asked for that security which they had lost when the Corn Laws had been repealed—a guaranteed 'just price' for their grain. With the spectre of famine knocking at their door, the Government agreed and sealed their pact with the farmers, first in the Corn Production Act of 1917 and later in the Agriculture Act of 1920. It marked a return to the old medieval economics—for a time. So the pressure of necessity drove man back to the neglected fields and to the eternal and inescapable natural rhythms, so richly symbolic, of ploughing and sowing, reaping and harvesting. In the rich brown corduroy of new ploughed land, in the green mist of springing corn, in wind-dappled

WINTERSTOKE

fields of wheat ripening to harvest, in standing stook and golden stubble, an ever-changing beauty returned to the fields on the slopes of the Wendle valley wherever the touch of Winterstoke had not irrevocably destroyed them. Thomas Winter even ploughed up the rough on the golf links at Emberley Hill; land which he had been reluctantly compelled to sell to the Winterstoke Golf Club a few years previously.

The springing corn might reaffirm the timeless triune partnership of God, man and nature which man in his wisdom had foresworn as 'primitive', but it represented no acknowledgment of error but only of the hour's necessity. Moreover, with men dying by the thousand in the fields of France there were all too few available who could return to till the neglected fields of England. So to remedy the deficiency the power of the internal combustion engine was brought into the fields to aid the power of horses and of steam cable tackle. Tractors imported from America, 'Titans' and 'Overtimes', made their appearance for the first time in the local fields. Cumbersome and unwieldy chain-driven machines looking not unlike miniature traction engines, they wheezed and panted laboriously along the furrows, their heavy horizontal engines in a perpetual paroxysm of vibration. But they were presently joined by the neater and far more compact Fordsons from Dearborne which were the shape of things to come.

After the Armistice of 1918 war-exhausted Europe began the task of setting its house in order and of picking up the threads of life which four years of the most destructive and costly war in history had broken. It soon became obvious that a bitter lesson had not been learnt and that the ruling slogan was to be 'business as usual'. It might have been otherwise had not the task of reconstruction fallen upon men of middle age who could only think in terms of the world of 1914 which had seemed to them so secure. For the younger generation who might have avoided at least some of their parents' mistakes had been virtually wiped out in the slaughter of the trenches. But if the people of England

WINTERSTOKE

had been sorely weakened by the war her industrial machine certainly had not. Quite the reverse. As a result of an insatiable and assured market for the weapons of the new industrial warfare, factories such as the Darley Bank Forge and the Great Ketton Steelworks emerged from the conflict larger and far more formidable than they had been before. So there was only a temporary lull while these great machines adapted their enhanced energies to different purposes and then the old ferocious economic struggle broke out again with more than the old fury. Now that 'the war to end war' was over and there were no longer any U-boats on the high seas to threaten starvation, England listened again to the siren voice of the industrial economist and thought of herself once more as 'the workshop of the world' despite all the growing evidence to the contrary. The result was inevitable. In 1922 when a bumper harvest on the American continent slumped the price of corn to 49s. a quarter, the Government of England betrayed the pledge they had given in time of peril by repealing that part of the Agriculture Act which regulated the price to the English farmer. History repeated itself. Thomas Winter passes once again into a neglected obscurity, returning to his moated Hall a sad and disillusioned man prepared to withstand another long and bitter economic siege. Once again the farmlands of the Wendle valley tumbled down to neglected ruin, to a worse state, as it proved, than they had been before. What matter? In the Winterstoke shops food was becoming cheaper and more plentiful. Great Ketton and Darley Bank flamed and thundered as of yore. Wages were higher and working hours shorter. What matter? Business was looking up. Perhaps that new world lay just round the corner after all.

Chapter Thirteen

BY THE TIME the Foster brothers returned from their war service in the R.A.S.C., Bob to his garage and Peter to his beloved buses, they had become men of middle age, but the years had done nothing to damp their enthusiasm and they were full of plans for the future. Old George Foster had managed to keep the family business ticking over through the war years, but no more, and he was glad to hand it over to his sons. To outward appearances the war had called a halt to the impetuous forward march of the internal combustion engine and such little evidence of progress as Winterstoke had seen had been in the fields or in the air. Car manufacturers had turned over their factories to war production. Petrol had been scarce and dear. Doctor Harald's Rolls-Royce had appeared with a billowing gas-bag mounted on its roof which did not enhance the dignity of the equipage and had to be frequently reinflated by the good offices of the Winterstoke Gas Light & Coke Company. As a result, there were fewer cars to be seen in the streets of Winterstoke at the end of the war than there had been at the beginning. But the prices at which cars changed hands was a sufficient indication of the demand which existed, and not only the pre-war builders with reputations already established, but a host of newcomers hastened to supply it. As the new models began to appear it soon became evident that the engineers had not in fact been marking time since 1914. The demands of the wartime aircraft industry for engines of greater power and less weight had brought about improvements in engine design and efficiency and, more important still, the development of new alloys of steel and aluminium capable of withstanding greatly increased stresses. These new metals were the vital sinews which enabled new engines of puny size, but running

WINTERSTOKE

at revolutions per minute hitherto unheard of, to produce more power than a steam engine of many times their weight.

Bob Foster did not return from the war with the mere intention of running the Winterstoke Motor Company (as the old 'Autocarists Depot' was now called) for the rest of his life, profitable though the taxi and garage business promised to be. He had greater ambitions. He had dreamed of designing and building a car of his own when peace returned, a 'light car', for, in England at all events, he believed that the future lay with the smaller machine owing to the high cost of petrol and the punitive horse-power tax. He was not alone in thinking this and he was right.

The first Foster 'Light Four' was built at the back of the garage in the High Street using a four cylinder side-valve engine of proprietary manufacture. With spindly artillery wheels and a box-like open four-seater body of extreme simplicity, it was scarcely a thing of beauty but it proved both reliable and economical. At £450 plus various 'extras' including even the headlamps, the horn and the driving mirror, it was a good selling proposition when it first took the road in 1920. So much so that the column in Bob Foster's order book very soon became far too long for his small assembly shop where there was not room to build more than two cars at a time. The advertisements of the Foster Car Company assured potential customers that each car was guaranteed and 'fully tested before leaving our works'. Had they realized that 'our works' consisted simply of a converted stable, the hopes of aspiring owners would have fallen somewhat. A remedy had to be found before they gave up in despair and cancelled their orders, so in 1921 the Foster Car Company purchased the premises of the Atlas Pressworks in Institute Road from its retiring owner. Here there was not only room to assemble more cars but to install new machinery and produce many of the component parts which the Company had hitherto been forced to purchase from others. It was an inspired stroke on Bob's part to retain the name of the old works. 'The Foster Car Company, Limited,

WINTERSTOKE

Atlas Works, Winterstoke' had a fine, impressive ring about it. It inspired confidence. Instead of a huddle of dingy brick buildings in a back street it suggested that each car was sustained by the strength of a mighty organization of fuming chimneys and titanic machines. Nevertheless there was a lot more elbow room in the Atlas works and it became remarkably efficient for its size. So much so that by 1925 the characteristic Foster radiator had become quite familiar on the English roads. Bob Foster placed his son in charge of the garage business of Winterstoke Motors so that he could devote his whole attention to car manufacture.

Meanwhile the increasing number of buses to be seen in the streets of Winterstoke showed that brother Peter had been no less enterprising. So as not to be confused with Bob's business, the name of the bus venture was changed from Foster Bros. to that of Midshire Motor Services. The buses bore the name in large gold letters emblazoned on their green side-panels. The original pre-war route between the railway station and Emberley Cross soon became a mere insignificant shuttle service lost in a continuously expanding network. Buses ran to Church Ambling, to Westerport, to Lobstock, to Summersend and Coltisham. Constantly thrusting out from its original nucleus at Winterstoke and buying out less powerful local concerns, the Midshire Motor Services spread over the roads of the county after the fashion of creeping buttercup. The long tentacle of some new service would take root in the form of a branch garage in the town at its extremity and from this root a fresh crop of flourishing offshoots would grow. In twelve years Peter could number his buses in hundreds and the name on their panels was shortened to the single word 'Midshire' as though to boast that they enjoyed a monopoly of the county's public road transport as, indeed, with but few stubborn exceptions, they did.

The Midshire buses did not compete directly with the Winterstoke trams except on a few short stages for they ranged further afield. But the success of the motor bus was too patent to be ignored. The town boundaries had thrust outwards since the tramways had been built, and when the Town Council were faced with the alternatives of extending the tram routes or scrapping them altogether and substituting buses the bus supporters carried the day. So the last trams clanked sadly away into the silence of the scrap-yard and in their place, wearing the same livery of cream and scarlet, the new 'Winterstoke District' double-decker buses appeared. But for some years after the old tramlines remained in the streets to trap incautious cyclists.

Before the war the proud railway companies, so confident in their long-held monopoly of passenger traffic, had hardly begun to regard the motor bus as a serious competitor. After the war its advance was so rapid that it caught the railways, if not napping, at least off guard. While they were making good the arrears of maintenance which had accrued during the war their nimble rival, operating on tracks provided by the State, had achieved an impregnable position by the time the railways fully realized the gravity of the threat to their traffic. The London & North Midland Railway, as the combined Grand Central and Great North-Western Companies now called themselves, sought to take over Midshire Motor Services outright or, alternatively to acquire a controlling interest. Such strategy had worked well enough a century before when the railways had gone to war against the Canal Companies, but they soon discovered that these new bus proprietors were made of tougher metal. Peter Foster refused to be overawed by the majesty of the London & North Midland and declined to surrender to their blandishments. A brief spell of intensified competition ended in the truce of a 'knock-for-knock' Agreement over rates and traffic on certain routes. If anything, the honours lay with the Midshire Company. Certainly the crowds on the platforms of Winterstoke station during the morning and evening rush periods were obviously less dense; there were vacant seats in compartments which had always been well-filled, and on many a local train the complement of coaches gradually fell from a crowded eight to a half-empty four. So the road had its revenge at last; it also gave the railways

WINTERSTOKE

a taste of the bitter medicine which they had meted out to the unfortunate canal companies.

The decline and eventual eclipse of the Lobstock Canal which accompanied the renaissance of the road makes sad reading. When the Great North-Western Railway Company obtained a controlling interest in the Midshire Union Canal Company they accepted that Company's obligation to maintain its waterways in a proper navigable condition. As the years went by, however, the railway masters showed themselves to be experts in the art of observing the letter of this obligation whilst totally ignoring its spirit. Superficially, the works appeared to be reasonably well-maintained, but the most vital maintenance work of all, that of dredging, was sedulously neglected. Traders had to reduce the payloads of their boats in order to struggle along the mud-choked channels, while 'stoppages' due to summer water shortage grew more frequent and prolonged as feeders and storage reservoirs became choked and silted. The Railway & Canal Traffic Act which was designed to remedy these abuses remained to all intents and purposes a dead letter. Canal traders appealed in vain to the Commissioners appointed under the Act but could obtain no redress. A small trader, owning, perhaps, half a dozen canal boats and scarcely able to sign his own name was no match for the Goliath of the Great North-Western which could afford to employ its own staff of legal experts to put up a barrage of casuistic argument in the event of attack. It was, indeed, scarcely to be expected that the North-Western should spend money in the interests of traders who competed with them for goods traffic. The only section of the Midshire Union Canal system which continued to flourish under railway control was one to the North which lay in the territory of the rival Grand Central Railway. Here the North-western concentrated the Midshire Carrying Company's fleet and harassed the Grand Central very successfully for many years until the amalgamation of the two Companies in 1921 put an end to the game and the Carrying Company was wound up. But the Lobstock Canal, running parallel with the North-

WINTERSTOKE

Western's own main line, was fated from the outset. The appearance, in Darley Bank Basin, shortly before the outbreak of war, of canal boats propelled by Bollinder semi-diesel engines seemed to promise a canal revival, but because nothing was done to reinforce the canal banks against the wash from their propellers, the effect of the new boats was to make the condition of the canal rapidly worse so that they defeated their own object. When the war called a temporary truce and both the railways and canals operated under Government control there was a revival of traffic on the Lobstock down to Winterstoke, and Ketton tunnel often reverberated with the steady, purposeful throbbing of the new boats. But so soon as peace returned the traffic fell away and it became increasingly clear that the canal was doomed.

The end came one night in 1925. The captain of a late travelling motor-boat and 'butty' tied up at 'The Boat' above Winterstoke top lock and, finding Joe Horner, the lengthman, occupying his usual seat in the bar, told him that he had 'felt a flush' as he was travelling through the tunnel. Investigation next day soon found the reason for this sudden and mysterious surge of water: part of the tunnel roof had collapsed, damming the canal with the debris of fallen bricks and spoil for a length of fifty yards. The theory which was advanced to account for the disaster was that the tunnel had been seriously weakened by the subsidence of old workings of the Ketton Colliery. It was hopefully rumoured that negotiations were going on between the railway company and the Great Ketton Steelworks and that as soon as an agreement was reached repairs to the tunnel would be put in hand. But time slid by: months became years and still nothing was done. The few boats in Darley Bank Basin which had at first been kept hopefully afloat leaned wearily away from the quay walls, snapped their rotten mooring lines and sank. Seams cracked and gaped on their cabin panelling as sun and rain bleached and rinsed away their brave decoration; bright painted castles became misty outlines and roses of red and yellow faded to the pallor of moonflowers. Paddle racks rusted, lock gates rotted and the

WINTERSTOKE

locks themselves became choked with old bicycle and perambulator frames, battered oil drums, tin cans and worn-out motor tyres, all the hideous and useless detritus of the most wasteful civilization that the world has ever known. Finally, after three years had passed, the London & North Midland Railway Company applied for powers to abandon the waterway on the grounds that during those years it had carried no traffic. The L. & N.M.R. Canals (Abandonment) Act, 1929, officially pronounced a sentence of death on the Lobstock Canal which had in fact been carried out long before.

This Abandonment Act meant more than the closing of an old highway; it brought to an end the small, closed world of the canal, an eighteenth century world which had stubbornly survived until the twentieth. Despite the contribution which the canal had made to the progress of industrial revolution, it had itself preserved the traces of that older, tougher, but freer England which had everywhere been overwhelmed when the black tide swamped the green. To meet one of the long, narrow boats, glowing with barbaric colour and aglint with polished brass gliding slowly along the lonely levels on Barnby Moors as dusk was falling was to be reminded, with a sudden pang of nostalgic anguish, with a sudden stirring of ancestral memory, of that lost England. In some strange way the life of these nomadic people seemed nearer to that of the Iron Age men who sleep in their long barrow on Summersend than to our own; nearer to the life those itinerant story-tellers and ballad singers knew who roamed England before ever the monk Ambrosius wrote his chronicles. A life of material poverty, hard, bitter, often cruel and yet mysteriously enriched. By what? By some brighter memory of lost Eden? As the reflected glow from its lighted cabin faded from the water the traceless passing of the boat would recall the words of the gipsy, Petulengro: 'There's night and day, brother, both sweet things; sun, moon, and stars, brother, all sweet things; there's likewise a wind on the heath. Life is very sweet, brother; who would wish to die?' But now the canal was dead. The long boats

WINTERSTOKE

would come no more to Winterstoke and, like the railway navvies before them, their people vanished without trace.

In the early 'thirties, Darley Bank Basin was transformed. The basin itself was filled in to make a new car park and central bus station. The surrounding warehouses and slum properties were demolished and in their place grew new shops, a new cinema and, occupying one whole side of the square, a great neo-Georgian building of five storeys which housed a new police station and the offices of various departments of local government. Wharf Square, as it was called, was graced by the statue of Henry, first Baron Winterstoke, which was removed from its original site at the junction of High Street and Bridge Street where it had become an obstruction to traffic. From his new eminence Lord Henry appeared to be conferring, with one uplifted hand, a perpetual benediction upon the new subterranean public lavatories (Gentlemen to the right of him, Ladies to the left) which supplemented the original conveniences of green-painted Gothic ironwork erected during his father's mayoralty.

Wharf Square was only one of many changes which the Age of Internal Combustion and Electricity brought to Winterstoke. The most remarkable of these changes was the migration from the centre of the town towards its suburbs. Whereas previously its people had crowded together in the black heart of the town in order to be near their work, now the cars and the buses gave wings to their impulse to escape from it. The canal and the railway with their prescribed ways of water and steel had been responsible for compact areas of urban growth, but the new transport, ranging quickly and freely over dustless black roads of tarmacadam, was entirely centrifugal in its effect upon the dense mass of the town. Winterstoke began to sprawl as it had never sprawled before, devouring the surrounding countryside at a prodigious rate. Shopkeepers ceased to live over their shops; houses were converted into offices. All who could afford to do so forsook the centre of the town, drawn outwards by an impulse to live in the country which,

WINTERSTOKE

because it was a mass impulse, defeated itself. Except for its cinemas and pubs, the centre of Winterstoke emptied itself each evening as soon as the shops closed and became a place of the dead inhabited only by strolling policemen and stray cats until the following morning when the engine-driven tide would turn and bring its population roaring back. Up Emberley Hill, along the Coltisham Road and along Park Road as far as St. John's Bridge and the new Wendle Bridge Hotel which replaced the Winterstoke Arms, the lines of neat detached villas advanced.

Because the new suburban Winterstoke has its exact counterpart in every sizeable town in England, there is no need for us to linger in this prim world of privet hedge and raw red tile, of pebble-dash and mock Tudor timbering, of grinning bay window, artificial stone bird bath and aubretia-covered rockery of sooty stone. It was a strange half-world of compromise and pretentious make-believe created by a people who imagined they could combine the advantages of town and country life without the disadvantages of either and succeeded in destroying both. How hygienic were these new 'all-electric homes', how convincing a demonstration of the blessings which material progress had showered upon mankind! How consoling to shut out the realities of life's mysterious and terrible adventure behind a ring fence of the office desk, the golf club, the bridge party, the wireless set, the weekly visit to the cinema and the week-end car ride! Compared with the old crowded courts of Camp, Hanger Lane or Darley Bank, life in these new suburbs was so eminently respectable and law-abiding, so disinfected and dehydrated, that they seemed almost as dead as the cemetery in Lower Leasowe.

The social strata were even more subtly graded and distinguished in these new suburbs than they had been in the older residential quarters of the town. All the best people lived along Park Road in detached houses set well back from the road in their sloping gardens so that their windows could peer over the park wall. The ghost of that 'night-shrouded splendour' of Winterstoke still seemed to haunt

WINTERSTOKE

the heavy trees of the park to make the neighbourhood, in the house agent's term, 'most exclusive'. Next in the social scale were the houses which climbed resolutely up Emberley Hill until they linked the old village with the town. Then followed the semi-detached villas which lined both sides of the Coltisham Road as far as Sir Richard Blenkinsop's Cedar Lodge, now a seedy guest-house hiding its shame behind a screen of overgrown laurel and rhododendron bushes.

Besides these contributions of the private builder to the growth of Winterstoke, the Town Council themselves were also active. As long ago as 1890 the Housing of the Working Classes Act had empowered them to 'acquire, rearrange and reconstruct an area proved insanitary'; also to acquire land on which to build, manage and let what were described in the Act as 'working-class lodging houses'. But in spite of being thus armed, until the outbreak of war, the back-to-back courts of Ketton, Camp, Hanger Lane and Darley Bank still stood intact. True, they were no longer so grossly overcrowded and they were provided with wash-houses and outside water-closets, but by no flight of fantasy could the most euphemistic house agent describe them as desirable. Even after the war the majority lingered on amidst their sombre slag tips, for the principle adopted by the Council was not to rebuild but to build anew elsewhere and as the demand for housing always seemed to exceed the supply, the rate of demolition by no means equalled that of new building. The Council sowed its first crop of new houses on the remaining lands of the Abbey home farm much to the consternation and impotent fury of the neighbouring residents in that hitherto exclusive neighbourhood. The old farm itself, which still showed remnants of the secular buildings of Winterstoke Abbey, was demolished and the Abbey Cinema now overlooks its site. Whereas this Abbey Estate, as it was called, was simply an extension of the existing rectangular trellis pattern of streets, the next municipal enterprise, the Wendleside Estate which was begun in 1934, was of different form and could be called an

WINTERSTOKE

early example of a 'planned conurbation'. Its road system was laid out in the shape of a wheel, a central green and an outer ring road being linked by the spokes of a series of radial avenues. As all the semi-detached council houses which bordered this geometrical pattern were exactly alike, the effect produced by this new estate upon a stranger visiting it for the first time, particularly after dark, was bewildering in the extreme. It was not unlike a maze whose centre was its inner ring where a sense of direction was easily lost. It possessed a certain nightmare quality. For having penetrated to this centre from the Coltisham Road it was possible to imagine oneself perambulating for ever round the disc of trampled turf unable to find the way out. This estate was laid out on the lands of Upper Mill Farm between the Coltisham Road and the river. The farm itself was pulled down. Latterly it had been one of the few prosperous farms in the neighbourhood, growing market-garden produce on a large scale for sale in Winterstoke Market and to several greengrocers in the town.

The effect of the daily tide of buses and cars which ebbed and flowed between the centre of Winterstoke and its suburbs combined with the rapidly increasing volume of through traffic passing east and west along the High Street and north and south between Church Ambling and Lobstock was to create a major traffic problem, particularly at the point of intersection of these two main thoroughfares. It was to relieve congestion at this point that the statue of Henry Blenkinsop was removed to Wharf Square. Yet the problem remained. Long lines of buses, cars and lorries throbbed and fumed head to tail in a haze of blue vapour while a sorely-tried police force struggled to prevent the engine-driven torrent from becoming irrevocably dammed up. Traffic signals, roundabouts, parking prohibitions, speed restrictions and one-way traffic schemes, all were introduced to assist the police and to prevent confusion from becoming worse confounded. Roads were widened where possible and a new bridge of reinforced concrete was built over the Wendle at St. John's beside the old medieval bridge which

WINTERSTOKE

was referred to as a 'bottle-neck' and was showing signs of strain under the continuous burden. Yet all these expedients were to a great extent nullified by the persistently increasing volume of traffic. After one August Bank Holiday a correspondent of the *Winterstoke Sentinel* reported the spectacle of a motionless line of vehicles extending from the High Street traffic lights as far as the Wendle bridge. Finally, in 1933, the Ministry of Transport authorized the construction of the Winterstoke By-pass.

This new road with its dual carriageways described an arc round the south-eastern part of the town. From a junction with the Lobstock Road near the entrance to the Great Ketton Steelworks it burrowed under the Ketton curve of the old Great North-Western Railway, skirted the station marshalling yards, and crossed the railway and the river at Upper Mill to join the Coltisham Road at a large new roundabout by 'The Cedars' guest house. Traffic travelling from west to east was thus able to avoid the centre of the town altogether by turning right in the direction of Camp and Darley Bank before reaching St. John's Bridge, left into the Lobstock Road at the 'Woodcolliers' (now a palatial establishment in the Tudor style) and from thence on to the by-pass. It was of equal value to the Coltisham—Lobstock traffic.

The prompt reaction of Winterstoke Motors to this new situation showed that, like his father, Steve Foster was not a man who allowed the grass to grow under his feet. Through his father, who was now a leading figure in the affairs of the town, he received the news of the impending by-pass before it was generally known and promptly bought the moribund Cedars Guest House from its impoverished and unsuspecting owners. Steve's business friends chaffed him for having, as they put it, 'bought a pup', but he merely smiled enigmatically and refused to be drawn. Ridicule turned to admiration not untinged with envy for what was called the Foster luck when the Cedars blossomed forth as a smart new roadhouse restaurant fronted by an impressive rank of electric petrol pumps. Steve sunk a

WINTERSTOKE

concrete bathing pool on what had once been Sir Richard Blenkinsop's croquet lawn and the 'Knave of Hearts', as it was now called in red neon lit letters, soon became a serious rival of the Wendle Bridge Hotel as a place of resort for the younger generation of the smarter suburbs. Steve Foster was not the only one who, to use a current phrase, 'got in on the ground floor' when the by-pass was built. Fred Isaacs, the enterprising proprietor of a fish and chip saloon in Canal Street, sank all his savings in the purchase and reconstruction of the long-derelict Upper Mill. As 'the Olde Mill Café', better known as 'Fred's', the venture was an immediate success and became a favourite port of call for long-distance lorry drivers. Advertising undoubtedly helped, for Fred erected boards which announced in bold letters 'Stop! Good Pull-In 200 yards ahead. Café open day and night. Always something to eat'. His road-signs were only one of many examples of commercial enterprise which advised the motorist to: 'Stop at the Wendle Bridge Hotel', 'Drink Blenkinsop's Ales', 'Take your troubles to Winterstoke Motors', 'Make a date with your favourite Stars at the Abbey—we have the best programmes', 'Smoke Wensums, all the best people do', 'Ask for Finnemans—you can't go wrong', 'Bake better cakes with Wendle Valley Flour—My Mummy does', 'Don't suffer in silence, Kilapane cures that after-eating agony'.

The Abbey Cinema's boast to have the best programmes was, needless to say, hotly contested by the 'Moviedrome' in Wharf Square and by the palatial 'Seville' which reared its brick bulk on a commanding site near the Wendleside Estate. The latter lured patrons with boasts of its mighty electric organ whose console, looking like a cross between a telephone exchange and a gigantic typewriter, rose on a lift from the depths of the orchestra pit into a blaze of coloured lights when occasion demanded. But the pulling power of this novelty began to wane when the film found its mechanical voice and all three cinemas proclaimed that they were 'All Talking, All Singing'. The pace set by these three strident monsters proved too hot for the older places of

WINTERSTOKE

entertainment. The 'Winterstoke Palace' in Bridge Street soon gave up the struggle. Its exotic façade was replaced by the familiar frontage of a famous chain-store whose proprietors purchased the site for a very handsome sum. The old Theatre Royal put up a more stubborn resistance but found, as its houses grew thinner, that the legitimate drama was no match for the new and massive entertainment machine with its highly-organized publicity which created a world-wide cult of star worshippers. For a time the theatre management tried the experiment of alternating films and stage plays, but the house was unsuitable for the showing of films and the youthful fans of Winterstoke who were forced to occupy seats to the side of the screen disliked seeing their phantom heroes and heroines of Hollywood appear with their faces abnormally elongated. So the theatre then became a second-rate variety house, fighting the cinema with the only weapons left in its armoury: the sex appeal of the real-life 'leg show', the strip-tease act and the 'blue' joking comedian. In this way the once-proud Theatre Royal, cherishing the memories of past greatness only in the faded signed photographs on its foyer walls, was able to struggle on until the Winterstoke Blitz in 1941 when five hundred pounds of high explosive administered the *coup-de-grace*.

The cinemas were by no means the only attractions against which the old theatre struggled to compete. There was the new greyhound racing track on Wendleside beyond Blenkinsop's Brewery. There was the Winterstoke United football ground off Cemetery Road which drew its roaring crowds every Saturday afternoon from September to May. And like the all-electric suburban homes with their many gadgets, the new amenities, from petrol pumps, and neon signs to super-cinemas, called for power. Needless to say, the demand far exceeded the capacity of the original power station. That station had gone at the same time that the trams ceased running. Winterstoke was now 'on the Grid', to use a phrase intelligible enough to us though quite incomprehensible to our ancestors. On the site of the old a new Grid Station displayed all the most modern apparatus of power:

high-pressure water tube boilers automatically stoked by chain grates and fed from huge hoppers filled by conveyors; more conveyors to clear the ash pits; a phalanx of chimneys and concrete cooling-towers breathing steam like immense cauldrons; tall steel pylons horned with high tension insulators which were irradiated at night with stray current from their leashed lightning as with St. Elmo's fire; pylons which marched away over the slopes of Emberley and High Hanger to supply half Midshire with current. Here there was a concentration of horse-power far in excess of anything Winterstoke had known before and far more formidable and frightening for its very lack of apparent movement or dramatic effort. There was a new impersonal and inhuman quality about the smooth black shapes, gleaming but quite immobile, of the turbo-alternators which filled the power house with a sound like that of a gale of wind and yet betrayed no flicker of motion, stirred no current in the warm acrid-smelling air. Formidable, too, the long frieze of black control panels with their rows of staring dials and their mysterious tell-tale lights winking red, green and amber eyes. This was the new heart of Winterstoke, dominating the town less dramatically and obtrusively than the old industries of iron and steel had done but much more effectually as it pumped out its life blood of electric current. This power station symbolized, too, the still accelerating tempo of technical progress. That great crescendo which had begun with the first laboured breath of the Newcomen beam engine had now become the tempest of the turbine.

Chapter Fourteen

THE HISTORY of the Darley Bank Forge after the first world war affords a good illustration of the irreparable damage which that war inflicted on 'the workshop of the world'. When the Forge resumed its peacetime work of locomotive building it was found that while it had been preoccupied with armament manufacture some of its best customers among the overseas railways had been forced, either to place their orders in the United States or to develop their own locomotive building plants. Nevertheless the world was wide, there were four years of lee-way to be made up, and so for a time the works throbbed with life and energy. The Nasmyth hammers thundered as of old as they forged the heavy crank-axles, the long coupling and connecting rods. Great glowing plates of steel slid out of the mouths of furnaces between the die blocks of the hydraulic flanging presses to be moulded as easily as tin foil by the slow but irresistible power of the ascending rams into the throat plate or tube plate for another new boiler. Electric cranes moaned and rumbled to and fro high under the roof girders. Over the foundry the air shimmered in the fiery breath of the cupolas, and from the boiler shop sounded the deafening staccato bombardment of pneumatic riveting hammers. Through the high doors of the erecting shop there emerged, slowly and majestically in their sober birthday suits of shop grey, the fruits of all this fiery and tumultuous travail: long, low metre gauge engines for Mysore State with bulbous spark-arresting chimneys and enormous headlamps; squat little shunting tank engines destined for a life of industrious obscurity in some colliery yard; eight-coupled monsters bound for Buenos Aires, engines which would have to be dismantled again before they left the works because they were too large to travel 'dead' over English metals to their port of shipment. All

WINTERSTOKE

these made their first slow journeys up and down the mixed gauge test track attended by watchful fitters.

But by the end of 1925 it became apparent that the pace of production at Darley Bank was beginning to slacken. It was not only in the locomotive building trade that the backlog of the war years had been overtaken and the advantage of temporary shortages lost. A war-inflated industrial machine was beginning to satiate its peacetime market and after a brief boom the shadow of yet another slump lurked in the offing. It was over the coal pits of High Hanger and Ketton that the shadow first fell. As the great Ruhr coalfield got into its stride once again the English coal owners found they were being priced out of their European market and their pithead gears no longer spun so merrily. To meet the threat they called for a reduction in the wartime level of wages and longer working hours. But despite the fact that England had just had its first disastrous Labour administration, the coal owners did not reckon with the new power of organized labour which had been steadily growing for a hundred years. The miners replied with the slogan: 'Not a penny off the pay, not a minute on the day', and won the support of the newly established General Council of the Trades Union Congress. Negotiations between the Government and the union leaders having broken down, union after union declared overwhelmingly in favour of strike action and, to the accompaniment of the singing of 'The Red Flag' by their leaders, the strike was called.

Winterstoke had experienced strikes before but never one like this. On Monday, May 3, 1926, a strange stillness fell over the town. It seemed as brooding and ominous as the breathless lull which falls before a thunderstorm. Not since the first Newcomen engine had begun its laborious life at High Hanger pit nearly two hundred years before had Winterstoke known such a silence. The great machine had stopped. There was no electric power; not a tram or a bus was to be seen; there were no newspapers. Over the Central station and the marshalling yards hung the same uncanny silence; not an engine moved and the bright rails

WINTERSTOKE

tarnished in the morning dew. The pit-head gears stood motionless and the hubbub of the steelworks was stilled; smokeless chimneys stood forlorn as the trunks of dead trees in an air of unaccustomed clarity. Only the Darley Bank Forge, the Atlas Works and a few minor undertakings maintained a half-hearted activity, crippled by lack of materials and electric power, until the engineers joined the rest of the strikers on the eleventh of the month.

The great strike petered out without achieving its object although the miners continued the fight until the following November, but though it failed it was a demonstration, bewildering to many, of the power which the leaders of labour now commanded. By the labour supporters the failure of the strike was looked upon as a victory for the entrenched power of unscrupulous employers and financiers. For the 'true blues' it represented the well-merited defeat of a gigantic piece of national blackmail inspired by 'Red' agitators. Both were wrong. Each side laid the blame upon the other for evils which had been inherent in the industrial system from the outset and which made instability inevitable. Had the strikers won the day they would only have hastened the onset of a slump which no financial manipulation, no juggling with the currency, could prevent. It began in Wall Street in 1929 when the bodies of suicidal stock jobbers who jumped from their skyscraper offices spattered the New York pavements like over-ripe fruit, and the ripples of this financial crash spread rapidly across the world. At Great Ketton, at Darley Bank and in the pits, more and more men were 'stood off' while most of those who were luckier were soon working 'short time'. Only one furnace remained in blast at 'Ketton Bar'. Never before in working hours were there so many men to be seen in the streets of Winterstoke; aimless men with no means to kill the time that hung so heavy on their idle hands; men squatting on their doorsteps or leaning in listless groups against the walls of street-corner pubs they were too poor to patronize. They represented only a small detachment of England's army of

WINTERSTOKE

unwanted men which by the autumn of 1931 had reached a strength of nearly three millions.

It was in 1930 that Winterstoke experienced its heaviest blow. The Darley Bank Forge could not weather the crisis. The Company went into liquidation and under the watchful eye of a Receiver the orders already in progress were completed. Then, when the last new locomotive had been hauled away to the marshalling yards, the heavy gates closed and the silence of death fell over empty shops and idle machines. The brazen voice of the Darley Bank steam bull no longer roared its daily summons. On office doors and entrance gates wandering out-of-works read and re-read as though unable to believe their eyes the laconic obituary notice: 'Works Closed. All inquiries should be addressed to the Official Receiver', and the following address. At the Receiver's sale all the plant was sold, most of it for scrap, and when the machinery dealers had done their work the deserted shops looked even more empty and desolate. Practically no evidence of past activity remained except a giant hydraulic riveting machine which no one had considered worth the labour of removal, and the black moulding sand on the foundry floor. So the old works stood forlorn for twelve months until a banner headline in the *Winterstoke Sentinel* brought hope to the workless. 'NEW HOME FOR FOSTER CAR', it read, 'MR. ROBERT FOSTER BUYS DARLEY BANK WORKS; EXPANSION OF PRODUCTION.'

The Foster Car Company was a member of a young and virile industry which, while by no means unaffected by the slump, was able to withstand it better than its older neighbours. Nevertheless, the outlook before the Atlas Works had not looked any too rosy to Bob Foster and he had come to the conclusion that unless he staked everything on further expansion the Foster car would soon be driven off the market by more powerful competitors. A visit he had paid, along with other English car manufacturers, to the Ford plant at Trafford Park on the invitation of that Company, had convinced him that his future lay in applying the methods of mass production which the Americans had so successfully

WINTERSTOKE

developed. The old individual methods he was using at the Atlas Works could not hope to compete against such a system; he must either arm himself before his rivals or lose the battle. But there was no room for further expansion in Institute Road. Where else then? The answer was obvious —at Darley Bank.

The Leeds family would have been almost as bewildered as any laymen if they could have seen the ingenious and complex machines which now re-animated Darley Bank. The tools introduced during Darley Bank's first transformation under the ægis of Henry Blenkinsop were childish and simple toys compared to these batteries of bar automatics and automatic capstan lathes which performed unbelievable feats of mechanical legerdemain behind dark, smoking screens of cutting oil or in a white stream of sour-smelling suds. A fabulous cosmopolitan company of machines, German machines, Swiss machines, American machines from Milwaukee and Ohio, assembled to roar, to whine, to chatter and to moan in the mechanical bedlam of the new Darley Bank works. Humming centreless grinders spewed out gleaming gudgeon pins into waiting stillages; complicated milling machines and boring lathes machined the several faces of a casting simultaneously; with remorseless mechanical deliberation the spined heads of a multi-spindle drilling machine closed like an Iron Maiden upon a cylinder block and crankcase casting; towering presses shaped chassis members and sheet steel body shells. The old foundry was revived in highly mechanized form with moulding machines and conveyor fed core ovens. But there was no longer any forge at Darley Bank. The Foster Company bought in their forgings, mostly light stampings, from specialists and the old forge became a hardening shop filled with glowing muffle furnaces and steaming vats of lethal looking liquids. The tributary streams of overhead conveyors bore away finished components to the old locomotive erecting shop. Here they joined the main river of the assembly tracks on which, in the course of one short journey, a bare chassis became a near-finished motor car.

WINTERSTOKE

When all these machines at Darley Bank had got into their stride the new Foster 'Flying Fours' began to pour off the assembly lines almost as fast as the bolts that fell from the bar automatics. What matter if a few old die-hard customers thought that a thin false shell of chromium-plated steel was a poor substitute for the handsome German silver radiator of the older Foster, or complained of inferior road holding and steering qualities, inaccessibility and shoddy workmanship? What matter if the little high revving engines did wear themselves out in fifty thousand miles? This was the new age of mass production and its machines had come to stay. The best way to keep costly machines busy and avoid slumps was to produce an article with a short life. Judicious advertising and the introduction of new gadgets would soon educate the public to the habit of discarding and replacing their cars as often as their worn-out shoes. The Foster 'Flying Four' made a substantial contribution to the traffic jams in the streets of Winterstoke because it was 'cheap'. Judged by standards of value based on quality of workmanship and materials, however, the new 'Flying Four' was very dear indeed compared with its predecessor from the old Atlas Works. The public would have been astonished had they known how little each car actually cost the Foster Company in materials and labour and how much of their purchase money represented overhead expenses, plant maintenance and depreciation, advertising, selling commission, and the steadily growing burden of the unproductive staff in the great new office block.

The continued success and expansion of the Foster Car Company during the 1930's did much to improve the employment position in Winterstoke. By a process of amalgamation with other less successful and weaker concerns, Bob Foster (Sir Robert Foster in 1937, first Baron Emberley in 1940) became the head of a vast commercial concern owning several plants in various parts of the Midlands, each as large as that at Darley Bank. Between these different factories production became highly specialized. Thus the Darley Bank factory ultimately became responsible for manufactur-

WINTERSTOKE

ing all the engines for the group, while car assembly was concentrated in another plant at Earlspool.

The natural tendency of ruthless commercial competition towards monopoly which first became apparent in the great railway age was a process which the widespread introduction of mass production methods greatly intensified. Only the most powerful of business organizations could afford the capital outlay which the new machinery involved and their weaker competitors found themselves faced with the choice between amalgamation and extinction. So rapid was this process in the motor industry that whereas in the nineteen-twenties there had been over a hundred firms in the trade, by 1939 six organizations were responsible for ninety per cent of the output of English cars. The same process was going on elsewhere though less obtrusively. Although the Great Ketton Steel Company retained a nominal identity, in fact, after the slump, it became a subsidiary of the Universal Steel Corporation. By the same token many of the small manufacturers in the town went out of business during the depression, and from the flux of closure and amalgamation there eventually emerged two new factories on the Winterstoke by-pass: The United Pressed Steel Company (known in the town as the 'U.P.S.') and Allied Iron Founders Limited. These were joined in 1937 by a new flotation of the Universal Steel Corporation known as Special Stress Alloys Limited, which worked in close association with Great Ketton. These new shops of brick and asbestos roofing with their rows of barrel-shaped ventilators were largely hidden from the by-pass by office blocks whose angular neon-lit façades defied architectural description. That there was a marked affinity between them and the architecture of the Seville Cinema was obvious. Their managements would probably have described them, if asked, as 'modern' or 'functional', though precisely what function their curious embellishments and the strange 'vertical features' which reared above their entrances performed it was hard to say.

A characteristic of all Winterstoke's industries, new and

WINTERSTOKE

old, in the nineteen-thirties was their impersonality. The complexity of their machinery was matched by a human organization which was equally complex. At the time that the Darley Bank Forge was reorganized by Henry Blenkinsop the elaborate hierarchy of control which he set up had seemed impersonal enough after the old régime of the Leeds family. But, at least, the whole pyramid from Henry downwards had still been based on Winterstoke. Henry might exist upon a height so exalted that many of his employees would never see him, but he was still known to be there, and was still the ultimate 'gaffer'. But now, in the era of mass production and monopoly, personal responsibility was so diffused, so lost in the financial and material ramifications of nation-wide organizations that, with the sole exception of the Foster Car Company, there was no longer any enthroned industrial deity in Winterstoke. The commercial destinies of the town were now determined by decisions reached in remote offices, offices in Sheffield, in Birmingham or in London's Victoria Street or Milbank. In Winterstoke there were only managements who were as much at the mercy of such decisions as the labourers who swept the factory floors. Commercial considerations of international scope quite beyond the ken of anybody on the spot might cause the Universal Steel Corporation to close down their Great Ketton steel plant with little regard for, or knowledge of, the local consequences of such a decision. Indeed at one time such a closure was actually contemplated. As individual industries disappeared one by one or became merged in huge and amorphous monopolies, the old 'Captains of Industry' disappeared also. Thus Robert Foster, first Baron Emberley, was the last in the line of great men who, by their enterprise, their immense energy and their boundless material ambition, rose from the ranks of their fellows to shape the course of this history of Winterstoke for good or for evil. Had their place been taken by better and wiser men less obsessed by ambition and the will to power we should have no cause to regret their passing. But an age which was learning, in the name of democracy, to disparage any mark of indi-

WINTERSTOKE

vidual greatness, good or bad, merely exchanged the devil for the deep blue sea of the Board, the Commission, the Committee and the Government department. This no less materialistic world was filled by men whose names find no place in this history; smaller men, place seekers, time servers and jealous little demagogues angling for the pomps and the heady vanities of power and authority but scrupulously avoiding the risks of power: its lonely insecurity and the great responsibility of individual decision.

This passing of commercial control away from Winterstoke was inevitably accompanied by a similar decline in the autonomy of local government. When a town is no longer in command of its commercial destinies, then every aspect of its local administration must become increasingly subordinated to centralized control or chaos may result. Hence the fact that civil servants representing the Ministry of this or the Ministry of that began to usurp the functions hitherto exercised by locally appointed men in the large new office block in Wharf Square.

Until 1930 industry had continued to observe the river boundary line by keeping itself to the south of the town, and Blenkinsop's Brewery had remained the sole interloper on the north bank. But, far below ground and unknown to most of the inhabitants of north Winterstoke, the miners of 'Ketton Deep' had tunnelled their way under the river like industrious moles and were working beneath their feet. It caused no little consternation amongst the inhabitants of the neat semi-detached villas along the north side of the Coltisham Road when these blackened troglodites from the hinterland of Ketton broke surface a mere quarter-mile away from the boundary of their back gardens. What had happened was this. In view of the need for economy in a struggling coal industry, the Ketton Company decided that the cost of underground haulage from such distant coal faces to the 'pit eye' at Ketton had become too great. So having acquired the necessary land they proceeded to sink a new shaft which became known as Emberley Heath Pit and to build from it a short mineral branch railway which crossed over the

WINTERSTOKE

Coltisham Road and joined the main line in a fan of new sidings near Summersend Junction. If Thomas Winter had not been forced, shortly before his death in 1925, to sell Low Emberley Farm, whose lands the new pit occupied, he might have resisted this intrusion although it is doubtful whether the impoverished lord of a diminishing manor could have successfully withstood the might of Great Ketton. The new owner of Low Emberley whose most profitable crop was the Coltisham Road villas, accepted with alacrity the handsome sum which the Steel Company offered for his farm. There is little room for regrets when the shoe pinches, and the place was worth next to nothing as a farm. No one but a sentimental fool would put any money into farming in 1930. So the spoil buckets from Emberley Heath Pit swung along on their overhead cables over the green fields to build new black mountains of waste, and the inhabitants of Coltisham Road soon enjoyed a similar landscape to that which their neighbours at Camp and Hanger Lane had for so many generations surveyed.

The society created by industrialism could be likened to an engine whose speed cannot be governed. Notwithstanding the feverish efforts of philosophers, politicians and economists to devise some more reliable method of control, periodically its speed rises to a pitch where catastrophic disintegration becomes inevitable. So far no mechanic has seriously suggested that this may be due to any fundamental error in the design of the whole machine; trouble with the governor is the invariable diagnosis for its every defect. So the engine is repaired and set running again and another cycle of acceleration and explosion begins. As at each rebuilding the engine is capable of running at higher revolutions, disintegration when it comes is the more disastrous. In the late 'thirties it became increasingly obvious even to the most optimistic that such another explosive breakdown was imminent. The Munich crisis of 1938 made it clear that the outbreak of a second European war was only a question of time and a phase of inertia was succeeded by one of pessimistic energy. Air-raid shelters were dug in

WINTERSTOKE

Winterstoke Park, and in every square, open space or street of sufficient width surface shelters and 'static water' tanks began to appear. In more and more gardens and backyards family shelters were to be seen, pathetic answers to the threatened terror from the skies. The Air Ministry requisitioned High Emberley Farm. A fleet of roaring bulldozers and graders swept away trees, hedgerows and buildings to make the prairie-like desolation of runways, camouflaged hangars and Nissen huts which constituted His Majesty's Royal Air Force Station, High Emberley. The Foster Car Company built what was called a 'shadow factory' at Darley Bank, and those who affected to be 'in the know' began to spread incredible rumours of great underground machine-shops quarried out of the heart of High Hanger Hill. A large new factory quite unlike its neighbours was built with remarkable speed near the eastern end of the by-pass. Covered with black and green camouflage paint its long, low single-storeyed buildings covered all the ground between the road and the railway. It did not advertise itself. Only an unpretentious bronze plate beside the office entrance announced that it was: 'Pre-fabricated and Hydraulic Aircraft Components (1938) Ltd.' Finally, in the following year another new factory of similar character appeared which called itself 'The Electronics Development Corporation, Ltd., Winterstoke Division.' Even among those who worked in these new by-pass factories, there were very few who knew the functions of the mysterious and complicated looking gadgets which they produced. Lorries hustled them away, carefully packed, to unknown destinations.

The declaration of war in September 1939 was marked by none of the scenes of jingoistic enthusiasm and excitement which had marked the previous declaration of August 1914. The new generation in Winterstoke knew better. Some found themselves anxiously scanning the skies, half-expecting that swift annihilation by aerial bombardment which the Jeremiahs had prophesied. Others were mainly concerned to get their children evacuated to 'safe areas' as quickly as possible. Long trainloads of 'evacuees' pulled out from the

WINTERSTOKE

Central Station, and when the children of Camp, Hanger Lane and Ketton arrived in the 'reception areas' their hosts were surprised and shocked to discover that England still had slums. They had hitherto associated slums with the England of Charles Dickens and were appalled by these verminous little creatures with the domestic habits of animals that had never been house-trained.

After all this foreboding and anxious preparation the 'phoney war' which lasted through the long hard winter and into the belated spring was an anti-climax, a wearisome prolongation of nervous tension. Then came the fall of France and the threat of invasion which brought the hastily constructed road blocks, the concrete blockhouses, the removal of signposts and the recruitment of the L.D.V. In September the first 'blitz' was launched on London; Winterstoke flew a circle of silver barrage balloons and at nightfall the bombers, heavy laden with their deadly freight, roared up from High Emberley in increasing strength on their missions of retaliation. During all this time Winterstoke lay every night expectant and silent under the dark apprehensive blanket of the black-out—but nothing happened. It was not until a night of full moon in March, a 'bombers' moon' they called it now, that Winterstoke heroically received its long dreaded 'baptism of fire'. It was the town's first experience of the 'total warfare' of industrial society since the Zeppelin raid of twenty-five years before. But how great the progress in the technique of destruction since then! The warning sirens had sounded many times before, but this time, as their wailing died away the whole sky, it seemed, began to pulse with the throbbing of high-flying aircraft. From the encircling hills of High Hanger, Summersend and Emberley, searchlight beams made a pyramid of light overhead and then suddenly the whole horizon seemed to become alight and alive with flashing fire as the deafening barrage of Bofors and naval guns opened up. The first wave of aircraft dropped a shower of well-directed incendiaries which, by an unlucky chance, set fire to the gasworks. Along this bright flare-path the following waves flew in to drop their loads of high ex-

WINTERSTOKE

plosive. The first bomb to fall was short of the target area. It scored a direct hit on 'Highways', the large house which Robert Foster had built for himself near the Winterstoke Golf Course, and the first Baron Emberley perished with all his family. By one of those ironical freaks which often occurred in the 'blitz', the last bomb of this stick fell in the centre of Wharf Square and toppled Henry Blenkinsop from his pedestal. Next morning his headless trunk was found half buried in a deep crater surrounded by fragments of glazed earthenware and twisted pipes which represented all that remained of the public lavatories. So a single bomb aimer, unknowing and unknown, put an end to the last of Winterstoke's great men.

The damage caused to the town by its one great air raid of the war was so haphazard, so irrational and purposeless that a visitor from some more rational age before man's conquest of the air would have found himself quite at a loss to account for it. Of all the legitimate targets for attack, only the Great Ketton Steel Works and the railway yards, neither of which were able to black-out their activities completely, suffered any substantial damage. The authorities congratulated themselves on the miraculous escape of Winterstoke's 'key industries' and her power station. That St. Cenodoc's Church was a roofless shell, the Theatre Royal destroyed and hundreds of homes either seriously damaged or reduced to rubble with great loss of life was deeply regrettable but of less account. The homes of the machines were safe; in this war of machines, that was of paramount importance.

The majority of the bombs had not fallen so very wide of the mark, for it was the quarters of the town nearest the mines and factories, Camp, Hanger Lane, Darley Bank and Ketton which were the hardest hit. The long overdue demolition which the Town Council had failed to accomplish had now been carried out in one night with remarkable efficiency. Had it not been for the death roll involved, this drastic surgery could scarcely have provided any cause for regret. Unfortunately, however, it cannot be said that the new rows of 'Pre-fabs' represented much of an improvement upon their predecessors. Admittedly they were described as temporary housing and they did, in the shortest possible time, provide shelter for the bombed-out families. But to-day these little white metal boxes, rather bleared now with grime, still terrace the slopes of the hills. For all their hideous squalor, at least the old courts suggested a kind of crude and violent life and a certain permanence. In fact they had proved all too permanent until war destroyed them. But the new 'pre-fabs' suggested neither life nor permanence. Resembling some ephemeral shanty town growing, mushroom-like, about a new oil well or a lucky gold strike; further removed from any conception of architecture or craftsmanship than the crude thatched huts of the railway navvies, these machine-made dormitories with their underground bolt-holes represented a civilization that was nearing the end of its tether.

In the first world war it was not until the submarine blockade began that the vulnerability of industrial England was realized. In 1939 the additional and far more deadly menace of far-ranging enemy bombers to a country dependent on supplies from overseas markets for over sixty per cent of its food was recognized from the moment that war was declared. Once again the fool's paradise of the industrial economist was rudely shattered and England was forced to look to her land as a source of life instead of as a blank space on the map waiting to be scribbled upon by the industrialist, the road maker, the town planner or the builder. So William Winter of Emberley found himself courted by Government, all unmindful in their panic anxiety of their predecessor's broken faith, just as his father had been twenty-five years before. A family who had obstinately refused tempting offers from speculative builders and who were regarded in Winterstoke as eccentrics, and obstructive, if not selfish, reactionaries, now emerged yet again into the limelight from their moated stronghold. Once more, as in 1917, the word went out to speed the plough, but this time there was a significant difference; the plough could no longer

WINTERSTOKE

speed so far as it had done before. Low Emberley Farm had been lost to the Universal Steel Corporation and Emberley Hill to the Air Ministry. Everywhere in the Wendle valley the green had been in full retreat since 1917 and fields which had then grown corn had been lost beyond any recall. In this respect the age of the internal combustion engine had been far more swiftly and extensively destructive than the whole century long age of steam. No crops would ever grow again on the rich market garden lands of Upper Mill or on the broad acres of the Abbey Home Farm. Along the by-pass with its sprawling factories, along the old main roads, everywhere the acid of an urban civilization had eaten its corrosive way into the green. Even those parts of Summersend and High Hanger Hills which had not been scarred past redemption by industry had been lost to agriculture forever. They now wore the dark, dense fleece of Forestry Commission conifer plantations and, when the time came to clear-fell them for pit props or pulp, their barren, acid soils would quickly leach away down the steep slopes to leave insufficient fertility to nourish even the hardiest of sheep. These ravished lands of the Wendle valley formed only a small part of the total of three and a half million acres which had been lost to agriculture in England and Wales since 1891. Yet there were now fourteen million more mouths to be fed. Because even fewer men could be spared to till the land than in the first world war, machinery invaded the fields upon a scale never before seen in England. More powerful tractors, multi-furrow ploughs, gyro tillers, combine drills, combine harvesting machines as large as cruiser tanks, all lumbered into the fields with one object—to cash in as speedily as possible upon the fertility which the fields had stored up during their years of neglect.

Whether William Winter, with generations of experience behind him, really approved of this new expediency farming it is impossible to say. For if he did not he had no option but to keep his thoughts to himself. His cropping policy was dictated by the Midshire War Agricultural Executive Committee, and the machines which roared over his land were

WINTERSTOKE

theirs. Perhaps, too, the knowledge that he was to be the last Winter of Emberley made him lose heart. His only son, Flight-Sergeant Hugh Winter, was rear gunner in one of the Wellingtons which roared away into the dusk one evening from High Emberley and never returned.

One day in 1944 in the test-house of Foster Motors (Aircraft Division) at Darley Bank three men gazed anxiously and intently, now through the observation window of a sound-proofed testing bay, now back to the dials on the control panel before them. Both the engine in the bay and its test rig looked strange. This was not one of the familiar Peregrine engines with its two inclined banks of six cylinders which the factory had turned out by the thousand during the war years. Here were none of the familiar fittings: carburettor and supercharger, intercooler and manifolds, the complicated ignition system and its nest of armoured high-tension leads. This engine was totally different in form. It could be said that it resembled an octopus or the head of a harpoon, a formidable-looking blunt head of curving pipes on a barrel-shaped body tapering away to a single circular orifice. The soundproof walls which had effectually subdued the roar of the Peregrine as it delivered its two thousand horse-power to dynamometer or wind tunnel propeller could scarcely contend with the howling tornado of sound which tore from this engine. It was not connected to any propeller or dynamometer; its only visible betrayal of power and motion was the tongue of flame that issued from its tapering tail. Yet the roar from the jet was so overwhelming and the scream of the compressor so excruciatingly intense and high pitched that the impression conveyed was one of a power and velocity too prodigious for any metals to withstand. This was the prototype Foster 'Wendle' jet engine undergoing its first full-power test. Just as the turbine had superseded the old steam reciprocating engine forty years before, so now the Peregrine piston engine would soon be obsolete. The pace of industrial revolution was still accelerating.

While the engineers of Foster Motors had been developing their jet engine at Darley Bank, work of even greater moment

WINTERSTOKE

was going on along the by-pass within the walls of that mysterious newcomer to Winterstoke, the Electronics Development Corporation. This highly secretive activity could be called a mystery within a mystery. The word Electronics was mysterious enough for most people whose only knowledge of this highly specialized science was that it had something to do with the Radar Station whose masts now encircled the long barrow on the crown of Summersend Hill. But this arcane research had nothing to do with electronics. That was merely a cloak of convenient obscurity. The work was finally carried to a successful conclusion in America, and it was just as well that Winterstoke did not experience its first-fruits. Indeed it was not for some time afterwards that the town learnt that it had unwittingly played its part in the successful obliteration of two cities by the power of atomic fission which marked the end of the second world war. Like the creaking Newcomen pump and the stuttering engine of the Foster Brothers' first horseless carriage, the explosions which destroyed Hiroshima and Nagasaki represented only the first tentative and puny stirrings of a new power. The 'atomic age' had dawned, the third, and in all probability the last, phase of the industrial revolution.

Chapter Fifteen

WE ARE NEARING the end of a long journey. Why should we hesitate upon the threshold of this, our own Atomic Age? Despite the war and the drastic rationing of food the great majority of the poor of Winterstoke are better off materially than they have ever been before. Thanks to the development of medical science they enjoy better health and a longer expectation of life. They have had the benefit of education, they work much shorter hours, are better clothed and better fed. They have electric light, gas, sanitation and rapid transport. They have their amusements: the cinema, the wireless and now television, the popular press, the greyhound track, the Saturday football match and the Pools. Unemployment is almost non-existent. Why should we not step back with relief from the past into such a present? Is it only the threat of the atomic bomb and the 'cold war' that makes us shrink from the new Winterstoke and look back with nostalgia down the road we have followed to a past that can never come again? No, it is not. The question is more difficult to answer. Something has died in this post-war Winterstoke that was alive even during the terrible years of the early nineteenth century, something which was intangible and yet seemed indestructible, something which awoke during the Winterstoke Blitz but now seems to have disappeared. It is as though the town had lost its soul. At Darley Bank and Ketton and along the by-pass the factories still hum, the pit wheels spin, traffic roars through the town and the long expresses slide into the central station; people crowd pavements, chain stores and market more densely than they ever did before. Yet somehow all this familiar activity seems to have become suddenly aimless and meaningless, like the automatic muscular con-

WINTERSTOKE

tractions in the body of a chicken after its head has been struck off. Life goes on in Winterstoke, but it seems a life without belief, without purpose either for good or evil, a life without faith in itself or hope for the future. It is not as though the industrial revolution has come to a standstill in the town by any means. There is a roar of jet engines on test from Darley Bank and the new machines from High Emberley Field scream overhead at the speed of sound. There is also a new Atomic Research Station in the fields below Summersend Hill to the east of the by-pass; a new village of impermanent-looking houses surrounding mysterious buildings of steel and concrete. The whole area is enclosed like a prison camp by a high ring-fence of barbed wire patrolled by security police. But who in Winterstoke was responsible for these new developments and with what object? Whose personal ambition or whose dream for the future of mankind do they represent? What successor to the Hanmers, the Leeds, the Blenkinsops and the Fosters, has now come forward to stand or fall by the success or failure of these new enterprises? The questions echo round an empty room. Nobody answers. Are they then a communal achievement, the creation of the people of Winterstoke, the expression of their corporate will? Once more there is no answer. It is as though the industrial revolution had acquired a momentum of its own, 'The Sorcerer's Apprentice' who was clever enough to set the genie to work now finds he knows no counter charm.

We have seen many changes pass over the face of Winterstoke. Once it was very fair. Then it became black, terrible and pitiless as Lucifer in smoke and furnace flame; yet always it has worn a human face. What makes the face of atomic Winterstoke so fearful is that it appears no longer human. It is neither beautiful nor ugly, neither good nor evil because the power to distinguish the one from the other has been lost. Like a death mask its steel and concrete face is expressionless. Yet power there must be somewhere or the wheels would run down. We have seen that power pass from family to family and then disperse in huge hydra-headed

WINTERSTOKE

industrial monopolies. Where now is the seat of power to be found? By one of those strange ironies of history it has come to rest in the corner of Winterstoke Park on the very spot where once the cloisters of the great Cistercian abbey stood. A warren of single-storeyed and flat-roofed buildings, it resembles the factory of the Electronics Development Corporation on the by-pass or the R.A.F. buildings at High Emberley. But, oddly enough, its interior is not unlike a cloister with its long, echoing corridors. True, there is much traffic upon them: Government messengers tramping to and fro with inter-departmental minutes and memos; officials with bulging brief cases; pert typists with armfuls of tape-tied files or carrying interminable cups of tea. Yet no laymen trespassing in the old monastic cloister could look more harassed or apprehensive than those members of the public who stray into these corridors to seek audience, chivied from department to department or waiting submissively at closed doors. Apart from their heat and the smell of stale tobacco, these offices, with their ink-stained trestle tables, wire letter-baskets, metal filing cabinets and hard chairs are as austere as that narrow stone cell in which the good Ambrosius wrote his *Chronicles* six hundred years ago.

These are the offices of the new Welfare State. Here preside the officials of the various Ministries whose task it is to regulate the life and work of the townspeople of Winterstoke in sickness or in health, for richer or poorer, in joy or in sorrow from the cradle to the grave. They have pitched their mansion here because the pre-war local government office block in Wharf Square was damaged in the blitz and was in any case far too small to house them all. Moreover, this encampment in Winterstoke Park only houses the elite corps of the great army of officials which a new régime has brought to Winterstoke.

By the consistent return of a Labour Member to Parliament ever since the election of 1922, the majority of the inhabitants of Winterstoke proclaimed their belief in the Socialist theory. Through the long years of poverty and grinding monotony in the squalor and unrelieved ugliness

WINTERSTOKE

of the back streets, in the darkness of the mine, in the roar of the machine-shop or in the heat of the furnace; through strike and lock-out and unemployment, they held fast to their faith in the Socialist State. For many of them it became a religion, promising deliverance from all the evils, the hardships and injustices of an inhuman system. How much braver and brighter this new doctrine, this splendid crusade for which all could fight, than the old religion of superstition which had advised them to be content with their lot and read their Bibles on the seventh day!

It was not until after the second world war when they secured an overwhelming majority in Parliament that the forces of labour at last had their opportunity to translate theory into practice. Two circumstances made their task easier. First, the demands of the new 'total war' had already vastly extended the powers of the State over industry and transport, over local government and over the lives of all its citizens. Only by such imitative methods had it been possible to counter the attack of totalitarian Germany. Secondly, just as Marx had forecast, a competitive industry had proceeded so far along the road to monopoly that it was ripe for plucking. For example, it would have been a difficult problem to nationalize the iron industry in the days of the Leeds family. In the case of an industry represented only by a few huge concerns such as the Universal Steel Corporation it became a relatively simple matter. 'Private enterprise' had come like a sheep to the slaughter; the transition was easy, so easy, in fact, that for a while it was a case of 'business as usual' in Winterstoke. There was little to indicate to the workers that the long-awaited Utopia was now at last in the making and that, to paraphrase the words of one of their spokesmen, 'they were the masters now'. They became the owners of the pits of Camp, High Hanger, Ketton Deep and Emberley Heath, of the London & North Midland Railway, of the Gas, Light & Coke Company, the Midshire Power Supply Company, and the Winterstoke General Hospital, yet it was strangely difficult to feel exactly proprietorial about them.

WINTERSTOKE

Soon, however, the new régime began to make itself evident in Winterstoke. 'Highways', Robert Foster's bomb-damaged house on Emberley Hill, was thoroughly reconditioned, enlarged and its dilapidated gardens restored to order. It was then reopened as the area headquarters of the National Coal Board. A block of bombed shops on Wharf Square was similarly rebuilt as regional offices for the Gas and Electricity Undertakings. The big 'Countess' class Pacifics which hauled the crack expresses of the London & North Midland Railway appeared, for a time, in a new livery of bright blue with a strange insignia on cab-sheets and tender sides. The L. & N.M.R. had now officially become the North Midland Region, and gradually the individuality of the old Company began to disappear. The people of Winterstoke had already heard over the wireless and read in the press what immense benefits the nationalization of transport would bring so soon as the system began to operate for the public good instead of for private profit. All forms of transport could now be fully utilized, while to ensure that the public had their say in this new and truly democratic organization, Users Consultative Committees would be set up. It therefore came as a surprise to many when the first important action of the new organization in Winterstoke was to close down the Summersend branch line. There were vigorous protests in the *Winterstoke Sentinel*. An aggrieved resident of Summersend wrote to the paper and explained precisely what a journey from Summersend to London with heavy luggage now involved. He pointed out that the Midshire bus, now the only link between Summersend and Winterstoke, had refused to handle his luggage. As a result he had been forced to hire a car and had missed his main line train. But such protests were vain. As well might Canute bid the tide recede. The private monopolies had been dictatorial enough, but it became increasingly apparent that these new State monopolies were virtually unassailable. As a last resort, an injured customer of one of the old public companies could always write to his M.P. and have the matter ventilated in the Commons. But now

WINTERSTOKE

there was no such redress. The responsible Minister would smoothly reply that he was not empowered to deal with questions affecting the day to day administration of the nationalized undertakings. As for the Consultative Committees, no one in Winterstoke seemed able to discover much about these bodies or how or where they functioned. Certainly no aggrieved local customer was ever invited to join one. He had to remain content with the practised evasions of some public relations officer.

If the new nationalized industries were a law unto themselves, how much more so were the officials in Winterstoke Park, those 'obedient servants' as they continued to sign themselves. For under their delegated powers they could not only make their own laws in the form of Ministerial Orders but, through committee and tribunal, act as judges in their own causes, a state of affairs which set at nought the ancient Common Laws of England. Yet not one of them could be held personally responsible for the consequences of his actions. The machinery of power was much too democratic, too complex and highly organized for that. None of these officials ever stated anything himself; he was always 'directed to state'; there was always a 'higher level' to which responsibility could be passed. No wonder the face of Winterstoke became blank and expressionless. No wonder freedom and initiative in the town was slowly but surely destroyed as its inhabitants became form-filling suppliants whose right to live depended on a rubber stamp.

The workers in the new national monopolies were told that they were now public servants working for the good of the community instead of being exploited by greedy capitalists. Yet somehow this fact remained singularly abstract and uninspiring. It was difficult to distinguish this new freedom from the old exploitation. The work in mine or machine shop became no less arduous or monotonous. Not only was there no 'gaffer', there was now no management either; only a growing army of officials harassed by mysterious and unknown 'higher levels': Area Boards, Purchasing, Finance, and Co-ordinating Committees to which decisions must be referred or requests made on the appropriate form in sextuplicate. It began to occur to some that the bureaucrat could become as heavy an incubus as the hated capitalist. For the greatest disillusionment of all was that the Socialist State did not appear to be a promised land overflowing with milk and honey after all. Their leaders had broken open the capitalist's till and seized that miser's hoard but where was the working man's long promised share? What had become of it? Why did not that obstinate gap between wages and prices now close? Prices should fall and wages increase now that a privileged class could no longer claim their pound of flesh. Yet instead the gap yawned as wide as ever and, instead of falling, the price of coal, of gas, electricity and transport rose rapidly. So did the cost of food. The workers of Winterstoke found themselves waging the same old battle for higher wages against their own leaders.

The sorry truth may have dawned on some that the sinister figure of the Capitalist was a mere turnip ghost and that the reason for the gap between wages and prices must lie much deeper, so deep that it called the whole industrial system in question. In truth, the effect of the revolution which caused Winterstoke to grow from a small, self-sufficient, regional community into a great town, was to create an ever wider gulf between the producer and the consumer. In that gulf there stood, not a mere clique of capitalist exploiters, but an enormous and ever-growing army of unproductive labour: chains of buyers and sellers and carriers, swollen offices filled with administrators, salesmen, planners, buyers, progress men, production experts, personnel managers and welfare workers, clerks and typists, each one adding his or her quota to the price of an article whose real value remains as it always was and ever will be the 'just price': the cost of the labour and the materials that have gone to its making. This was the bitter lesson which Winterstoke began to learn as it not only paid more instead of less for its goods and services but staggered under a weight of taxation so heavy that it destroyed all incentive. This was the price of the Welfare State, the pound of flesh demanded, not by the old

WINTERSTOKE

enemy but by those obedient servants in Winterstoke Park.

There is no neat conclusion to this story of Winterstoke, no tidy tying of its many stranded threads. The story goes on as these words are written into a future that we can neither follow nor forecast. We may visit its long past in imagination, hearing again the shrill scream of the peacocks on Richard Hanmer's lawn or the music of the virginals, the churning of the mill wheel, the thud of Alfred Darley's first tilt hammer. We can watch the swaying beam of the High Hanger Newcomen, see the glare of Bedlam Furnace, ride with Brindley through the woods of Deepforest or on the footplate of *Typhoon* as she hauls the first train down the valley. We can walk through those splendid rooms of the Earls of Winterstoke or through the thunderous forge at Darley Bank. Thus far imagination will carry us, but not into the future; that is hidden.

But it would be a mistake to suppose that the prospect before the town is necessarily dark. We should not be misled into despair by the blank expressionless face which it now wears; by the bewilderment and the lack of purpose; by the loss of freedom and initiative and the weight of frustration and apathy which that loss has bred. Appearances are always deceptive. To despair would be to lose faith in life itself with its eternal capacity for regeneration and renewal. For however forbidding and inscrutable the face of Winterstoke may appear, beneath that exterior there are thousands of individual human souls, each with a capacity for good as well as for evil. If another war were to come they would display the same heroism and self-sacrifice as they did in the last. Such a life current may be woefully misdirected and abused, but no tyranny of industrialist, bureaucrat or machine can ever altogether prevail against it. Though seemingly weak it can overthrow tyranny as a green shoot will lift and crack a paving slab. There is doubt and uncertainty now because both versions of the materialistic philosophy have been tried and found wanting, the second threatening a form of tyranny worse than the first. But nature abhors a vacuum, and angels are as likely

WINTERSTOKE

to fill this void as devils. What is needed is a religious faith by which alone the one species can be distinguished from the other. Modern materialistic philosophers have tried to paint life in Winterstoke a uniform dirty grey and have succeeded in creating a very fair semblance of their vision. In medieval Winterstoke they had a much more realistic conception of that life as a continual struggle between black and white, between the world of men and the natural world of God.

There are so many different strands in the complex pattern of the Winterstoke of 1953, some promising good, others evil, that we cannot tell what the outcome will be. The offices in Winterstoke Park are still the seat of power though they are not quite so thickly populated with officials as they were. The land has not been forsaken as it was after the previous world war. The fields of the Wendle Valley are still under the plough, for there will be little more 'cheap' food from overseas. Despite the cries of 'more exports' that pipe-dream of the workshop of the world has dissolved for ever. The world has other workshops now, each with the same problem of a swollen population clamouring for a higher standard of living. One threat that Winterstoke will certainly face before many years have passed will be that of starvation, but out of that suffering may come good: the restoration of those broken links between the town and the country; the return of man to the land. But as yet this danger is not fully recognized and good land is still being squandered.

Another more immediate and terrible threat comes from that final apotheosis of scientific progress under Summersend Hill; that sinister wired enclosure where the work of the Summersend Atomic Research Establishment goes forward. Here the old human pride which once flared in Bedlam Furnace rides on towards its ultimate and most deadly fall. Yet even this has been countered by the return of an even older humility. For in one respect the wheel has already come full circle. As we turn our backs upon the town, ascend Emberley Hill for the last time and pass the tall elms which screen the Old Hall, so we may hear, very

WINTERSTOKE

faintly, the ancient music of Gregorian chant, elemental and timeless as the surge of the sea, as monks sing their office. For William Winter has bequeathed his hall to the church. After four hundred years the Cistercians have come back to Winterstoke and confront another wilderness.

Chronology

Date		Page
1072?	Emberley Castle built by Hugh Fitzwinter	11
1085?	Chapel built by Hugh Fitzwinter on site of first church of St. Cenodoc	11–12
1132	William Fitzwinter grants lands to Benedictines of Citeaux; Winterstoke Abbey founded	12
1133–	River Wendle embanked	13–15
1210?	St. John's Bridge constructed	15
1348–9	The Black Death	20–21
1385?	Robert Fitzwinter builds Emberley Hall on site of Norman Castle	29
1433–67	Luttrell tower and new Lodging built by Abbot Thomas Luttrell	22–23
1510?	First 'water bloomery' built on the Wendle	25–26
1539	Dissolution of Winterstoke Abbey	27–28
1542–	Abbey lands granted to Richard Hanmer, first Earl of Winterstoke. Abbey church destroyed. Abbots' Lodging rebuilt as Winterstoke Place	30–32
1548 (*circa*)	Certain Common lands enclosed	35–36
1550–1600	Ironworks concentrated in Lob Valley	39, 42–47
1585	First coal pit sunk at High Hanger	42
1594	First charcoal blast furnace built at Darley Bank	43
1636	First water powered slitting mill at Darley Bank	51–52
1642–9	Civil War: St. John's Bridge damaged, ironworks raided and Emberley Hall sacked	52–54
1682–4	Winterstoke Place rebuilt by Henry Hanmer, fourth Earl	79–80
1708	Darley Bank Company founded by Josiah Leeds I	57
1710	Lower Wendle Navigation Company incorporated	61

CHRONOLOGY

Date		Page
1711	First pound locks built on River Wendle	61–62
1712	'Bedlam' Furnace blown in on coke fuel	65–66
	(First Newcomen engine built near Dudley)	68
1715	Darley Bank Company takes over High Hanger pits	72
1720	Second forge and slitting mill built at Darley Bank	66
1722	First Newcomen cylinder cast at Darley Bank	67–68
1730	Wooden wagonways built from High Hanger to Darley Bank	72–73
1733	(Savery's steam engine Patent lapses)	69, 70
1734	First Newcomen engine in Winterstoke installed at High Hanger Pit	70, 76
1742	Newcomen engine installed at Darley Bank and a second engine at High Hanger	91
1755	'Bedlam' furnace rebuilt and Newcomen engine built to pump water to the bellows wheel	91
1766	Cast-iron plateway constructed from High Hanger to Darley Bank and river wharf	101–2
1766	Lobstock Canal projected, James Brindley, Engineer	103–5
1767	Reverbatory Furnace at Darley Bank produces coke smelted forge pig iron	93
1768	Lobstock Canal Act passed	105
1772	Westerport – Winterstoke – Coltisham Road becomes a Turnpike Trust	103
	Winterstoke Enclosure Act passed	85–86
1773–6	Winterstoke Place rebuilt by James Wyatt	83–85
	Winterstoke Park laid out by Lancelot Brown	85–90
	Old village and church destroyed and new village constructed including church by James Wyatt	88–90
1775	Lobstock Canal completed and opened	109–10
1779	New iron bridge constructed over the Wendle	88
	Wilkinson cylinder boring lathe installed at Darley Bank	96
1780	New Bank Furnace with Watt direct blast engine blown in	92, 95

CHRONOLOGY

Date		Page
1782	Watt rotative beam engine installed in new Darley Bank Forge	95
1788	New rolling and slitting mill built at Darley Bank powered by Watt rotative engine	95
1791	Heslop winding engine built at High Hanger Pit	98–99
1810	Poor House built at Winterstoke	122, 123
1812	New military barracks built at Church Ambling	121
	New County Gaol built at Church Ambling	122
1825	Combination Laws repealed; Winterstoke Mechanics Union recognized and Mechanics Institute opened	131
1826	Wendle Navigation improved, horse towingpath built and locks reconstructed	133
1827–8	Lobstock Canal improved by Thomas Telford	133–4
1832	Reform Bill passed; Winterstoke becomes a new borough	131
1834	London & Earlspool Railway promoted	135–8
1835	Municipal Corporations Act passed; Winterstoke ratepayers enfranchised	131
1836	London & Earlspool Railway Act passed	138
1837	First steam locomotive built by the Darley Bank Co.	139–40
1840	London & Earlspool Railway opened	140–41
1842	Corn Laws repealed; effect on local agriculture	157–8
1846	Lobstock Canal becomes part of the Midshire Union Canal Company by amalgamation	144
	Midshire Union Canal Carrying Company formed	144
	Great North-Western Railway promoted	145
1847	London & Earlspool Railway becomes the Grand Central Railway by amalgamation	145
1849	Great North-Western Railway Act passed	146
	Great North-Western Railway Company obtains a controlling interest in the Midshire Union Canal and Carrying Companies	146

CHRONOLOGY

Date		Page
1850	Winterstoke Brewery built by Richard Blenkinsop	162, 165
1852	Winterstoke Steam Mills opened by Richard Blenkinsop	162, 165–6
1853	Great North-Western Railway opened	148
	Camp Colliery opened by the Darley Bank Company	160
1853–5	War between rival railway companies for Winterstoke traffic ends in two disasters	150
1854	Winterstoke Gasworks opened	174
1856	Bedlam and New Bank furnaces rebuilt	160
	(Bessemer Converter introduced)	161
1861	New Market Hall built	173
1863	New Town Hall opened	174
1865	Summersend Branch Line completed	148
1866	(Siemens Martin open hearth process of steel-making introduced)	161
1866	Great Ketton Steel Company formed	161–2
1866–8	Great Ketton Steelworks and Ketton Deep Pit opened	163–5
1872	Winterstoke Theatre Royal opened	175–6
1875–6	Death of Thomas Leeds; Darley Bank Company wound up; Darley Bank Forge and High Hanger & Camp Colliery Companies formed	166–9
1876	Darley Bank Ironworks dismantled	169–70
1888	Local Government Act; Winterstoke becomes a County Borough	131
1889	Free Library, Museum and Art Gallery opened	175
1895	First motor car seen in Winterstoke	182–3
1896	National Telephone Company Exchange opened	186
1901	Winterstoke Electric Generating Station opened	185–6
	Electric Tramway system opened	184
1906	First regular motor bus service inaugurated	187–8
1909	Winterstoke Electric Theatre opened	189
1912	First aeroplane seen over Winterstoke	188

CHRONOLOGY

Date		Page
1914–18	First World War; Darley Bank Forge builds tanks; Zeppelin raid	190
	Winterstoke Park becomes a War Emergency Hospital	194
1920	Winterstoke Park destroyed by fire	194–5
	Foster Car Company established by Robert Foster	201
1921	Grand Central and Great North-Western Railway Companies amalgamate as London & North Midland Railway	203
	Midshire Motor Services established by Peter Foster	202
1921	Midshire Union Canal Carrying Co. wound up	204
1923	Winterstoke Park presented to the town by Bernard Blenkinsop	195
1925	Collapse of Ketton canal tunnel	205
1926	Abbey Building Estate completed and Abbey Cinema opened	209
	Trams cease running and are superseded by buses	203
	General strike in Winterstoke	216–7
1929	Lobstock Canal abandoned by Act of Parliament	206
1929	New road bridge built at St. John's	210
	New Grid Power Station built	213–4
1930	Darley Bank Forge closes down; Company goes into liquidation	218
	Great Ketton Steel Company becomes a subsidiary of the Universal Steel Corporation	221
	Emberley Heath Pit opened	223–4
1931	Darley Bank Forge buildings taken over by Foster Car Company and re-equipped for mass production	218–9
1932	Darley Bank canal basin filled in to make new Wharf Square and new Government offices built	207
1933–4	Winterstoke By-pass constructed	211–2
	Wendleside Estate and Seville Cinema built	209–10
	Allied Iron Founders Ltd. factory opened	221

CHRONOLOGY

Date		Page
1935	United Pressed Steel Company's factory opened	221
1937	Special Stress Alloys Ltd., factory opened	221
1938	R.A.F. station, High Emberley, built	225
	Air-raid shelters dug in Winterstoke Park	224–5
	Foster Car Company build shadow factory at Darley Bank	225
	Pre-fabricated & Hydraulic Aircraft Components Ltd. factory built	225
1939	Electronics Development Corporation factory built	225
1939–45	Second World War; Winterstoke 'Blitz' and damage caused; death of Robert Foster	225–8
1944	First Foster 'Wendle' jet engine produced at Darley Bank	230
1946	New government offices established in Winterstoke Park	234
1946–48	Railways, collieries, Gas and Electricity undertakings nationalized	235–7
1949	'Highways', Emberley, reconstructed as offices for the National Coal Board	236
1950	Summersend Branch Line closed	236
1951	Atomic Research Establishment completed	233, 240
1952	William Winter grants Emberley Hall to the Benedictines of Citeaux	241